Forgiving *Lies*

Also by Molly McAdams

From Ashes
Taking Chances

Forgiving *Lies*

MOLLY McADAMS

wm

WILLIAM MORROW
An Imprint of HarperCollins*Publishers*

FORGIVING LIES. Copyright © 2013 by Molly Jester. All rights reserved. Printed in the United States of America. No part of this book may be used or reproduced in any manner whatsoever without written permission except in the case of brief quotations embodied in critical articles and reviews. For information address HarperCollins Publishers, 10 East 53rd Street, New York, NY 10022.

HarperCollins books may be purchased for educational, business, or sales promotional use. For information please e-mail the Special Markets Department at SPsales@harpercollins.com.

FIRST EDITION

Designed by Diahann Sturge

Library of Congress Cataloging-in-Publication Data

McAdams, Molly.
  Forgiving lies : a novel / Molly McAdams.—First edition.
    pages cm
    ISBN 978-0-06-226774-0
  1. Undercover operations—Florida—Tampa Bay—Fiction.   I. Title.
PS3613.C25F67 2013
813'.6—dc23

                                                      2013016454

13 14 15 16 17   OV/RRD   10 9 8 7 6 5 4 3 2 1

To Amanda and Nikki, for convincing me that hot guys with lip rings deserve names like Kash. Love my soul friends. xoxo

Acknowledgments

As ALWAYS, a huge thank-you to my incredible husband, Cory. He puts up with so much, and even more than usual with this book. I'm often lost in the world of my characters, but I don't think he was prepared for me to get lost in Blake. Ha ha! Sorry, babe! Love you!

Thank you, thank you, thank you to my agent, Kevan Lyon, and my editor, Tessa Woodward. Y'all are the best. I don't know what I would do without either of you. Kevan, just admit it. You *love* Kash's lip ring! Tessa . . . you know I love you, and thank you for not letting me trash this book!

Kelly Elliott, oh my word, what would I do without our weekly lunches? Love you so much. Thank you for keeping me sane!

Amanda Stone, my soul friend, I love you even though there are too many miles separating us. No one else would sit on the phone with me for hours while I write. People just don't understand the awesomeness that is *us*.

A. L. Jackson, Kristen Proby, and Rebecca Shea—thank you all so, so much for the daily sprinting and encouragement. I don't know how I would ever get the motivation to hit my word goals if it weren't for y'all!

To all the bloggers and readers who helped pimp out the cover reveal and teasers for this book, thank you! I adore each and every one of you, and appreciate what you do more than you could possibly know.

1

Rachel

"CANDICE, YOU NEED to focus. You have got to pass this final or they aren't going to let you coach this summer."

She snorted and her eyes went wide as she leaned even closer to the mirror and tried to re-create her snort. "Oh my God! Why didn't you tell me how ugly I look when I do that!?"

I face-planted into the pillow and mumbled, "Oh dear Lord, this isn't happening." Lifting my head, I sent her a weak glare. "Snorts aren't meant to be cute. Otherwise they wouldn't be called something as awkward as 'snort.'"

"But my—"

"Final, Candice. You need to study for your final."

"I'm waiting on you," she said in a singsong voice. "You're supposed to be quizzing me."

I loved Candice. I really did. Even though I currently wanted to wring her neck. She wasn't just my best friend; she was like a sister to me and was the closest thing to family I had left. On the first day of kindergarten, a boy with glasses pushed me down on the playground. While he was still laughing at me, Candice grabbed his glasses and smashed them on the ground. That's playground love. And since then we've never spent more than a handful of days apart.

By the time we started thinking about college, it was just assumed we would go away together. But then my parents died right before my senior year of high school started, and nothing seemed to matter anymore. They had gone on a weekend getaway with two partners from my dad's law firm and their wives and were on their way home when the company jet's engine failed and went down near Shaver Lake.

Candice's family took me in without a second thought since the only relatives I had lived across the country and I hardly knew them; if it weren't for them I don't know how I would have made it through that time. They made sure I continued going to school, kept my grades up, and attempted to live as normal a life as possible. I no longer cared about graduating or going away to college, but because of them, I followed through with my plans of getting away and making my own life. I would forever be grateful to the Jenkins family.

I applied to every college Candice did and let her decide where we were going. She'd been a cheerleader for as long as I could remember, so it shouldn't have surprised me when she decided on a university based on the football team and school spirit. And granted, she was given an amazing scholarship. But Texas? Really? She chose the University of Texas at Austin and started buying everything she found in that god-awful burnt-orange color. I wasn't exactly thrilled to be a "Longhorn," but whatever got me away from my hometown was fine by me . . . and I guess the University of Texas accomplished that.

When we first arrived I remember it felt like walking into a sauna, it was so hot and humid; of course the first thing Candice said was, "What am I going to do with my *hair*?!" Her hair had already begun frizzing, and not more than five minutes later she was rocking a fro. We got used to the humidity and crazy weather changes soon enough though, and to my surprise, I *loved* Texas. I had been expecting dirt roads, tumbleweeds, and cowboys—let me tell you, I had never been so happy to be wrong. Downtown Austin's buildings reminded me of Los Angeles, and the city was unbelievably green everywhere and had lakes and rivers perfect for hanging out with friends. Oh, and I'd only seen a couple of cowboys in the almost three years we'd been there, not that I was complaining when I did. I had also worried when we arrived that with Candice's new burnt-orange fetish, people were going to be able to spot us like Asian tourists at Disneyland. Thankfully, the majority of Austin was packed with UT Longhorn gear, and it was common to see a burnt-orange truck on the road.

Now we were a little less than two weeks away from finishing our junior year and I couldn't wait for the time off. Normally we went to California to see Candice's family during the winter and summer breaks, but she was working at a cheer camp for elementary-school girls that summer, so we were getting an apartment that we planned to keep as we finished our senior year.

That is, if we ever got Candice to pass this damn final.

Before I could even ask my first question, Candice gasped loudly. "Oh my God, the pores on my nose are huge."

Grabbing the pillow under me, I launched it at her and failed miserably at hitting anything, including her. At least it got her attention. Her mouth snapped shut, she turned to look at the pillow lying a few feet from her, then she turned around with a huff to walk back to her desk.

Finally. "Okay, what is—"

"So are you ever going to go on a date with Blake?"

"Candice!"

"What?" She shot me an innocent look. "He's been asking you out for a year!"

"This—you need—forget it." I slammed the book shut and rolled off my bed, stretching quickly before going to drop the heavy book on my desk. "Forget it, we'll just see if we can get our deposit on the apartment back. I swear to God, it's like trying to study with a five-year-old."

"You never answered my question."

"What question?"

"Are you going to go on a date with Blake?"

I sighed and fell into the chair at my desk. "One, he's your *cousin.* Two, he works for UT now; that's just . . . kinda weird. Three, no."

"It's not like he's your professor! He isn't even a professor, period. And do you realize that if you marry him, we'll actually be family?"

"Marry? Candice— Wait . . . how do you even jump from me going on a date with him to marrying him? I'm not going to marry your cousin; sorry. And I don't care if he's a professor or not, it doesn't change the fact that he works for the school. Besides, he's not even my type."

"Not your type?" she said, deadpan, and one perfect blond eyebrow shot straight up. "I seem to remember you having the *biggest* crush on him when we were growing up. And I know he's family, but I can still say that he's gorgeous. I'm pretty sure he's everyone's type."

I had to agree with her on that. Blake West was tall, blond, and blue eyed and had a body like a god's. One of these days he was going to show up on a Calvin Klein billboard. "I had a crush on him when we were thirteen. That was eight years ago."

"But you had a crush on him for years. Years. You were devastated when he moved away."

"And like I said, I was thirteen. I was ridiculous."

Blake was five years older than Candice and me, but even so, all of my childhood memories included him. He was always at Candice's house to hang out with her older brother, Eli, and we followed them everywhere. I'd viewed both Eli and Blake as awesome older brothers until the day Blake saved my life.

Okay, that's a little dramatic. He didn't actually save my life.

I was nine at the time; we'd been playing on a rope swing and jumping into a little lake not far from our houses. When I'd gone to jump, my foot slipped into the foot hole and I ended up swinging back toward land headfirst, screaming the whole way. Blake was standing on the bank and caught me, swinging me into his arms before I could make the trip back toward the water.

In that moment, he became my hero, and I fell in love. Or at least my nine-year-old version of love. My infatuation with him grew over the next few years, but he never saw me as anything other than his "little cousin's best friend." I'm sure if I'd been older, that would have been a blow to my ego, but I just kept following him around like I'd always done. When he graduated from high school, he immediately joined the air force and moved away from me. I remember throwing a few "my life is over" fits to Candice, but then I got boobs and hips and the other boys my age started noticing me. And then it was something along the lines of, "Blake who?"

He'd been out of the air force for four years now and had pretty much been off the grid until last fall, when he'd moved to Austin and started working at UT. Candice had flipped out over having her cousin near her again. And I'd just straight flipped out. But then I saw him. He looked like freakin' Adonis standing there in his godlike, too-beautiful-for-his-own-good glory. Every straight female within a mile radius seemed to flock to him, and he loved every second of it.

That is why I refused to go on a date with him.

"Rachel," Candice snapped.

I turned my wide gaze to her.

"Did you even hear me?"

"Not unless we're done talking about Blake."

"We are if you've decided to say yes to him."

I rolled my eyes. "Why is it so important to you if I go on a date with him or not?"

"Because he's been asking you out all year! He's my cousin and you're my best friend and I love you both and I want to see you two together."

"Well, I'm pretty sure you and Blake are the only two who feel that way. I have absolutely no desire to date a guy who has women literally hanging on him all the time." *Stupid air force, turning him into sex on a stick.*

Suddenly she was sporting her signature pouty face. "Rach? How much do you love me?"

"Nope. No, I'm not going."

"Are you saying you don't love me?" I was already shaking my head to say no when she turned on the puppy eyes and continued. "So will you please do this for me? Pleeeeaaasse? I thought you were my best friend."

I can't even believe we're doing this right now! "If I go on *one* date with him, will you drop this forever?"

She squeaked and did a happy clap. "Thank you, I love you, you're the best!"

"I didn't say I would, I said *if.*"

"But I know you'll go."

"He works for the school!" I whined, going back to my original argument. Even though he wasn't a professor at UT, he did work there as a personal trainer and helped out in the athletics department. Since I was majoring in athletic training and Candice in kinesiology and health ed, we saw him almost daily in classroom-type settings. That just . . . didn't sit right with me.

"Rachel." She twisted back around to face me. "Seriously, that is getting old. He already checked it out and it's a nonissue. Stop acting like you don't want to date him."

"I don't! Who wants to date a man-whore?"

"He isn't a—well . . . eh." She made a face. "Well, yeah."

"Exactly!" Blake was rumored to be screwing most of the females he trained as well as . . . well . . . he was rumored to be screwing pretty much any female he passed. Whether the rumors were true or not was up for debate. But seeing as he didn't try to squash them and the horde of bimbos was never far from him, I was leaning toward their being true.

"You haven't dated anyone since Daniel. You need to get back out there."

"Yes I have. Candi, just because I'm not constantly seen with a guy, like you are, doesn't mean I don't date."

I had gotten kind of serious with Daniel at the beginning of our second year at UT. But apparently six months was too long to make him wait to have sex and he ended up cheating on me. I found out two days after I'd given him my virginity.

Asshole.

After him I'd gone out with a few guys, but they didn't last much longer than a date or two and an "I'll call you later." Not that there was anything wrong with those guys, I was just more interested in being done with school and Texas than getting my "MRS degree" or risking catching a disease.

I sighed to myself and headed toward our door.

"Are you going to find Blake?!" Candice was bouncing in her seat and her face was all lit up like a kid's on Christmas morning.

"What—Candice, no. It's after midnight! I'm just done talking about this. I'm going to wash my face so I can go to sleep. And I'm not gonna hunt him down either; *if* he asks me out again, then I'll say yes." I grabbed my face wash and was reaching for the knob when someone knocked on the door. I don't know who I was expecting it to be, but I wouldn't have thought Blake West would be the one standing there in all his cocky glory. From the look on his face, there was no doubting he'd heard part, if not all, of our conversation. What the eff was he doing in our dorm?

He pulled one long-stemmed red rose—that was unexpected—from behind his back and looked over my shoulder, and his cocky expression went completely serious. "Hey, Candi. Do you mind if I steal Rachel for a few minutes?"

I turned around to look at her and she was grinning like the Cheshire Cat. *Traitor.* I looked back at Blake and he let out a short laugh at my question-mark expression.

"That is, unless you're busy or don't want to. It looks like you were headed somewhere." He looked pointedly at the hand that wasn't holding on to the door.

It took me a few seconds to look down at my hand and realize he was looking at my face wash. "Oh . . . um, not. No. I mean. Busy. Not busy. I'm not busy." *Wow, that was brilliant.*

Blake's lips twitched and his head fell down and to the side to hide the grin he was failing at keeping back.

Trying not to continue looking like a complete idiot, I took a deep breath in and actually thought about my next question two different times before asking it. Okay, fine, I thought about it four times. "So, what can I do for you?" Yeah, I know. Now you understand why that required a lot of thought.

"I was wondering if I could talk to you for a few minutes."

"Uh, you do realize it's almost one in the morning, right?"

His head lifted and he looked sheepish. That look on this man was so different from anything I'd ever seen, and I almost didn't know how to respond to it. "Yeah, sorry. I think I fought with myself for so long on whether or not I should actually come up here and talk to you, it got a lot later than I realized." He jerked the rose up in front of him like he'd just remembered it was there. "This is for you, by the way."

"And here I was thinking you just walk around holding roses all the time." I awkwardly took the rose from him, looked at it for a few seconds, then let it hang from the tips of my fingers. "So, Blake . . ." I trailed off and searched his eyes for a second before he took a step back.

"Can I talk to you out here for just a minute? I promise I won't keep you long."

Yeah, well, the fact that I've turned you down for the amount of time it takes to make a baby and now you're standing at my dorm room door at one in the morning is kind of creepy. But of course we have history, you're incredibly hot now, and I'm thinking about as clearly as Candice does. So, sure. Why the hell not? I followed him out into the hall and shut the door behind us but stayed pressed up against it.

"Rachel . . ." He ran a nervous hand through his hair and paused for a second, as if trying to figure out what to say. "The school year is about to end and you'll be going back to Cali over the summer. I feel like I'm about to miss any chance with you I may have. And I don't want to. I know you liked me when we were growing up. But, Rach, you were way too young back then."

"I'm still five years younger; that hasn't changed."

He smirked. "You and I both know a relationship between a thirteen-year-old and eighteen-year-old, and a twenty-one- and twenty-six-year-old are completely different."

So? That doesn't help my argument right now. "Well, you and I have both changed over the last eight years. Feelings change—"

"Yes." He cut me off and his blue eyes darkened as he gave me a once-over. "They do."

I hated that my body was responding to his look. But honestly, I think it'd have been impossible for anyone not to respond to him. Like I said. Adonis. "Uh, Blake. Up here." He smiled wryly, and dear Lord, that smile was way too perfect. "Look, honestly? I have an issue with the fact that you're constantly surrounded by very eager and willing females. It's not like I'd put some claim on you if we went on a couple dates, but you ask me out *while* these girls are touching you and drooling all over you. It's insulting that you would ask me out while your next lay is already practically stripping for you."

His expression darkened and he tilted his head to the side. "You think I'm fucking them like everyone else?"

Ah, frick. Um, yes? "If you are, then that's your business. I shouldn't have said that, I'm sorry. But whether you are or not, you don't even attempt to push them away. Since you moved here, I've never seen you with less than two women touching you. You don't find that weird?" Was I *really* the only person who found this odd?

Suddenly pushing off the wall he'd been leaning against, he took the two steps toward me and I tried to mold myself to the door. A heart-stopping smile and bright blue eyes now replaced his darkened features as he completely invaded my personal space. If he weren't so damn beautiful I'd have karate-chopped him and reminded him of personal bubbles. Or gone all Stuart from *MADtv* on him and told him he was a stranger and to stay away from my danger. Instead, I tried to control my breathing and swallow through the dryness in my mouth.

"No, Rachel. What I find weird is that you don't seem to realize that I don't even notice those other women or what they're doing because all I see is you. I look forward to seeing you every day. I don't think you realize you are the best part of my weekdays. I moved here for this job before I even knew you and Candice were going to school here, and seeing you again for the first time in years—God, Rachel, you were so beautiful and I had no idea that it was you. You literally stopped me in my tracks and I couldn't do anything but watch you.

"And you have this way about you that draws people to you . . . always have. It has nothing to do with how devastatingly beautiful you are—though that doesn't hurt . . ." He smirked and searched my face. "But you have this personality that is rare. And it bursts from you. You're sweet and caring, you're genuinely happy, and it makes people around you happy. And you have a smile and laugh that is contagious."

Only men like Blake West could get away with saying things like that and still have my heart racing instead of making me laugh in their faces.

"You're not like other women. Even though these are the years for it, you don't seem like the type of girl to just have flings, and I can assure you, that's not what I'm into, nor what I'm looking for with you. So I don't see those other women; all I'm seeing is you. Do you understand that now?"

Holy shit. He was serious?

"Rachel?"

I nodded and he smiled.

"So, will you please let me take you out this weekend?"

For the first time since he'd come back into my life, he actually looked unsure of himself. I was still in complete shock, but I somehow managed to nod again and mumble, "Sure, where do you want to go?"

He smiled wide and exhaled in relief. "It's a surprise."

I frowned. How did he have a surprise planned if he hadn't even known I was going to say yes? "And by 'surprise,' do you mean you have no clue?"

"No, it's just a surprise."

I started to turn into Candice and whine that I wouldn't know what to wear but was interrupted by my own huge yawn, which made me sound more like Chewbacca. I covered as much of my face as possible with the hand that wasn't holding the rose and ed awkwardly. "Oh my word, that's embarrassing."

His laugh was deep and rich. "It's late and I stopped you from going to sleep. If for some reason I don't see you for the rest of the week, I'll pick you up at seven on Friday. That sound all right?"

"That sounds perfect. I'll see you then, and, uh, thanks for my rose." Before he could say anything else, I turned the doorknob, gave him a small smile, backed up into the room, and shut the door in his still-smirking face. "Holy hell," I whispered, and let my forehead fall against the door.

"Tell. Me. *Everything!*" Candice practically shrieked, and I turned to narrow my eyes at her.

Like she hadn't been listening.

"We're going on a date Friday. That's about it."

"That is *so* not all that was said, Rachel! Ohmigod, did you swoon when he said all he's seeing is you?"

"Swoon, Candice? Really? This isn't one of your romance novels." And yeah . . . I did kind of swoon. "And that's exactly why I'm not telling you. You eavesdrop anyway, so what's the point in going over it all again?"

"Because I want details of how he looked at you and how you reacted to him."

Oh dear God, this was going to be a long night.

WHY BLAKE THOUGHT we wouldn't see each other the rest of the week was beyond me, because sure enough he was the first person I saw when I walked into the athletic center the next afternoon. And surprise, surprise . . . he only had four girls around him that day. That wasn't including the one he was stretching out on the ground.

Candice's constant talking faded out as I watched him explaining why he was stretching those particular muscles. But I knew the girl wasn't paying attention; all she could care about was that he was practically in between her legs.

The girl on the ground said something I couldn't hear, and the runway-beautiful, mocha-skinned girl standing closest to me practically purred as she reached for his forearm, "Well, that's just because Blake's so good with his . . . *hands*." The other four girls started giggling and I wanted to gag.

Blake's head shot up and I realized I must have actually gagged out loud. *Whoops.* Our eyes locked for a few seconds before he quickly looked at the girls surrounding him and his position with the one on the floor. When he looked back at me, his blue eyes were pleading, but I just shook my head and walked off toward the back to get my out-of-the-classroom part of my course over with.

"Hey." Candice nudged me. "Don't get upset about that. They aren't the ones who have a date with him on Friday."

"I'm not upset about that." I was upset about the fact that *that* pissed me off. What, did I expect him to change overnight just because we were going to go on one date? Or did his words last night really have me thinking I'd imagined his robot bimbo herd all year? And sheesh, why did I care at all? I didn't even want to go on a date with him! Not really . . .

An hour and a half later, I'd successfully avoided his gaze, which I could feel like a laser on my back. But when I turned to put some equipment away, he was right there and there was no way I could avoid Blake in all his real-life Calvin Klein model–ness.

"You're mad," he said, and began taking the equipment out of my arms and putting it in the closet.

"Um . . . not? And I can put this away myself."

"Rachel, I told you. I only see you."

"Yeah, no, I heard you." As soon as everything was put up, I turned away, only to quickly turn back around and face him. "Look, Blake, I don't think Friday is a good idea."

"Why isn't it?"

"Well, it's—you know . . . it's just not. So thank you for your offer. But once again, and hopefully for the last time, I'm not going to go on a date with you. If you ever move back to California, I really hope this doesn't make family dinners awkward."

The corners of his lips turned up slightly. "All right. You done for the day?"

This was the first rejection he'd taken well, and it threw me off for a moment. "Um, yes?"

"Let's go then."

"Whoa, wait. Go where? Its Wednesday, not Friday. And I said no anyway."

"You said no to a date with me. The date was on Friday. So we aren't going on a date. We're just going to go walk, hang out, whatever you want. But it's not a date." He stepped close enough that we were sharing the same air and his voice got low and husky. "If you want to call it something, we can call it exercising or seeing Austin. You can hardly count that as a date, Rach."

I was momentarily stunned by the effect his voice and blue eyes had on me. "Um . . ." I blinked rapidly and looked down to clear my head. "I've lived here almost three years, I don't need to see the sights."

"Perfect, I don't get out much other than to come to work, so I do. You can be my tour guide."

"Blake—"

"Come on, Rachel."

Not giving me an option, he grabbed on to my arm and began

towing me out of the building. I caught sight of Candice and she waved excitedly as she watched us leave.

Why was she smiling? I sure as hell wasn't smiling, and Blake was practically dragging me away! He could have been hauling me off to slaughter me and leave my remains on a pig farm for all she knew, and Candice was just going to sit there and wave like a lunatic? Playground. Love. Over. Best-friend card officially revoked.

As soon as we were outside, I yanked my arm free and continued to follow Blake as he made his way off campus. Well, at least he was right about one thing: I couldn't count this as a date. No way would I have worn baggy sweats cut off at my calves and a tight tank on a date.

"Are you still mad?"

I glanced up to see his stupid smirk, which I kind of hated right now. "Why would I be mad? I was just dragged out of a building to go *walk* with a guy I turned down for a date."

His smirk turned into a full-blown smile. "Still mad," he said, and looked ahead. "Although I always did find your temper adorable, let me know when you're not."

Thirty minutes later I was getting tired of following him around. Tour guide my nonexistent ass. He wasn't looking at anything. He was walking with a purpose and hadn't looked back at me since he'd asked if I was mad.

"So, this has been awesome and all. Are you going to tell me where we're going now?"

"Are you going to tell me what you're mad about?"

"I'm not mad!"

He slowed his pace so he was directly next to me and I was surprised to see him looking at me completely seriously. "Yes you are, Rach. If you didn't want to go on the date on Friday, you would have never agreed, and you wouldn't be following me right now." I opened my mouth but he cut me off. "You would have gone back to your dorm and you know it. I was two steps ahead of you the entire time; you could have turned back if you were really mad at me."

"You didn't even give me an option to say no!" He raised an eyebrow and I huffed, "All right. Fine. Maybe I am mad."

"And you're mad at me."

"Yeah, Blake, I am."

"But not because I pulled you out of the building."

Oh my word, he was so infuriating! "Uh, yeah, I'm pretty sure that's why I'm mad. Are you going to start telling me I'm not hungry either? Since you all of a sudden seem to know me so well?"

He pulled me to a stop and moved to stand directly in front of me, tipping my head back with his fingers under my chin. "You're mad because of the girls around me when you walked in this afternoon."

"I—"

"And I told you I only see you. I'll tell you that over and over again until you understand that. They mean nothing, nor do I notice anything other than the fact that they talk like they're in middle school."

"I don't care about them the way you think I do. When I saw it, it just reminded me why I never wanted to go on a date with you in the first place. Nothing more, nothing less."

"You're lying, Rachel." I could smell the mint from his gum and feel his breath on my lips, and suddenly I was wondering if I *was* lying. There must have been something in his gum that put me in a daze. "It's fine to admit you were getting jealous. I hate seeing the way Aaron looks at you, and you work with him every day."

I was so not getting jeal— Wait. What?! Aaron's gay. I leaned away from his nearness and started to tell him when I realized we were on top of a bridge surrounded by a bunch of people just standing there looking toward the side like they were waiting for something. I pointed toward the people. "Uh . . . am I missing something?"

Blake looked a little smug as he glanced at his watch, then the sky. "Nope, give it a couple minutes. We got here just in time."

Aaron, his sexuality, and the fact that Blake had gotten jealous over my flaming gay friend completely forgotten, I looked at the sky, then pulled out my phone to check the time. There was nothing special about the time from what I could tell. As for the sky, it was nearly dusk, and although it was beautiful I didn't know why that was anything worth noting either. Glancing at the people and the street around us, I turned and saw the street sign and did a double take. We were on Congress Avenue.

"Oh no. No, no, no, no, no!" I started backing up but ended up against Blake's chest. His arms circled around me, effectively keeping me there. I felt his silent laughter.

"I take it you know about this then. Ever seen it?"

"No, and there's a reason. I'm terrified of—" Just then, close to a million bats took flight from underneath the bridge. A small shriek escaped my lips and I clamped my hands over my mouth, like my sound would attract the bats to me.

There was nothing silent about his next laugh. Blake tightened his arms around me and I leaned into him more. I'd like to say it was purely because my biggest fear was flying out around me, but I'd be lying if I said his musky cologne, strong arms, and chest had nothing to do with it either. This was something I'd wanted for years, and I almost couldn't believe that I was finally there, in his arms.

I continued to watch in utter horror and slight fascination as the stream of bats, which seemed to never end, continued to leave the shelter of the bridge and fly out into the slowly darkening sky.

Minutes later, Blake leaned in and put his lips up against my ear. "Was that really so bad?"

Forcing my hand from my mouth, I exhaled shakily and shook my head. "Not as bad as I'd imagined. Doesn't change the fact that they are ugly and easily the grossest thing I've ever seen."

"But now you can say you've faced one of your fears."

"The biggest."

"See?" He let go of me and started walking again in the direction we'd come from. "You up for a drink?"

I realized I was still shaking so I nodded my head and followed him. "Just one though."

We walked for well over half an hour while Blake tried to recreate my shriek at seeing the bats and I accused him of doing that with every girl so he'd have an excuse to put his arms around her. The air between us was much more relaxed this time as he asked about my life after he'd joined the air force. I told him all about the end of middle school and high school but never once mentioned my parents. I wasn't sure if he knew about them or not, but there was no point in bringing up that hurt. Besides, if he had known, he hadn't even come back for the funeral. Just as we were passing the school, Blake slid his hand down my arm and intertwined our fingers.

"Rachel, why did you finally agree to go out with me?"

When I looked up, I was surprised at his somber expression. I would have expected something a little more taunting. "Do you want me to answer that honestly?"

"I'd appreciate it. I've asked you out for . . . shit. I don't know, nine months now? No matter what I said, your answer was always no. Until last night."

"Well . . ." I looked down at the sidewalk passing beneath our feet.

"You can tell me, it's fine. You never were one to hide your feelings. And your hate for me lately has been a little more than apparent. I'm already expecting the worst."

"I don't hate you. I just don't exactly like you . . . anymore." I squinted up at him and nudged his side with the arm he still had a firm grip on.

He gave a little grunt with a forced smile.

"Um, Candice is always bugging me for turning you down. She said she would stop if I agreed to one date with you." I know, I know, I could have made something up that wasn't so harsh. But I didn't. If I hadn't looked back down, I probably would have missed the pause in his step.

"Figures." We walked for a few more minutes before he paused and turned to me. "I'm not going to make you go out with me."

"You aren't. I said I'd go."

He raised an eyebrow, making it disappear under his shaggy hair. "You also told me earlier today that we weren't going anymore. I'm just letting you know I'll stop. All of it. Asking you all the time, what I did today. And I'll talk to Candice."

"Blake—"

"No, Rach, I should have stopped a long time ago. I'm sorry you felt pressured into it last night. I want you to *want* to go on a date with me. I don't want you to go just so she'll drop it or because you want me to quit asking. Which I will." I couldn't tell if he looked more embarrassed or hurt.

Is it ridiculous that I want to comfort him? "I want to go."

"No, you don't."

Okay, still somewhat true. "I didn't . . . before." *Ugh, who am I kidding. He knows I'm lying anyway.* "Look, I don't know what you want me to say. You can't exactly blame me for not wanting to go out with you." He looked as if I'd slapped him. I hurried on before I could chicken out on the rest. "I mean, come on, Blake, you were rumored to be screwing all these students, coworkers, and faculty. And not once did you try to shut down those rumors. Add to that, the Blake I grew up with is completely gone; now you're usually kind of a douche. Why *would* I want to go out with someone like that?"

"Rumors are going to spread no matter what I do. The more I try to stop them, the guiltier I look. Trust me. As for you thinking I'm a douche . . ." His voice trailed off and he ran a hand through his hair. "Try seeing it from my side. The only girl I've wanted for years now and can't get out of my head no matter what I do repeatedly blows me off like I'm nothing."

Did he say years?

Letting go of my hand, he turned away from me and ran a hand agitatedly through his hair. "Come on, I'll walk you back to your dorm."

"What about drinks?"

"I'm not going to make you do this, Rachel."

"Blake, why can't you just be like this all the time? If how you were growing up, last night, and the last hour was how you always were . . . I probably wouldn't have ever turned you down."

He huffed a sad laugh. "Yeah, well . . . obviously I've already fucked that up."

I watched him begin walking in the direction of the dorms and squeezed my eyes shut as I called after him, "You know, you kinda traumatized me tonight. I feel like you owe me a beer." Peeking through my eyelashes, I saw him stop but not turn around. "And maybe dinner on Friday night?"

When Blake turned to face me, his smile was wide and breathtaking.

2

Rachel

Drinks with Blake had actually been more fun than I would have thought, and we'd ended up spending Thursday afternoon and evening together as well. He seemed to slip back into the Blake that Candice and I had spent years following around. On Friday, when I stepped into the athletic center, I was met with three red roses and a heart-stopping grin. He'd said that regardless of his reasoning on Wednesday afternoon, he was counting the bats and bar on Wednesday, and movies on the couch in my dorm room on Thursday, as dates. So Friday night would be our third and deserved three roses.

I'm not gonna lie, I totally did the *aww, you're so sweet* girly thing as I took the roses from him and kissed his cheek in front of the circle of girls he was doing pretty well at fully ignoring.

When Candice dragged me out of the center not even an hour later to go get a pedicure and have me start getting ready for the date, she pressed me for every single detail of my time with Blake thus far. She was really rooting for this whole actually-being-related thing.

He was sweet, attentive, and completely down-to-earth. But I was glad he was still giving me my space. Even being alone in the dorm room with me for three movies, he never once tried to pull me into his arms and had yet to try to kiss me. Which Candice was taking as a bad sign. I rolled my eyes at that assumption. Now that Blake was finally getting his dates, he was letting me take this at the speed I wanted, and I couldn't have been more thankful.

But then Friday night was just . . . odd.

Blake picked me up in his silver Lexus convertible and took me to the Oasis, a restaurant sitting on the lake with the most amazing view as the sun set, which it began to do just after we'd arrived. I honestly don't think I'd ever seen anything more beautiful, and just as I began to tell Blake that, our waiter arrived to take our drink order. Without a word, Blake handed him both menus and placed our order for our food and drinks. I hadn't even looked at the menu yet. The food was just as he said it would be, to die for. But from the way he continued to treat me I was expecting him to cut my meat and feed me himself by the time our food got there.

Conversation was at a standstill until we were back in his car.

"Want to go for drinks again?" he asked suddenly, halfway back to campus.

Obviously he had missed how awkward the last hour had been. "Two margaritas are more than enough for me. I'm good."

His laugh boomed throughout the small car as his hand fell onto my upper thigh and gave a little squeeze. "Okay, no drinks. Anything else you want to do?"

"Um . . ."

"Do you like horses?"

"Horses?" That wasn't something I'd been expecting. "Of course I like horses."

"So how about we go for a carriage ride down Sixth Street before I take you home? Sound good?"

"I don't know."

"Rachel, did I do something? I feel like we've gone back a few steps."

"No, I'm sorry . . . I'm just tired. I've felt off all day. Is it okay if you take me back?"

"Of course there's always tomorrow!"

I stifled a groan and smashed myself as close to the side of the car as possible. The entire way back he kept his hand on my thigh and continued to rub his thumb back and forth. In an effort to not smack it away, I crossed my arms under my chest and resorted to burning imaginary holes in his hand with my eyes. After we got to campus he walked me all the way to my room before trapping me against the door frame and leaning in. I turned my head away at the last minute but that didn't seem to faze him. Grabbing my hips and pressing his body closer to mine, he started kissing a line down my neck, and I swear he smelled my hair before groaning. I tried not to gag.

"Blake, please? Can we not do this?"

He pulled back and his blue eyes flared. "Fine." The way he looked at me from under his eyelashes caused a chill to run down my spine. And not a good one. "I'll see you later." Without another word he pushed off me, turned, and stalked down the hallway.

"RACH, WAKE UP and tell. Me. *Every*thing!"

Cracking my eyes open the next morning, I looked at a too-perky Candice and groaned. "Where were you when I got back last night?"

"With Jeff." She dismissed his name with a wave of her hand. "Now, tell me about your date!"

"Wow, Jeff too, huh? Nice, Candi."

"Don't stall!"

Pulling myself up so I was resting on my elbows, I didn't even feel like sugarcoating the prior night. "It was awful."

Her eyes went wide. "What do you mean? What'd you do?"

Bitch. "Why is it that I had to do something?"

"Um, let's see." She started counting on her fingers. "One, you didn't want to go out with him in the first place. Two, unlike Wednesday and Thursday, Blake didn't text me after to tell me about your time together. Three, you didn't want to go out with him in the first place."

"You already said that."

"Exactly, that's a big enough one that it counts for two! So what happened?"

I sighed and flopped onto my bed. "It was just weird. It's like we had nothing to talk about. Which was crazy because we talked the entire time we were together on Wednesday and Thursday. And he didn't even let me see a menu; he ordered for me. Like I was a three-year-old or something."

"Is that all?"

"Well, yeah. Oh! And when we were on our way back he just

started acting like the night had been completely normal and not awkward in any way. Then when we got back, he pushed me up against the door and started kissing my neck. I kind of asked him to stop and he got weird. Like creepy, scary weird . . . and then he just up and left. I don't know, the whole night was just a bust."

Candice didn't say anything; she just sat there staring at me.

"What?"

"Are you insane? You told him to stop kissing you?!"

Really? That was all she got from what I told her? "Yeah, we had a bad date; why would I want him to kiss me? Maybe if it had gone something like the first two nights I wouldn't have—"

"No, no. Rachel. Oh my God. We need to fix this. I can't believe you still managed to mess up the date after everything I went over with you yesterday!"

"Wow." I shook my head and let my arms give out so I face-planted into my pillow again. I was so dumbfounded I didn't even know what to say anymore.

After running to a café to grab a quick breakfast, we made our way back to *hopefully* study for finals, which were next week. But from the way Candice had tried to lecture me on all I probably had done wrong on the date during breakfast, I doubted much studying would take place if it involved her.

Not even two minutes after getting back into our room, there was a knock on the door. And surprise freaking surprise. Blake West. With *four* red roses.

"You do realize it's not even nine on a Saturday," I said. And yes, I laid the California-bitch tone on thick.

Blake didn't miss a beat, and his smirk didn't falter. "Morning, Rach. Can I take you out to breakfast?"

"Oh, we just ate!" *Darn.* I didn't even try to sound disappointed.

Candice gave me a look that I pretended not to notice.

"Well, that's okay." His smile was full of easy confidence. "How about we go grab some coffee instead?"

"I actually need to start studying for my finals."

"All the more reason for coffee now; it'll keep you awake."

Dear Lord, what is it with him and Candice? Do they not get hints? Must come from her mom's side of the family. "Sure, why don't we all go? Candice, you want to get coffee?"

"Nah, I'm good. I just texted Eric to come over in a few to help me, um, study."

Traitor. I glanced back at a victorious-looking Blake. "Could you give me a couple minutes?"

"See you down there." He handed me the four roses, winked, and walked down the hall.

"Eric today, huh? I'm sure you two will get tons of studying done. Maybe I should stay and help you; you can't afford to fail this thing.

"You better go!" She looked me over and raised an annoyed eyebrow. "Please tell me you're going to change."

I looked down at my yoga pants and off-the-shoulder Iron Maiden concert shirt. "Ha! No, definitely not. It's early in the morning, and we're just getting coffee. Which means I get to stay skanked up."

"You do not stay skanked up when you're trying to get the man of your dreams to fall in love with you! You stay skanked up if no one is going to see you! You know this, Rachel."

Love? God, this whole dating-her-cousin thing was making her more dramatic than usual. I threw my long, dark hair up into a cute messy bun, grabbed my purse, and sighed heavily. "See you later."

Blake didn't say a word to me as I slid into the passenger seat of his car, and he continued to stay silent as we drove to one of the Starbucks near campus. The only acknowledgment he made of my presence was to put his hand high up on my thigh again and hold tight. Too tight. And not much changed once we were finally in the shop. Conversation didn't happen, his hand was back on my thigh, and we had four different stare-downs.

I only won one of those.

At least he let me order my own coffee. That was honestly the only good part of this morning.

I was barely able to hold in my sigh of relief when my phone chimed.

"Who is that?" Blake's eyebrows were pulled down, and he seemed more than a little annoyed.

Only checking the text preview on the lock screen, I shrugged. "Oh, it's just a friend, he wants to get a study group together tonight." I started to put my phone back in my purse when his hand shot out and grabbed on to my arm, effectively keeping it suspended above my purse.

"Well, it's rude to keep him waiting. Aren't you going to answer him?" He looked like he was struggling to keep himself in check.

I tried to pull my arm back and he finally released it. Sheesh, what was his problem? It was just a text. "Sure, I guess."

"Just let him know you can't go."

"Excuse me?"

He leaned forward and his eyes narrowed. "I'd prefer that you study with Candice."

Now I was getting mad. He didn't own me, he definitely wasn't my boyfriend, and this was Aaron. The same gay guy that Blake didn't like "looking at me." "And since when do you get to decide who I hang out with? Look, maybe I've been giving you the wrong impression over the last few days, but we aren't together. You have no say in what I do."

Like a switch had been flipped, his face went back to its usual smooth, sexy expression. "You're right. Actually I think it's a good idea for you to study with some other people besides Candice; I'm sure you wouldn't get anywhere with her."

Wait. What? The sudden change in his mood made me almost feel dizzy. It was like I had my own personal Dr. Jekyll and Mr. Hyde sitting next to me.

When I could finally get my mouth to stop opening and shutting like a fish, I shook my head and exhaled roughly. "Speaking of, I really need to get back to campus." I stood to leave without giving him the chance to say no.

Without another word, Blake followed me out to the car. We didn't say anything on the drive back but he put his hand on my thigh again. Was I imagining how tight he was holding it? When we arrived at the dorm, he parked in one of the spaces rather than letting me out in front. I grabbed the handle to open the door and he pushed down on my thigh, gripping it tighter. I turned to look at him and was surprised to see he still looked light and easygoing.

"I'll get the door for you. Wait here for just a second."

Crap, I hope he isn't going to walk me to my room. I bet Candice still has Eric in there with the door locked. As soon as he released me, my thigh throbbed from the relief of the pressure he'd put on it and I almost wished I was wearing shorts so I could look at the damage I was making myself believe he'd done. The passenger door opened and I stepped out without looking up at him. We walked without saying anything and I made sure to put some distance between us. I was relieved when he began to slow down as we reached the main entrance of the dorm.

"Well, thanks for the coff—"

He caught me around the waist, pushed me up against the wall, and kissed me roughly, interrupting my good-bye. Before I had time to realize what was happening and push him away, his body left mine and he started backing up toward his car.

"I'll see you later." He winked, then turned away from me.

I have no idea what my face looked like; I couldn't even pin down an emotion. I was disgusted, annoyed, confused, and pissed. It took a second before I was able to compose myself. I shook out my arms and walked up to my room.

I didn't know if I was ready to tell Candice about this, or if I even wanted to. Knowing her, she'd somehow turn it around so that I had done something wrong or I didn't know how to kiss. Needless to say, I was dreading facing her. Luck was on my side. Eric must still have been in there, because the door was locked, and on the mini whiteboard attached to our wall in Candice's writing were the words "DON'T come in." I texted Candice, asking her to put my laptop and books outside while I went to the bathroom so I wouldn't be subjected to a flushed and rumpled Candice and Eric. After I picked those up, I went back to the common room and pulled out my phone to finally text Aaron back.

Sounds good. What time and where?

AARON:
7p @ Starbucks

Great. Like I wanted to go there again. I sighed, cracked open a book, and tried not to think about Blake.

WITH THE STUDYING I'd done before the group and the five hours with them, I felt fully prepared for this final and was glad it was on Monday. Once that was out of the way, I only had two days left of easy finals and this year would be over.

I was still wired from all the espresso I'd sucked down in the last few hours, and since it was a twenty-four-hour Starbucks, I decided to stay in the café and write in my journal. After my parents' accident, Candice's parents tried everything to get me to talk. I think they were afraid I would never come out of my depression. Her brother, Eli, had been the only one who had known how to handle me—so to speak. He'd been home from college for the summer when the accident happened, and unlike his first few years away, he came back every weekend to see me once school started up again. He would hold me while I stared off into space and never spoke a word. Eli's form of healing was my favorite, since it was silent, but we all knew he couldn't be there for me forever. One night when I got home from school there was a journal on my bed with a note from Candice's dad, George. He suggested using the journal to write to my parents like they were still here. At first it freaked me out, but I told him I would try, and I'm glad I did. Even I could see the difference in myself. I wrote to them every day, even if it was just a few lines. But I viewed it as a way of continuing our family time. Every night after dinner while I was growing up, we'd pile on the couches, turn on the TV, and talk about our day while watching whatever shows were on that night. So that's what I did. I just told them what was going on in my life like I would have if they were still there.

When I finished a couple hours later, I put everything in my purse and called out good-byes to the too-awake baristas. As soon as I pushed open the door and walked out into the muggy night air, my phone went off and the words on the screen caused me to stumble and a chill to shoot through my body.

BLAKE:
You look beautiful tonight.

Instead of bolting for my car like any sane person would have, I looked around until I found him. Well, running to my car wouldn't have helped much; he was parked right next to it and leaning against the driver's door of his shiny little Lexus.

How did he know I was here? If he didn't know I was here, what is he doing here at two in the morning? Oh my word, he's been following me! No, that's ridiculous; come on, Rachel, get a grip. He is not following you. Frick, I really need to stop thinking the world and everyone in it revolves around me. He just happened to be here and saw your car. That's all. Right? Right.

I took a few steps closer to the cars and took a deep breath as I dropped my phone back into my purse, trying to calm myself down. "Hi, Blake."

"I was starting to think you would never leave. I've been out here for hours."

Oh God, he has been waiting for me! Those words were creepy enough, but paired with the sexy, innocent smile they seemed even worse. I meant for my voice to sound strong and annoyed but it was barely a whisper. "Why are you following me?"

"Following you? I'm not following you. Candice told me you were waiting for me to pick you up from the study group.

Jesus, Rachel, you look like you've just seen a ghost; are you all right?"

"Candice said what? No, I was definitely not waiting for you; I drove myself here. That should be obvious, since you're parked next to my Jeep." I didn't know what was going on, but I wanted to get out of there and away from him. Now.

"Yeah, but your car isn't starting. Which is why I'm here." He said every word slowly, like I was a child or something. "Don't you remember, Rachel? You called her almost three hours ago, but she was busy, so you told her to call me. Are you feeling okay? Come on, get in the car. I'll get you back to your room."

"I am *not* getting in your car, I'll drive myself back!" With that I took the last few steps to my car, got in, locked the door, and put the key in the ignition. I turned it but nothing happened. There wasn't even a click. What had happened to my car? I knew I hadn't called Candice. And even then, if I'd wanted Blake to pick me up I would have called him myself. Someone tapped on the window and even though I knew who it was, I still jumped.

"Come on, Rach, this is dumb. Just get in the car and I'll take you back. I'll get your car towed in a couple hours."

There was no point in trying to call someone else. It was two in the morning, everyone was asleep, and I definitely couldn't walk back at this hour. I grimaced and opened the door.

"That's my girl. Come on, let's go." He helped me into his car, then got in beside me. This time he didn't put his hand on my thigh.

The short drive to the dorm seemed to take forever, and besides his asking me a few times if I was feeling all right, there was no conversation. Blake seemed genuinely concerned about me. Had I called Candice? Did I just forget about everything while I was writing to my parents? Is that why I went in to write to them in the first place? Maybe all the studying mixed with my caffeine high, which was turning into a major crash, had my mind all jumbled. I must have just forgotten. It would have been easy to grab my phone and check the recent call history, but something inside me tightened and I knew it would be the wrong thing to do. We finally reached the dorm, and just like that morning, Blake parked in the lot. Aces.

"Are you sure you're feeling okay?" he asked for the fifth time since we'd gotten in the car. "You freaked when you saw me."

"I'm fine, really, don't worry about me. I probably just forgot and lost track of time in there." I tried to make my smile convincing; I didn't want him to walk me to my room. I got out of the car, ducked my head back in to thank him, and saw he was getting out too. Crap.

"You don't really think I'm going to let you walk up there by yourself, do you?"

"Of course not," I muttered. "I was just trying to be polite. It's late and you've already been waiting on me for hours . . . apparently."

He just laughed as he walked toward me, put his arm around my waist, and led me to my room. When we got there he reached out to open the door for me; at least the good-bye would be quick. But my happiness was short-lived; he walked me into the empty room and then turned to shut and lock the door behind us.

"Where's Candice?" I couldn't stop my voice from shaking. How weird that just Thursday I'd spent hours alone with him in this room and had felt comfortable and enjoyed my time with him. But now, being in here with him felt . . . wrong.

"She didn't tell you when you talked? All she told me was she was busy," he said a little too innocently.

I turned to face the room again to see if her cell was around; if it wasn't I was going to call her immediately. Before I could find—or hopefully *not* find—her phone, Blake came up behind me and began kissing the back of my neck.

"Uh, Blake? Can you not do that right now? I need to find out where Candice is."

Instead of stopping, he turned me around, pushed me up against my wardrobe, and resumed his place on my neck. I tried pushing him back, but it was useless. The guy was a rock and he wasn't budging.

"She'll be back when she's ready to come back," he breathed between kisses and little bites.

Well, I wasn't about to wait for that to happen. I wanted him out of my room *now*. "Okay, I'm really ti—"

He quickly moved up to my lips, shutting me up, and his kisses became rough and possessive. Just as they'd been that morning, only these weren't lasting three seconds. We were close enough to the door that he reached out to flip off the lights and caught me around my waist again before I could take advantage of the break in his strong hold. He started backing me up toward the bed, and I pushed as hard as I could against the hand holding my head in place. His only response was to push against me harder. My bed was high enough that it hit at the small of my back and helped me stay standing when he tried to push me down. When I didn't immediately fall onto the bed, he pulled my head back to look at me, giving me the break I needed.

"You need to leave. Now!" My arms had been caught between us, but with the new space I put them against his chest and tried to push him back farther. Instead of moving away, he got a smile that turned my body to ice and my arms to Jell-O. This is what I imagined a crazy person looked like.

"You don't mean that," he growled as he pulled my face back to his.

Did he really think I was just playing hard to get? I wanted him off me! He let go of my waist and began searching for the bottom of my shirt, but even though my waist was free I still couldn't move; I was caught between him and the bed. When he found it he didn't waste time traveling up to grab my chest. I could feel him getting excited and it made me want to throw up. His lips moved back to my neck.

"Please. Stop." I hated how small my voice sounded.

"This would be over sooner if you'd just lie down and shut up."

Grabbing both sides of my waist, he lifted me onto the bed, pushed me down, and climbed on top of me. I tried to tell him to stop again, but nothing was coming out except for my rapid breathing. My body was shaking violently and I was danger-ously close to hyperventilating. He bit my bottom lip, causing me to gasp enough that he could slide his tongue into my mouth. Blake's knees were pinning my legs to the bed and I bucked my hips and pushed against his shoulders, but he still didn't move. He gathered both my wrists in one hand and pinned them above my head. Tears pricked at the back of my eyes. I tried to move my head to the side so I could scream for help but he moved with me as he thrust his tongue in my mouth over and over again. I froze for all of five seconds before biting down on his tongue as hard as I could. He flew back with a pained cry and I tasted blood in my mouth. I was going to throw up. Before I could scream, his free hand slammed down on my throat and his face was directly above mine again. He growled as his blue eyes turned to ice and he just stared at me as I gasped for air.

"You're going to regret doing that, sweetheart." My vision blurred from my tears; the outer edges were turning black as I struggled to stay conscious.

Blake's breathing deepened and the look that crossed his painfully handsome face terrified me. My mouth opened and shut, but I couldn't pull in any air and I couldn't make a sound. My arms gave up their fight seconds before my bucking hips did the same, and soon I could hardly focus on Blake at all. I prayed that someone would come and save me as the hand that had been holding my hands down on the mattress slid down and cupped me through my thin yoga pants.

I felt his hot breath on my ear. "I'll make sure you never want to fight me again, Rachel."

The hand that was cupping me went up and slid under my pants and underwear. I tried to roll away but it was taking everything in me to stay awake. Tears spilled over and fell down my cheeks. Just as my mind started shutting down, the hand clasped around my throat was gone and I began gasping for air.

Waves of dizziness washed over me, and the blackness slowly faded away. I heard the distinct sound of his zipper over my gasps and sobs and my head shook slowly back and forth. I felt like I was underwater and couldn't find my way to the surface. His hand closed around my throat again and I frantically tried to pull in air and claw at his hand, but it was useless. My arms lost function quickly and the edges of my vision were going black again, and I begged the darkness to come quicker when he began moving inside me. I didn't want to be conscious through what he was doing. I didn't want to remember this. The sweet numbness began claiming me, and at that moment, the most beautiful sound in the world came from outside the door.

Candice's voice.

Blake was off the bed and putting himself back in his shorts in seconds while I wildly tried to take in as much oxygen as possible. He roughly pulled my pants up just as the key could be heard in the lock and took the few steps toward the door to flip the light on before coming back to my side. When the door opened, Blake was standing at the side of my bed looking down at me. The light brush of his fingers over my throat and his solid glare were clearly a warning. But I was still on the verge of fainting, now from trying too roughly to inhale.

Candice said good-bye to whomever she'd been talking to as she shut the door. "Oh, hey, cuz! I didn't mean to—" Blake turned to look at her and Candice's eyes went wide when she saw me. "Oh my God, Rachel, are you okay?!"

She rushed over to me, but Blake touched her arm and pulled her away. "She was attacked by a couple guys outside Starbucks tonight. She called me about half an hour ago. She's in shock but she'll be okay."

"What?!" Candice screamed, and tears instantly filled her eyes.

What? No. No, no, no. My head shook back and forth as I choked on a sob and my breathing got even faster and heavier. I tried to tell her that was wrong, that he was lying, but all that came out was the ragged sound of my breathing.

I could see Candice and Blake's mouths moving, but I couldn't hear anything else. Everything tilted to the side and the blackness came back full force. I reached out for Candice but missed her arm as the dark claimed me.

3

Kash

"DO YOU KNOW what we're being pulled in for?"

I glanced over at Mason like he'd missed the massive pink elephant in the room. "Oh, I don't know. Maybe if you hadn't punched Juarez in the face . . ." I trailed off.

"That little piece of shit spit on me with his meth saliva! You expect me to let that go?"

"Not like it was the first time you've been spit on."

"He'd just taken a hit not even ten minutes before!"

"Mason." I shook my head as I held my badge up so we could get into the locked doors. "The dude was so strung out he couldn't stay standing and he was in cuffs." As soon as we were in the door, I smiled at the ladies behind the plate-glass windows and continued back to Chief's office. "Not to mention the guy is so thin he gives a new meaning to the phrase *skin and bones* and you look like you're on steroids."

"Whatever, for what we put up with from him and his crew for the last six months, he deserved it."

"And that's probably why we're here. Swear to God, Mase. If you get me put behind a desk for this shit, I'll hate you for life."

He snorted nonchalantly, but I could tell the thought of being a desk bitch instead of on the streets terrified him. "You can't hate me for more than a day. Who would feed you?"

"Oh, I'd still make you feed me. I'd just hate you." We got to Chief's door and we both stopped to collect ourselves. I looked over at my best friend and work partner and clapped his shoulder. "Ready to see what your latest fuckup has gotten us?"

"Fuck you, Kash," he sneered, but he was fighting a smile.

Mason and I had met while going through the police academy, and for some genius—or more likely stupid—reason they'd partnered us not long after we'd both gotten hired on at Tampa Bay Police Department. We had barely gotten out of our time with our different field-training officers and been put on patrol before we were partnered up and moved to a whole new scene of TBPD: the undercover narcotics division. And I promise you, it's not as exciting as it sounds or looks on TV.

With my half sleeves of tattoos, and with Mason looking like a 'roided-out freak, Chief thought we'd be perfect for it. And though we liked to complain about it, I could say for both of us that we loved what we did. Not that what we did was something either of our families were okay with, but it was our job, and one that a lot of cops didn't want. In the last three and a half years of being undercover, we'd successfully taken down three different major suppliers in the Tampa Bay area. Mason and I didn't break down doors or run in with the SWAT team to do drug busts. We were the ones who had to be manhandled and cuffed and put in the back of cars until everyone involved in that drug ring was hauled away. Only then were we let out and able to lead the rest of the officers to where all the goods and money were. That way our cover was never blown.

Until now.

We'd never gotten in with a crew faster than we did with Juarez's, and we'd also never taken one down as fast. But as soon as our guys burst in, we realized why. We'd never fooled Juarez for a second and his boys had guns drawn on Mason and me the minute the door flew open. Thank God they'd all just taken hits and weren't coherent enough to get shots off before they were taken down, which led to Juarez spitting in Mason's face and Mason breaking his nose in return. And that leads us to now.

Mason knocked, and after a quick murmur from the other side of the door, he let us in. Once we were seated, I knew our days infiltrating drug dealers were over. The look on Chief's face said it all.

"He was cuffed, Gates." Chief spoke low to Mason, but Mason knew better than to reply yet. "Man was cuffed, and you punched him in the face. You have ruined not only your undercover career but Ryan's as well." He gestured toward me. "Wanna tell me your side of the story, gentlemen?"

"Cover was already blown. They knew; they all had guns pointed at our heads the minute the narcotics team busted down the door," Mason answered, and I nodded my agreement. My heart still raced when I thought about that moment.

Our jobs meant living with scum and dealing with drugs, lots of money, and idiots who had no idea how to handle weapons on a daily basis. But yesterday morning had been the first time in our three different takedowns that I was scared for my life. Our guys knew not to ever hurt Mason or myself, no matter what was going down. And we knew how to stay out of the way and help them out if a bust resulted in gunfire. But to have five guns drawn on you by meth heads was another thing all in itself.

"So, because your cover was blown, you felt it appropriate to punch him. He's lawyered up and is going for police brutality, Gates."

Mason snorted. "Please." But he quickly snapped his mouth shut when he saw Chief's look.

The room stayed tense as we all stared at each other in silence for what felt like hours. Finally, Chief sighed and handed two files to each of us. "Look, we'll take care of the police-brutality thing, but I don't think it should come as a shock to you that you are out of the undercover narcotics division."

Do. Not. Say. Desk.

"But since Juarez already had his suspicions of the two of you, he had guys lined up in case he was taken down. And we just caught wind of it this morning. There's a hit out on both of you."

"What the fuck?" I whispered mostly to myself as I looked through the top file. There were new credit cards, a driver's license . . . everything I would need to start over. Except the name didn't say Logan Kash Ryan. And the state sure as shit wasn't Florida. In its place was Logan Kash Hendricks. Texas. I glanced over at Mason, who was now scrambling to see what was in his file, before looking at Chief. "Chief, for the last three and a half years we've lived—almost the entire time—with thugs, dealers, and druggies. When don't we have someone wanting us dead?"

"This is a serious hit. What we're doing isn't exactly witness protection. But it's getting you away from here until things calm down, and before you say anything"—he held his hand up and I snapped my mouth shut—"you'll still be working. Just not with narcotics. You'll still be undercover." He grabbed both files that had been under the ones with our new identities and opened them. "Do you remember the college girl who went missing and was found tortured to death in that basement about two years ago?"

I skimmed quickly over the file and newspaper clippings. We'd been neck-deep in another operation at the time and hadn't been paying much attention to the news. But that had been huge. She'd been the third girl in what they were now calling the Carnation Murders. All the girls had looked alike and each had been found tortured, murdered, and with one white-and-pink carnation lying on her chest. The last girl had been right in our backyard.

"A few of our detectives have found some things other than physical appearance, type of torture, and the flower that are starting to link all of them together. Whether we're about to go on a wild-goose chase or not, we don't know. But they've been studying this trail for a few months now and we just got the okay to send in some of our guys."

"All right. And . . . ?"

"And we're sending the two of you."

Glancing down at my new ID, I peeked at Mason's file and saw that he had a Texas driver's license with the last name Hendricks as well. "I'm sorry. Let me see if I'm understanding all this. You're getting us away from a hit that may or may not be out for us, we have *Texas* IDs all of a sudden, and you're *sending* us somewhere. You're sending us to cowboy country?!"

"You always were a quick one, Ryan," Chief said, deadpan. "Or should I say, Hendricks."

"If you've followed this trail to Texas then it's out of our jurisdiction. Let Texas law enforcement deal with it."

"Austin detectives have already been sent all of the information we've collected on this James Camden guy, and they're expecting you on Monday."

"Monday?!"

Chief continued like we hadn't spoken. "Mind you, there's never been an actual suspect that has had any credibility, and when the victims' family and friends were shown a picture of James Camden, no one had ever seen him before. And no one can actually track Camden down, so it's possible his identity has been stolen."

Just looking at the balding now-forty-year-old put a bad taste in my mouth. His mug shot from a petty theft six years ago looked like a photo from a story you'd see on the news about a child molester. I studied his face and every description of him as Mason and Chief argued over the fact that we wouldn't be able to tell our families where we were going but would be able to keep some forms of contact with them. This was the weirdest form of protection I'd ever heard of. And I blamed Mason for all of it.

"We have jobs set up for you as bartenders at the two places his paper trail has led to in Austin, but other than that we have nothing on him. You have bank accounts set up with money you'll need to set up an apartment we've already rented out for you."

"We aren't—" Mason said, but was quickly cut off.

"I know you don't bartend, and so do the owners. They have been informed of the situation, but the staff hasn't. Just try to blend in and find Camden. This is a college town, so we have to assume he's looking for his next victim. You will check in with the Austin police department same as you would do here for undercover assignments; you will be on their payroll for now. You are now cousins, but the rest of the cover story will be up to the two of you to decide upon. As I said before, you cannot tell your family where you are moving to, only that you are going away on another undercover assignment. Now, get out of my office and get your asses to Texas."

As soon as we were out in the hall, I turned my glare on Mason. "Texas? Really? Your mess-up has us moving to Texas?"

"You can't put this shit on me, Kash. Juarez had us pegged and listed already; this has nothing to do with me punching him."

"You know my mom is going to flip and try to figure out where we're going."

"Your mom?" he asked incredulously. "I just told my parents and little sister I'd be there for her graduation this weekend and now I won't. And I won't be able to give them a reason. You know my ma, she'll go freakin' ballistic."

True. She would. As we made our way out of the building, I came up with our immediate plans and shared them when we hit the parking lot. "We each get one small bag. Essentials only. Leave the apartment looking like it always does. That way if the guys Juarez hired come looking for us, it'll look like we're still around. I'm having dinner with my parents, then we'll leave at ten tonight. When we get home, I'll go in first to make sure it's all right. Then I'm gonna go put gas in my truck and pick up my bike from storage before I head to my parents'. I'll let you know when I leave so you can go in after; that way we don't look suspicious. Try to crash on your parents' couch for a few hours at least before dinner; I want to drive as much as possible tonight." Holding up the new Texas license plates that had been in my file, I sighed as I looked at my Florida plates. "I guess we'll change these out sometime tomorrow. Keep them hidden for now."

Mason stopped outside the door of his truck and looked at the ground, playing with his keys. "You telling them you're going on assignment?"

Do I ever? "Nope."

He nodded. "All right. Call you at ten when I get in my truck. I'll have mine filled up too."

"Later." I climbed in my truck and placed the files and plates on the passenger seat. Taking a deep breath, I told myself it was just another assignment. Just like the last three. Clearing my mind, I started preparing myself to once again say good-bye to my parents without their realizing what I was doing.

I HOPPED OUT of my truck, and Mason did the same. "You got the keys and everything?" he asked as he stretched.

"Yep. I'm guessing it's . . . this way? Twenty-one oh four. First floor, Chief? Really? That's just asking to be broken into."

Mason followed me to the second door on the left and we both stayed silent as I put my ear up against the door. No noise. Mason inspected the handle, said it looked clean and was still locked. We'd already discussed trying not to scare any of our neighbors, so we both had our guns in their holsters on our hips under our shirts. But with the hit and the fact that this apartment had been set up for us, it felt unnatural to go in unprepared.

With a look confirming that we were both ready, he unlocked and opened the door and I stepped in with Mason directly behind me. As soon as we were in, he shut the door silently and we both had our weapons drawn as we cleared the unit. Satisfied with our search, we reholstered and opened all the blinds in the dark apartment before heading out to grab our bags.

"Mason—what the fuck?" I slammed the door to my truck shut and slung my bag over my shoulder. "I said one bag each."

He hefted a box out of the backseat of his truck and reached in for another. "Yeah, you also said the essentials."

"What do you deem essential?" I walked quickly over and opened the top. "I told you to leave the apartment looking like we still lived there, dumbass! How is taking this looking like we still live there?" Folding the flaps over each other, I pushed the box with our Blu-ray player and all our Blu-rays aside and checked the next box. "Our Xbox is not essential!"

"Dude, how can you even say that? Of course it is."

"Not when we're on assignment," I hissed.

"We're supposed to look normal. And when aren't we playing Xbox when on assignment? We killed Juarez and his boys in all our online tournaments."

Okay. He had a point. We were always playing. "But still, Mason. If someone goes to our place and sees our Xbox, the controllers, games, and headsets gone, not to mention the hundred or so movies and Blu-ray player . . . you don't think they'll find that suspicious?"

"Well . . ." He stood up and raked a hand through his hair. "Whatever. They were essential."

"God, I fucking hate you sometimes."

He shrugged, then picked up his bag and one of the boxes. "You know you'd be bitching in a week if I'd left them. You're welcome in advance."

"Hey, boys."

We turned to see a short, freaking gorgeous blonde in next to nothing standing there with a coy smile crossing her face.

"I'm Candice." She bounced once on her toes and the bikini top she was wearing didn't do much in the way of helping keep her girls in. "I take it you're just moving in?"

"Thank the good Lord above," Mason whispered next to me, and I huffed a laugh. "We are. I'm Mason. This is my cousin Logan."

"Cousins? Wow." Her eyes went wide and she dragged her teeth over her bottom lip as she stuck her chest out even farther. God, could this girl have been any more obvious? "Do you need any help moving in?"

I almost laughed. She was the size of a toothpick. "Uh, no. We're good, this is all we have. Thanks anyway."

Her brow furrowed as she took in the two small boxes and bags but quickly smoothed out. "So, you're moving into the apartment directly across from ours. We'll be neighbors."

Oh, joy. I sucked on my lip ring and watched Mason walk right up next to her.

"Really now? Lucky me, unless . . . you said 'ours.' You aren't living with your boyfriend or anything, are you?"

"No!" She slapped Mason's arm and giggled. Actually. Freaking. Giggled. Like a damn toddler. "It's me and Rachel, she's my best friend. She's not here right now, but I'm sure you'll like her. All the guys do, she's the pretty one." She pouted and I'm pretty sure I did laugh then.

Good God. I'd only been around this girl for two minutes and already she was annoying me. I was a guy. I didn't mind if you wanted to walk around in your bikini. But the way she continued to bounce and stick her chest out as she devoured us and fished for compliments was a sure way to get me to lose interest fast. Girls who had to try that hard were better fitted for Mason. Obviously. But shit, if Candice was like this, I couldn't imagine how bad her friend was. I didn't want to put up with this during an assignment; living across from them was going to be a nightmare. I didn't like first-floor apartments anyway. I wondered if Chief would let us change.

Leaving them to blow smoke up each other's asses, I walked back to our unit and dumped the box in the living room and the bag in one of the bedrooms. We needed to go shopping for beds and couches soon. But I was too damn tired for that after all the driving we'd done. When I walked back outside, Candice was practically leaning against Mason and he was eating it up. I shook my head and punched his shoulder as I passed them.

"Help me get my bike down."

My Harley was my baby. Usually when we were on assignments, she went into storage, but not this time. I didn't know how long we were gonna be in Texas, and I'd already gone long enough without her. So there was no way I was leaving her in Florida. Besides, Chief had left Texas plates for her too.

"Gonna go put gas in her," I told Mason when we put the tailgate back up.

"All right. Candice wants the four of us to go out to dinner tonight. You game?"

With cheerleaders one and two? Fuck. "Sure. Not like we have food anyway."

"Sweet. See you when you get back. Don't get lost."

"Okay, Mom."

Rachel

THE LAST FEW weeks had gone by in a blur. Finals had been easier than I'd hoped, and I'd gotten pretty decent grades in all of my classes. Blake hadn't bothered me since that horrible weekend and Candice and I had moved into our apartment two weeks ago. She was starting cheer camp next week and couldn't wait. I was excited for her, and for me. Because all I wanted was some time to myself. What had happened with Blake had shaken me more than I'd expected it to, and I was finding it difficult to move past it. It didn't help that Candice still viewed him as her perfect older cousin who could do no wrong.

THE DAY AFTER Blake attacked me, I woke up late in the afternoon, and the first thing I noticed was the pain in my throat and lower body and stinging in my eyes. That morning came flooding back to me and my body instantly started shaking. Candice had been sitting at her desk, but when she heard me stir, she grabbed her drink and came to sit on my bed with me.

"Are you okay, Rach? You had a rough night last night." Candice spoke slowly and carefully, making sure not to say anything that would set me off again.

My head shook quickly back and forth and I wrapped my arms around her, squeezing her as tight as my shaky body would allow. She had no idea how thankful I was for her and her timing.

"Those guys didn't hurt you too bad, did they, Rach? They didn't—they didn't . . ."

"No. Candice. No. Blake—"

"I know, Rach. Blake took such good care of you last night, he was so sweet to you."

No! A sob broke free and the tears poured down my cheeks as I tried to tell her how wrong she was. "No. Blake—my car—he . . . he did something and I—I thought I was going crazy!"

"It's okay, sweetie. He took me to pick up your Jeep from Starbucks a few hours ago. It's in the parking lot."

"W-what?"

"Aww, Rach. I'm sorry I wasn't here for you last night. I'm so sorry. I can't believe that happened to you. I'm so thankful Blake was there for you."

A bone-deep shudder rocked my body and I tried to pull back from her; she wasn't understanding! "You're not listening! Blake's the one who attacked me!"

"Rachel! Why the hell would you say something like that?!"

"Because he did! Before you came back!"

She pushed away from my bed and faced me with a cold glare. "How dare you accuse my family of something like that! I know you had a rough night, Rachel, and I'm sorry! But you can't just pin it on Blake. I can't—" She huffed loudly. "I can't believe you would do something like this. Why do you hate him so much? If you don't want to date him, then fine, but don't blame him for something like that. God, I feel like I don't even know you."

My phone rang from my desk, and she stormed across the room to go to answer it.

"Hello? Hey, Blake, yeah, she's finally awake . . . She's okay, still shaken up from it . . . No, you're so sweet, but I'll take care of her today . . . Yeah, I'm sure . . . Okay, love you too. Here she is."

My head was shaking a no when Candice tried to hand me the phone, and she eventually just shoved it into my palm. I just stood there staring at the front of it in horror. Candice huffed and forced my hand so the phone was pressed to my ear and went to sit back at her desk.

"Y-you—"

"Took care of you," he said, cutting me off. "I have a witness."

"No," I whispered, and glanced up at Candice.

"Who's going to believe anything you say, Rachel? My own cousin and your best friend saw me taking care of you after you'd been attacked. She saw me hold you after you fainted. She watched me vow I would never let anyone touch you again as you slept. And trust me when I say, Rachel, I will never let anyone else touch what is mine. And you. Are. Mine."

Who was this man? Where was the Blake I'd grown up with? My heartbeat felt like it stuttered and I sat there in silence as I thought through every different outcome of telling people about what had happened last night.

When I didn't say anything for a while, Blake spoke again. "Did you just realize that I'd come out the hero no matter what?"

"Stay away from me," I said shakily, and took a deep breath in as I tried to put some strength behind my words as I repeated them: "Stay away from me, Blake."

I hit the *end* button and let my phone fall to my bed before pressing my fist to my mouth to muffle my new sobs.

Candice snatched my phone from me and walked back to her desk. When she was seated she turned her glare on me. "You're probably just having a freak-out because Blake was the one to take care of you after your traumatic experience."

"You're supposed to be my best friend! Why won't you listen to me?"

"Because even though I love you and I hate what happened to you, you're being a bitch by accusing Blake!"

I jerked back on the bed. Oh my God. How did she not understand any of this? I wanted to scream at her to listen to me. But I knew Blake was right; no one would believe me. Especially Candice. He was perfect in her eyes. He was perfect in everyone's eyes. And what proof did I have? None. Nothing but horrific memories.

"Have you told Blake we're moving into an apartment here this summer?"

"No . . ." She drew the word out and tilted her head to the side. "Why?"

"I don't want him to know, Candice. I don't want to see him, I don't want to talk to him. I don't—I just don't want anything to do with him."

"You're being ridiculous," she whispered.

"Please, just don't! If you won't believe me, then please just do this for me."

She shook her head quickly and straightened her back. After a few deep breaths she opened her eyes again. "I know this is all just because you're going through a lot. I think we should spend a minute apart. Take a Xanax, lie down, and rest. I'll go pick up some Chinese food and a pint of Ben and Jerry's. Then, after you've had time to relax, we'll talk about what really happened to you, okay?" Before I could respond, she grabbed her purse and practically ran out of the room.

I SPENT THE morning and early afternoon writing to my parents at Starbucks, and though it usually left me feeling closer to them, connected somehow, today just wasn't cutting it. It could've had something to do with the fact that I was pulled over by an APD officer for going thirty-nine in a thirty-five, or that Starbucks got my order way wrong. Honestly, how is an iced vanilla latte con-fused for an iced coffee with caramel? Or it could've had some-thing to do with the sporty silver Lexus convertible that had pulled up next to my car and had me in a near panic attack in the middle of the café since I had a big chair next to a window with a perfect view of the parking lot. Didn't matter that it was a woman with dark hair driving it. I'd already started my minor freak-out. There was no stopping it. Any one of those things could have made it so I didn't enjoy writing to them, but I was in a funk now, regardless.

I shut my eyes and listened to the remainder of "I'll Be" by Edwin McCain in my car before preparing to get out. My dad used to sing that to my mom when they thought I wasn't look-ing. He'd pull her close in the kitchen and dance with her slowly as he softly sang each word in her ear. My dad was sweet like that, and I remember thinking I wanted a guy just like him. A rugged-looking softy who would take the time to dance with his wife for no reason at all. He looked at her like she was the world. And I'd vowed to never settle for less. But after Daniel and Blake, I was considering becoming a nun, or a crazy cat lady like our new neighbor Mrs. Adams. Either sounded pretty perfect to me.

As soon as Edwin's voice and the saxophone drifted off, I turned my car off, and opened my door. A short shriek burst from my chest and I tried to slam my door shut, but I already had one leg out and ended up just causing more pain and damage than I would've if I'd left the door alone. I pushed it back open, avoiding the motorcycle that had almost had a collision with my door, and rubbed my leg. That shit hurt.

The roar of the motorcycle stopped, and the rider whipped off his sunglasses. "Are you trying to get your door taken off?"

My heart had stopped the minute I'd looked into his piercing gray eyes, but anger quickly took over everything. "Do you always swing into parking spaces when someone is opening their door?" I rubbed my leg once more and stumbled awkwardly out of my car. I realized he hadn't answered me, and after shutting my door and locking the car, I turned to face him, a frown tugging at my lips when I saw him smirking. "I'm fine, if you're wondering."

He sat up straight on his Harley and took a deep breath in. "I'm sorry I made you hurt yourself. I'm Kash, by the way."

"Cash . . . like money? Or Johnny?"

"Um, I guess we can go with Johnny, but with a *K*."

"Kash with a *K*. Got it. That's a, uh . . . very interesting name. Fits the image, I guess."

His head jerked back. "I'm sorry, what?"

I took a few steps toward the apartments before turning to look at him, my hand waving over his frame, which was now hunched back over his bike. I wondered who he was here to see. "You know, the whole 'bad boy' thing you've got going on there. Tattoos, lip ring, Harley. Makes sense you'd have a nickname and try to make it, I don't know, awesome or something by having it start with a *K*. Have a nice day; try not to almost take any more car doors off, Kash with a *K*."

Kash huffed a short laugh and his brow creased; he opened his mouth to speak but I turned and found my way to my apartment before he could say anything else. I was in a pissy mood, and I really didn't want to deal with someone like him. Didn't matter if my heart had skipped a few beats and butterflies had taken up residence in my stomach when I first saw him. I'd had issues with two perfectly normal-looking guys; a bad boy was definitely not in my future. Guys, in general, weren't in my future.

"Candi, I'm home," I called, and walked through the living room to my room to kick off my shoes and toss my purse and cell on the bed.

"Ohmigod!" she screeched as she followed me into my room. "You have *got* to see the guys who just moved in across the hall from us!"

"No thanks," I mumbled.

"Seriously, Rach, these guys are hot with a capital *hot*. Mason and Logan, they're cousins. You've got to meet them."

"Like I said—" I turned and stopped short when I saw her. "Candice, please tell me you haven't met them yet."

"Of course I have!"

"Were you wearing that?"

She rolled her eyes and turned to check herself out in my full-length mirror. "Duh, I had to show them the goods that will be living next to them!"

"Candice! You're in cheer shorts and a bikini top! Did you even go to the pool today?"

"Uh, no. But anyway, it doesn't matter if you want to meet them or not. We're going out for dinner with both of them to-night." She grabbed my hand and pulled me back to our living room, pushing back the curtain and peeking through the blinds at the unit directly across from ours. It looked the same as it always did. No activity.

"You might be going out for dinner. I'm not going anywhere. Besides, this way you have two guys all to yourself." I stepped away from the window and headed toward my room, looking back over my shoulder at her as I said, "You might want to warn them that you aren't a one-guy kind of girl, though."

She flipped me off without taking her gaze from the window.

"Oh, you know I'm kidding . . . but for real, warn them."

"So hateful." She shook her head and dropped the blinds and curtains before walking past me toward her own room. "Whatever, I'll be lucky if either is interested in me after they've seen you. I'm going to hop in the shower, and you should start getting ready soon. We're leaving at seven."

"I'm not going, Candice!" But it didn't matter; she'd already shut her bedroom door.

With a sigh, I turned and went to my bathroom. Stripping out of my comfy clothes, I turned the shower on and waited until the room was filled with steam before stepping in.

And no, I still wasn't going.

That's what I continued to tell myself when I was doing my makeup almost forty-five minutes later and when I did large, loose curls throughout the bottom half of my long hair. Not going. Just getting ready to sit around the apartment looking pretty. When my hair was done, I checked my makeup one more time, making sure the smoky eyes were just enough to make my blue eyes pop but not so much that I looked like I was going clubbing. I flossed and brushed my teeth, told myself one more time I wasn't going to go, then went to my closet to pick out something to wear.

Candice burst into my room thirty minutes later, and I was standing there in a bra and underwear, just staring at my closet.

"I can't believe you're not dressed yet! I told you to get ready! They're going to be here in, like, five minutes!"

"I think this is a sign that I shouldn't go."

She huffed and pushed me out of my closet before walking in. "You can tell yourself all you want that you're not going. But even if you'd stayed all skanked out like you were earlier, I would've still dragged you out the door with us."

I wanted to sneer at her and ask why it was okay to stay skanked out with these guys and not Blake, but I kept my mouth shut. We hadn't talked about the situation with Blake since Candice had come back to the dorm with food and ice cream that afternoon. It was just easier this way.

In less than two minutes, Candice was walking out of my closet and throwing my outfit onto the bed. "There. Get dressed."

"Heels? Candice, are these guys even tall?" I'm five eight. And these were four-and-a-half-inch stilettos.

"Yeah, they're ginormous, they're going to be here any second, get dressed!"

"Gah, so pushy." I dressed in my faded skinny jeans, black stilettos, and a loose black tank. The kind you have to wear a camisole underneath unless you feel like showing the entire world what Victoria's Secret really is. As soon as I was done, Candice was in front of me, her lips pursed as she critiqued my outfit. "Well?"

She stamped her foot—yes, Candice still stamped her foot like a five-year-old—and her pursed lips turned into a pout. "This is so not fair! Can I have your boobs for just *one* night?"

"Yeah, sure . . . let me just take them off," I said, deadpan. "Tell me, Candi, do I look all right?"

"Uh, yeah. I'd do you."

I snorted, "You're disgusting."

"You love me."

Rolling my eyes, I walked into my bathroom and put on some perfume. "It's true."

Just then there was a knock on the door. Candice squealed, did her little happy clap, and left my room. I took everything I would need out of my monster of a purse and threw it in the dark green clutch Candice had dropped on my bed as well. With one last breath and look in the mirror, I stepped out into the living room and tripped over myself when I saw them. My hand shot out to the wall to keep myself somewhat vertical, and both guys standing near the door with Candice took a step toward me with eyes wide and arms out. Like they could catch me from over twenty feet away.

This is not happening.

"Wow, smooth, Rach." Candice sighed and shook her head.

When I righted myself, I tried to keep my eyes on the ground or anywhere but on him. But of course I found myself locked in his steely gaze. Recognition flashed in them and that stupid smirk crossed his face.

"Guys, this is my roommate and best friend, Rachel. Rachel, this is Mason and Logan."

Swallowing the last of my pride, I walked over to them, this time without any incident, and reached out to shake their hands. They looked a lot alike. Both were tall—still a few inches taller than me even with those heels on—tan, and had dark just-got-out-of-bed hair. The one standing closest to Candice, who reintroduced himself as Mason, had arms so massive, I swear the sleeves of his shirt were about to tear from how much they were stretching against the bulging muscles. To be honest, they were kind of frightening. He had tribal tattoos coming down both arms, stopping halfway down; a killer smile; and dominating eyes. But then he picked me up in a big bear hug, and all freaky thoughts of him melted away. Massive teddy bear.

I laughed and pushed away from him when he set me back down, and I turned my narrowed eyes on the guy standing next to him. "I like the name Logan. You should stick with it. It sounds much better than Kash."

Mason snorted and Candice groaned into her hand before gasping and pointing at me. "Wait! You know him?"

"Yeah, he tried to take my car door off this afternoon when I got back."

Kash . . . Logan—whatever his name was—stopped sucking on his lip ring and I had the strangest urge to take over that lovely task for him. "You know, we could always turn that around and say you tried to ruin my bike."

"You pulled into the spot *way* too fast, and I'd been opening my door!"

"Fast? Sweetheart, I promise I wasn't going fast, and I'd already been turning in before you opened your door. It's not my fault you threw your door open."

"I did not throw my door open! And don't call me sweetheart. You don't know me."

"Uh, Rach. You do kinda throw your door open."

"Candice." I turned to look at her and gave her a *Whose side are you on?* look. "So not helping right now!"

"So," Mason said loudly, and clapped his hands, "I'm starving. We going?"

Just as I was about to say I was going to stay home, and actually mean it this time, Candice grabbed my hand and walked me toward the door. "Yep!"

I turned, waiting for Logan to exit the apartment so I could lock the door, and found him directly in front of me. I inhaled sharply, and his eyes slowly worked their way down my body and back up. When his liquid-steel eyes met mine, I swear I shivered and my skin was instantly covered with goose bumps. That stupid smirk came back and I narrowed my eyes at him as I tried to ignore the way my heart was pounding.

Calm down, Rachel. He's annoying, and he's not even cute. Those eyes do not put you in a daze, that smile does not pierce you to the floor. You do not want to bite down on that ring on the left side of his bottom lip. You do not want to rip his shirt off to see the muscles that fill it out perfectly. And you do not want to spend hours studying his tattoo sleeves. Not. At. All.

Candice couldn't have been more obvious when she suggested we take my Jeep or that Logan ride in front with me. But there was no point in arguing. Candice always got her way. Obviously.

"So, let's take the guys to the Oasis, Rach. That way they can see the lake."

Thank God I hadn't started driving yet, because I slammed on the brake even though I was still in park. "No!" Everyone in the car jerked back. "I mean, um . . . it's just always so crowded there. And on a summer night, it's gonna be crazy." Anything that reminded me of Blake, I definitely wanted to avoid.

"Oh . . . kay. Well then." Candice thought for a second before saying warily, "Are you going to freak out if I suggest Hula Hut?"

"No, I'm not. And I—I didn't freak out."

"Whatever, Rachel. Just drive."

I glanced in the rearview mirror to see her give me a *Cool it* look before turning to whisper in Mason's ear.

"Hey, are you gonna be okay to drive?" Logan asked softly in my ear. "You look sick all of a sudden."

"Thanks," I said through clenched teeth, and shot him a glare as I backed out of my space.

"I didn't— Jesus," he huffed, and sat back. "Forget it."

I took a shaky breath in and held it for a few seconds before releasing it. I knew I was being rude. But it was like I couldn't stop. "So why'd you tell me your name is Kash if it's Logan? Are you a part of some motorcycle gang or something and you got stuck with the shitty nickname? Or do you just sing like Johnny Cash?" He definitely had a voice deep and smooth enough for that to be a possibility.

Logan made a noise between a scoff and a laugh and shook his head. "First off, they're called motorcycle *clubs,* not gangs. And no, I'm not a part of one; I just love motorcycles. Second, you were wrong earlier, and you're wrong now. Kash isn't a nickname. It's my middle name, and I've gone by Kash my entire life. It was my grandpa's name."

Oh sweet baby Jesus, someone please give me a time machine so I can restart today. "Um . . ." I tilted my head to the side and grimaced. "I'm just going to throw myself out of the car now."

"Didn't mean to make you think I'd lied to you or something. Mason was the one who introduced us to your roommate and I was on my way out to fill my bike up with gas, so I didn't have time to talk to her. He always introduces me as Logan. Not really sure why."

"I'm really sorry. I've—" I quickly broke off. There was no point in explaining I'd had a bad day. I'd been a bitch, and there was really no excuse for that. "I'm sorry."

"Don't worry about it."

"So," I said a couple minutes later, "you just moved in? Are you from the Austin area, or . . ." I trailed off and glanced over to see him sucking on the damn lip ring again. Why was that so hot?

"Ah, no. We're from . . . far East Texas."

Vague. "Um. Okay. What brought you here?"

"Change of pace mostly. How about you? You from the area?"

"We're from *far* West Texas." I let that linger for a moment before turning and shooting him a grin. "Otherwise known as California."

"Smart-ass." He smiled wide and I forced my eyes back on the road. Oh Lord, that smile was perfect. "Let me guess. College?"

"Yep."

"Isn't it summer? Wouldn't you want to go home during vacation?"

"Uh, yeah. It is . . . but Candice has a cheer camp for elementary-school girls she's working at this summer. And where Candice goes, I go."

He huffed softly and looked back at Candice and Mason. "Cheerleader. Yeah, I'd already kinda pegged her as one; she looks like it."

At barely over five feet, with bleached blond hair, bright green eyes, and an ever-present smile and bounce in her step, yeah, she definitely looked like it.

"So you're a cheerleader too?"

"Ha! Um, no. Definitely not." Candice usually had to drag me to games and was always getting on me about my lack of enthusiasm for sports. Not my fault they reminded me of my dad. I would always sit on the couch with him while he watched whatever games were playing. He'd taught me everything there was to know about each sport, and watching them now, I could still hear him calling out fouls, flags, and strikes before the refs or umps did it themselves.

"So . . ." Kash drew out the word and turned his body so his back was against the door and he was facing me.

"So, what?"

"You're not a cheerleader; what are you?"

For such an innocent question, it hit me deep. I felt like I was walking around lost half the time, and the other half I was just following Candice to be near someone I considered family so I wouldn't break down. I'd only majored in athletic training because it was close to Candice's major. I didn't want to do anything with it when I graduated—to be honest, I had no idea what I wanted to do when I graduated. I didn't know who I was, let alone who, and what, I *wanted* to be.

"I'm just Rachel," I finally answered, and flickered a glance toward Kash to see his brow furrow as he studied me.

We got to the restaurant without my having a minor freak-out or impulsively slamming on the brakes again. But hell if I didn't start drifting into the lanes next to us a few times because I kept sneaking glances at Kash. And by the way the corners of his mouth kept tilting up like he was fighting off a grin, I knew he was aware of why I was currently not helping women's driving statistics.

Candice and I ordered margaritas while the guys ordered beers, and I downed my margarita so fast, the guys were looking at me like I was a crazy alcoholic, and Candice just looked embarrassed. I really didn't even care anymore what they all thought. I'd had a bad day and instead of its getting better, I'd continued to make it worse. Looking at the large glass, which only had ice left in it, I frowned and set it back down on the table. Whenever I was the one driving, I only allowed myself to have one drink, and now I was regretting not enjoying that.

"Do you want another?" Kash asked with a lazy smile that I wasn't sure if I hated or loved yet.

"No, I drove. One's enough."

"I'll drive us back if you want." We were in a small booth, and Candice had made it a point to sit with Mason, which put Kash and me in a position to get all up close and personal whether we wanted to or not. And now he was leaning in and the smell of his musky cologne was calling my name. "You look like you need more than one."

His cologne had officially stopped talking to me. I sat back so I was smashed against the wall and raised an eyebrow at him. "Just like I look sick? You really are quite the charmer, aren't you?"

He didn't miss a beat. "And you really know how to turn shit around so I look like an asshole, don't you?"

I huffed a laugh. "Just saying . . . girls don't like to hear they look bad. I'm almost waiting for you to tell me I look tired next."

Kash's eyes roamed my face. "Well, I wasn't planning on mentioning it . . ."

"Wow." My jaw dropped and I blinked rapidly. "I don't need to do a thing. You make yourself look like an asshole all on your own."

He laughed loudly and leaned in closer than he'd been before. "I don't know what happened in the car earlier, but you looked like you'd seen a ghost. And right now, you're putting off an uncomfortable vibe that I'm sure half the restaurant can feel. You know you look beautiful, but that doesn't hide the underlying stress that is rolling off you." Before I could say anything, he continued. "So that makes me assume you've had a really bad day, which is why I offered to drive us all home so you could have another drink or two. If you honestly think what I've said means you look bad, then that's your own problem you'll have to deal with. And as long as you're giving some attitude, be prepared to get some in return."

Oh. Wow. If he hadn't already bothered me so much, I'd have wanted to make him my new best friend. Or maybe that was the tequila already hitting my completely empty stomach. He cocked an eyebrow and I decided it was definitely the tequila talking.

When he sat back, I turned to look at the table and busied myself by eating chips and salsa, and the next time the waiter passed us, Kash ordered me another margarita. He and I didn't say anything to each other or the flirting duo across from us until it was delivered to the table.

Pushing it toward me, he smiled softly and kept his eyes on the drink. "I'll get us back to the complex. Just relax, and maybe try to enjoy this one, yeah?"

I laughed and his eyes flashed down to mine. Taking the drink, I took a sip and relaxed into the back of the booth. I didn't understand this guy sitting next to me, and although I wanted to hate him, I found myself smiling as I thought about his no-bullshit attitude. I'd had a bad day and taken it out on a stranger—a gorgeous stranger, no less—and while I still felt embarrassed about the first and second impressions I was leaving, I couldn't help but be intrigued by him.

But then thoughts of Blake crept back into my mind and I pushed down any feelings that may have started making themselves known about Kash as I scooted closer to the wall of the booth. Getting caught up in a guy was the last thing I needed right now.

4

Kash

"WHAT THE HELL are you thinking?"

"Uh . . . that she's hot and I need to get laid?" Mason looked at me like I was missing something completely obvious.

"You really think it's smart to get involved with someone while we're in the middle of an assignment?"

He sighed heavily and dropped to the floor, leaning up against one of the walls. "You can't tell me this assignment isn't completely different from anything we've done. The only reason we can't tell our families where we are is because of the hit. But other than that, what we're doing—it's like we're detectives."

"Yeah, and we're still *undercover*."

"Whatever, Kash, you think detectives don't have relationships? Don't have families?"

I groaned and raked a hand through my hair. He wasn't getting it. "Of course they have relationships and families. They're allowed to have lives. *This*"—I motioned to our empty apartment—"isn't our life. We aren't here to start new lives, Mason. We're here to find a serial killer and stay hidden. All the rest of this is just for show. The minute we forget that is the minute James Camden slips through our fingers and another girl ends up dead. Do you want that on you?"

"What the fuck, Kash? Of course I don't! Jesus, it's not like I want to marry her. And from what she was saying last night, Candice isn't the type of girl to be tied to one guy at a time. I don't have to worry about her being clingy or wanting a relationship. So back off and instead of putting this shit on me, maybe worry about the fact that you couldn't take your eyes off Rachel all night."

My gaze quickly darted to the window that gave me a perfect view of the girls' apartment. "She's hot, sue me. But I'm not thinking about letting her get in the way of what we're here for."

"Perfect." He stood up and stretched before heading to the front door. "I'm not going to let Candice get in the way either. But since we don't check in 'til Monday, you can be damn sure I'm using this weekend to my advantage. See ya."

"Have you forgotten we have no furniture?"

"Ask Rachel to go with you to pick out some stuff. I'm sure she'd be happy to *do* it." He wagged his eyebrows and I groaned.

Just as he turned the doorknob, I slapped my hand down on the door to keep it shut and spoke low. "What we do? The lives we live? There's no room for family or relationships, Mason. How many voice mails has your mom already left sobbing?" Mason ground his jaw but stayed quiet. "We've only been gone two days and they're already freaking out. Because even though we didn't tell them, they know what's going on, and they're fucking terrified. You hate doing that to your parents and sister; would you really want to bring a girlfriend or wife into what we do? Leaving them without notice for months or years at a time while we live the way those drug dealers do. You really want that for someone else?"

With a hard shove, he narrowed his eyes at me. "No, I wouldn't do that. And what's about to happen in that apartment"—he pointed toward the door—"will never make it that far. Even if it did, I would get out of undercover if I was getting serious with someone. You can't do this for the rest of your life, Kash. And like I said, I'm not the one you need to be worried about. The way you were looking at Rachel last night . . . I've never seen you look at a girl like that, not even Megan. So stop freakin' preaching to me and focus on yourself."

Megan and I had dated all throughout high school, through the first couple years of college, and when I went through the academy. When Mason and I got moved to undercover, I told her as much as I could, but it wasn't enough for her. She was engaged to some guy she'd met in one of her classes by the time we finished our first assignment. Mason knew I'd planned to marry her, and having Megan leave me put everything in perspective for me. I was happy for her now; she deserved someone who she could count on to be home for dinner, and I wasn't that guy.

"Like I said, Rachel's hot! Any guy with a working dick isn't going to be able to stop looking at her. But whatever you're thinking is happening for me with her, you're wrong. She's a grade-A bitch."

Mason snorted. "Whatever, Kash. You weren't just looking

at her. You were studying her, like you were trying to figure her out. I know you better than anyone and I say if anyone here is in danger of losing focus, it's you. Do me a favor, bro. Go get laid or something, lighten the hell up, and then we can focus on this case." With that, he opened the door and practically charged across the hall.

The girls' door opened, and like every other time I'd seen her, it felt like I'd gotten punched in the gut, all the air in my body leaving in one heavy rush. Rachel really was the most beautiful girl I'd ever seen. There was no doubting that. With long, dark hair; eyes so blue I'd found myself trying to see if she was wearing colored contacts—she wasn't, by the way; and a soft smile that made me want to fall to my knees, it wasn't hard to see why I couldn't stop looking at her. And those legs. My eyes traveled down to her bare legs as she let Mason into their apartment and I subconsciously started sucking on my lip ring again. Dear God, those legs were freakin' long and perfect . . . and headed right toward me.

My eyes snapped up and she looked back at her apartment door, which had just slammed shut, before meeting my gaze. "Morning, Kash."

"Good morning."

"Mason said you needed me for something in here."

Oh hell no, he told her I needed to get laid? I was gonna kill him. I locked my jaw and spoke low. "I don't need anything from you." *Especially pity sex.*

Her blue eyes widened and she rocked back on her heels. "Wow, um, noted. Remind me never to come to you if something breaks or I need help moving heavy things. Have a nice day." I swear I heard her mumble "*asshole*" when she turned and walked back to her door, then smacked right into it when she tried to open it and walk in at the same time. "What the— Oh *hell* no. Candice! Open the door!" She pounded her hand against the door. "Candice Marie Jenkins! I am in my pajamas and do not have my purse, cell phone, or keys. Open the damn door! I hear you two laughing!"

If I hadn't been so pissed off at Mason for sending Rachel over here and for her agreeing to it, I'd have been laughing too.

"I swear, if you do not unlock this door and let me in, I will go Cali bitch on your asses!"

Okay, now I was laughing.

The door next to ours opened and a middle-aged man looked between Rachel and me. He had his cell in his hand like he couldn't decide if he was going to call the cops or not.

"I will cut you!" Rachel swore and continued beating on the door; my neighbor looked at his phone and I groaned.

Pushing away from the wall, I took the few steps over to Rachel, grabbed around her waist, and pulled her back with me.

"Let me go, Kash. Candice! Open the door!"

"Calm down, you're freaking the neighbors out."

"I don't care! I do not want to be locked out of my apartment so I'm forced to spend time with you! You're rude, did you know that?"

I couldn't help but laugh at her. "I'm rude? If you hate me so much, you should have never agreed to come 'help' me." I nodded and gave a reassuring smile to the now-confused-looking neighbor before walking us into my apartment and releasing her.

"Excuse me for trying to be nice! That's what people do, they *help* people, especially when they're new to the— Holy crap, where's all your stuff?" She looked around at our living room, which was mostly bare save for the two boxes Mason brought.

"We—"

"Is this what Mason was talking about? He said I'd know it when I saw it."

Wait. What? "What are you talking about?"

"Mason said you needed me for something in here. I asked him what that *something* was, and he said as soon as I walked into the apartment I'd see what you needed help with."

Fuck. Me. "Oh shit, Rachel. Um . . ."

"When is all your furniture coming?" She began walking around the place and her eyes got bigger with each empty room she came across. "Did you guys sleep in here last night?"

"Uh, yeah. Good news? Floor is actually pretty comfortable. So there's that."

"Bad news?"

"We don't have anything coming, we need to go buy new stuff." I took a deep breath and blew it out quickly. "And I'm starting to think that's what Mason was sending you over here for."

She'd been slowly nodding her head at the beginning, but then she stopped and tilted it to the side. "Starting to? What did you think we were talking about earlier?"

"Uh—so would you like to go furniture shopping with me?" I scratched the back of my neck nervously and she narrowed her beautiful eyes at me.

"No! I would not like to go furniture shopping with you, Kash. Did you already forget *just* telling me that you didn't need anything from me?"

"I—that was a misunderstanding. I thought you . . . that

Mason . . . it doesn't matter. Like I said, misunderstanding. If you don't want to come with me, that's fine. You can hang out here, but obviously, you'd just be sitting on the floor."

"What misunderstanding? What did you think was happening?"

I groaned and grabbed the keys out of my pocket. "Forget it, Rachel."

"No, I deserve to know why you were so rude when I was offering to help you!"

I flung my arm out to the side and practically growled at her, "I thought he sent you over here to fuck me, and I thought you agreed to it!"

Instead of laughing at me, like I'd have expected any normal person to do, her stubborn expression fell, and all color drained from her face. Her mouth fell open and she quickly shut it, licking her lips as she forcibly swallowed. "I d-don't want . . . I don't want to have sex with you," she whispered, and backed up until she hit the wall.

"Okay, Rachel, that's fine." I spoke like I was talking to a scared victim. What was going on with her? "That's good to know, I don't want to have sex with you either, that's why I was an asshole earlier."

That was a lie. I'd even freakin' dreamed about this girl last night and woken with a painful hard-on I had to take care of in the shower, all the while Rachel flashing through my mind. And I'd lied to Mason earlier. Rachel wasn't a bitch, though she'd definitely shown her bitchy side at our first meeting and before we got to the restaurant last night. But it didn't take more than a handful of minutes watching her to realize it was her shield. It was her way of protecting herself. What she was hiding, I had no idea, and apparently it'd been obvious I was trying to figure it out last night. But there was something, and for some reason, I wanted to find out what it was and be whatever shield she needed.

And that was dangerous.

I'd been serious when I was talking to Mason about keeping focused, but he'd seen through my bullshit. I'd needed to say it to someone so I could try to get it through my head too. Anything with Rachel would be a bad idea. It wasn't that I couldn't have meaningless hookups; Mason and I had faced that a couple times with different groups we'd had to get into. To say we were paranoid about making sure we were still clean after being with those girls was an understatement. But from the moment Rachel had practically fallen out of her car yesterday afternoon, there was no doubting there was something different about her. There's no such thing as meaningless when you find a girl like Rachel.

Rachel squeezed her eyes shut and took two deep breaths in and out before opening them again. But she wouldn't look at me.

"Rachel?"

"What?" she snapped.

Shield. "Are you feeling okay, do you need something to eat or drink? I don't have anything here but I can go get something."

"I'm fine." She took one more deep breath and forced her eyes to my face. "Tell me why you thought that's why Mason would have me come over here."

"It's just something we were talking about."

"You were talking about having sex with me?!"

"No! Jesus, no. We just—" I groaned and shifted my weight. "He was going over there to be with Candice and told me I needed to get laid. That's all. Then you showed up saying what you said . . . and I just thought . . . It doesn't matter."

"Okay. Look, can we get out of your apartment? I'll go help you pick out furniture or whatever. I just don't feel comfortable being in here with you right now." Her chest started rising and falling quickly and I just stood there staring at her.

I was scaring her? She was scared of me! That was fucking awesome. I couldn't think about anything but getting to know her in every damn way possible, and I was freaking scaring her. Perfect. "Yeah, let's go."

We walked in silence out to my truck, and no, it didn't escape my notice that she stayed an awkward distance from me. As soon as she was in the passenger seat, I ran to the driver's side and hopped in. Just as I turned the ignition she cleared her throat and looked down at her hands, which she was twisting together. "Can we just get it out there right now that I don't want anything with you or from you?"

I'm not going to lie; it felt like she'd punched me. But I still nodded.

"I'm not looking for, or interested in, a relationship. It's nothing against you. I just—I can't—I don't. Um, I—"

"Rachel." I waited until she looked up at me and again found myself wishing I could figure out what she was hiding from me. Did she have a boyfriend? Just get out of a bad relationship? "It's fine. Nothing between us, I got it."

With a quick breath in, she nodded her head and forced a smile. "We kind of got off on the wrong foot, but since we're going to be neighbors I'd like it if we were friends. I'm sorry for how I was toward you when I met you, and I'm sorry for the confusion this morning—can we just start over?"

Only being friends with her sounded about as fun as kicking puppies right now. But this was good; I didn't have time for a distraction and Rachel would definitely be a distraction . . . I don't know why I even try lying to myself. The real problem was I couldn't put Rachel in my world. I couldn't put her in this danger, and being with her would put her right in the middle of it. So friends it was, then. "Sure," I said softly, and watched a genuine smile cross her face.

She stuck out her hand. "I'm Rachel Masters, from far West Texas."

God, she was cute. I grabbed her hand and tried to ignore the warmth coming from her body and how I wanted to lean into her, press my mouth to her neck, and breathe in the sweet scent coming from her. "Logan . . . Hendricks, from far East Texas. But you can call me Kash. It's good to meet you, Rachel."

"You too, Kash with a *K*."

"You know, my apartment is pretty bare."

"That's an understatement," she whispered on a laugh as she sat back and put her seat belt on. "I happen to be locked out of my apartment and have nothing to do today . . ."

"You want to help me pick out new furniture?"

"Took you long enough to ask me!"

I smiled and threw my truck in reverse. "Smart-ass."

"So tell me honestly."

I glanced over at Rachel, who was lying down beside me, and raised an eyebrow.

"Can you feel it, Kash?" Her eyes widened and she slapped down on the mattress. "Can you *feel* the difference this mattress makes?"

The saleswoman kept rambling on about the statistics of this bed and I tried not to laugh as Rachel acted as if what she was saying was from the Bible.

"Isn't this one just great?" The woman leaned over the bed to look at us. Her drawl was so thick that her *great* sounded more like *gright*.

"Feels just like a cloud, you were so right!" Rachel smiled sweetly at her.

"Oh, I *knew* y'all would just love this one! But c'mon over to the other side of the store, I have a few more to show you. And they just blow this one right out of the water," she said, and walked away to the next set of mattresses.

Rachel swung her legs over to the side and looked back at me, that same sweet smile plastered on her face. "It feels exactly like the last six except it's an extra two thousand dollars. So that just makes it so much better!" She scrunched up her nose on the last few words and smacked her hand down on the mattress again.

I rolled off the mattress and pulled her with me as I followed the saleswoman. "You look like a Miss America contestant on shrooms," I whispered to Rachel, and she snorted.

She began waving at no one in particular like she was in a pageant, and her smile widened. "In case you're wondering, the snozberries *do* taste like snozberries."

"Oh, I thought y'all were right behind me!" The saleswoman had stopped and turned to face us a good twenty feet ahead. "Well c'mon, you two, you're gonna love this next one!"

I groaned and Rachel's fake smile faltered. "Since when does *me* sound like *maaayyy*?" I asked quietly when she began walking again.

"She reminds me of Dolly Parton. She has got to go."

I barked out a laugh and tried not to picture the saleswoman as a Dolly clone.

Three beds and four couches later and I thought I was going to strangle the Dolly impersonator. And we still weren't done with this store. How had I gone day in and day out with drugged-out scum and hookers and not clawed my eyes out, but an hour with this woman had me wanting nothing more than to take off running out of the store while screaming at Rachel that it was every man for himself?

I swear, if it weren't for Rachel and her smart-ass comments, I would have been hiding underneath one of the beds. But even Rachel was starting to look worn out. Her fake smiles were a little less Barbie and a little more ermahgerd, and she looked ready to pass out on the couch I'd just gotten up from.

"Hmm." Dolly 2.0 tapped her chin and turned to look around her. "Ah! I got the perfect set over here!"

"That's it," Rachel whispered, a horrified look on her beautiful face. "This is where I die. In a furniture store the size of freakin' Costco!" She shuffled off after the saleswoman and I quickly caught up to her side. When I got there, her psychotic-Barbie look was back. "Did you know the leather couches we're about to look at have a warranty for ten years? No cracks!"

"Oh, well in that case, I have to buy these. Right?"

"Of course." She got oddly silent as we followed along and out of nowhere started dancing all crazy and lip-syncing to the song playing throughout the store.

I stopped, my eyes going wide as I watched her. As soon as the chorus ended she stopped, and just in time, since our saleswoman had turned to see why we weren't with her.

"Y'all coming?"

"Yes, ma'am!" Rachel answered since I was still looking at her with my jaw dropped. Her serene expression began cracking and she bit down on her bottom lip to keep from laughing. Glancing over at me, she gave me a soft nudge and winked before walking over to the next living room set, leaving me staring after her before I burst out laughing.

Damn, I'm pretty sure I just fell in love with Rachel Masters.

RACHEL FLOPPED DOWN onto the love seat and I stretched out on the couch with a groan. How do women like full days of shopping? This shit was exhausting. After we had finished at the furniture store, we'd gone to pick out lamps and other things Rachel deemed necessary before heading to the grocery store; I was ready to crash and not wake up until I needed to be at the department on Monday. But then all the furniture had arrived and we'd started "decorating."

"You're insane, woman."

She grunted some form of agreement. "But you're finished. You're fully moved in."

"I'm gonna kill Mason for not helping."

"Yeah, well . . . I'm used to this by now."

I rolled over so I could look at her. God, this girl was all long, tan legs. Thank God she'd still been in her pajamas when they locked her out. I'd had the best view all day. "Used to helping random guys pick out everything for their apartment?"

She laughed softly and rolled her head like she was trying to relieve the tension in her neck. I wanted to help with that, but I was pretty sure friends didn't do that. Or if they did they didn't think about following it by tracing the curve of her neck with their mouth. "No, I mean I'm used to being kicked out. I thought it would be different once we got our apartment, since I could just go into my room. But she still fully kicks me out whenever she's hooking up with someone."

My brow wrinkled. "You're serious?"

"Uh-huh."

"Do you get kicked out a lot?" She didn't answer; she just turned to look at me with raised eyebrows. *I'll take that as a yes.* "Where do you go?"

"I've become really close with the baristas at one of the twenty-four-hour Starbucks."

What in the actual fuck? And Candice was supposed to be her best friend? She and Mason had been locked in the apartment for almost twelve hours. "And do you do the same?"

Judging by her wide blue eyes, my gruff tone surprised both of us. I hadn't meant to ask. I didn't really want to know if Rachel was like Candice, but something in me needed to know. From Candice's drunk rambling the night before, I knew Rachel was single, but that didn't mean a whole hell of a lot.

"I'm sorry . . . what?"

I tried to smirk at her, but I'm positive it came off as more of a scowl. "Do you kick Candice out too?"

She fidgeted and broke eye contact with me. "There's never a need to."

Never as in she's never? Or never as in—not in a while? Before I could say anything else, she sat up and cleared her throat.

"Tell me, Kash. What is it you and Mason do?"

And so it begins. I got comfortable and flashed her a lazy smile. "We just got here yesterday. You gonna give us some time to try and find something?"

"How old are you?"

"Are we playing twenty questions now, sweetheart?"

Her eyes narrowed and she continued to stare at me.

"I'm twenty-five. You?"

"Twenty-one." She shook her head dismissively. "But that's beside the point. You're twenty-five, and I'm guessing Mason is around the same age?" When I nodded she continued. "And sorry for being nosy, but since I happened to be with you all day, I also saw how much you spent on setting up your new apartment. I know you didn't move here for a job, but I figured if you have that much just to blow on furniture and such, you must've had a pretty cushy job in Bullshit, Texas."

"*Cushy* is about the exact opposite of what we had. As for the money? We have rich parents." Well, technically that was true. But still, I hadn't lived off my parents' money since I was seventeen. "And you really have an issue with where I'm from, don't you?"

"I don't like liars."

"So now I'm lying? Why is it so hard to believe I'm from East Texas? Maybe I just don't want you to know which town because I like to keep my life private."

"Maybe because you don't sound like you're from Texas." She shrugged, but her stare was still full of a challenge. "Like, at all. Neither does Mason."

"So, you're saying . . ." I rolled off the couch and took the few steps toward her. If she wanted me to sound like I was from Texas, then I was about to sound like I was from motherfucking Texas. ". . . if I had a drawl, you'd believe me?" Her breath hitched when I leaned over her body and put my hands on the couch on either side of her head. Our faces were just inches apart and I swear I almost groaned when she quickly licked her lips.

Leaning in so my lips brushed her ear, I spoke soft and low. And yeah, with a fucking drawl. "Just say the word, darlin'. I'll talk however you want me to."

Rachel shivered beneath me and I'm almost positive I stopped breathing for a few seconds. Her cheek brushed against mine as she turned into me, and I moved so our lips were centimeters apart. Her blue eyes were hooded as they searched mine, and I took the rapid rise and fall of her chest as a sign that she wanted this just as much as I did. My nose brushed hers and as I leaned closer to press my lips to hers, the door burst open and Rachel's hands shot out to push against my chest.

"Oh, well if I wasn't gone long enough, I can come back." Mason laughed loudly and Rachel slipped out from under my arm and took off for the door. Without a glance at either of us, she rushed out and over to her own apartment. "Jesus, Kash. You kiss that bad?"

I was still leaning against the couch. My eyes had been wide with confusion but were now narrowed at Mason's words. "Shut up, man. I didn't even touch her."

"Well you did something. She took off like she couldn't get away from you fast enough."

"I said shut the fuck up," I growled, and sank back onto the couch I'd originally been on. What the hell had just happened? She had turned her head toward me, she'd wanted *something;* the look in her eyes had said it all.

Even with the friends-only talk we'd had that morning, something had changed between us as the day had gone on. Yeah, the shopping had been exhausting, but doing it with Rachel had made it entertaining. Her shield had been gone, and the girl underneath it was nothing less than incredible. She was still a smart-ass, but she was funny and sweet. And sexy—God, she was so damn sexy, and I was positive she didn't have a clue. More than anything, Rachel didn't try to impress me. She was who she was and didn't care how that came across to others.

I'd been thinking there was no way I could go day in and day out with this girl and not have her be mine. But after what had just happened, I was pretty sure I'd caused her shield to go back up.

"Wow, you guys did a great job today." Mason's words broke through my thoughts and I looked around the living room.

"Yeah, no thanks to you."

"I trusted you to get good shit. And this TV . . . mmm. Sixty-inch? I'm so proud. I've taught you well."

I rolled my eyes. "You really thought I'd get a shitty TV? Do you not know me at all?"

He shrugged and clapped his hands together once. "Well, since there's nothing for me to do here"—I narrowed my eyes at him—"we're gonna have pizza with the girls. So let's go."

"Rach and I went and got food today, we can make something for all of us."

"Aww, you guys went grocery shopping too? So cute."

I threw a pillow at him; he caught it easily and launched it back at me.

"I already ordered the pizza. Let's go."

"I'll meet you over there. I need a shower." *A very* cold *shower.*

5

Rachel

DRAINING THE REST of my lukewarm tea, I rinsed out the mug and was about to put it in the dishwasher when there was a knock on the door. I quickly thought about the day and looked over at the clock on the microwave. Was it sad that this was only the third Thursday since we'd moved in, and I already knew it would be Mrs. Adams? I set the mug down and made my way over to the door. When I opened it I saw a frazzled-looking Mrs. Adams standing there worrying her hands.

"Oh, Rachel dear! Thank heavens you're here! All my babies, they're gone. I need your help finding them, please come help me!" Without another word directed toward me, she began calling for Snickers and searching for her cats.

Mrs. Adams was the definition of a *crazy* cat lady. She was in her seventies, her husband had died ten years ago—as I'd come to find out from the son who brought her groceries three times a week and had seen me helping her the previous week—and she had absolutely no cats. She just *thought* she had them. When in reality, all of her cats were a bunch of stuffed animals, or pillows and blankets with pictures of cute little fur-balls on them. I never saw her unless it was a Thursday, and the first time she'd told me all her cats had escaped, I'd felt bad for the poor woman. That is, until I finally got an emotional Mrs. Adams back into her apartment and she began clinging to her stuffed animals, begging them never to leave her again. I'd left quickly after that, and when she'd shown up crying at half past eight again last week, claiming all her cats had run away again, I'd decided she needed someone to believe her for her five minutes of weekly crazy.

Like the previous two weeks, it was eight thirty on the dot, and this week we were searching for all her babies, but mainly Snickers. I followed behind her calling for the mischievous Snickers, and as she'd point under things, I'd fall to the ground and act like I was searching really hard for a cat I knew I'd never find.

"Oh, oh! Up there, what if they're up there? I'm positive Mr. Snickers would have led them up there."

So Snickers is a he? Good to know; that will help in the missing-cat search. I ran up the stairs to the second floor and continued to call out for the cats before making my way back downstairs to lead Mrs. Adams into the apartment directly to the left of ours.

"You know what, Mrs. Adams? I'm pretty sure I saw Snickers lead all the kittens into your apartment!"

"Oh, oh yes, I'm sure that's what he's done. He must have, those poor dears must've been so worried following him around—"

She broke off suddenly when we made it into her apartment and let out a little shriek before shuffle-running over to one of her pillows and hugging it close to her chest. "My babies are back! Mama missed you, don't ever leave me again!"

"Do you need anything else, Mrs. Adams?"

She turned and it broke my heart that her eyes were full of tears. How could her son leave her in an apartment alone like this? She needed someone with her all the time. "No, dear. Thank you. I'll see you tomorrow."

I just smiled and walked out of her wide-open front door, and right into a nicely muscled chest.

"Jesus, Kash!"

"What are you doing?"

"What are *you* doing? Why are you just standing out here like a creeper?"

He smirked and followed me over to my apartment. "I'm trying to figure out why you're army-crawling all over the breeze-way and shouting for a candy bar."

"I'm not shouting for a candy bar, I'm looking for a cat that isn't there."

One of his thick eyebrows rose and he bit down on his lip ring to try to hide his smile as he held my door open for us.

"Mrs. Adams . . . isn't exactly all there. She thinks she has cats and she doesn't. And every Thursday since we moved in, she's come knocking at eight thirty asking for me to help her look for them."

"And you help her, knowing they aren't there?"

"Well, I didn't know the first time until I got into her apartment. Her cats are really stuffed animals and pillows."

"But you helped her every other time knowing what you know?" He'd stopped biting on that ring and his lips kept tilting up as he tried to control his smile.

"Yeah, Kash, I did. Because no one else does, and don't laugh at me! It's not funny, I feel really bad for her! You should see how upset she gets over this."

I turned to walk into my room, but he caught me around my waist and hauled my body back to his. "I'm not laughing at you, Rach," he mumbled huskily, and his gray eyes roamed my face. "I think it's adorable that you help her. You're really just a big softy, aren't you?" Laughing when I growled at him, he continued to piss me off even more. "You're like Sour Patch Kids candy."

"What the hell?"

"Sour . . . then sweet."

"I will castrate you if you don't let me go right now." My eyes narrowed and he lost his fight as he grinned widely at me and kept me in his arms. When I realized he wasn't letting go, I sighed as I gave in. "Look, it breaks my heart. She shouldn't be there by herself. Her son drops off food three times a week and he's only here for about twenty minutes or so each time. She needs someone with her all the time. Instead she's just—she's alone. I hate that for her."

Kash's face softened and his hold on me got a little tighter. My heart picked up its pace and I blinked quickly as I looked away and pushed out of his strong grip.

"Do you want breakfast?"

"Uh, yeah. Sure." Clearing his throat, he looked behind him, toward the kitchen. "What are you gonna make me, woman?"

I snorted. "When you call me that, I literally just want to give you a bowl of cereal." But even as I said the words, I pulled the sausage out of the fridge and grabbed the pancake mix.

"You know you like it." I jumped when his voice came from directly behind me. He took the food out of my hands and put it on the counter before grabbing the skillet out of the cupboard. "If you didn't, you wouldn't keep cooking for me."

Rolling my eyes, I tried to act like his voice and nearness didn't have any kind of effect on me. But I'm sure I wasn't succeeding. I was positive he could hear the way my heart was pounding, the way my breaths were coming far too quickly, and see the goose bumps covering my arms.

We worked quickly and easily together in the kitchen, and soon my body relaxed as I remembered we could only be friends and we slipped into the comfortable banter Kash and I had shared over the last week.

Just as we were finishing up and I was grabbing plates out of the cabinet, Mason walked in without knocking and announced, "Kash, we gotta go."

"Breakfast," was his only reply.

"Nope, now."

I set down the plates just in time to be picked up in one of Mason's bear hugs, and he kissed the top of my head as he set me down. "You want breakfast, Mase?" I asked.

"Thanks, sweetheart, but we need to get going." He picked a piece of sausage out of the pile of paper towels and shoved it in his mouth.

"Dude, we just finished making this. Let me—"

"Kash." They shared a look for a moment. "We need to go work out."

Kash's eyes widened and he glanced over at me. "Rach, I'm sorry, I forgot today was Thursday. I'll make it up to you to-morrow."

Before I could respond, they were both walking out the door, and I was left there with enough breakfast to feed five of me.

"CANDICE, ARE YOU serious? I've been kicked out twice this week already. I don't feel like going to Starbucks again tonight."

"No one said you had to go to Starbucks every time I have someone over."

"Well where else am I supposed to go?"

She dropped her towel and began putting on pink lingerie. Why she even bothered with the lingerie, I had no idea. "You could go hang out with, oh, I don't know, Kash. Especially to-night. He'll be lonely." She winked.

"It's not Kash's job to babysit me when you decide you need to get some. And Mason . . . again? Really?"

"Ohmigod. Rach, he's incredible. He does this thing—"

"I don't want to know!" I shouted, and slammed my hands over my ears. "Mason is like Eli to me."

She made a face and shuddered.

Since the past weekend, I'd spent most of my time with Mason and Kash. They were usually home during the day while Can-dice was at cheer camp, and on Tuesday Kash had begun bar-tending at a bar/restaurant near campus. Mason had gotten the same position at a different bar downtown the next day. I was surprised they found work so quickly, but I guessed when you looked like them, it wasn't hard to find jobs.

I was happy for them. They were both only part-time, but it was something for now, Kash said, and they seemed happy about it. Throughout the almost-week with them, Mason had quickly taken on the role of the big brother I'd never wanted. But honestly, I loved the guy. His cousin, on the other hand . . . I wished I could view him the way I saw Mason, but every thought I had about Kash Hendricks was anything but sisterly. And while I knew we needed to remain friends, it was a near-constant struggle to get my body and heart to understand that too.

Mason walked into the apartment without knocking, as was becoming his usual routine, and I rolled off Candice's bed and went to grab my purse, phone, and keys. Mason grabbed me in another big hug and kissed my head. "Kash isn't working tonight."

I grumbled to myself and started picking everything up off the entryway table. "Just call me when I'm allowed back in." I'd barely stepped outside when they shut the door and locked it behind me. "Rude."

Taking a few steps toward the parking lot, I paused and shifted my weight a few times as I looked at the guys' door. With a deep breath, I gritted my teeth and walked quickly over to the door before knocking on it. Kash opened it after a moment in nothing but a pair of low-slung jeans and my mouth went dry.

"Rach." He laughed low and my eyes snapped up to his. "What's up?"

"Oh, um . . ." *This was a really bad idea. Would I look like a complete freak if I took off running for my car right now?* "Well, I . . ."

"Yes . . . ?"

"You, uh, wanna have a lock-out night with me?"

He mouthed the words *lock-out night* before recognition flashed through his gray eyes. "Mason with Candice?"

"Yep."

"You don't have to ask or have a reason, Rach. You're welcome here whenever."

My eyes drifted over the colorful artwork covering his shoulders and arms and I somehow made it into the apartment without running into anything. I wanted to study the tattoos but he was still smirking, so I forced my eyes onto the TV and walked past him.

"So did you get tired of hanging out at Starbucks for hours on end, or did they finally kick you out?"

I huffed and shook my head. *Such an ass.* Spinning around, I began walking right back to the front door. *I don't care that he's half-naked and I have to use superhuman strength to not throw myself at him and explore his sculpted body with my hands and mouth. He's just such a freaking pain.*

"I don't think so, Sour Patch." He grabbed my arm and pulled me back until I was standing in front of the couch. "Sit."

"I'm not a dog."

He rolled his eyes. "Sit down, woman. I'll be right back." With a shove strong enough to send me down to the couch, he smiled wryly and turned toward his bedroom.

"Put a shirt on while you're in there!"

He snorted.

Kash

HELL NO, I'M not putting a shirt on. She could act all she wanted. There was no mistaking that she was, at the very least, attracted to me. Her cheeks would flush whenever her eyes trailed over me, completely giving her away.

No need to make it easy for her by covering up.

Looking over my shoulder to make sure she was still on the couch, I shut my door and grabbed at my things. We'd *just* gotten back from being at the department for last-minute meetings all day, and my gun, holster, badge, and card to get into the department were all sitting on the bed. I walked quickly into the closet and put everything but my gun on the top shelf, where even I couldn't see them, before going back and putting my gun in the nightstand. After taking one more look around to make sure I hadn't missed anything, I walked back out to the living room.

Rachel's brow furrowed for a minute when she saw me, but not two seconds later, a blush stained her cheeks. Quickly averting her eyes, she looked back at the TV and continued scrolling through the guide. When she gasped, I rushed toward her, but she just looked up at me with the widest grin before pressing more buttons on the remote.

"Wait. Do you already have this movie?"

"*The A-Team*? No."

With a disappointed shake of her head, she hit *record* and clicked on the channel as the credits ran from the previous movie. "You're not allowed to delete this recording then."

I flopped down next to her on the love seat rather than going to the couch and tried not to smile when she inched away. "I'm guessing it's a good movie?"

She did a quick double take when my words finally clicked. "Are you— Wait. You're joking, right? You . . . you have to have seen this. You're a guy!"

"And?"

"Oh my word. You really haven't seen this? I'm pretty sure that's like . . . a sin. Or against the law, at the very least. This movie is amazing." She jumped off the couch and went over to browse through our Blu-ray collection, and when she turned back around to join me on the love seat, her face was full of pity. "It's okay, Kash. I'll educate you."

Rachel set about looking up movies on the guide and setting them to record whenever they were coming on next. Some I'd seen previews for during commercials and looked funny. Some I shook my head at when she hit the *record* button. Others were just not okay.

"Hell. No. I'm not going to watch a movie called *Bridesmaids.*"

"Um, actually, you will, and I'll bet you one hundred dollars right now that you'll willingly watch it more than once."

"I'll bet you *two* hundred and a week's worth of pancakes for breakfast that I won't make it twenty minutes in."

Her eyes never left the screen, and her hand never stopped clicking buttons on the remote as she set up endless movies to record, but a smug grin crossed her face and she held her free hand out to shake on the bet. "Deal."

After we finished watching *The A-Team,* which was actually good—though I honestly think the best part was how damn cute Rachel looked as she quoted the entire thing—we got two movies on demand. After we finished the first one, Rachel and I wandered into the kitchen.

"This is no good."

I stopped grabbing stuff out of the pantry and looked at her standing in front of the opened freezer. "What's no good?"

"First, you have no taste in movies, and now you have no Ben and Jerry's. Really, Kash . . . how did you survive all these years?"

I snorted. "We have great taste in moves. We have all the *Alien* movies, *Rocky, Rambo,* the *Die Hard* movies . . ."

"Exactly, nothing funny."

"We have *Office Space!*"

"True. You deserve a gold star for that one." She shut the freezer and faced me. "But literally, your collection probably came off a list of the top hundred guy movies or something. You need a little variety, and you need good ice cream. So thank the good Lord above I finally have a legit reason to ask you to put a shirt on, because we need to run to the store."

I set everything back in the pantry haphazardly and shut the door before stepping right up to her and backing her into the refrigerator. "Why can't you just admit you're attracted to me, Rachel?" I asked into her ear as I pressed my body against hers.

She swallowed audibly and shook her head as if to clear her mind before speaking. "Because I'm not? I'm not attracted to guys who look like they're Photoshopped and who have bigger chests than most girls I know."

I couldn't help it. I laughed loudly and had to pull back slightly when the movement and being pressed up against her made my jeans shrink a size. "Liar." Even if her voice hadn't gone all breathy, I still hadn't forgotten her blush.

"And I really hate your tattoos."

"No you don't."

"And your lip ring and your eyes. And your hair, it drives me nuts. You really need to cut it. Or better yet, one morning you'll wake up and I will have shaved it off while you slept."

I smiled and let my nose run along her jaw, loving the quick breath she took and how her eyes fluttered shut when I did.

"Good to know your favorite things about me, Sour Patch. And if you're wondering . . . everything about you is my favorite."

"They're not. And I wasn't."

"Keep telling yourself that if it helps you sleep at night. But do you think we could wrap up this meeting about how much you want me? I *really* need to go buy about a dozen pints of ice cream so I can work at not looking Photoshopped anymore."

Her eyes snapped open and darkened as she narrowed them at me. "God, you're annoying."

"And you're keeping me from eating."

"I'm not the one who isn't dressed."

Touché. "I think I should go like this. Maybe there will be a woman there who appreciates the way I look." I grinned when her blue eyes narrowed and started singing "No Shoes, No Shirt, No Problems" by Kenny Chesney as I backed out of the kitchen.

I *needed* her to stay away from me, but damn if I wasn't grinning like an idiot knowing that Rachel was falling for me just as hard as I was falling for her.

6

Rachel

STUPID TEXAS AND stupid allergies.

I'd never had allergies until I moved to Texas. And although I still had yet to determine what exactly it was I was allergic to, whenever it hit, it hit with a vengeance. I couldn't breathe through my nose, I sounded like a man, my face felt like it was going to break from being so congested, and my eyes were watering so bad it looked like I was constantly crying.

It was sexy.

I threw away the last empty box of Kleenex and went into the bathroom to grab a roll of toilet paper to take back to the couch with me. The front door opened as I was headed out of my bedroom and I saw Kash closing the door behind him. I would've sworn I'd locked that when Candice left for camp that morning.

Kash looked up when I entered the living room, and his eyes went wide. "You okay, Rach?"

"Ugh."

"I'll take that as a no," he murmured, and bit back a smile when he saw the roll of toilet paper I was carrying with me. "Do you have the flu?"

I shook my head and flopped down on the couch dramatically. "Whachoo want?"

Walking quickly over to me, he knelt down and put the back of his hand to my forehead. I swatted at it but he held down my hands and tried to decide if I had a fever. "You just have a cold then?"

"Allergies. Stupid mold or cedar or . . . air."

"Have you taken anything?"

"Nope. Juss woke up. Cantchoo tell?" I waved a hand over my pajama-covered body and wiped my tears away.

He smiled softly and stood up. "You still look beautiful. Let me find you something to take."

I wanted to have an *aww* moment, but just then I started in on a string of sneezes.

"Only six sneezes?" Kash called from the kitchen. "Come on, Rach. You're slacking. Next time go for eight at least."

I flipped him off and then there was a knock at the door. "Ugh." That was quickly becoming my favorite word. Rolling to the side, I tried to get my legs on the ground to get off the couch, but I rolled too far and my feet didn't move fast enough and I landed with a thud on the floor. "Fuck my life."

Kash barked out a laugh as I sluggishly got to my feet. "Get back on the couch, I'll get it."

"No, no. My door. I answer."

"It's eight thirty, it's going to be Mrs. Adams."

He remembered? "Crap. I forgod it was Thursday."

"Oh, you *forgod,* did you?"

I looked up at Kash's wicked smile and wished I had the energy to punch him. "Shuddup."

He beat me to the door and opened it as I came up behind him.

"Ra— Oh, you're a boy. Um . . ." Mrs. Adams stood there wringing her hands. "Uh, well . . . is Rachel here? She needs to help me, my cats are all gone."

"Hi, Mrs. Adams." I stepped up and tried to smile.

"Rachel dear! They're all gone, come quick!"

"Umb, I'm a little sick."

She shook her head. "The cats, dear."

I couldn't close my mouth and I'm pretty sure snot was starting to come out of my nose. Could she not see this?

"I'll help you, Mrs. Adams," Kash said with a charming smile.

"Butters won't respond to a boy."

Pushing past Kash, I looked at Mrs. Adams. "Well, let's find them, then."

"Yes, of course." She turned and began searching. "Butters!"

"Budders," I called lamely, and was suddenly being pulled backward. "Kash, stop. She needs help."

"Go get on the couch. I'm not going to tell you again." He pushed me back toward my door and gave me a stern look. "I'll help her today."

I stood there long enough to see Mrs. Adams look at him like he had three heads and Kash look underneath a bench before I walked back into the kitchen. After searching through the mostly bare medicine cabinet, I grabbed the bottle I was looking for and took a big swig before shuffling back to the couch.

Kash walked in a few minutes later and immediately went to the kitchen. Opening the same cabinet I'd just been in, he looked around before shutting it and looking over the counter at me. "Rach, there's nothing here you can take. I'll run to the st— What's in your hand?"

I lifted up the toilet paper roll.

"Other hand."

I lifted up the NyQuil.

"It's eight thirty in the morning. You're taking NyQuil?"

"Ugh." That's sick-talk for *Yes, I am, stop bitching at me.*

"All right, give me that." He pried the NyQuil from my hand and bent close. "I'll go to the store and get something for whenever you wake back up. Is there anything you need or want?"

"Nope." I rolled to my side and hugged the roll of toilet paper as I curled into a ball. I just wanted to go back to sleep and not have my nose feel like it was about to fall off.

A few moments later Kash was laying my comforter on me and lifting my head up to stuff my pillow beneath it. After a quick kiss to the top of my head, he was gone. He so deserved pancakes tomorrow morning.

Another round of sneezes tore through me. *Only five? Fail.*

Maybe his pancakes would have to wait until Saturday.

WHEN I WOKE up a few hours later, the apartment was empty, but the coffee table had boxes of Kleenex, cold and allergy medicine, a bottle of water, and a note on it.

Rach,
 Had to run to the bar to take inventory. Mason's running errands, call me if you need anything. The rest is in the kitchen.

*And if you eat my green ones, I will not take pity on you just
because you're sick.*
    Kash

Green ones? I walked into the kitchen and laughed out loud.
The counter had four cans of chicken noodle soup, eight Gatorade bottles, and three boxes of Sour Patch Kids on it. I put
away everything except for one of the boxes and went back to my
makeshift bed on the couch. Kash was either the worst . . . or the
absolute best at taking care of someone. Either way, I was falling
so in love with that man.

And yeah, I ate the green ones. I'd have to remember to hide
the other two boxes before he came over again.

Kash

"Chicken noodle soup and Gatorade?" Mason laughed and
opened the door to the police department. "She said she had allergies, not the flu."

"Well shit, I don't know! She really looked like she didn't feel
good, so I just got her everything I could think of."

"You're so whipped and you're not even screwing her."

I shook my head and tried not to punch him. "Shut up, Mase."

We walked in silence the rest of the way to the conference
room and both stopped when we got in the room. What the hell
was our chief from Tampa Bay doing here?

He didn't look at or acknowledge us in any way during our
three-hour meeting on Camden, possible leads, and some new
courses of action. The millions of reasons he could have been

there in Texas ran through my mind the entire time, and to be honest, at the end of the meeting I couldn't remember the actual details of it. I wasn't sure what Mason thought of his being there, but from the fact that his face was drained of color, I figured it was the same as me. Chief wouldn't have been there for good news.

"Gentlemen," he said by way of greeting once the room was finally cleared out, "sounds like you're doing your jobs well. Had a meeting with Detective Ryder before everyone was called in and we went over some things."

"You're checking up on us? Are you kidding me?" Mason looked annoyed but relieved that that was all he was there for. "When have we ever not done everything and more than what was asked of us at our jobs?"

Chief raised one graying eyebrow. "You're right. You *do* do more. Surely you haven't forgotten about what you did to get the police-brutality charge brought against you, right, Gates?"

Mason shut his mouth.

"And I'm not checking up on you to make sure you're doing well. If I didn't think you two were some of the best I've ever worked with, I wouldn't have given you this opportunity after what went down last month. I would have just suspended you before sending you to a desk."

Fuck . . . Mason was *about to make us desk bitches.*

"The charge was dropped, by the way; you're welcome."

"Thanks, Chief," Mason mumbled.

"No disrespect, sir, but why *are* you here?" I hurried to finish before he could get mad. "I mean, your being here kind of scared the shit out of us. The only reason I could come up with for it is that bad shit went down back home. So is everything okay?"

He took his time sitting back down in one of the chairs and straightening out his tie. "Things are great for you, gentlemen. My wife and I are here visiting family in Houston and I got the call yesterday morning that the guys hired to take the two of you out are now in prison awaiting trial for first-degree murder."

"That—" I looked over at Mason and straightened up a bit. "That's good. So we're not hiding anymore?"

"No, but for the duration of this case, you will continue to stay where you are, working where you are, and doing what you've been doing. If you want to tell your family where you're at, that's up to you."

"Understood," Mason answered when I got quiet.

"You boys work tonight?"

"No, sir."

"Let's go grab a beer and talk about this case and what's going to happen when you come back to Tampa Bay. I'm not exactly in a rush to get back to my wife's family," he said as his eyes widened in dread.

"MASE, WE NEED to talk about this."

"About what?"

"About not being in hiding."

He nodded his head and lifted one hand from the steering wheel to run it over his face. "I don't think we should tell our families where we are."

"Agreed. And I don't think we should tell the girls who we are yet."

"What? Why?"

"Same reason we don't want to tell our families where we are. We need to keep them safe. As soon as we tell them who we are, we'll have to tell them about our lives . . . at least back in Florida. They're going to know why we're here even if they don't know about the case. Their knowing anything is dangerous."

"It makes sense, but are you going to be able to stay away from her?"

I rolled my eyes. "It's not like you've been staying away from Candice."

"It's different, and you know it."

"I'm not going to put Rachel in danger, and we need to be in agreement with this. So do you agree or not?"

"Yeah, whatever. I agree, Mr. Chicken Noodle."

"Fuck off." As soon as he pulled into an empty space, I was out of the truck and walking to the girls' apartment. The door was locked, and after knocking quietly and getting no response, I wasted no time at all picking the lock and letting myself in.

A smile tugged at my lips as I took in Rachel wrapped up in the comforter like a burrito, Kleenex everywhere, a half-empty Gatorade bottle on the floor next to the couch, and an empty box of Sour Patch Kids on the table next to the cold and allergy medicine. I brushed the back of my hand against her forehead, making sure she hadn't gotten a fever since I'd left her, and she rolled toward me on a groan.

"Rach, wake up," I whispered close to her ear, and let my fingers trail down her cheek.

She grumbled again as her eyes slowly cracked open. "Time is it?"

"Almost five. You hungry?"

Shaking her head, she closed her eyes again.

Laughing softly, I kissed her forehead and spoke against it.

"It's probably because you ate the green ones when I told you not to."

Her body went rigid for all of three seconds before she began burrowing herself deeper into the comforter and away from me.

My next laugh was louder. "Take some more medicine, and go take a hot shower; the steam will help. I'll make you soup for when you get out."

As soon as she was vertical and headed toward her room, I ran back to my apartment to rid myself of my badge and gun before going back to take care of her. Mason raised an eyebrow and mentioned something about lying to her for longer than necessary, but I ignored it. Lying for now meant keeping her safe. And that's what mattered most.

7

Rachel

I was on my way into the kitchen when there was a knock on the door. Glancing at the clock on the microwave, I sighed when I saw it was only half past eight. Was it already Thursday? Poor Mrs. Adams.

Walking over to the door, I flipped the locks and swung open the door, a bright smile plastered on my face, prepared for her weekly crazy. What I saw on the other side of the door had my stomach dropping and all the blood draining from my head. I thought I was going to pass out in the split second it took for me to grab the door and try to slam it shut.

Blake caught the door before it closed and pushed it open enough to get in. "Good morning to you too."

"Get out!"

"Aww. Come on, baby, don't be like that." He locked the

*door behind him and walked toward me with his arms open.
I matched each step with one of my own.*

"Don't call me that."

"What would you prefer? Princess? Sweetheart? My girl?"

*"None of the above. Get. Out." By that time I was close
enough to my room that I spun around, made it in there, and
locked the door behind me before Blake came crashing into it.*

"Open the damn door, Rachel!" he yelled, beating on it.

*I ran over to my nightstand and grabbed my phone to call
Kash, but my fingers were moving so slowly I still hadn't
gotten my password in when Blake broke the door right off
the hinges. I screamed as he turned me around and shoved
me into the wall, my head cracking against it. I started seeing
black spots and struggled to keep myself standing.*

*"Why do you always do this? You know you do this to me,
baby! I don't want to hurt you!"*

*I tried to take a step to the side but ended up falling over.
Blake caught me before I could hit the ground. He scooped me
into his arms and placed me gently on the bed as he brought
his mouth to mine. I pressed my lips into a hard line and
turned my head away from him.*

*"Stop! Please!" I screamed again, hoping that someone
would hear.*

*"If you can't keep that mouth of yours shut, I'll keep it
shut for you. Do you understand me?"*

*I gathered what saliva I had and spit in his eye, earning
me a hard blow across my face. I cried out in pain and tried
to bring my hands up to block another in case it came, but I
couldn't force them to move. He reached into his back pocket
and pulled out a roll of duct tape.*

I tried to ask why he was doing this to me, but my words came out as more of a whimper than anything. The next thing I knew, he was placing a strip of tape over my mouth and gathering my hands over my head to tape my wrists together. I was choking on a sob, and I worked hard to keep it down so I could continue to breathe.

"It doesn't have to be like this, sweetheart. Why do you have to be so difficult?" he crooned as he kissed my forehead, cheeks, and nose.

Blake took his time making a trail of kisses up and down my neck, eventually leading toward my chest. He grabbed the bottom of my shirt and pulled it up so it was covering my face, leaving my breasts bare. I tried turning my body away from him but he crushed his weight onto my hips, keeping me on my back. He explored every inch of my torso and chest before pulling down my pajama shorts and underwear. I wasn't able to hold back my sob any longer. I tried kicking at him but he was still pinning my legs down.

"I know you want me and this whole playing-hard-to-get act is getting old. I will have you, so stop fighting." I could feel his warm breath coming through the shirt covering my face, and his lips went to my ear. "Or don't, it's up to you. If you want it rough, then that's how I'll give it to you. But one way or another, I will break you, and I will own you. You. Are. Mine."

My body stopped shaking momentarily as a chill ran down my spine and I became covered in goose bumps.

"That's what I thought."

Tears burned my eyes as I shook violently, my sobs growing weaker and weaker as Blake claimed my body. Why wasn't anyone coming to save me? How had no one heard my screams or Blake breaking down the door? Kash's face flashed through my mind and I clung to that image while my body lay there lifelessly. I turned my face to the side and stared into nothingness as tears fell onto my shirt. I wondered if anyone had ever felt the kind of hate I felt for this man.

When it was over, Blake lowered his body onto mine and kissed my neck before whispering in my ear, "You're mine, Rachel. I'll never let you go."

I jerked upright and let out a scream. Confused, I looked around me at the perfectly messy bedroom and my hands flew to my face. It was wet with tears, but there was no duct tape. My bedroom door was intact, and I was alone in my bed. Falling back onto the pillows, I tried to slow my racing heart and looked at the clock on my nightstand. It was almost eight. I must have fallen asleep again after Candice left for cheer camp. A sob hitched in my throat and finally broke free in relief. It was only a dream. Blake wasn't here.

But it had felt so real.

Needing to get out of that bed, I jumped up, tore the sweat-soaked sheets off the bed, and put them in the wash. My body was still violently shaking as I turned the water on in the shower as hot as it would go. This wasn't the first nightmare I'd had of him, not even close. But it was by far the worst. I welcomed the burn of the water and scrubbed every inch of my body three times before stepping back out. My skin was red and blotchy as I shakily grabbed my toothbrush and brushed my teeth twice.

I still didn't feel clean.

Dream or not, I felt violated all over again. Everything from the night with Blake came flooding back to me and mixed with what my subconscious had tortured me with. I could still feel his weight on me—feel him in me. I could hear his voice ringing in my ears, and my cheeks stung like I'd actually been hit.

I dressed in loose sweatpants, threw on a tank top, and pulled my dad's old rugby sweatshirt on. It was the middle of the summer, and our apartment wasn't very cool, but I was still shaking and felt a chill that was bone-deep working its way through my body.

Making my way through the living room, I'd almost reached the kitchen when there was a knock on the door. Dread filled me and my eyes immediately flashed to the clock on the microwave. Half past eight. Oh God. Oh no. Another knock and I forced my gaze back to the door as my tears spilled over.

"Rachel, dear? Are you there?"

A half sob, half sigh burst from my chest and I slowly made my way to the door, unlocked the dead bolt, and opened it. "H-hi, M-Mrs. Adams."

"Oh, Rachel! There you are! You must come quick, all the cats have disappeared."

"I-I . . . I can't today, Mrs.—"

"No, you must! Come quick, they're all gone!" She grabbed my hand and I jerked back; she didn't notice as she began rambling about all of her cats leaving her.

The door directly across from mine opened, revealing Kash and Mason in nothing but workout shorts and running shoes. They laughed at something and Kash turned toward me; a smile covered his face the instant he saw me there with Mrs. Adams but fell when his eyes narrowed in on me.

"Rach?" he called, and hit Mason's arm. Mason turned from

locking their door as Kash took the few steps toward us. "Rachel, what's wrong?"

"The cats, dear." Mrs. Adams looked at him with a worried expression. "They've all gone! Rachel must help me find them."

His wide eyes searched my face and I dropped my head quickly; my wet hair fell like a useless curtain and I flinched when Kash grabbed my free wrist. He dropped it quickly and spoke softly. "You know, Mrs. Adams, Rachel isn't feeling well. I'll help you find your cats today."

"Oh, but—you're a boy! They won't respond to a boy!"

"Yes they will, Mrs. Adams. I helped you find them last week, don't you remember?"

"Well then come, hurry! We need to find them." She turned and shuffled back toward her door. "Smokey! Honey, come back to Mama!"

"Rachel, are—"

The buzzer on the washer sounded and I jumped back, hitting the half-open door and almost falling when it swung the rest of the way from my weight.

"Christ, Rach!" Kash grabbed for me and his eyes got wide again when he felt my body vibrating. "Mase! Take her into our apartment, I'll be right back."

"N-no. I'm fine." I pulled away from him, but he brought me out of the doorway and handed me to Mason. Jerking back again, I pleaded on a sob, "Stop touching me!"

Both guys dropped their hold on me and their hands went up, as if they were surrendering. Mason's deep voice was soft and slow. "Sweetheart, come on. I won't touch you. Let's just get you in our apartment. All right? Are you feeling sick? Do you want me to call Candice?"

"No! Please don't—don't call her!"

"Okay, I won't. Come on, sweetheart. We'll take care of you."

I glanced over to see Kash looking at me helplessly as I followed Mason toward their door. With one last worried look, he shut my front door, turned, and began calling out for Smokey as he tried to get Mrs. Adams to go back into her apartment.

Kash

WHAT THE FUCK *just happened?* I looked at the door to my apartment once more as I followed Mrs. Adams into hers.

"There you go, Mrs. Adams. There they all are."

"Oh, dears! Why did you scare Mama like that? I've missed you so!" She grabbed a pillow off her chair and hugged it tight.

"Do you need anything else, Mrs. Adams?" *Please, God, say no.* I was itching to get back to my apartment and Rachel.

"No, thank you, boy! You helped save all my babies."

I smiled and backed out of her apartment. "See you next Thursday, Mrs. Adams." I was out the door and running the few steps over to mine before she could say anything else.

As soon as I entered, my eyes searched until they landed on Rachel, knees up to her chest, chin on her knees, and arms wrapped tightly around her legs. She wasn't looking at me, but it was obvious she didn't want to be. I took one step toward her before Mason cleared his throat and nodded toward his room. Grinding my teeth, I looked at Rachel once more and followed him into his room.

"Did she say anything?"

"No, but, dude. You—I think maybe . . . well, she . . ." He trailed off.

"What, Mason? Spit it the fuck out."

He leaned closer. "Remember when we were in with Luis and his boys?"

That was our first undercover; how was I supposed to forget anything about that time? "Yeah, Rach isn't on crack."

"No, no. Not that. Do you remember the girls they'd pass around? Not the hookers," he added before I could respond.

"Yes," I hissed, and looked at the shut door, then back to him. "Don't tell me she—"

"Kash, I'm sorry. But she's acting just like they did. It's already over ninety degrees and she's shaking in sweats. She's not sick, she looks like she's just gotten out of a shower, and she freaked when we touched her. Think about it."

"No, no way." I shook my head and took a few steps away from him.

"Look, I know what she means to you," he whispered, "but try to look past what you feel for her. Did you see how she was curling in on herself when you walked in? We've seen this enough times before to know what's going on."

I raked my hands through my hair and tried to force the images out of my mind. "I'll kill anyone that's laid a finger on her." Turning, I started storming out of his room, but he put a hand on my chest and pushed back.

"Maybe I should be the one to handle this; you should go."

"The fuck I will!" I hissed, and smacked his arm away.

"*If* what I think happened to her *has* happened, then she needs someone to comfort her and make her feel safe. You going in there already pissed off that someone may have raped her isn't going to help her; you're going to scare her more!"

I swallowed back bile and took deep breaths through my nose. "When would this have even happened? Someone is always with her."

"No, we're not, there's days when Candice doesn't get home for hours after we've already gone into work. Not including the days we have to go to the pol—bar . . . for meetings. It could have been at any time. But, Kash, we don't know that it has happened yet. So let me handle this."

"No, you need to go. She means the world to me, not you. I need to be there for her."

"That's exactly why it needs to be me!" he said, and I knew he was right but I didn't care.

"Mase. Go. Now."

"You're going to—"

"*Go.*"

He sighed heavily. "Don't fuck this up, Kash."

When he was gone, I took my time just breathing and trying to rein in my temper before walking back out into the empty living room. *What the hell?* She was gone. I rushed over to the front door, but Rachel walked out of my bedroom putting her hair up. The fakest smile I'd ever seen crossed her face when she spared me a glance.

"Have you eaten breakfast? I can make pancakes."

What? "I'm not hungry, Rach, come talk to me."

"You're always hungry." She walked past me and into the kitchen.

"If you're hungry, we can get something later. But for now, come talk to me about what just happened."

She faltered somewhat but kept walking into the kitchen. When she hit the pantry she shrugged and looked over her shoulder at me. "Mrs. Adams caught me at a bad time, I was just getting out of the shower. I didn't feel like helping her this week."

"Bullshit, you're the only one who will help her. You said she needs it. Why were you crying?"

"Cramps."

"Woman, get the fuck out of the kitchen and come talk to me!"

Her body went rigid as she turned to completely face me. Her blue eyes were massive and after a few seconds she laughed awkwardly and turned back to the open pantry. "First time in the history of the world a female was told to get *out* of the kitchen."

"Damn it, Rachel. I'm not kidding! I want to know what the fuck happened to you; you're done throwing up your damn shield with me!" *Calm down, man. Calm the hell down. You're going to scare her and she's going to run rather than talk to you.* "Rachel." I lowered my voice and spoke softly. "Get your ass on the couch. Now."

Without a word, she made her way back into the living room and sat on the far corner of the main couch, exactly where she'd been when I walked in earlier. Taking another deep breath, I forced myself to sit on the opposite side when all I wanted to do was pace or pull her into my arms. I waited until I'd fully calmed down before saying anything. She still had yet to look at me since she'd sat down, and I decided this was the day I'd throw out that shield for good. I never wanted her to use it around me again.

Praying to God that Mason and I were wrong about this, I started off how I would with anyone else I was questioning. Like I knew exactly what they were hiding. "Tell me who the guy is who did this to you."

Her head snapped up and her eyes widened before she could

look away. "I don't know what you're talking about." Her body started shaking again and she pulled her knees up to her chest like earlier.

Oh fuck. No, Rach . . . God, no. Swallowing the lump in my throat, I kept going. "When did it happen?"

"I don't know what you're talking about," she repeated.

"What's his name?"

"Whose?"

"Do you know him, or was it a stranger?"

She paused before answering. "I don't know what you're talking about, Kash."

"You know him. Does Candice know about this?"

"Why are you doing this?" she whispered.

God, baby, trust me, I don't want to be. "When did it happen?"

We continued to go in circles as I asked the same questions over and over, and then asked somewhat different variations of the same questions, every now and then throwing in an assumption, and after almost ten minutes, the tears started falling down her face. It killed me, but I couldn't stop. I kept my voice monotone and forced myself to stay in my spot on the couch as her body tried hopelessly to curl in on itself while it vibrated almost forcefully. When I finally had her on the edge, I softened my voice and asked the question I didn't want to know the answer to but needed to.

"When were you raped, Rachel?"

"I wasn't raped!" she yelled, and her hands flew up to her face as a sob left her. Her shoulders began shaking harder with the sobs that were now coming, and I ground my jaw as I waited for her. "He didn't—he wasn't able to finish—Candice came back!"

she cried. "He tried . . . he started to, but she came back. I tried to get him off me! He was choking me, I couldn't breathe."

"So, Candice knows?"

Her head shook furiously back and forth. "I tried—tried to tell her. She wouldn't listen, and she won't believe me. She . . . *everyone* thinks he can do no wrong. But he's crazy, Logan." She looked at me, her tear-streaked face breaking my heart as she willed me to understand. "He told me no one would believe me, he said I was his and he wouldn't let anyone touch me. H-he's crazy, I swear!"

"What's his name?" She shook her head again and I wanted to shake her. "I need to know his name, Rach. What's his name?"

"He works at the school. I have to see him every day because of my major. Candice too. But no one will believe you. Everyone loves him."

This sick fuck is a professor? "Name. What's his name?" When she didn't respond, I went back to my earlier questions. "Did this happen last night?"

She jerked back and stared at me. "N-no! I haven't seen him since that night. It was the week before school let out."

"This morning?"

"I had another nightmare about him. He showed up at the door. This time—" She broke off on a sob. "No one was there to stop him before he finished this time."

Rachel. I wanted nothing more than to hold her, but with how she'd flinched away from us earlier, that would have been anything but helpful. My heart continued to break as she mumbled, "It felt so real," over and over again.

Giving her a second, I stood up and walked into my room,

threw a pair of sweatpants over my shorts, and shrugged into a sweatshirt. God, how was she shivering? I was already sweating with this on. But if I couldn't comfort her in the way I wanted to, I was going to do it in the only other way I knew how. I'd just be there for her. When I walked back through the living room, her sobs had quieted, but she was still in a ball. Heading into the kitchen, I grabbed two bottled waters, a spoon, and the pint of Ben and Jerry's she always made sure I had in the freezer. I put everything on the coffee table, grabbed the remote, and searched the DVR until I found *Bridesmaids*. I didn't give a shit about the two hundred dollars or breakfasts I would owe her for this.

Sitting down next to her this time, I picked up the water and ice cream, balanced them on my legs, and turned the volume up. When the movie started, she brought her red face up and glanced at the TV with a furrowed brow before looking over at me. Her eyebrows shot straight up when she saw me.

"What are you wearing?" Her voice was hoarse from crying and I handed her the bottle of water.

"Well, you came over in sweats. I figured I missed the memo or something and had to get in on the party."

She looked at the TV and back to me, and a small smile cracked when she took the ice cream and spoon from me.

I'd pushed her enough today. I hated knowing what I knew and vowed to one day find out who this guy was. Hopefully now that she knew she could talk to me, she'd open up more when she was ready. But anything more today would be too much. So I settled into the couch and pretended to watch the movie instead of her every move. After a while, she handed me back the half-empty container and leaned against my shoulder. My arm automatically went around her and I pulled her close to my side.

"Thank you, Kash," she whispered a couple minutes later.

"Anything for you, Rach. I'm here whenever you need to talk." Pressing my lips to her forehead, I kept them there as I said, "And I will always protect you."

We were still sitting there watching the movie when Mason came back from his run. He nodded at us, and when he came back out of his room after a shower, he was dressed in sweats as well. He grabbed the melting ice cream and tried to squeeze himself onto the couch on the other side of Rachel.

She laughed and curled closer into my side. "You guys are the best."

"You think we're going to let you veg on the couch alone?" Mason said, scoffing. "Sweetheart, you obviously don't know us that well. I mean, it's gonna be a hundred degrees today. How else would I spend the day than in sweats?"

Rachel kicked at his leg and he squeezed her knee. After a few minutes of watching the movie, Mason caught my gaze over Rachel's head. He quickly looked down at her and raised an eyebrow, the question clear in his eyes. I nodded once and the color drained from his face. He swallowed hard and grabbed one of Rachel's hands. She laughed lightly at something from the movie and his eyes came back to mine. They were determined, and he looked like he was struggling at relaxing his now-murderous expression.

I knew exactly how he felt.

He didn't have to say anything to me. We'd worked together long enough to know that we'd both just agreed to find the bastard. And make him pay.

8

Kash

"WOMAN!" I SHOUTED, and shook Rachel's bed roughly. "Wake up."

She shot straight up, her eyes wide in panic as she looked around her room before settling them on me. "God, I thought earthquakes had followed me to Texas." Taking a calming breath, she brushed her wild hair back from her face and scowled at me. "What is wrong with you? And what time is it—seven? Really, Kash?"

"Get up and get ready."

"No." Pulling the covers up past her shoulders, she sank back into the mattress and shut her eyes.

Hell. No. "This is your last warning, Rach. Get up."

A single snort was her only reply.

"Such a pain in my ass," I mumbled, and walked to the foot of the bed. Grabbing the bottom of the comforter, I ripped it off the bed and dropped it on the ground.

"Oh my God, what if I had been naked?!"

I raised an eyebrow and let my gaze run over her body. I wouldn't have minded. Ah shit, now I was getting hard and the jersey material of these shorts wouldn't hide that fact. *Think about Mrs. Adams and her fake cats. Think about Mrs. Adams and her fake cats!* "Moot point; you're not. Now, get your ass out of bed."

"Give me at least another couple hours. I just went to sleep."

"Not my fault, and you've had more than enough chances to get up yourself."

"Kash, please," she whined.

"Don't whine. It's not attractive." Without giving her any more time, I scooped her into my arms and threw her over my shoulder before heading toward her bathroom.

A low *oompf* left her before she began bitching at me. "I am going to gut you, you freakin' asshole! Seven in the damn morning, what the hell is wrong with you?! Put me down—ugh! Easy, this shit hurts. You have really bony shoulders, has anyone ever told you that?" She gasped when I turned the shower water on. "Put me down right now, Logan Hendricks, or I swear to all that is holy you will regret the day you moved in across from me and almost took my Jeep door off!"

"No can do, my little Sour Patch." Thank God I was still only in my workout shorts. Kicking off my running shoes, I stepped into the large tub and winced when she shrieked.

"You evil bastard, let me go!"

"You sure have a mouth on you when you wake up."

"I will murder you!"

I couldn't help but smile. She was just so damn cute. "And you're a little dramatic."

"This water is freezing," she whined, and I'd bet she was pouting just as bad as Candice usually did. At least her anger was dying down and her fists had stopped pounding on my back. "What did I ever do to you?"

"I gave you every opportunity to get yourself ready. You were the one who wouldn't get out of bed."

"I had barely gone to sleep!"

"Rach," I snorted, "it's seven in the morning and you left my place at nine last night. Why had you just gone to sleep?"

She didn't answer and stopped wiggling against me. She just hung there, limp.

"What—no more threats? No more whining?"

Silence.

"Woman, I swear to God, if you fell asleep on my damn shoulder . . ." I trailed off when I heard her mumble something. "What'd you say?"

"I was afraid to fall back asleep," she whispered, and my eyes clenched shut.

"Ah, Rach." I slid her awkwardly down my body until she was standing in front of me. I tried to block the water that was directed at her, but little droplets were bouncing off my bare shoulders and hitting her face. She blinked rapidly against them before dropping her head. "Why didn't you call me or something?"

She huffed and shook her head. "What for, Kash? To make you sit there with me in sweats longer? So you could act like what happened yesterday morning *didn't*? I don't need you to babysit me when I'm being ridiculous."

"That's not ridiculous." With a heavy sigh, I turned off the water and leaned toward the towel rack to grab a towel and wrap it around her. "Get some dry clothes on, I'll be back in a few minutes."

Once I helped her out of the tub and wrung out my soaked shorts as much as possible, I grabbed my shoes and headed for my apartment.

Rachel had stayed with Mase and me all day yesterday. Once Candice was home from cheer camp, she came over and questioned our wardrobe for a moment but dropped it soon after. Mason took her to pick up food for everyone and I'd hoped to question Rachel some more, but she was finally giving real smiles and I couldn't stomach upsetting her again at that point. After tossing and turning for hours last night, I'd come to the conclusion that I was going to make sure she was never alone, and I was going to find out exactly what had gone down between her and Professor Sickfuck.

Walking back over to the girls' apartment, I let myself in and was met with a pissed-off Rachel. My favorite kind. I smiled lazily at her and looked at the timer on the microwave I'd set before waking the monster.

"Why are there cinnamon rolls baking in my oven?"

"Because you have a sweet tooth and I figured you'd be pissed at me for waking you up. It was the least I could do."

She raised a brow and crossed her arms. "And how did you get in here this morning?"

I picked the lock like I always do. "Candice left it unlocked for me."

"Whatever," Rachel mumbled on a sigh, and went to flop down on one of the couches. "So are you ever going to tell me why you woke me up so early?"

"After breakfast." I went to pull the cinnamon rolls out of the oven and grabbed the icing packets. "Hey, Rach, why aren't you working this summer?"

Her head snapped up. "Because I didn't feel like getting a job. Why does it matter to you?"

"I was just wondering." I shrugged. "Are your parents paying for your share of the apartment as well?"

"My—"

Her voice cut off so suddenly that I looked back over at her, to see that her face had completely drained of color. Dropping the icing, I quickly started toward her, but she shook her head fiercely and sniffed as she leveled another glare at me.

"You aren't exactly in a position to give me crap for living off my parents seeing as you dropped twenty grand of your daddy's money on furnishing your apartment."

I had to take a few deep breaths before I could say anything to her. I knew she was just throwing up her shield again, but God, she knew how to piss me off. Leaning close to her on the couch, I matched her stare and held it. "I'll find out why you have this shield too. But for now . . . drop the attitude, Sour Patch, or I will take you over my knee and spank your ass so hard you won't be able to sit for a week."

Her blue eyes went wide before blinking a few times. When she finally looked away I noticed the blush that had crept up her cheeks, and damn if my pants didn't shrink a size at her reaction to my threat.

Mrs. Adams and her fake cats. Mrs. Adams . . .

Turning back toward the kitchen, I kept my focus on the cinnamon rolls and off spanking Rachel. "It was a simple question,

Rach. I wasn't getting on you for living off them. You're in college. That's normal. I just wanted to know if you didn't get a job for a reason, and if you were needing money, the bar I work at is looking for waitresses. After yesterday, I'm guessing that even if you had planned on getting a job this summer, what happened to you with that guy pushed those plans aside. And I think a job would be good for you. It would give you something to do, rather than having too much time to be alone and think about it." I risked a glance at her, only to see her staring out the window and chewing on her bottom lip. "It's up to you, but like I said, this would be good for you. It would help you start moving on."

"I *have* moved on," she whispered.

"If you're still having nightmares, you haven't."

I walked a plate of cinnamon rolls over to the couch and sat next to her, putting the plate between us. She ate, but she never looked back at me; she just continued to stare off at nothing. I didn't say anything else until we were done.

"Have you told anyone other than me about what happened?" When she shook her head, I continued. "Not even your parents or the police?"

So slowly, she turned to look at me, eyes narrowed into slits. Her mouth popped open to deliver whatever pissed-off answer she had waiting, but I cut her off.

"No more shields, Sour Patch."

"I hate when you call me that," she said through gritted teeth.

"Well, I hate when you act like a bitch as a defense mechanism."

She stared at me in shock for a full minute before smiling shyly at me and looking away again. "Old habit." She shrugged.

Grabbing her chin, I forced her to look at me again. "I'm serious, Rachel. When you're with me, no more shields."

"You don't understand—"

"I do," I told her. "You hide your pain behind them. This is how you think you're protecting yourself. I'm sure it works with some people, but all you're doing is pushing them away. If you're hurting, tell me. I'm here for you, and your bullshit isn't going to work on me because I'm not going to let you push me away. Got it?"

"Yeah."

"Again, you didn't tell your parents or the police?"

She looked past my head, her mouth open, before shutting it again. And after long moments she finally shifted her eyes back to mine. "No one else knows."

Releasing her chin, I leaned into the couch but kept my voice firm. "I need you to tell me exactly what happened."

"No, no—"

"Rach, I know it'll be hard. But you need to tell someone. And right now, I'm the only one who knows." She was still shaking her head back and forth. "This is the first step in your moving on. You need to face it. Completely."

We sat there in silence for a handful of minutes before she softly told me everything that had happened with her and this guy she still refused to put a name to. My years undercover had helped me keep a straight face during the worst situations you can imagine. But listening to *this* girl tell me what had happened to her . . . my hands weren't able to relax from their fists the entire time and my body was vibrating with the need to have this guy get up close and personal with my duty weapon. Despite Rachel's insistence that she hadn't been raped, that's exactly what had happened. He hadn't been able to finish what he started—thank Christ for that and Candice—but that didn't change what he had done to her. I wanted to kill the son of a bitch.

After she was done telling me her story and had calmed down again, I pulled her into my arms and laid back against the couch. She stiffened at first but soon relaxed.

"I can't imagine how hard that was for you, Rach. But I'm proud of you." I kissed the top of her head and continued to whisper, "Not right now maybe, but soon you'll feel better that you've told someone. No one should have to go through that, and definitely not alone. I won't make you decide anything right now, but I really want you to consider applying at the bar, okay?"

"I will." She spoke softly against my chest.

"And I want you to think about telling your parents what you just told me."

Her body tensed beneath my arms again, and when she lifted her head, her eyes were full of tears. "I can't." Her words had barely any sound behind them. But I'd understood.

"Just think about it."

An odd pained look crossed her face and she grimaced. " 'Kay."

"I gotta run some errands with Mase this morning, so I need to get going. If you want to apply for the job, Rod is one of the owners as well as the manager at the bar, and he'll be there sometime before noon. He's the guy you'll want to talk to, all right?" When she simply nodded, I sat us back up and pressed my lips to her forehead. "You're brave, Rach. I'm proud of you. And I'll make sure nothing like that ever happens to you again."

Before she could respond, I pushed up off the couch and left her apartment.

When I got home, Mason was standing there waiting for me.

"About damn time. I know Rachel put you in the friend zone so I know you weren't getting any. What took you so long? Painting each other's nails and gossiping? We're gonna be late and I really don't feel like hearing any crap from Detective Ryder today. That guy scares the shit out of me."

Once I had my wallet, phone, and keys, I turned and faced him. "I'll make sure to let him know, I'm sure that will make his day." Lowering my voice once we were outside, I glanced over at the girls' door and whispered, "Rachel was telling me about what happened."

Mason stopped walking and turned toward their door. "Ah, shit . . . Rach."

"Yeah." Pushing him toward the parking lot, I kept talking. "Sorry, I didn't feel like rushing that."

"She okay?"

He and I both knew that was a dumb question; of course she wasn't. But he was just as worried about her as I was. He loved her too, just in a completely different way.

"She will be. She got it all out for the first time, so eventually. I gave her some things to think about while we were gone today. Hopefully she'll take them into consideration." Cranking the engine, I pulled out of the parking lot and switched gears. "Read me the e-mail from Ryder again. I want to know what new things they have on Camden and what we have."

"They're thinking he may be getting close to another murder, but at least he's getting sloppier. The two times he slipped up with using his card last week, it was double what he normally spends. And I checked the receipts—I doubt he's eating two meals by himself."

"And those were at the restaurant you work at?"

"Yeah, both nights I wasn't working though. I reviewed all the cameras we have set up in there and checked them against everyone who came in. The only people who didn't match up with cards paid in cash. I don't know how he's doing this."

"Waitress or waiter remember anything?"

"Ryder told me we couldn't question her. She'd served too many people that night, and it'd raise flags if we started questioning staff. What about your bar?"

"I check things when I get there early to see if his card was used and we just missed it. He hasn't been at my bar in weeks. There've been three times we've had people leave without paying. First was a homeless guy I see all the time. Next was this ancient woman who comes in almost every day. I don't think she even realized she hadn't paid when she left, because she always does. Last was a man in a business suit who took off running out of the bar when he got a phone call. But he came in the next day and paid what was owed. Other than that, I keep a record of the table, date, and time when people pay cash. Every Wednesday I check them on our cameras. Never seen Camden."

"Shit. This whole two-meals thing is something to worry about, though. And I think that's why Ryder is calling us in today. Now that Camden might be closing in on someone, I'm sure he'll want all of us working a lot more."

"Good, we need to until he's found."

Mason lifted his left hand, curled into a fist. "Anything to bring the fuckers down, right?"

We'd been saying that since our first undercover assignment. I smiled and pounded his fist. "Always."

Rachel

"So WE NEED to go out and celebrate."

I rolled over on Candice's bed and watched as she held up different shirts and studied herself in her full-length mirror. "Oh really? And what is it we're celebrating?"

"You getting a job. Duh."

"Candice." I laughed softly. "Is it really so exciting that I got a job that we need to go out and celebrate? It's waitressing. It isn't like I made partner at a firm or—" I broke off quickly when I realized what I'd just said.

Candice was quiet for a second and her eyes lifted to look at me through the mirror. "Are we going to go back to California for the anniversary?"

"I don't—I don't think so." Every year Candice's family went to my parents' graves on the anniversary of their death. But I hadn't. I couldn't. I wasn't even there when they were lowered into the ground. I couldn't stand the thought of watching them go six feet into the earth. And by staying away from the grave, it kept it not as real for me.

"Are you ever going to go, Rach?"

Swallowing audibly, I dropped my head and studied the details of Candice's comforter instead. "Someday, maybe. I just can't yet . . . can we not talk about this?"

"Yeah," she said softly, then more resolutely, "Yeah! Waitress or not, we need to celebrate!"

I loved Candice so much for being able to get us out of uncomfortable conversations so easily. "Candice, we can go out for drinks anytime. We don't need a reason, especially not this one."

"Don't be lame, Rach. I want to celebrate you getting a job. So we're going to do it. Are the boys home?"

I grunted what I thought sounded like an affirmation.

"Maybe they can—" She cut herself off when her phone rang beside me on the bed.

"It's Eli." I answered it for her and put it on speaker.

"Hey, big brother!" we said in unison, and he laughed.

"How are my favorite girls?"

"Good, but Rachel's being lame. She got a job and I want to go celebrate. She thinks it's stupid."

"Ah, well, we have to celebrate that." *What "we"?* I thought. "But can we please take my rental? Because it looks so much better than Rach's Liberty; don't you ever wash this thing?"

Candice gasped and hurried to get dressed, but I was already running out of her room and out the front door. I didn't spare a glance at Kash's place as I turned and literally squealed when I saw Eli standing in front of my Jeep.

"Eli!" I screamed, and ran full speed at him. He caught me and just barely kept us from falling over as he laughed and hugged me close.

"Good to see you too, sis."

"I can't believe you're here!"

He kissed my cheek and turned me to walk back toward the apartment with an arm slung around my shoulders. "Figured I'd surprise you girls."

"How long are you staying?"

"Just until tomorrow evening. I'm only here on business."

I pouted but didn't have time to say anything else, because as soon as we were in the apartment, Candice launched herself at him much the same way I had. She said my words verbatim and I couldn't help but laugh. Candice and I were so different but at the same time so similar it scared me.

"Well, now we definitely have to go celebrate," Candice said as she bounced up and down on her toes. "Do you have any more meetings today?"

"Nope, done until the morning." He patted his flat stomach and looked at his watch. "I'm starving, though, and I heard the Mexican food here is completely different than what we have in California."

"Then Mexican it is," I said with a huge smile. "Let me go change, I'll be ready in two seconds!"

I felt lighter than I had in a long time. Eli had always had a calming effect on me and I was so thankful for it now. He'd seemed to be more mature than other guys his age when we were growing up, and he had this silent intensity about him that I had clung to after my parents had died. He knew words wouldn't help in those hard times and his presence alone had helped me more than anyone else could have until I was given my journal. But even in times that were happy, like now, that intensity rolled off him and washed over me, making it feel like a huge weight had been lifted. The anniversary of my parents' death and the Blake situation were forgotten. Complete peace.

Until three hours into our drinking and eating, anyway.

"Hey, so I heard Blake was in Austin."

I froze and Candice eyed me warily before downing the rest of her margarita. I grabbed my beer and followed suit.

"Got in touch with him this afternoon. I'm supposed to go

meet up with him in about half an hour. I told him I'd bring you two with me."

This wasn't happening. "Um . . ."

"I'm game!" Candice said, and nudged Eli's side. "I haven't seen him since school let out anyway. I miss him."

Eli laughed and drained his beer. "I haven't seen him since all that shit went down with Jenn. He left for the air force right after."

My heart rate had kicked up, but at the mention of Blake's girlfriend before he moved away, it halted. I hadn't known anything bad happened between the two of them. I just remembered hating her for being with Blake. She'd been tall, with long, dark hair and blue eyes. I remembered not understanding why he would like her and not me; the only thing she had that I didn't was boobs. "What—um . . ." I cleared my voice and tried to sound as uninterested as I could in my questioning. "What went down between Blake and Jenn? I thought they were happy before he left."

Candice's eyes narrowed at me. She knew I was searching. Eli shook his head and stretched his arms over his head before responding. "They had been happy. Jenn was attacked by some guys walking home from a party one night, ended up in the hospital . . . she was really fucked up. I went with Blake to wait for her to wake up, and when she did she didn't want to talk to him. It tore him up. He kept trying to talk to her and see her, and she refused to. She and her family moved away the week after she got out of the hospital. Blake had to leave for boot camp right after."

I'd officially stopped breathing.

Was Blake the one who attacked her? Is that why she didn't want to see him? I glanced over to Candice to see her shaking her head at me. She wasn't glaring anymore, but she looked disappointed in me. Like she knew exactly where my train of thought had gone and was upset I was still putting the blame on her cousin who could do no wrong.

Eli handed his card to our waiter and drummed his hands against the tabletop. "So does that sound good? We're gonna meet him in the bar of the hotel I'm staying in. I can get you girls a room."

"No."

"Rach"—Eli smirked—"I'm not gonna be able to drive the two of you back to your place after. Unless you want him to meet us at your apartment?"

"No!" I said too loudly, and people at the surrounding tables looked awkwardly at us. "I don't want to go. I'll just go back to the apartment."

"What? Rachel, why?"

Candice cleared her throat and straightened her spine. "Rachel can't stand Blake."

Eli laughed softly. "Right. You only had the biggest crush on him growing up."

My eyebrows shot up. "You knew about that?"

"Who didn't know about that? You weren't exactly subtle about your feelings for him." His expression darkened suddenly. "I could've killed him for that."

Wait . . . What?! "Killed him for what? For me having a crush on him? It's not like it was his fault." Oh my God, was I really sitting here defending Blake West for *anything*?

"No," he snorted. "I was making fun of him because he never dated or hooked up with anyone. He told me he was just waiting for you to get older, that he was going to marry you someday. I thought he was joking at first, but I was wrong. Do you remember when Blake got in that fight and his nose got broken?" When

Candice and I both nodded, he continued. "That was because of that. Dad had to pull me off him."

"You beat him up because he wanted to be with me?" I wanted to pull Eli away and tell him everything that had happened. Candice didn't believe me, but Eli would.

"Of course I did. You were like my sister, but it wasn't just that. You were only twelve at the time and he was . . . what, seventeen? It was fucking disgusting."

So that was why Blake had started ignoring me. I'll never forget the way he looked after that fight. I had run up to him wanting to take care of him and began fawning all over him. He'd pushed me away and started dating Jenn not long after. I still saw him all the time since he was always with Eli, but it was like I didn't exist to him anymore after that. I'd been hurt, but not discouraged in my quest to win his affection.

Chills spread through my body. Eli's words made everything that had happened with Blake so much worse. And the fact that Jenn had been an older version of me was now incredibly disturbing. "Um . . . well. Things changed. I grew up. And I don't like the person he's become."

Candice made a frustrated noise but played it off by looking at her phone when Eli looked at her questioningly.

"What do you mean? What's he like now?"

I ground my teeth and locked my jaw. Pulling my phone out of my purse, I typed out a quick *Rescue me* text to Kash with the name of the restaurant and tried not to scream at Candice when she responded.

"Rachel just doesn't like the fact that he's a player now."

Eli barked out another laugh and signed the check. "I'm sure she doesn't. You girls ready?"

"I'm going to go back to the apartment," I said softly as I grabbed my purse and got out of the booth.

"You're serious, you really aren't going to come?"

"No. But let me know if I can see you tomorrow before you have to fly back to California, 'kay?" I hugged him tight and wondered again why he couldn't have been the one to save me from Blake.

He kissed my temple and began leading me out to the parking lot. "Well, I'm still going to drive you back."

"No, it's fine. I have a friend coming to pick me up. You two go meet up with him."

"Oh . . . well, then. All right, I guess." It came out as more of a question, and I couldn't blame him.

I would never normally have passed on spending time with him, especially since Candice and I never got to see him anymore. But if they were going to be with Blake . . . I just couldn't.

They waited with me until Kash pulled up, and Eli instantly took on the big-brother stance. "Do I need to have a talk with this guy?"

Candice and I both laughed but I just hugged Eli and kissed his cheek before heading toward the truck. "He's harmless, Eli, promise. His only problem is that he has a bad habit of waking me up early and forcing me to make pancakes, but he's just our neighbor."

"Just." Candice snickered and grinned mischievously at me.

"You should really ask Candice about her relationship with his cousin." I made a faux-shocked face before blowing a kiss to Candice and practically throwing myself into Kash's truck.

"Bitch!" was her muffled response, and I grinned at Kash until I saw the hard set of his jaw and mocking eyes.

"So she's the lucky winner tonight?" he asked after a few minutes of silent driving.

"Excuse me?"

"Kinda surprised you're not more upset about it."

"Well, I kinda want to know what I'm supposed to be upset about." I crossed my arms under my chest and turned so my back was resting against the door so I could look at him more easily. *What is his problem? I made the douche bag pancakes two days ago! And I told him all about Blake this morning. That was hard for me; now he's going to treat me like this?* "I got the job, by the way, in case you were wondering."

He shook his head and rested his forearms on the steering wheel while he waited for the light to turn green. "Knew you would, and Rod called me this afternoon so I already knew that you *did*. You start tomorrow night?"

"Mmm-hmm. Are you going to tell me why I'm supposed to be upset?"

"Because that guy is taking Candice home tonight instead of you."

My head jerked back and I could only imagine the disgust dripping from my expression. "Ew! What?!"

Kash looked quickly between the road and me a couple of times. "That guy. I saw you launch yourself at him earlier. He kept kissing your cheek, and now he's taking Candice back to his place."

I slammed my fist over my mouth and swallowed. "Oh God, I just threw up a little bit in my mouth."

"Shit, do you need me to pull over?"

"No, no. Oh, just *ew*, Kash! You and Mase kiss my head all the time. Mason picks me up almost every time I see him."

"So?"

"So? So! So, Eli is Candice's older brother that I grew up with and I actually view like my own brother. Besides Candice he was the best friend I had. He helped me through—" I cut myself off quickly and blew out a deep breath. "He helped me through a lot when I was younger. But I have never once viewed him as anything other than family and a friend. He even calls me *sis,* for crying out loud. Candice isn't going *home* with him, they're going to meet up with their cousin for drinks and I didn't want to go."

Kash's face relaxed, and though I expected him to look embarrassed, he just turned and raised an eyebrow. "You don't like him?"

"Seriously, this conversation is grossing me out."

He blew out a deep breath and the corners of his mouth tipped up. "Why didn't you want to go to drinks with their cousin?"

Don't shake. Don't shake. I gripped the seat belt like it was a lifeline and worked at keeping my heart rate under control. "He and I have bad history, I really don't like him." God, even I could hear the shakiness in my response. Before Kash could comment on it, I forced myself to sound as normal as possible, but I sounded like a cracked-out Valley girl instead. I definitely wouldn't be winning any Oscars in my life. "Logan Hendricks, were you jealous of Eli?"

"What? Come on, Rach, I just didn't like that he was playing both of you like that. Or that I thought he was, anyway." He started sucking on that lip ring again and my eyes zeroed in on the action.

We'd just pulled into a parking spot, so I took off my seat belt, leaned in close enough that I could smell his cinnamon gum, and whispered, "Liar," before throwing open my door and hopping out of his truck.

"I wasn't jealous," he grumbled as he joined me on the concrete.

Such a baby. "Whatever you say, Kash. What do you say to a pseudo lock-out night? Neither of us are locked out, but I'm going to be bored . . . I'll even let you pick out the movie this time."

He immediately stopped sucking on his lip ring and I frowned. "Let's go." He grabbed my hand and began leading me to his apartment, but I pulled back.

"No way, crazy. You finished off the Ben and Jerry's in your apartment the other night. My place tonight."

"I have the better TV."

"But I'm Rachel."

His head jerked back and his shoulders scrunched up as he looked at me like he was lost. "What—what does that have to do with anything?"

Oh, good question. "I'm not sure. Give me a bit to come up with an answer. But for now, it means you'll let me get my way."

Kash's eyes narrowed and he sucked in a deep breath, but then he shut his mouth and shook his head. "I was going to say something that probably would've resulted in me getting slapped right now . . . but it would also mean you wouldn't cook pancakes for me anymore."

"Probably smart to keep your mouth shut then."

"Unfortunately." He sighed. "All right, lead the way to the ice cream. I don't want to look like I'm Photoshopped anymore and you really need an ass."

I slapped him.

Hard.

9

Rachel

YOU EVER HAVE that feeling when you *know* someone is in the room with you, even though you should be alone?

Yeah. I was having it right now.

I kept my eyes closed and tried to keep my breathing steady, but I was on the verge of a full-blown Rachel freak-out before I caught the scent of cinnamon. Cracking one eye open, I saw Kash sitting on the edge of my bed just staring at me with an amused expression.

"Can I help you?" I mumbled against the pillow.

"I'm hungry and want pancakes."

"You want . . . What are you, five?! Make your own. I even bought the easy-make pancakes last weekend. All you have to do is add water." I rolled over and groaned. "Seven thirty? Kash, we didn't get back from work until after one. You have got to stop waking me up so early. And how are you even in here?"

He looked like he was fighting a smile and his eyes kept flashing up above mine. "Candice let me in."

Trying to act like I didn't notice where his eyes kept going, and like I wasn't flipping out because I was sure my hair looked like a hot mess, I slowly brought my arm up to brush back the hair from my face when my hand hit something that tugged at my forehead. "What the hell?" I tried to look straight up and even leaned my head back to try to follow whatever was at the very top of my forehead. I saw a blue tip and grabbed at it before yanking it off and holding it in front of my eyes. *"A Nerf dart?!"*

Kash shamelessly pulled up a Nerf gun and waved it at his side. His eyes slid back up to my forehead and a hard laugh burst from his chest. Rolling back, he fell off the bed and landed with a dull thump on the floor.

"What?" I snapped, and scrambled out of bed. As I made my way to the bathroom, I was hit once in the butt and once on my calf by more darts. "You're such a child, Kash!" Flipping on the light, I blinked against the brightness before focusing on the mirror. A loud gasp filled the small room. "Logan Kash Hendricks! What did you *do*?"

He was still cracking up as he got to his feet and came to stand behind me. "I just had to make sure it was on there real good. So I tested it a few times . . . you're a really heavy sleeper, by the way."

"There is a *hickey* on my forehead!"

His body was shaking from the laughter he was trying to keep in now.

"It's not funny! This better be gone by the time we go to work tonight."

"Don't be mad, Sour Patch." He planted his chin at the top of my head and brushed at my bangs. "You have those, they'll cover it. Can we have pancakes now?"

My eyes went wide and my jaw dropped as I continued to stare at him in the mirror. "No! Go make them yourself."

He frowned and brought the toy gun up in front of us. "I'll let you shoot me."

I chewed on my bottom lip for a moment. Pancakes sounded *really* good right now. With a heavy sigh, I held my hand out. "Give me the gun." As soon as it was in my hand, I went around collecting the three darts and put them back in with the other three still in there before aiming it right at his forehead.

Kash smiled, closed his eyes, and took all six darts like a champ. When I was done he had little red marks all over his forehead, and though I knew his would be gone in a few minutes, I felt like he'd gotten it worse than I did.

"Feel better?"

"A little." I handed the gun back to him and turned toward my door. "Let's go make pancakes." I'd barely hit the kitchen when I realized I didn't hear him behind me. "And don't even think about shooting me again, or you'll be on your own for breakfast!"

Whirling around, I saw him lower the gun that had been aimed at me and, with a pathetic frown, let it drop onto the couch.

I gave him the silent treatment while he pulled out the skillet and mix and I began whisking together the batter. I really wasn't mad at him—okay, that's not exactly true; I still couldn't believe he'd given me a hickey on my forehead with a freaking suction-cup dart. But it was hard to stay mad at Kash when we worked together in the kitchen. He always found reasons to brush up against me, and whenever I thought he wasn't looking, I'd take my time studying what I could see of his half sleeves and usually made my way up to his full lips. When I saw him sucking on that lip ring, my belly started heating and my mouth went dry. Every. Time. It never failed. So how was I supposed to be mad when I was currently finding it difficult to remember why I kept us as just friends?

"Damn, that's a good hickey."

Oh, right. That's how.

I frowned down at the fully mixed batter. My poor not-yet-made pancakes . . . it was fun while it lasted. The next time he turned to check the skillet, I pulled the whisk out and set it gently on the counter. I really wasn't worried about messes right now. Grabbing the bowl with both hands, I stepped right up behind him, reached my arms up high, and tipped it over. The sense of glee I got as I watched his entire body stiffen and all that batter fall onto his head was kind of alarming. No wonder he'd been so proud of his suction-cup hickey. I was damn proud of this mess.

When only a little dribble was falling from the bowl, I brought the bowl away from his head, set it on the counter, and had only taken two steps when he grabbed me around my waist and hauled me back to him. The movement made him lose his footing on the now-slippery tile and we both crashed down to the floor.

Quickly getting up on my hands and knees, I slip-crawled a few feet before my legs went out and I fell back to the floor. Kash dragged me back by my legs and I was laughing so hard I couldn't even attempt to try to crawl away as he flipped me over on my back and slipped toward me until he was covering my body.

I laughed harder and wiped at his cheek, which was completely covered. "You, uh, got a little something there."

His eyes were silver as he growled, "*Now* do you feel better?"

"Much!"

"I probably deserved that."

"A little bit." My laughter finally quieted and I smiled widely at him.

"Rachel . . ." His voice dropped and the huskiness alone caused my breathing to deepen.

When I realized that our bodies were flush, mine started warming again, and my eyelids fluttered shut when he brought one hand up to cup my cheek.

When he repeated my name, I could feel his breath against my lips and they parted in anticipation. His hand left my cheek and he leaned closer to whisper in my ear, "Your hickey looks really lonely."

Wait. What?! My eyes flew open just as he wiped a hand covered in batter across my face. "You son of a bitch!"

Kash laughed loudly and attempted to move some of the batter so it wasn't in my eyes.

"I will end you," I said, making him laugh harder. "I hate you."

"Don't lie, Sour Patch, you love me."

He was joking, I knew he was joking—but my heart still took off at his assumption. Kash must have noticed the change somehow, because he immediately stopped laughing and his gray eyes turned silver.

"Rachel?"

"I, uh—we should clean this up." I attempted to slide out from under him, but he kept his weight on me and brought his hand up to my cheek again. I stopped moving beneath him and locked up my body as his gaze held mine.

His silver eyes fell over my face as his head inched down, and in the torturous seconds where his lips hovered over mine again, I told myself a dozen times I needed to push him away.

But needing and wanting are two completely different things.

Kash closed the distance between us and pressed his lips to mine, and in that instant, I felt like I was exactly where I belonged and my body relaxed between him and the tile floor. He parted my mouth with his own and a soft whimper left me when our tongues met and moved against each other. Kissing my bottom lip softly, he pulled back a fraction of an inch to look into my eyes again and smiled before leaning back in.

The door burst open and we jolted away from each other as much as our positions allowed as Mason ran into the apartment, a loud war cry following him into my room, where it abruptly cut off.

Kash's chest moved roughly as we both came back to reality, and after a heavy silence he turned his head and called out, "Mase?"

I blew out the breath I'd been holding and refused to look back up at Kash as I silently berated myself for my actions over the last few minutes. That wasn't supposed to have happened, and it couldn't happen again. We both knew that.

My inner scolding stopped abruptly when Mason slowly walked over to the kitchen with a Nerf gun in hand. In a black wife-beater and cargo pants, with a bandanna around his forehead . . . he almost looked like Rambo.

"What the hell are you wearing?" Kash asked as he cautiously lifted himself off me.

Mase looked down at himself, then back up. "I saw you coming in here on my way back from my run with your gun. I thought we were gonna have a Nerf fight."

Oh. Dear. God.

Even with the tension coming from Kash and me, I couldn't help it. I burst into laughter until I was crying and snorting uncontrollably.

IT WAS NIGHTS like this I wished I didn't have a job.

The bar had been slammed for the first half of my shift. Normally, I wouldn't have complained; it made the shift go by faster and it meant more tips for me. But one of my tables during the rush was a couple with their toddler who thought it was hilarious to throw food off the table and at me, as well as continuously knock over her parents' drinks. You'd think maybe they'd—I don't know—move the drinks away from the baby. Or feed the baby rather than let her have her own plate *right* in front of her. Or maybe, just maybe, apologize for the fact that I was now covered in sour cream and refried beans instead of sitting there arguing with each other about who was better at playing Angry Birds. Just a thought, but what did I know? I was just the food-covered waitress with a smile on her face. That, added to the fact that Kash and I hadn't mentioned our kiss once, and that Eve had decided to remind me of original sin by bringing me my monthly gift, and I now had cramps bad enough to bring Chuck Norris down . . . equaled one incredibly grumpy me.

I then began messing up orders and spilling drinks, and, in an attempt to save a woman's white blouse, I tipped my tray back my way so a full bowl of salsa fell on me instead of her. I'm pretty sure my shirt had been craving salsa anyway.

The after-work rush had just begun to taper off when Kash pushed me down the hall toward the bathrooms and handed me a new work shirt.

"Go change, Rach."

"What, you don't like what I'm wearing now?" I laughed humorlessly and grabbed the shirt from him.

He smiled wickedly at me and leaned over so his lips were at my ear. "You look so . . . very . . ." His lips brushed my ear before he leaned back.

I cleared my throat and tried not to lean toward him. "I look what? Edible?" I asked, pointing at my newest addition to my shirt.

Sucking on the metal in his lip, he gave me a once-over, and when his eyes came back up to mine they were heated. Completely not fitting his next statement. "I was going to say *disgusting*. But sure, *edible* works too."

"You're such an asshole." I smacked his arm and turned toward the bathroom.

He laughed and backed up in the direction of the dining area. "Cheer up, Sour Patch."

Until I was home, in my pajamas, and had a pint of Ben and Jerry's in front of me, that wasn't likely to happen.

A part of me hated that he could so easily go back to how we'd been, without so much as a hint of what had happened that morning—but I knew that's how it needed to be and was thankful that at least it hadn't changed the friendship I'd come to love from him. I changed shirts, tried to wipe off as much as possible on my other shirt before throwing it in a to-go bag and putting it in my purse, and planted another fake smile on my face. I could get through the rest of the shift. Three more hours was nothing. Right? My cramps made their presence known and my back started aching.

I'd lied. Three hours would feel like forever.

Over two hours later, I'd successfully avoided spilling anything else on myself. And thank God there were no more evil food-throwing babies.

I was clearing some plates off a table when I heard the familiar strum of guitar chords. My heart clenched painfully as I slowly made my way to the kitchen. Tonight was another open-mic night, and while I enjoyed having live music playing throughout the bar and dining room, I didn't usually pay that much attention to it. But there was no way to miss this song. The deep, husky voice began crooning through the speakers as I came back out of the kitchen empty-handed. And I couldn't shake the feeling that I knew that voice as I made my way to a spot where I could see the stage.

I rubbed a hand over my aching chest and stopped suddenly when I saw Kash sitting on the stool in front of the mic with a guitar in his hands. What was he doing? Since when did he play guitar and sing? And why this song? His eyes searched the dining area and landed on me just as he began the first chorus of "I'll Be." Tears pricked the back of my eyes and my entire body warmed under his intense stare as he continued through words that meant more to me than he could have known. Not once did he take his eyes from me, and my mind and heart fought over my conflicting feelings. Part of me wanted to yell that he was the guy I'd been waiting for. That I was in love with him and was done being only his friend. The other part wanted to know why he was torturing me with this song. With everything else that had happened tonight and the fourth anniversary of my parents' death less than two months away, I wanted to run away from there, to curl in a ball and mourn what I had lost and would never have. I couldn't call my mom and tell her I'd met a guy whose presence alone made me dizzy. Who sang to me the same song Dad had always sung to her. I couldn't tell my parents that no matter how hard I fought my feelings and pushed Kash away, I knew I'd met the man I wanted to marry.

The haunting words drifted to an end, and soon the chords did too. When Kash was finished, he put the guitar on the stand and began walking in my direction. Throughout all of this, his eyes still hadn't left mine. Before he could reach me, the bitter side of me won out and I turned on my heel and rushed back to my customers. I kept myself busy for the rest of the hour and whenever I had to go over to the bar, I made sure to go to Bryce's side so I wouldn't have to face Kash again.

I knew I was being ridiculous, but if it had been any song other than that one, if it had been on a night that wasn't wearing me completely down, I may have been brave enough to finally fight for what I wanted. But right now all I could think of was finishing out this shift at work and staying far from Logan Hendricks. Somehow, he knew how to get to me. And somehow, I knew that our being together was right. But especially after that morning, everything about him—and us together—scared me. And I wasn't sure I could handle that right now.

People say that being in love is amazing.

They lie. It's freaking terrifying.

"WHAT'S UP, LADY, how was work?"

I looked at Candice and groaned. "It sucked so bad!" I went into the kitchen, where she was searching for dinner, and jumped on the counter as I told her about the entire night—including Kash's song.

"Oh my God! Did you tell him about that song and what it means to you?"

"No! We've never even talked about it. I really think it was just some freaky coincidence but it—God, it hurt, Candi." I wanted to tell her about the kiss that morning, but Candice and I hadn't talked about guys for *me* since the whole Blake incident, and I didn't know how to bring it up now.

She looked like she was about to cry. My parents' death had been almost as hard on her. "Well, what did you say to him after?"

"Nothing. He was walking toward me and I turned and ran back into my part of the dining room. I avoided him the rest of my shift."

"Rach, I'm sorry." She sniffed and blinked back tears that were threatening to fall as she fanned at her eyes rapidly. "Screw this. Tonight is a Chinese-food-and-Ben-and-Jerry's kind of night." She grabbed the Lean Cuisine she'd taken out, put it back in the freezer, and looked at our stock. "I'm going to go get food and another couple pints; we're running low and I have a feeling we'll go through a lot this week."

I smiled weakly at her and slid off the counter. "I'll go with you."

"No, go get comfy and take some Midol. I'll be right back."

"Love you, Candi."

She wrapped her arms around my waist and squeezed me tight. "Love you back. Always."

I was in my pajamas and had just finished downing the pills and a glass of water when the door opened and Kash walked in. *Candice has* seriously *got to start locking that door when she leaves.*

"Are you locked out tonight?" I asked, but didn't look up at him.

"No. I want to know what's going on with you."

Shrugging, I put the cup in the dishwasher and walked over to the couch. "Nothing."

"So you just walked away from me and avoided me for the rest of the night . . . because you felt like it?"

"Pretty much."

He walked over until he was standing directly in front of me, blocking my view of the TV, but I still didn't look at him. "We talked about this."

When he didn't continue, I snorted. "We talk about a lot, Kash. You expect me to know what conversation you're referring to just because *you* know which one you're talking about? Can you move? You're in the way."

He moved. But it was to grab the remote out of my hand to turn the TV off. "You're shielding again. Why? Did I push things too far tonight? Did something happen to you? Are you having nightmares again?"

"I'm just having a shitty night. Isn't that enough?"

"Then tell me! Don't throw your shield at me. I told you, no shields with us; if something is wrong, I want you to tell me. I can't help you through whatever is going on if you shut me out."

"I don't need you to help me, I need you to back off! You're not my boyfriend, you're not supposed to be there to fix things."

His eyes turned silver and his brow furrowed. "Where's *my* Rachel, huh? The girl who just this morning dumped an entire bowl of pancake batter on my head and was kissing me . . . where is she?"

"First of all, you don't have a Rachel. And as for this morning, we'll say it was a moment of stupidity on my part."

"A mo—" His eyebrows shot up and he took a step back as he

shook his head. "A moment of *stupidity*? That's really what you're going to call that?"

It was a moment in my life I wanted to relive over and over again. But it *was* stupid. I shoved off the couch and headed for my room. "Since you like to let yourself in, see yourself out."

Before I made it to my door, he grabbed on to my wrist and yanked me back toward him. "Stop with the goddamn shields!"

"Fine! You don't want shields? Then they're gone!" I tried to free my wrist, but it was no use. "I had a shitty night at work. Which you already mostly know about, seeing as you had to buy me a new shirt. Bad shifts happen, people get over it. As for the kiss . . . can I remind you that you were acting like it'd never happened as well? We shouldn't have let it happen in the first place."

"And why the fuck not?"

I kept talking over him. "And then you had to go and sing that song! Why did you pick *that* song?"

His head jerked back slightly and his eyes lost some of their fierceness. "You're mad about me singing the song? You love that song. You play it all the time."

I finally succeeded at freeing my wrist and crossed my arms under my chest. "And how the hell would you know that? I know I've never played that song in front of you!"

"Seriously? You leave your windows open! We live right across from each other. I can hear it from my apartment."

Oh. "Well, that's private. It's for my parents. You don't understand what it could possibly mean to me for you to sing that song to me."

Confusion crossed his face and he shook his head. "For your parents?"

"Yes! And since we're throwing the shields out, I lied to you, Kash."

"About what?" he said through gritted teeth, and called my name when I turned and dashed into my room. "Damn it, woman, stop running from me!"

"I'm not running. I never told my parents about what happened to me like I promised you I would," I mumbled as I grabbed underneath my mattress for my journal. Turning back to him, I held it up so he could see it and dropped it on the bed. "*That* is how I told my parents."

His eyes were narrowed again as they bounced between the journal and me. "Why?"

"Why did I lie to you? Because you kept telling me I should tell them. And . . . well . . . technically, I did. I wrote it to them, so I guess I wasn't exactly lying, because this"—I picked the journal back up—"is the only way I can talk to them."

"What are you—"

"They're *gone*, Kash. My parents died almost four years ago! I told you I couldn't tell them. But I wasn't ready for you to know why; no one in Texas other than Candice knows about it. And that's how I like it."

Kash's face fell and he took a few steps closer to me. "Rach . . ."

"No, Kash. You didn't want any more shields. Now there aren't any. That song you sang tonight, my dad used to sing to my mom when they thought no one was watching. He would pull her close and dance with her in the kitchen while he did it, and it's my favorite memory of them. So I'm *sorry* if I didn't know how to react to you singing it to me, but that song means so much to me."

"Rachel, I'm sorry."

I threw my arms up and planted them on his chest so he wouldn't come any closer. "Is this what you wanted? You know everything now. Are you happy . . . are you glad the shields are gone?"

He pulled me into his arms and held me close. "I had no idea, I'm so sorry. I—I'm just sorry. For hurting you, for pushing you to tell me, for upsetting you with the song . . . all of it. I swear to you that isn't what I wanted."

My anger was quickly fading and I blinked back tears. "I know, I just . . ."

"That song is special to you. I get it, Rach." He tipped my head back and brushed his lips across my forehead before capturing my eyes with his. "You need to know—"

"Rach, I'm back!" Candice called. "Time to start this junk-food night!"

Kash didn't let me go, and I didn't move. We continued to stare at each other, and when we heard Candice messing with the food in the kitchen, he leaned close and whispered in my ear. "You need to know that *you're* special to me. I meant every single word I sang to you tonight and I will never regret that kiss." He quickly let me go, then walked out of my room and out of the apartment.

I was staring at my empty doorway when Candice rushed in, eyes and mouth wide. "Oh my God, he was here?!"

Nodding, I just kept staring at the space Kash had just left through and replaying his words in my head. *You're special to me. I meant every single word.*

"Well are you okay, what did he say? Did you tell him?"

"Yeah." My voice was hoarse and I had to clear my throat a few times. "I did."

Before I could even attempt to stop them, heavy tears rolled down my cheeks and a sob tore from my chest. Candice caught me just as my legs gave out and awkwardly sat us both down. We clung to each other and cried for what felt like hours. Since my phone call to Candice early in the morning after their plane had gone down, I hadn't actually told anyone about my parents. Dad had been well-known, so people found out in their own ways, but I'd never repeated those words again. And even Candice and her parents hardly ever brought my parents up. Eli refused to talk about them.

Most people attempt to heal from loss. They grieve and deal with the pain that comes with it, and somehow try to keep moving forward in their lives. I hadn't done that. I'd felt like I'd died with them in that wreck, and instead of grieving and moving on, I'd shut down and built walls around me to keep the pain out and tried to act like it had never happened. Kash had been so right; he'd pegged me from the beginning. I shielded myself from the pain and in doing that pushed everyone except Candice and her family away. But no matter how hard I tried to push him, he pushed right back . . . and I wasn't sure yet if I loved or hated him for that. Regardless, I loved that man.

Once our tears had run dry, Candice and I made our way to the kitchen, piled up our plates, and grabbed a pint of Ben and Jerry's each before heading to the couches. Halfway through the movie, she fell asleep, so after getting her to her bed, I set about cleaning everything up and went to take a long shower. As I got ready for bed, I continuously replayed Kash's words and the sound of his gravelly voice as he sang to me. Each time, the memory of that sound and the heated look in his eyes gave me chills, and each time I think I fell for him a little more.

10

Kash

THE CORNERS OF my lips tilted up at the sound of Rachel's laugh. I loved it, and though she laughed a lot more now than when I first met her, I didn't get to hear it near enough.

"Dude, at least tell me you're hitting that," the other bartender, Bryce, pleaded as he finished up on a couple drinks.

"What are you talking about?"

"You and your fucking ridiculous constant smiling whenever she's here with you." His head jerked in the direction of the tables and I glanced over at Rach, my eyes narrowing as a guy at one of her tables made a grab for her. "*That.* That's what I'm talking about. Y'all say you're just friends, but she's always looking over at you . . . and you act like the possessive boyfriend when another guy looks at her. And to be honest, it's kind of disgusting the way y'all are with each other. So why not just admit you're sleeping with each other?"

I tore my eyes from the asshole who was now fully turned in his chair to keep looking at Rachel as she passed by their table again and looked at Bryce. "Because we're not."

"I call bullshit."

"Call whatever you want. She's the most amazing girl I know, but for now, all she is . . . is my best friend."

I'm in love with Rachel. There is no doubting that. And while I have a strong sense that she feels something similar, she isn't ready for anything yet. What happened after our kiss is proof. At first, I wasn't ready for a relationship since I was keeping too much from her, but that wouldn't stop me now. I wanted her to be mine; I was just afraid of pushing her again. As much as I hated not being in control of this, I needed to let her make the decisions.

Things had been different since the night I sang to her; something had changed. She was still a bitch and loved throwing her attitude at me, but I didn't want her any other way. Rachel was easily the most beautiful girl I'd ever seen, and that was what had originally caught my attention, but her attitude was what hooked me. In an attempt to give her the time she needed, I had gone back to being exactly like I always was with her. As if there had never been a kiss, as if I'd never sung for her and told her what she meant to me. The last couple weeks though, through the bickering and friends-only relationship, there had been a charge between us. Well, more than usual, anyway. It was constant, and it didn't make things awkward; it was almost as if it just made us both more aware of each other physically at all times. And I'm not gonna lie. I. Fucking. Loved it. The way she gasped softly whenever I would brush against her, how her arms would be covered in goose bumps when I pulled away from kissing the top of her head, and how she always seemed to shift closer to me without even realizing it.

"Kash."

I focused back on Bryce and realized he was shaking his head at me and had one hand stretched out toward me. "Hand in your man card. Now."

My expression was deadpan as I grabbed a stein to fill with beer for one of the regulars who had just walked in.

"I'm so serious. Do you even hear yourself? She's amazing and she's your best friend? Dude. I just wanted you to admit you were fucking her, not turn into a chick."

I threw one of the bar towels at him. "Come talk to me again when you fall in love with someone and stop screwing half of Texas."

Bryce's eyes went wide and his jaw dropped. "You're in love with Rachel. And you aren't dating *or* screwing her?"

"Bryce!"

We both looked over to the redhead who had just snapped his name. Her expression gave a whole new meaning to the phrase *if looks could kill*. I laughed when Bryce groaned and said under my breath as I walked past him, "My point exactly."

"Hey there, sugar," Bryce said smoothly. He called all his girls *sugar* because he couldn't remember their names half the time anyway, and when he could he was afraid of mixing them up.

"Don't 'sugar' me. Who was the bitch who just kicked me out of your apartment?"

"Depends on what she looks like. But I'd bet it was either my sister or the cleaning lady."

Redhead cocked a hip and planted a hand firmly on it while the other slammed down on the bar. "Your place is always a dump; you ain't got no cleaning lady. And from the things she was shoutin' at me, she ain't your sister. So tell me who the fuck she is and why she has a key to your apartment."

All of our customers at the bar were good, and none of the waitresses had any orders they were waiting on, so I clapped Bryce on the shoulder and spoke softly. "Get her to leave before she causes more drama, or I will when I get back." He nodded and I headed toward the restroom.

When I was walking back down the hall toward the restaurant, I could hear the redhead running her mouth, and from the sound of it, she wasn't yelling at Bryce anymore. I groaned and quickened my pace. Bryce needed to stop telling his lays where he worked, and he needed to stop making all of them a key to his apartment.

". . . assure you, you don't mean shit to him. I do, bitch. Let's get that clear right now. Don't look at him! You have no reason to look at him!" *Good God, her voice sounds like nails on a chalkboard.* "Run along, you little slut—"

"Um, no. You have five seconds to get your hands off me."

Shit. I would know that California-bitch tone anywhere. I rounded the corner to see Rachel give a warning glare to Red, grab four steins full of beer off the bar, and give Bryce a look before turning back to the restaurant, muttering something under her breath.

Red gasped and reared back. "What'd you just call me?"

Rachel didn't look back at her, just took another two steps toward the tables, but Red grabbed the back of her shirt and yanked her so that Rachel tripped over herself and landed hard on her ass, most of the beer spilling out of the steins and covering her and the floor.

"Are you kidding me?!" Rachel set the steins on the floor and got herself upright. When she stood back up from grabbing the mostly empty mugs off the ground Red slapped her hard across the face and I practically ran the rest of the way to them.

Red's arms were out like she was waiting for Rachel to retaliate, but Rachel was still standing there just staring at her. I grabbed both of Red's hands and brought them behind her back, twisting them slightly and bringing the backs of her hands together so I could hold them with one of my own. I realized too late that with that move, I probably looked like exactly what I was, but most people were focused on Rachel at the moment.

"Get off me, asshole!"

"Unless you want this to end up a lot worse for you, I suggest you shut the fuck up," I growled, and pushed her past Rachel, but stopped so I could brush my hand down the red side of Rach's face. "You okay, sweetheart?"

"Fine." She flashed a tentative smile at me and turned to put the glasses on top of the bar.

I took Red out of the restaurant and away from the windows before releasing her and bringing my hand up. "Key to Bryce's apartment."

"What? No!"

"Lady . . ." I let my face grow cold and stepped right up to her. "I'm only going to say this once. You do not step foot in that place again. You don't contact Bryce again, and if you ever touch that girl again? I swear to you I will make sure there are charges brought against you." Her eyes widened and her face paled. Oh, I knew that look well. "I'm betting you have warrants from the look on your face, so I know you'll do as I say. Now, give me the damn key and leave."

She licked her lips quickly and looked to the side as she rummaged through her bag until she found her keys. Her hands shook as she kept trying to get the key off, and as soon as it was in my hand, she took off. I wondered just what kind of warrants that piece of trash had. Bryce really needed to set higher standards.

I jogged back into the restaurant and found Bryce mopping up the floor. I glared at him as I slammed his key on the bar in front of him. "I'll talk to you later. Where's Rachel?"

"Rod pulled her into his office. Look, man, I'm sorry. I didn't know she'd do that."

"Grow the fuck up, Bryce. You're a great guy and all, but you're in your thirties, and you're still doing the same shit that guys are doing in high school and college. Act your damn age. Get a girlfriend or something and settle down." I didn't wait for him to respond, I just walked back to the office. I smiled when I heard Rachel.

"I'm fine. I'll just clean up, and we'll all get over it."

"Rachel, I would feel a lot better if you would just take the rest of the night off."

"I agree with Rod." Rachel turned to glare at me and I smirked at her. "You only have a few hours left. Just go home."

Rod gestured toward me. "You're outnumbered. Go home. I'm sorry about what happened tonight."

She huffed and quickly left the office, but I grabbed her arm and brought her back to me when she hit the hallway. "I'm fine, Kash. You're both being ridiculous."

"I know you are," I said softly, and brushed her cheek. She flinched when I touched the red mark. "But you have a handprint on your face, and you're covered in beer, and I swear to God if anyone touches or looks at you again I won't be able to stop myself from ripping into them."

Her blue eyes softened and she momentarily leaned into my hand. "That was actually a really impressive slap. It shocked me."

A grin tugged at my mouth and I brushed a kiss over her forehead. "I could tell. I'm proud of you for not reacting though. It would've just caused more trouble, and since you work here, it wouldn't have gone over well. What did you call her though?"

"A two-dollar whore."

God, she was cute. "And she got mad? I think that's a compliment for her."

"Right?" Rachel pushed at my stomach. "Go back to work. I'll see you tomorrow."

"Sleep well, Sour Patch."

Rachel

"RACH?"

I looked over toward the parking lot and offered up a small smile as Kash came running over to me.

"Please tell me you haven't been sitting out here this whole time."

"Um, I haven't?"

He closed his eyes and muttered something too low for me to hear. "Is she in there with Mason?"

"Yep, and neither are answering their phones."

"Shit, I should've just come home with you. I'm so sorry."

"No, no, it's fine." I struggled to get up but almost fell over from my butt being numb and legs being asleep.

Kash caught me around my waist and held me close until he was sure I could stay standing. My heart started pounding being this close to him again and I prayed to God he wouldn't hear it. I licked my suddenly dry lips and forced my hands to not curl into his shirt. I could feel the hard planes of his chest beneath my fingers and part of me wanted to run my hands over him, though the other part was telling me I needed to push him back. That voice was very small right now, though.

I'd let my guard slip and somewhere along the way I'd let Kash in. It terrified and thrilled me, but I couldn't keep pretending anymore. I couldn't act like my world didn't practically revolve around him. Like our "lock-out" times together weren't something I secretly craved. And like I didn't think about that damn kiss every second of every day. Kash took care of me and treated me like I was the only person in the world who mattered, even though I'd made it clear we could only ever be friends. He wouldn't be like Blake or Daniel. He'd never hurt me in any way, and he'd always protect me. Tonight was proof.

He cleared his throat and took a step back. "So, lock-out night?" His voice was rough and low, and after a few moments he had to force his eyes from mine before he turned for his apartment.

"Uh, yeah. Yeah, lock-out night. Do you mind if I take a shower first? I'm still covered in beer."

Did Kash just growl?

"None of Bryce's girls will be bothering you again, Rachel. I promise. And yes, you know you can take a shower, you don't have to ask. Just grab whatever clothes you need. I'll get the movie ready. Any preferences?"

I shook my head and started toward his room, but he grabbed my arm and brought me back to him. I could feel the heat coming from his body and tried not to let my eyes flutter shut as I caught a hint of his cologne and cinnamon gum.

"You sure you're okay after what happened tonight?" His gray eyes searched my face when I could only nod, and he brushed his lips against my forehead; the metal from his lip ring had goose bumps running up and down my body. "I'm sorry I wasn't there to stop it right away. But like I said earlier, I am proud of you for how you handled it." He whispered against my forehead and pressed his lips there one more time. "Go take a shower, Rach. I'll be waiting for you."

I wanted to say those kisses started meaning so much more after our kiss on my kitchen floor. But that would have been a lie. They'd been making my entire body warm and knees weak for weeks before the kiss had ever happened. I stumbled toward his room and into the bathroom. After turning the water on, I put my hair high up in a bun and shrugged out of my beer-covered clothes. It felt like I was in a fog as I slowly washed my body and dried off. I opened the side drawer that held an extra toothbrush and deodorant for me in case of nights like these, freshened up, and turned off the light. By the time I was standing in Kash's room again in nothing but a towel, I had made up my mind.

Mostly.

I wanted whatever this was with him. I was tired of keeping him at arm's length, and honestly, I didn't know how we'd even lasted this long. As I went over the last couple months with him, it seemed so obvious that we were meant to be together and I could hardly remember why I'd told him we could only be friends.

Grabbing and putting on one of his old T-shirts, which hit me right at midthigh, I glanced at the top drawer that held all of his boxers and workout shorts but didn't open it this time. Pulling my hair out of the bun, I ran my fingers through it and tried to give it some fluff before taking a deep breath in. My heart was already racing and my hands were shaking, and I was still alone in his room. Looking down at my bare legs, I made sure the shirt covered me enough and then almost laughed out loud at how ridiculous that thought was with what I wanted to do. Before I could change my mind, I turned off the light in his room and rounded the corner to the living room.

Kash was sitting on the couch, the room dark except for the glow from the TV. He was pressing buttons on the remote and turned to look at me, then did a double take. Through the light coming from the screen, I watched his eyes drift over me as I walked toward him. Without saying anything, I pulled the remote out of his hand and dropped it onto the coffee table before placing one knee on the couch, followed by the other so I was straddling him.

"Rachel . . . ," he whispered, and looked down to where I was almost sitting on him before meeting my gaze.

I placed one hand on his chest and smiled softly when I felt his heart beating just as fast as mine. "I'm done playing this game, Kash. I'm done hiding."

His hands cupped my cheeks as he continued to stare at me, and slowly—so slowly—he brought my face down to his and brushed my lips with his once . . . then twice, before pressing them firmly against my own. And just like the first time, I had the overwhelming feeling that I was exactly where I belonged.

Pulling away, he looked at me for a few heavy moments. "You're sure?"

Hoping my actions would be answer enough, I lowered myself until I was sitting on his lap, his growing erection pressed firmly against my heat, and I almost moaned as I captured his mouth. Our lips moved against each other, and soon, his tongue was torturing mine in the sweetest way possible. I rocked against him, and the goose bumps came back full force when he moaned into my mouth. His hands left my cheeks, slowly sliding down my neck and breasts, his thumbs brushing over my hardened nipples before continuing down until he was grabbing my hips and pressing us closer together.

Our kisses started getting rougher, our breathing heavier as I continued to rock my hips against him. Running my tongue across his bottom lip, I hit metal and lightly bit down and tugged on his ring. The sexiest growl I've ever heard worked its way from Kash's chest, and his hands left my hips to slip under the bottom of the shirt I was wearing. I lifted myself off his lap and his warm hands moved up my thighs, over my hips, and to my butt, where they stilled momentarily before quickly going back to my hips.

Kash leaned away and looked down at my legs as his hands made their journey back to my butt. A devilish grin flashed across his face before his lips made a trail up my throat as one hand came back around my hip to my thigh. "You're not wearing anything under this shirt?" he asked softly against the sensitive skin behind my ear.

"Kash . . ." I pulled his head back to press my lips to his and pleaded, "Touch me."

The hand on my thigh slowly trailed over and up but continued to stay just on the inside of my thigh. I started to lower myself, but the hand on my butt flew to my hip, and both hands squeezed to keep me where I was. An aggravated groan left me, and Kash laughed softly against my mouth.

"Be patient."

He released his hold and I didn't move as he dipped his head to suck on my breast through the shirt. The hand on the inside of my thigh went back to making lazy circles, each one bringing him closer to where I was aching for him. My breathing was getting rapid and I had to grab on to the back of the couch for support as he continued to tease me. I thought I would die if he didn't touch me soon. Each circle on my thigh and teasing bite to my hard nipples had the heat in my stomach growing. My whole body was buzzing and I was so turned on I was afraid I'd fall apart the second he finally did touch me.

Just when I was about to start begging, his fingers trailed against my heat, his thumb stopping on the sensitive bud as his fingers teased my opening before he slid one inside me.

"Fuck, Rachel." He growled and smashed our mouths together.

I kissed him with everything I had and whimpered when he added a second finger and started teasing my aching bud as he worked me slowly. The knot in my stomach tightened and I pressed harder into his hand as his fingers started going faster. I was so close. I broke off our kiss and tilted my head back as I rode his hand. Just before I went crashing over the edge, his hand was gone and my head snapped forward.

"Wha—" I broke off when I saw that devilish grin again. "You—I—why . . . stop teasing me!"

"Woman, I'm nowhere near done teasing you," he said softly, and pressed his lips to mine.

I wanted it rough. I wanted his hand back on me, *in* me. And he was smiling at me like he knew I was seconds from screaming in frustration and kissing me soft as a feather.

"Enjoy that frustration for a bit." He spoke around my lips and kissed me once before lifting me off him and standing up.

"What . . . just . . . what?!"

With a wink, he turned and walked into Mason's room. I was going to kill him. Or cry. I couldn't decide which. I knew as soon as my aggravation died down I was going to be mortified that I'd been that bold with him, and he'd spent countless minutes teasing me before finally giving me what I wanted, only to stop before it got to the best part. And why was he in Mason's room?!

Shakily getting to my feet, I swallowed the rejection that had just hit me and turned toward Kash's room to put some more clothes on. I didn't care if Mason and Candice kept it up all night; I'd rather have sat in front of my apartment than let Kash know how much he'd just crushed me. Before I made it to his door, his arms were suddenly on me, turning me around and pushing me up against the wall. His mouth slammed down on mine and he pressed his hips into me. His hard-on against my stomach had my knees going weak again. But before I could get lost in the feelings he stirred up in me, I pushed against his chest and turned my head.

"Kash—"

"You want to see what a little frustration will do?" he asked huskily as his fingers trailed against me before he slid two back inside me.

I moaned and my back arched off the wall as my body instantly reacted to his touch. The knot and heat were back and stronger than before, and I couldn't talk anymore. I could hardly think, only feel. In less than a minute he had me right back to where I'd been on the couch, my body tensed, and I felt like I was suspended in air for torturous seconds before everything in me shattered and I couldn't help the loud moan that escaped me.

Kash's mouth was back on mine, swallowing my moans as he continued to work me through the most earth-shattering orgasm I'd ever experienced. My knees gave out and he caught me before I could crumple to the floor. Slowly, he pulled his fingers out of me and let them trail back against me; a whimper sounded in my throat when they ran across my overly sensitive area.

I took in a shaky breath and face-planted into his chest. *Frustrated orgasms. Best. Ever.*

He laughed out loud and the sound warmed my body. "C'mon, Rach." As he lifted me into his arms, I instinctively wrapped my legs around his waist and let him walk me toward his bed. When he set me down, he brought my head back, pushed some hair behind my ear, and cupped my cheek. My hands reached for the button on his low-slung jeans but he twisted away from me. "Don't pout, woman." Kissing my lips once, he pulled back again and looked me in the eye. "Tell me what's going on with us, what you're wanting, because I—Rachel, if we do this . . . I'm all in. I want all of you . . . *need* all of you. I won't do what Candice and Mason are doing. If that's what you want, I'm sorry, but I can't give that to you."

A huge smile spread across my face. "Logan," I whispered, and loved the way his gray eyes turned to molten silver when I used his first name like this. Taking the hand that was holding my cheek, I placed it on my chest and just sat there staring at him for a while. "No one has ever made me feel like my heart is flying away but still holding me to this earth. No one has ever made me feel so at peace and crazy with one look. No one has ever made me feel so in love and terrified at the same time. No one until you." I kissed his shocked face and rested my forehead against his, our eyes locked on each other. "Trust me when I say, I'm completely yours."

"You love me." It wasn't a question, but I nodded my head anyway. "I want to hear you say it."

"I love you, Logan," I whispered, and had barely gotten his name out when his mouth was on mine and he was lowering my body onto the bed.

"Rachel, I can't begin to explain how in love with you I am." He spoke through our kiss, and I swear my heart was about to burst.

He slid me closer to the edge of the bed and slowly pulled his shirt off me. His breath caught and he lowered me onto the bed as he shamelessly took in my completely naked body. Heat rushed up my chest and to my cheeks, my legs tried to close even though they were still wrapped around him, and my arms came up to my chest. It was one thing to not have anything under the shirt, but that had been like another shield to hide behind. And now that shield was gone too.

Kash's eyes burned as he removed my arms, placing them gently on the bed, and opened my legs back up. "You're so damn beautiful," he whispered, and looked back into my eyes. "Please don't cover yourself with me."

My eyelids fluttered shut when his hands began their slow exploration of my body, and I had to force them back open so I could watch him. He sucked on his lip ring and looked up at me through hooded eyelids, and my body began burning for him. Sitting up quickly, I grabbed the back of his neck and brought his face to mine. Our kiss was slow and teasing, with soft bites and unhurried tongue strokes. I reached for the bottom of his shirt; he helped me get it off and I let my fingertips trail down his toned chest and stomach. I broke off the kiss to watch the path my hands were taking and only glanced at him for a moment when I began unbuttoning his low-slung jeans.

His erection was straining against the zipper, and my eyes widened when I pulled the denim off his hips and the only thing hiding him was a pair of boxer-briefs. I ran my hand over him and was rewarded with a low sound of pleasure in his throat. Letting the tips of my fingers run along the inside of the briefs' band before pulling them lower, I bit my lip to hide my smile when his body shuddered. I grabbed his length in my hands and ran them slowly up and down, placed two openmouthed kisses on his chest, and looked up at him. He was breathing heavily, his mouth slightly open, and there was no doubting the look in his eyes.

"Do you . . ." I trailed off, the blush returning at my minimal experience with this.

Kash seemed to understand as he grabbed at the jeans hanging on his thighs and took a couple foil packets out of the pocket. "Mason's good for something, I guess."

I laughed and continued to work him with one hand as I

pushed his pants and boxer-briefs off the rest of the way. He tilted my head up with his hands around my face, his thumbs brushing my jaw, and kissed me deeply.

"Rachel," he whispered against my lips before pulling back an inch to look into my eyes, "can I have you?"

A lump formed in my throat when I realized what he was asking. I'd already told him I was his, but that wasn't what this was. He knew about Daniel and the situation with Blake. One pushing, the other taking. Kash was asking. I nodded and squeezed my eyes tightly shut as I kissed him hard.

Pushing me farther back on the bed, he stepped out of his pants and tore open one of the foil packets. I watched as he rolled the condom on and reached for him when he finished. He grabbed the outstretched hand, kissed my palm, and intertwined our fingers as he crawled onto the bed and over me. I lay back and let him pull me up higher. When his lips found my throat, I wrapped my legs around his body and whimpered when his length pressed against me. He rolled his hips against me and I thought I would go mad if I didn't have him soon.

"Please, I don't want to wait anymore."

He leaned back and positioned himself at my entrance. The hand holding mine gripped tighter and his eyes locked on mine as he slowly pushed inside of me. A breathy moan left me and he groaned as I stretched around him. Kash didn't move for a few moments as we just felt each other. And with that lazy smile I loved, he pulled almost completely out and pushed back in harder. His name left my mouth and I brought his body down toward mine to capture his lips. Our joined hands were now pinned to the bed, his long fingers still entwined with mine and now clutching the comforter in them as well as we moved together. His other hand was in my hair, and his elbow was pressing into the mattress to keep his weight off me and give him the leverage he needed to move completely, but slowly, inside me.

My body was on fire for him, the heat in my belly growing rapidly. Our breaths were labored and our kisses were changing from slow and passionate to rough and needy. I urged him to move faster as I felt the familiar tightening low in my stomach and cried out when he leaned away and slammed into me. The heat in his eyes held me captive, and I'd never felt as beautiful or wanted as I did right now, in this moment with him. The hand that had been in my hair moved down my body, and the second his fingers rolled around my sensitive bud, my body shattered around him and I roughly whispered his name as I lost myself to him. He worked me through my orgasm, and when my body felt limp and sated, he curled back over me and placed his head in the crook of my neck. With a few more thrusts, his entire body tensed before shuddering, and he bit down on my collarbone as he groaned out his release.

His body was gently shaking when he pushed himself up, and I wrapped my arms around his broad back, bringing him closer to me. His arms gave out and I welcomed his weight for the moment before he rolled us onto our sides. Placing a soft kiss where he'd bitten down, he looked up at me and claimed my mouth next. We lay there holding each other for a few moments; the only sound was our heavy breathing as we stared into each other's eyes. A soft whimper escaped my lips when his body left mine, and he kissed me quickly on the forehead before rolling off the bed and walking into the bathroom. He smiled when he came back in and saw me under the covers.

"I love seeing you there," Kash said roughly as he crawled in with me. He wrapped an arm around my waist and pulled me close to him. "Are you okay after that?"

I snuggled in closer to his hard chest and sighed happily. "Much better than okay. I—" I broke off and kissed his warm skin.

"You what?" When I didn't respond, he tilted my head back and searched my eyes. "What, Rach? You can tell me."

Wishing I'd kept my mouth shut, I smiled softly and internally cringed, hoping I wouldn't ruin this night. "I was afraid I'd end up breaking down during. I was afraid he would find a way to ruin this for me."

"Did—"

"No!" I cut him off quickly and tightened my hold on his waist. "No, everything with you is just—it's perfect." I shrugged and hoped he could see the sincerity in my eyes. "It was just you; I felt safe and cherished, like I always do with you."

He kissed me softly. "I *do* cherish you. I love you, Rachel." My chest warmed as I whispered my love for him back. He held me close and I was almost asleep when he said softly, "You begin school again soon. He'll be there, and I—I don't know how to protect you if I don't know who he is."

"It doesn't matter. He won't do anything at school, and you wouldn't be able to protect me from him anyway. You can't go to my classes with me. It just—it doesn't matter. He won't bother me there."

"I wish you would tell me."

"Why, Kash? So you can have a name? It won't change anything."

He opened his mouth but then shut it and breathed heavily through his nose. "Okay, I'm sorry. You're right. I shouldn't have asked again. I don't want this between us right now. I just want you."

I kissed his jaw and silently cursed myself for saying anything. Relaxing into his embrace and the pillows, I tried to go over every second that I'd just shared with Kash and attempted to push thoughts of Blake away. After a few minutes of my internal battling, Kash began humming "Fall into Me" by Brantley Gilbert and I felt my body fully relax into him. I hadn't even realized I'd tensed up again.

His lips brushed across my cheek and he broke off humming to whisper in my ear, "Sleep, Rach. I'll keep you safe."

When he continued, he wasn't humming anymore; he was whispering the words, and my heart swelled. Sleep came quickly in Kash's arms as he softly sang to me. If I hadn't been sure before, I was now. I wanted to spend forever with this man.

11

Rachel

WORK WAS PICKING up now that summer was coming to a close and more people were returning from their vacations. I didn't have time to sit there just talking with Kash at the bar, but it didn't matter. The steady flow of customers made the work hours fly by, and then it was just Kash and me when it was all over. We didn't spend every night together, but more often than not, we both ended up in one of our beds. I preferred those nights. I'd never slept as well as I did with him, but with how raw our relationship was, it was good that we still spent some nights apart.

I grabbed for four bottles of beer and giggled against his lips when Kash leaned over the bar and pulled me in for a slow kiss. A few of the people around us hollered and a couple jokingly told us to get a room, and my face was bright red by the time we broke apart. We didn't show affection often at work, but we had an understanding: if someone was hitting on one of us, the other made sure to let him or her know we were taken and not interested. My eyes glanced over the people sitting at the bar and spotted a few girls at the end who had witnessed the exchange and were whispering to each other. I couldn't hide my smile and winked at Kash as I grabbed the bottles and turned to take them to the awaiting group of businessmen.

My phone vibrated in my pocket as I checked to see if they were ready to order yet, and after getting their order put in, I walked back toward the kitchen. As soon as I was around the corner, I pulled my phone out and my blood ran cold.

> BLAKE:
> I saw that

Oh my God, he's here. My body started shaking and my breathing turned shallow. I looked around the empty, short hallway and had begun putting my phone back in my pocket when it vibrated again. I squeezed my eyes shut and pulled in two deep breaths before looking down again.

> BLAKE:
> And I didn't like it. You seem to have forgotten whom you belong to.

A whimper escaped my throat and I turned to run into the women's restroom. I threw up bile and continued to dry-heave for a few minutes before sliding down the wall to the ground.

"Rach? Are you in here, sweetie?" Tina appeared in the stall—I hadn't had the time to shut and lock it when I ran in there—and her hands flew up to her mouth, then shot out in front of her. "Oh no, are you okay?"

Was I okay? No. I was definitely not okay. I was the opposite of okay. I was freaking the fuck out and coming dangerously close to hyperventilating and dry-heaving again. My hands shook as I pushed a few loose strands of hair away from my face.

"Do you want me to get Kash?"

"No!" Kash would flip the second he knew who was here. My mind ran wild with different possible scenarios. Kash beating the shit out of Blake and getting fired. Kash making me quit work and hiding me in his apartment. I never wanted to see Blake again, but I knew Kash would try to protect me and would go way overboard. "No, I'm fine, Tina. I just . . . got sick for a minute. But I'm fine."

"You sure? Do you want me to tell Rod that you need to go home?"

Yes, I wanted to go home. But if Blake was here, he could follow me. And Kash was here; he wouldn't let anything happen to me. "No, really. I need a few minutes and I'll be fine."

She looked at me, a little unsure at first, then smiled sadly. "Okay, well one of your orders is up, but I'll get it taken out to the table."

"Thank you, Tina. I'll be right out."

Once she was gone, I pulled myself up and had to grip the wall when I thought I'd fall right back down. When I regained my ability to stay standing and breathe normally, I went to the sinks and washed my hands. The cool water felt so good I let it run all over my arms and splashed a bit on my face. After drying back off, I shook out my body and chanted to myself that we were in public. That he wouldn't do anything to me here, and the worst he could do he'd already done. I could do this.

I opened the door and walked out of the hall and into the packed restaurant, and I realized, no. I could *not* do this. My eyes darted around the customers in search of a mentally disturbed Adonis, and I silently prayed he'd left while I was in the restroom. When I didn't see him, I went back into the kitchen, picked up my next order, and delivered it to the table. Checking on the rest of my tables and refilling drinks didn't ease any of my worry or occupy my mind like I'd hoped it would. I was afraid to look anywhere but straight ahead of me, and my heart stopped each time I had to turn around.

Walking back to the bar for refills, I went over to where Bryce was mixing drinks and gave him my order. I couldn't face Kash right now. He would know something was wrong . . . he would—

"Babe, you okay? You look like you've seen a ghost. Did something happen?"

—do that. "I'm fine." I tried to smile at him, but it felt wrong and his expression told me he wasn't buying it for a second.

"Rach, don't lie to me."

Bryce's eyes bounced between us as he handed me my drinks.

"I'm fine," I repeated, and thanked Bryce before taking the drinks to the table.

Making my way across the restaurant to clear off an empty table, my body froze and all the air left my lungs in one hard rush when I heard him directly behind me.

"To refresh your memory, sweetheart, you belong to me."

Please let this be a nightmare. His large hand touched my lower back as he came up to my side and my body began shaking.

"Long time, no see," he said, and lowered his voice. "Hiding, Rachel?"

Oh God, did Candice tell him where I work? "Leave me alone." I hated how small my voice sounded, but I couldn't force out anything more than a whisper. I refused to look over at him, and when he stepped closer, I dropped my head to stare at the floor.

His other hand came up to my stomach and brushed gently back and forth, just above the top of my shorts, and I prayed I wouldn't start dry-heaving in the middle of the restaurant. "Never. I gave you the summer to realize that you needed me, wanted me. Obviously you need more time, but make no mistake, you are mine. What I'm not okay with is someone else touching you. Kissing you."

"Please leave."

"Who is he, Rachel? Boyfriend? Fuck buddy? And before you answer that, know that either of those two answers would be the wrong one."

"Rach, everything okay here?" Kash grabbed the arm farthest from Blake and pulled me into him. Blake's fingers dug into my back momentarily, but he let me go. I still couldn't take my eyes off the floor.

"Everything's fine. We were just catching up for a second," Blake answered. His voice had dropped the threatening tone and was the smooth and silky voice everyone else knew and loved. "I haven't seen Rachel since school ended."

"Babe . . . ," Kash whispered softly.

Blake's arm shot out in front of me and I cringed back. "Blake West. Rach and I go way back."

"Logan . . . Hendricks. Rachel's boyfriend." He accepted Blake's hand and shook it hard once before dropping it.

"You're a very lucky guy," Blake said tightly. "Rachel is extremely picky when it comes to dating and has broken more than a few hearts with her rejections."

No one said anything as I was caught in the middle of a testosterone-filled staring contest. Kash's hand ran up and down my back slowly and Blake finally cleared his throat.

"It was good to meet you, Logan. Take care of Rachel for me, will you?" He took a step closer and Kash's hand stopped on my back. I could feel his body vibrating as it tensed up. "I'll be talking to you very soon, Rach."

As soon as he left, I took in a deep breath and Kash leaned close to kiss my cheek and whisper in my ear, "Who was that and how do you know him?"

"That's Candice's cousin."

"I thought you said you had a bad history with him," Kash said accusatorily as he held me close.

"I do."

"Then why the fuck was he touching you?"

I'd been afraid Kash would overreact if he knew what was going on, but none of that mattered now that I'd seen Blake and his hands had been on me again. Everything in me was screaming to pull Kash into the back and tell him exactly who Blake was to me. But I didn't want to voice those words at all, and especially not at work. I couldn't break down in front of everyone. I needed a distraction. Or to leave. Something, anything to take my mind off Blake.

"Rachel, can you help me with table twelve? I have a party of ten that is driving me crazy."

Big party. Distraction. I almost cried out in relief. I nodded my head at Amy and began pulling away from Kash. He tightened his arms around me and I looked into his concerned eyes, which didn't match the furrowed brow and set jaw.

"No more shields. We'll talk later tonight. But we *are* talking about him."

" 'Kay." I forced out the word, and when I turned this time, he let me go.

The next three hours dragged. Every time the door opened, I was afraid it would be Blake walking in again. And every time I had to go to the bar or looked over at it, Kash was staring at me with the concerned/pissed look. How he managed to look both, I didn't know. But he had it nailed. He waited for me to get off and followed me home on his motorcycle.

"Are you ready to talk now?" he asked as we walked toward my apartment.

"Not really, can we do this tomorrow?" My body had been tensed and my breathing ragged for the last few hours. I was exhausted and felt like I didn't have long before I collapsed and didn't move for an entire day. All I wanted to do was get out of the clothes that Blake had touched and make myself clean again.

"No, we can't. Because I had to watch another guy touch you. I had to sit there and watch another guy whisper in your ear. And you've been avoiding me since you saw him. You told me you had bad history, and that sure as shit isn't what it looked like. So we'll talk about him now," he demanded as we walked through the door.

I looked up and saw Candice standing in the kitchen and felt a small stab of betrayal. Had she told Blake where I was? She took one look at us and her eyebrows shot up.

"Just the girl I wanted to see," Kash declared, and clapped his hands together loudly once. "What is Blake West to Rachel?"

Oh shit.

Candice's eyes went wide. "My cousin? He's her ex. They dated a couple months ag—"

"He is not my ex!"

Kash's eyes narrowed. "So you're still with him, is that what you're saying?"

"No!"

Candice put something back in the fridge and walked quickly to the front door. Pointing awkwardly in the direction of the guys' apartment and waving, she opened the door. "I'm just going to see what Mason's up to."

I turned for my room and practically ran in there. I needed to get out of those clothes.

"Rachel. I'm not going to do this with you. Tell me who he is, or I'll just go with my original assumption. Now that I think about it, you were acting weird before I saw you with him. Was it because he and I were in the same place? You didn't want your two boyfriends to accidentally run into each other?"

"He was *never* my boyfriend!"

"Well then what, Rachel? You don't just act like this for no reason. You don't just shut me out. And he was *touching* you, Rach. So explain it."

Stop reminding me that he was touching me! I quickly took my shorts and shirt off and threw them into the trash in the bathroom. Turning the shower on high, I reached for the hook on my bra and shrugged out of it and my underwear.

"That's not the hamper," he said drily, and scoffed when I didn't respond. "So this is how you're going to do this. Just ignore me? You can't even be decent enough to tell me about him? To break up with me like a normal person?"

"I'm not breaking up with you!" I practically shrieked, and tried to step into the shower, but Kash caught my arm and I turned on him. "Who do you think he was, Kash? Who the fuck do you think he is to me?"

"Other than Candice's cousin, I don't know! I want you to explain what I saw." He reached around me and tried to turn off the shower but I smacked his arm back.

"No! I need to get clean, please!"

"You can take a shower after we've talked this out."

"Think about it!" I shrieked, and whirled on him. "Did I look like I was enjoying seeing him? I couldn't even *look* at him. Think about when Candice said I was 'dating' him. Think. About. It." Steam was filling the tiny bathroom and again, I tried to go into the shower. I just needed to wash him away. "Please, let me get clean," I cried.

"Clean," he whispered like that word had finally sunk in, and sucked in a quick gasp. "Oh my God, Rach—"

"I hate him, Kash. I hate him with everything in me. If I never see or hear from him again, it will be too soon! He tried to ruin me. And today—he saw us kiss. He started texting me. He said I forgot who I belonged to."

Kash's hand dropped from my arm and I cried in relief when my body hit the stinging water. I grabbed a loofah and poured shower gel on it before hastily scrubbing at my body. I was grabbing for more shower gel when Kash caught my wrist. I looked up at him and saw his horrified expression.

"Baby, please—don't . . . don't tell me he was right there and I did nothing."

My jaw trembled and I blinked back the tears that began to cloud my vision.

Kash's face drained of color and his shoulders slumped. "Son of a bitch. You said he worked at UT, I thought—I thought he was a professor. I was expecting some old, sick bastard, not . . . that."

I shook my head quickly and began scrubbing myself again. "He's a personal trainer there. He's only twenty-six."

His body swayed before going rigid, his eyes wide. "And he's Candice's cousin? Her goddamn cousin raped you?!"

Sobs filled the bathroom and I continued to scrub vigorously. "That's why she didn't believe me," I explained when I could take a deep enough breath in. "She was so mad, said I was just accusing him because I didn't want to date him."

"What the fuck? She—how could she—"

"He's her family. She loves him, I get it."

"There's nothing to get. That shouldn't make a difference. Rachel, I'm so sorry. I'm . . . I'm sorry." He grabbed the loofah out of my hand and tossed it in the tub. Cupping his hands to catch the water, he tried to help wash the suds off me and turned the water off when I was soap free. "You don't need to get clean, baby. You aren't dirty. You're okay." He wrapped a large towel around my body and pulled me close as I trembled. "You're okay. I'm so sorry I didn't realize, I'm sorry I was upset with you."

I face-planted into his chest and let him lead me into my bedroom. Letting me go for a moment, he flipped off the lights, quickly undressed until he was only in his boxer-briefs, and walked back up to me. Grabbing the comforter off the bed, he had me let go of the wet towel and let it fall to the floor before wrapping me up in the comforter. I climbed onto the bed after him, and he got under the sheet and pulled me close to him, his arms tightening around my shaking body.

"I've got you," he whispered against the top of my head. "You're safe."

My eyes shut and my body melted against his. I focused on nothing but his arms holding me close, the sound of his steady breaths, and his soothing words. Nothing else mattered as long as I was in his arms.

Kash

MY FEET SLOWED their pounding against the concrete as I turned into our breezeway and stopped completely when I saw him.

"What the hell?" I breathed, and got closer. "Can I help you?"

The man looking in Rachel and Candice's windows jerked back and faced me. "I'm sorry, do you live here?"

Uh, no. I ask questions. "Can I ask what you're doing looking in windows?"

"I was trying to see if I had the right apartment."

"Same question. Different answer, or I call the cops." *They've already been alerted. But that's just a technicality and I'd rather not use my job around here.*

He laughed awkwardly and brought his hands up in front of him. "No, no! I'm sorry; I didn't mean to scare you. I'm here visiting my daughter. I came to surprise her, but she isn't answering the door. I was just making sure I had the correct apartment."

"And you didn't think to call her? Who's your daughter?"

"Oh, if you live around here you probably know her. Rachel Masters?"

Who the fuck was this guy? I kept a straight face, but every inch of me wanted to pull him into my apartment and interrogate him. "Heard of her. Not sure which apartment is hers. And to be honest, I don't feel comfortable with you going around looking in windows. So until your *daughter* is here to show you which apartment is hers and let you in, you'll leave. Or I'll call the cops. And I can assure you it won't take more than a few seconds for them to get here."

His phone started ringing and I watched as he answered with an overenthusiastic "Hey, sweetheart! Whatcha doin'?" He pointed at the phone and mouthed *daughter*. "Oh, you're out with Candice, huh? That's great. When are you gonna be back home? Uh-huh. Uh-huh. Okay, I can meet you there. Okay, love you too."

Did this dumbass really just forget telling me he came here to surprise her?

He put the phone back in his pocket and pointed in the direction of the parking lot. "She's having breakfast with a friend. I'm going to go meet them there."

"You do that." I smiled and watched him walk back to the parking lot. As he got in his dark green Explorer, I took in as much as possible and waited for him to leave before pushing through my door. Mason was standing right there, arms crossed, expression furious.

"That motherfu—"

"Stop!" I hissed, and searched for a pen and paper. God, why is it that you can never find both! Giving up, I grabbed a cereal box and wrote down the license plate, make and model of the car, and every detail I could remember about the creep. Once I was done, I turned to Mason. "You heard that?"

"Yeah, and we had a real similar conversation when I came back from working out."

"Shit." Walking quietly, I opened my bedroom door and blew out air I hadn't realized I was holding in as my eyes landed on my sleeping girl. Thank God we'd both come back to my apartment last night. I already hated knowing that she'd been there alone while Mason and I were both gone, but I would've been sick if she'd been in her place and that guy had been trying to find a way in.

I brushed the top of her head with my lips, grabbed her phone, and walked back out to the living room, closing the door silently behind me. I wasn't dumb; I knew Rachel hadn't called that guy, whoever he was, but I needed to know if someone was trying to contact her. Sitting on the couch, I started going through her calls and texts as Mason kept an eye on the window. When I didn't find anything out of the ordinary, I went back to the counter and grabbed the cereal box and my phone.

Detective Ryder answered, and after giving the information on the car and what had been going on with the man, I told him to e-mail me the findings and hung up before facing Mason again.

"Who do you think he was?" Mason asked.

"I have no idea. But he's sloppy. Even if I didn't know Rachel's dad was dead, I would have thought something was weird with the guy. There were too many contradictions in his story. And whoever he is, he obviously doesn't know that Candice is at cheer camp during the week."

"Yeah, I noticed that too." He sighed and roughly ran a hand through his hair. "We gotta keep a watch out for him. I told him to leave, and not twenty minutes later he was back and looking through the windows, trying the door."

"He was trying—" I caught myself and took a few deep breaths before lowering my voice. "He was trying the door?"

"Yeah, I called you to see where you were, but you left your phone here and as soon as I started calling the cops, you showed up."

Running a hand over my face, I looked over at my closed bedroom door and thought for a few moments. "If we arrest him, people around us will know what we are. *Rachel* would know what we are. I can't put her in that position."

"I agree, the farther we're getting into this case, the more I'm with you that we need to stay as undercover as possible. Not including the meetings at the department."

I nodded. "So now, if he comes back . . . do we call the police, or do we watch and take down everything?"

"I don't know, man." Mase sat down on the opposite couch and sighed heavily. "If you didn't know who was living in that apartment, what would you do?"

"Call it in to dispatch, see if he is who he says he is . . . and if he came back I'd arrest him or call APD and get them to do it."

"But because it's Rachel and Candice?"

"I wanna know who is claiming to be Rach's dad and why."

He didn't respond for a while and we both continued to look out the window. "If we have him arrested, we can see if Ryder will let us question him. Or at least watch it on the cameras while someone else does it."

"You know he wouldn't. He'd want to know why we were so interested in this. Just like Rachel doesn't know about that part of my life . . . that part of my life won't know about her. I need to make sure they don't have a possibility of colliding."

"All right. I get you. Let's watch. If he even comes back over the weekend, we'll watch everything he does and then decide."

"Sounds good." I heaved myself off the couch, walked over to the door, and glanced into the parking lot. The spot the Explorer had vacated was still empty, and I didn't see any sign of him. But if he'd waited twenty minutes after Mason confronted him, I was betting he'd wait a while longer before coming back after both of us had. "Gonna go take a shower, keep an eye out."

My phone chimed, and after checking and forwarding the e-mail to Mason, I read off everything about our Peeping Tom.

"Marvin Cross. Five feet eleven inches. One hundred and ninety pounds. Caucasian, black hair, brown eyes. Born in sixty-eight . . . Texas resident, no priors. Fucking awesome. I've never seen him before at the bar; either he's checking on Rachel for someone, or she knows him through the school somehow."

"If you hadn't just met the bastard who raped her last week, that would've been my first line of thought."

"Mine too. Let's open the windows and keep the blinds cracked. The sun goes right into our windows, so it should keep him from seeing us, but I want to hear him. Whoever called him played along with that bullshit about her and Candice being together. If he gets another call, I want to know what's said."

Just as we'd finished with the windows and blinds, my door cracked open. I turned and smiled at the most beautiful girl I'd ever seen. "Morning, babe."

She smiled and stumbled out of the room.

"Sleep well?" I asked against her hair when she walked into my arms.

"Mmm-hmm. You already go for a run?"

"Yep, I need to shower. Wanna join me?"

She peeked around me to look at Mason, then looked back up at me and blushed as she gently nodded her head. I pushed her back in the direction of my room, and as soon as her back was to me, I tossed her cell to Mason so she wouldn't ask why I had it and looked back at him in time to see him nod at me.

Whatever this Marvin guy was doing, we would find out. I just needed to find a way to keep Rachel away from the apartments completely while we watched for him.

12

Rachel

"I'M EXHAUSTED," CANDICE moaned, "but we needed this day."

"I agree. I just want to go home and crash for the rest of the night . . . we did big today."

"Yeah, we did! How many outfits did we get combined? And the shoes—oh, the shoes. Maybe we should go out with the guys tonight instead. Take them to a club downtown or something. I need an excuse to wear some of my new stuff."

A club sounded like the exact opposite of fun right now. Not when my comfortable bed and fluffy pillows were calling my name.

With Candice at the cheer camp during the day and me work-ing half the nights during the week and spending the rest with

Kash, we never saw each other anymore. Kash and Mason had set it up so Candice and I could go to the movies last night, and today we'd gotten pedicures before going on an all-day shopping spree. It was good to be with her again, but I was already missing just being with Kash. Even before we'd stopped playing games with each other, I'd craved being near him. And now—I couldn't get enough of him.

Yes, my bed was definitely calling my name. But I didn't see sleep coming any time soon.

I grinned to myself and hoped Candice wouldn't ask why I'd started blushing suddenly. "I don't think I'm up for a club tonight, Candi. Maybe next weekend, when we haven't been on our feet all day?"

"Oh, did you already have plans with . . . someone?"

"Someone like Kash?"

She shrugged slowly. "Or just someone."

Uh . . . what? "No." I drew out the word as I looked at her expectant expression. "Am I supposed to? And who else would I be with? I only ever hang out with you, Kash, and Mase."

Candice didn't respond for almost an entire minute. She just stared like she was waiting for something from me. Like a switch being flipped, her expression went back to normal and she bounced in her seat. "Well, anyway! Next week's perfect. We can celebrate me being done with cheer camp and our senior year starting!"

I was about to tell Candice we needed to see if she was bipolar or had multiple personalities when what she'd said registered in my mind. "School, that's, uh—just a little over a week away, isn't it?" All the color drained from my face at the thought of having to see Blake on an almost-daily basis again. I wasn't ready to face him, especially after the way he had been that night at work.

"Yeah, can you believe how fast this summer went by? I'm kind of bummed the camp took up all of my time, but next summer, after graduation, we're going on a trip somewhere and we're celebrating for a few weeks. Just us, a bunch of hot guys we won't remember the names of, endless drinks, and the beach." She sighed contentedly. "Doesn't that sound perfect?"

I forced a smile as I attempted to remember what she'd just said. "Uh, minus the nameless guys . . . yeah, it does."

She scoffed. "You're no fun now that you're dating Kash."

"Candice, when have you ever known me to want to hook up with a bunch of guys?"

"Okay, true."

We got out of the car and, loaded down with our dozens of bags, made our way to the apartment.

"So, you're not going out tonight?" she asked as we walked through the living room toward our doors.

What the hell was with her right now? "No, Candice. I'm not. I just want to relax for a while. Make one of your booty calls; I'm sure one of your guys is free."

Before she could respond, I dumped all the bags on my bed and walked into my bathroom to turn on the tub. Giving my sink a double take, I studied it for a second before walking back into my room to get undressed and start pulling things out of the bags. Once everything was laid out on the bed, I hurried back into the bathroom, turned off the faucet, and slipped into the hot water.

After a few minutes in there, Candice poked her head in. "I'm going over to Charlie's place. I'll probably be back tomorrow."

Wow, I hadn't heard of a Charlie yet. "Be safe. Hey, did you take anything out of my bathroom?"

"No, why?"

"My sink just looks . . . kind of bare, I guess. I'm not sure, it caught my eye when I came in but I can't figure out what—if anything—is missing."

She studied the contents on top of my counter before shrugging. "It does look like something's missing. But I haven't taken anything. Maybe you just took some more things over to Kash's and forgot about it?"

"Maybe," I muttered, but I really didn't think that was it.

"All right, I gotta go. Call me if you need anything. Love you, Rach."

"Love you back," I mumbled.

After she was gone, I took my time relaxing in the tub until the water was cold before stepping out. As soon as I walked back into my room, I knew something was wrong. I looked at my bed and my eyes flitted over the few things that were on it. Over half of what I'd bought wasn't there anymore.

"What the hell?" I whispered, and checked all the empty bags, making sure I hadn't left some of my things in there and forgotten. Turning to check Candice's room, a scream to rival those in horror movies left me and I jumped back, clutching my towel to my chest. "Jesus, Kash! Make yourself known!"

"I called your name when I came in. Why are you so jumpy? You okay?"

"No, I feel like I'm going crazy. First I thought there was stuff missing from my bathroom, and now I swear most of what I bought today isn't here anymore!"

He offered a small smile and pulled me into his arms before

kissing me softly. "Sorry, babe. I should have told you when I came back in while you were in the tub. I've been taking your stuff. I packed a bag for you. We're going on a little trip."

"We are? Wait. Who's 'we'?"

"You and me. Get dressed, we're leaving in a couple minutes."

"Kash!" He whirled back around to look at me, and though he was exuding patience, he began pushing me over to my dresser and pulling out thin sweats and an off-the-shoulder top I only ever wore to bed. "Are you packing those too?"

"No, put them on."

"What—no. First, we can't just leave; we both have work. How long are we going for anyway? And you can't just expect me to get ready and leave in two seconds. If you were in here while I was in the tub, you should have told me. I would have gotten out sooner and started getting ready then. I'm not wearing this to wherever we're going."

Kash turned me and held me close as he caught my gaze. "I promise you don't need to dress up for where we're going; I doubt anyone will see you but me. I didn't tell you because I didn't want you to have time to get ready or to know about it. As for work, I took care of it." He leaned in close and kissed me softly once but didn't move back as he continued to talk against my lips. "But I planned something for us, and we need to get going. Will you please just put on these clothes?"

I'm pretty sure I wanted to keep arguing with him, or at least demand to pack my own bag. But my stomach had gone all fluttery on me and I had a ridiculous smile on my face as I nodded, letting my nose trail against his, and kissed him once more. "Okay."

He pulled away and was walking into the living room when his phone rang. I made quick work of finding a bra and underwear and putting them on before throwing on the clothes he'd pulled out for me. I had just taken my hair out of its high bun and was braiding it low and off to the side when he walked back into my room.

"See? You look beautiful."

"Liar."

He rolled his eyes and tugged at the bottom of my long braid before kissing my forehead. "You ready?"

I shrugged and looked around my room. "I mean, I guess. It feels weird not packing anything. Are you going to tell me where we're going?"

"No." He grabbed my hand and pulled me out of the apartment. Mason was standing outside by his truck, looking awkward and like he was keeping watch, but he smiled when he saw us.

"You coming with us, Mase?"

"Nah, just got done loading the truck up." He threw a set of keys at Kash and Kash led me toward Mason's truck.

"We're taking his?"

"Bigger cab." Kash shrugged and got me situated in the passenger seat. After he shut the door he spoke softly enough to Mason that I couldn't hear what they were saying, and then he jogged around to the driver's side.

"There's a lot of food in here. You went shopping?"

He grinned before reversing out of the spot. "You were gone for a long time today."

I turned to look in the backseat again and shook my head, my mouth still partially open. I couldn't believe that he'd planned a trip for us, and to go through all of this? "But, Kash, there's like . . . *a lot* of food here. I guess it's safe to say we aren't going to a hotel . . . or a bed-and-breakfast?"

"Eh. There aren't many places to eat where we're going. Well, there's one, but other than that you have to drive a ways. But I don't plan on leaving where we'll be." His gray eyes darkened and he flashed that arrogant smirk I loved before squeezing my thigh and leaving his hand there.

I instantly hated Mason's truck for having a center console. From Kash's throaty laugh and the way he began sucking on his lip ring, he knew I was frustrated. And he knew why.

"How long will it take us to get there?"

"Anxious?" He raised an eyebrow and winked. "An hour or less."

Drumming the fingers of my left hand on the center console, I worried my bottom lip and studied his profile as he drove. "Drive fast."

Kash

I LOOKED OVER at Rachel, who was practically pressed up against the window as we drove through the country. She'd originally laughed and asked why I was taking her to Florence, Texas . . . but the farther into Florence we drove, the wider her eyes got. And I couldn't wait to see how she'd react when we finally got to The Vineyard. From all the pictures on their website, it was gorgeous property and secluded. Out in the middle of nowhere. Hardly any cell phone service. Perfect for hiding Rachel from this guy who Mason and I now knew was stalking her for reasons that made me want to hide Rachel forever, but I knew I couldn't.

As soon as I'd heard Marvin Cross say the name *West* that day,

I was done. Mason had continued to watch for him as I'd made countless calls, looked up dozens of secluded places close by that could easily be passed off as a romantic getaway, and then went about getting everything ready. It was one thing for the girl who meant everything to me to have been raped by someone she was close to. It was another thing entirely to have someone stalking her. But to have the guy who raped her hiring people to track and stalk her? That was crossing a line that was sure to blow my cover.

I was already pushing it with the department taking these three nights off, but Mason was picking up my slack, and I was thankful. Mase and I hoped by taking Rachel away for a little bit, this guy posing as her dad would cut back on hanging around the apartment and following her wherever she went, but only time would tell.

Slowing down when The Vineyard came into view, I turned onto the property and drove to the main building to check us in and grab the keys. As soon as I was in the car, Rachel started talking again.

"Are we going wine tasting? Kash, you told me I didn't need to dress up!"

"We're not going—"

"Oh my word!" She gasped. "This place is . . . oh . . . wow. Look at this."

I leaned onto the steering wheel as we passed the gates and slowly drove down the dirt path. I had to agree with Rachel. Damn. Pictures didn't do it justice. We began driving past the villas and pulled into a smaller one that we would be staying in for the next few days. As soon as I parked the car, I turned to look at her and couldn't help but laugh through my smile. Her eyes were bigger than a kid's on Christmas morning. Her hand was covering her mouth, which was still open from gasping at everything, and she was looking back and forth between the villa and me.

"Is this where we're staying?" She spoke softly behind her hand, like she was in awe. I just nodded and enjoyed watching her take it in. "Kash, it's beautiful. I can't believe we're staying here! This whole place is beautiful."

"Well, do you want to see the inside, or do you want to sleep in the car and just admire it from out here?"

She smacked my arm and hopped out of the truck, bouncing up on the balls of her feet as she waited for me to join her. "When did you do this?"

"I told you, you were gone for a long time today."

Her expression was deadpan for all of three seconds before brightening again. "Come on, I want to see the inside!"

Kissing the top of her head, I led her around to a side door and let us in. Even I was shocked by what we walked in on. I'd seen the pictures of our villa, but this was insane. The villa matched the vineyard, and it was as if we'd stepped into Italy, but out back was the best view of nothing but pure country.

I could get used to this.

Rachel was turning slowly, with her mouth still wide open, so I told her to go look around and went back out to the truck to start bringing everything in. I was finishing up putting all of the food on the kitchen counter when I heard her clear her throat behind me.

Looking over my shoulder, I shot a confused look at the face she was making. "Uh . . . do you not like the rest of it?"

Her blue eyes sparkled as she fought off a grin. "Oh no, I do. It's gorgeous here. The bedroom's my favorite."

I couldn't even come back with a suggestive remark like I wanted to. She was still looking at me weird. "Okay . . . ?"

"Good to know we're on our honeymoon. Apparently I missed something."

My head jerked back and my brow furrowed. "Uh, what?"

"Oh, so you didn't know either? Go check the bedroom. I'll wait here."

I made my way to the bedroom and stopped short when I finally found it. *What . . . in the actual fuck?* On the bed were rose petals in the shape of a massive heart, and above the heart, spelled out in Hershey's Kisses, were two words. *Just. Married.* Um. What?

There was a letter lying on the rose petals, as if Rachel hadn't bothered to fold it back up, and I grabbed at it.

Mr. and Mrs. Logan Hendricks,

We are pleased you have chosen The Vineyard at Florence as your honeymoon destination and hope you enjoy your stay here. In the kitchen you will find vouchers for free brunch every day of your stay, as well as complimentary chocolate-dipped strawberries in the refrigerator and some of our finest wine.

Congratulations on your recent nuptials.

Sincerely,

The staff of The Vineyard at Florence

One, I was going to kill Mason after I shook his hand for somehow pulling this off. Two, I really hoped Rachel wasn't freaking out over this. At the moment, I couldn't remember what she'd looked like when she told me about this; had she been mad or scared? Three . . . I placed my thumb over the name *Hendricks* and swallowed hard. I let the image of the girl I'd left in the kitchen be forefront in my mind and pictured the surname *Ryan* instead. My heart started racing as I imagined it all.

Rachel in a white dress, her blue eyes and beautiful smile directed at me as we exchanged vows. Rachel with my parents and Mason's family. Us at the beach in Florida. Rachel's stomach round with my hands pressed softly against it.

I let my focus come back to the bedroom of the villa and blew out a hard breath. It didn't matter that I'd only known her a little over two months. I'd known that first day that she was a game changer, and I was sure now that I couldn't live without her. I wanted to marry her; I wanted everything I'd just envisioned. And I wanted it now.

Letting the letter drop back onto the rose heart, I walked through the house to find Rachel shutting the pantry door; she'd put away all the food while I'd been in there. With a secretive smile, she nodded her head in the direction of the refrigerator and my body relaxed when I caught the brightness in her eyes again. She wasn't mad. She wasn't scared about what any of that meant; she wasn't accusing me of anything even though she couldn't have known that it was all Mason. I opened the door to the fridge and right in the middle was a tray of huge chocolate-covered strawberries, just as the letter had said. And off on a side counter were the wines.

Without a word, I grabbed Rachel's hand and towed her back outside. She laughed and tugged against me, but I wasn't letting her win this one.

"Kash, what? Did you forget stuff in the truck?"

"Nope." I stopped suddenly, whirled around, and knocked her legs out from under her, catching her and cradling her in my arms before she could hit the ground. She gasped and glared at me, but I kissed her soundly to silence any snide remark she could have made. She wasn't about to ruin this. "I forgot this." I met her blue death stare and waited for it to soften before speaking again. "Mrs. Hendricks . . ." *Wrong name. Wrong. Name.* "Isn't it tradition to carry your new bride across the threshold?"

Her head tilted back and she laughed. "Isn't it tradition for the bride to be aware that she got married?"

I paused with one foot in the villa and one out. "You're ruining it, woman," I growled.

"Well, husband"—her laugh died down and she ran her hand down the side of my face to my neck—"we should probably continue with tradition and consummate the marriage."

Kissing her lips once, I left my mouth hovering over hers as I took the last step into the villa. "Let's get to it, wife."

I didn't miss her near-silent inhale on the last word or the way her blue eyes had taken on a darkness I'd never seen before. And I wondered if she was seeing a future similar to the one I'd been seeing in the bedroom.

"I LOVE YOUR tattoos," she whispered softly, and I cracked open my eyes to watch as hers followed her trailing finger on my arm.

"Do you?"

"Mmm-hmm."

I grinned and helped her by turning my arm when she reached where it rested against the bed. "Who's the liar now?" When her brow scrunched together, I continued. "I seem to remember you telling me you hated them, along with my lip ring . . . my hair . . ."

Her soft laugh filled the room and I tried to commit the sound to memory. "I was lying."

"Exactly, so who's the liar now?"

She shrugged with the shoulder that wasn't against the mattress. "But those were forgiving lies."

"*What* lies?"

"Forgiving lies, the only kind I'll tell." Forgetting her study of my arm, she crawled up the bed and rested her head on the pillow next to mine so our noses were almost touching. "You know, like white lies."

I pulled her closer and let the tips of my fingers trail up and down her bare spine. "So why not just call them white lies?"

"Because they're usually lies you tell people to protect them or be polite . . . right?" I just raised an eyebrow as confirmation and she smoothed it out. "It's like you telling me I looked beautiful when I was sick, or how I had to keep telling Candice I was fine when I wasn't, and acting like I wasn't upset with her even though I was. And with you? You and I both knew I was lying anyway . . . so they're lies. But they're the kind of lies that people forgive and forget about because they're so minor. But when people tell harmful lies, or ones that can shatter trusts, and the other person finds out about them . . . they always say what they did was unforgivable. So if lies that can hurt people are unforgivable, then why can't the ones that are meant to be polite be forgiving lies?"

I prayed she didn't notice how tense my body had become. I searched her face for any indication that she knew I was hiding things from her, but when I found nothing, I worked at slowing my heart rate and relaxing every muscle in my body. Realizing I'd stopped my trail at the top of her back, I began slowly going up and down again.

"*Forgiving* makes more sense when you put it that way. And you did look beautiful that day; you always do." My tone was gruff and I hoped like hell she wouldn't try to figure out why.

Liar, she mouthed.

I shook my head, wishing I could say I wasn't. I wasn't lying about her always being beautiful. But being a liar was pretty much in my job description. So instead, I said the one thing that wasn't, and never would be, a lie. "I love you, Rachel."

"I know." She smiled and ducked down to kiss along my jaw. "And I love you too."

One of her hands trailed down my stomach and I caught it before it could get to where I was already hard. I wanted her, but she'd just unknowingly called me out on everything I was doing to her, and the guilt I had from lying to her had just tripled and was eating at me. I didn't deserve anything from her right now; but she just rolled to her knees and began the same descent with her other hand. Capturing that one as well, I intertwined our fingers and pinned our hands to the bed.

"Rachel . . . ," I said when she grinned devilishly at me.

Bending low, she placed a kiss on my right hip before trailing her tongue along the muscles of my lower abdomen. "Shut up, Kash."

Flashing her blue eyes up at me, she winked and leaned back before letting her lips slowly trail up my length. My fingers dug into the top of her hands and pressed them harder against the comforter when they wrapped around the tip and her tongue darted out to taste me teasingly before releasing me. A growl worked its way out of my chest and cut off abruptly when she took me in completely, never once taking her eyes off me. My head fell so I was looking up at the ceiling before my eyes rolled back and I fought with hating myself for lying to her and loving everything she was giving to me, including her complete and utter trust. I released her hands and whispered, "Forgive me, Rachel," to the ceiling low enough that I knew she couldn't hear me as I grabbed her shoulders and pulled her up my body.

I crushed our mouths together and squeezed her closer to me as I rolled us over and brought my knee up between her legs, parting them while I searched blindly for another condom. She wrapped her long legs around my back and flicked her tongue against my lip ring before tugging on it gently, and I groaned as I attacked her mouth again. I dug my hips harder against hers and we both stopped moving when I was pressed at her entrance. We stared at each other, our breathing ragged as I began teasing and sliding against her, and when I'd barely started to slip inside her, her face turned pleading.

"Please, Kash. Don't stop."

Stop. Stop. You need to stop . . . motherfucker, stop. "Shit." I reached over to the nightstand and slapped my hand down on a condom.

Tearing it open with my teeth, I had it rolled on and was slamming into Rachel within seconds. She yelled my name and gripped my shoulders tight as I pounded into her and I almost lost it a few minutes later when she whispered for me to go harder. Raising myself up even more on one forearm, I reached down between us and watched her beautiful face respond to my touching her and as she came undone beneath me. I came crashing down with her and when I couldn't support my weight anymore, I lowered my body onto hers.

"Holy hell," she breathed, and let her hands run through my hair and down my back. "Just . . . wow."

I didn't know what to say. I didn't know what I *could* say. I knew I was being a selfish bastard by keeping her when I was hiding everything that I was. And instead of breaking down and telling her everything, I'd just responded by claiming her. Curling one arm underneath her body and pressing my mouth to the soft skin at the base of her neck, I breathed her in and prayed that the day I told her everything wouldn't also be the day I lost her.

Rachel

I BROUGHT MY legs up on my chair as I stared at the darkening sky. It was beautiful out here, so quiet, and just perfect. Vineyard on one side, and Texas country on the other . . . I preferred the country side. I was sitting out on the patio, enjoying our last night at The Vineyard, exactly as we had the first two nights. I loved listening to the cicadas, watching the sun set, and looking at the stars after. You just couldn't get this atmosphere in Austin, and I was sad we were going back tomorrow. This impromptu trip had been incredible, and I loved Kash for it.

Looking over my shoulder through the windows, I caught a glimpse of him in the kitchen and a smile tugged at my lips. We'd been living up the honeymoon joke Mason had played on us, and though I knew it was just that—a joke—every time he called me his wife, it warmed my entire body, and I got a rush out of calling him my husband. My rational side kept telling me it was just the newness of being in love with him. That it was absolutely ridiculous to have a craving for this to be our reality. I mean honestly, who meets someone and a little over two months later knows without a doubt that they want to spend the rest of their life with that person?

Me.

I'd known even before we came here that I would spend the rest of my life with him. But this weekend had changed even that. It wasn't just that I knew I would. I could *see* it now. I could see our lives together, and the absurd thing about all of that was that I now couldn't see anything wrong with feeling this way after we'd only known each other for two months.

See? I was crazy. This is how fourteen-year-olds in puppy love think. Not twenty-one-year-olds who, honest to God, a few months ago couldn't have cared less if they ever got married. My rational side started spouting off divorce rates and the increase in those rates when marriage happens so quickly . . . but then I thought about my parents. They'd met and were married within four months and loved each other fiercely up until the end. Was it still possible to find that kind of love?

The door opened and Kash walked out carrying two bowls of pasta. Handing one to me, he pulled the other chair up closer and sat down in front of me. Grabbing both my ankles in one of his hands, he extended my legs and set my feet down on his lap as he got comfortable.

"What were you thinking about so hard when I walked out?"

Er . . . nothing I want to share with you right now. "I'm sad to be going back. I've had a really good time with you here."

He raised an eyebrow as he chewed some of his food and waited until he could swallow to respond. "So you only have a good time with me when we're here?"

I nudged his stomach with one of my feet and he smirked at me. "No, it's just been nice. No work, no Candice, no pancakes . . ."

"You love pancakes. Don't lie."

"Not as much as some people, apparently." Rolling my eyes, I snuggled deeper into my chair and took a bite of food.

Kash was quiet throughout the rest of dinner; he didn't look at me, just stared out at the scenery like I had been doing before he'd joined me. We could sit in comfortable silence or even spend hours together with him on one side of the room playing his guitar and me on the other writing to my parents. But this wasn't comfortable; it was weighted. I knew he wanted to say something, but I also knew he would say it whenever he was ready. So I finished my dinner and waited until he was. Sometime after he'd set his bowl down on the patio, he turned to me, and the depth in his gray eyes startled me.

"I've missed pancakes. But I'll miss being married to you more." Without another word, he moved my legs to the ground, grabbed both our bowls, and kissed my forehead before going back into the villa.

I was frozen. My heart had stopped and I wasn't sure whether it had started back up again or not. How had he taken something as asinine as pancakes and turned it into a beautiful statement? But I knew right then I had my answer. It was definitely still possible to find that kind of love.

And I'd found it in him.

I stood and walked out onto the grass a ways to enjoy the night for a little longer and think about this revelation without his too-knowing eyes on me. Not two minutes later, his arms were wrapping around my waist and his lips were on my shoulder.

"I want you to be my wife, Rachel."

My body froze but my heart began racing. What was he saying? "I thought I already was," I said teasingly, and forced out a light laugh.

"No, uh, I don't want this to end here. I—" He sighed and turned me so I was facing him. His darkened eyes searched mine and he shook his head marginally. "I get it, this is crazy. But I want this with you, what we've had this weekend. I don't want it to end, tomorrow or ever. I want you, forever."

"Logan . . . what?"

"Marry me."

My mouth popped open and every rational thought that was screaming at me was quickly shut up when I saw the love he had for me pouring out of him. My head shook negatively for a split second before my mind realized that was the wrong direction and I furiously nodded. "Y-yes." *Oh my God, I can't even figure out what word I'm supposed to say right now!*

"Yes?" he asked in shock, and gripped my shoulders in his hands.

"Yes!"

Crushing my body to his, he captured my mouth and kissed me through our smiles. "You're going to marry me?" he asked somewhat breathlessly, and kissed me harder. "You'll be my wife?" I couldn't respond against his forceful kisses so I just nodded again and he smiled. "I love you, so much."

"I love you too, Logan."

13

Rachel

I FELT A body slip into bed behind me and instantly knew it wasn't Kash. It was much too small, definitely smaller than my own . . . and the second her arms went around mine I knew exactly who it was. I patted at one of her hands and heard her sigh.

"You're awake then?" Candice asked in a shaky voice.

"Yeah, I'm up."

"Can't believe it's already here."

"I know." It was August nineteenth. It was a Saturday, not that the day of the week mattered; it just happened to be the day it fell on this year. The four-year anniversary of my parents' death. I continued to stare blankly at my clock as the minutes ticked by and laughed softly. "Now, girls," I said, imitating my mom's voice perfectly, "how are you going to get guys to notice you if you spend all weekend in bed?"

Candice's body shook with laughter and a happier sigh sounded behind me. "But, Rebecca, the sun isn't even up. All the cute guys are still asleep. Go away," Candice whined.

I mimicked throwing open the curtains, like my mom always would after Candice and I would complain. "Oh, they are?! Perfect! Then we can do the unattractive things now before they wake up."

Candice rolled out of bed and threw the comforter off me. "Ready for the unattractive things, Rach?"

"Meet you in three!"

I jumped off the bed and went to brush my teeth, put on some deodorant, and throw on a bra. It was tradition. Whenever weekends began at my house, my mom would wake us up the same way. And even though we knew what was coming, we'd always complain about her waking us up so early on a weekend. Deep down, she knew we loved it. We'd go get breakfast completely skanked out. The only thing Mom would let us do was the essentials: put on a bra, brush teeth, and wear deodorant. Every time we'd order the same thing: hash browns, biscuits and gravy, and a ham-and-cheese omelet. We'd split all of it, and when we were done stuffing our faces, we'd go out for pedicures. My mom thought you should always look your best for guys, but girls needed to indulge every now and then, and doing it at the ass crack of dawn was her method for getting away with it. And now, every year on the anniversary, Candice and I honored that memory.

After I slid the shirt I'd slept in back on and stepped into my flip-flops, I ran into the living room at the same time Candice was coming out of her room. We grinned awkwardly at each other and she grabbed me in a big hug before we left the apartment. Bittersweet memories . . . but definitely the best way to start off this day.

TURNING OFF MY car, I wiped the tears from under my eyes and tried to catch my breath from laughing too hard. "Oh my word, Candice, I had completely forgotten about that."

"You forgot about that?! How? Seriously, your dad was the funniest guy I knew!" She fanned at her tear-streaked face and we both got out of my car.

After breakfast and pedicures, we'd gone back to the apartment, taken showers, and gotten ready for the day. We went window-shopping at an outdoor mall called The Domain, not only because we couldn't afford much of anything from those shops anyway but because it was another thing we'd done with my mom. She'd take us to Rodeo Drive in Beverly Hills just for the fun of looking at everything. We never once bought anything, just browsed. And since Rodeo Drive was a little too far to get to this year, the pricey shops at The Domain were our replacements.

Once we got our fill of browsing, we went to the movies, picked a comedy, and got the biggest tub of popcorn and three boxes. Candice and I filled the boxes with popcorn and we each sat one on our lap, placed one on the seat next to her, and put the tub of popcorn next to me. My dad always said he was the man so he got to hold the tub, but really he just wanted all the extra butter that was sitting in it; we just let him think we never figured him out. Their popcorn remained untouched, as it had every August nineteenth over the last three years, and when Candice saw my face when we went to throw the leftover popcorn away, she immediately picked back up telling funny stories about my parents and kept it up all the way home.

"You remember when he taught all of us how to slide on the hardwood like Tom Cruise?" I said as we walked to our unit.

Candice threw her head back and laughed loudly. "Oh God, we spent hours learning how to do that. We were all so bruised from falling! Didn't you get hurt?"

"Dislocated my shoulder."

"That's right! I'm still really good at that. I wish we had hardwood floors in our apartment."

I laughed and searched for the key to our door. "Yeah . . . I haven't done that in years." My eyebrows scrunched together when Candice began walking over to Kash and Mason's apartment. "Where are you going?"

"I'll see you tomorrow." She smiled knowingly at me and her eyes began watering for a completely different reason when she held her hand over her heart. "Love you, Rach. Miss them."

She was going to leave me for Mason on a night like tonight? "Love you back," I whispered, and walked inside, screaming when I turned to find Kash standing right there. "For real! You need a freakin' bell on you— Oooh, it smells good in here."

He laughed low and pulled me close to whisper against my lips, "My Sour Patch."

I growled unimpressively at him and he smiled. He knew I couldn't stand that name, but I'm sure that's why he continued to call me that. I would have preferred something like *fiancée,* but we still hadn't told anyone in the few days since we'd been back and only talked about it during the nights we were in bed with each other. He wanted to wait until I had a ring, but a piece of jewelry didn't make a difference to me. I just hadn't realized how terrified I would be for Candice to find out. Well, not so much Candice as her cousin . . . and somehow I knew that if the Jenkinses knew, he would know as well. Mentally shaking off thoughts of Blake, I focused on my *fiancé,* who was now leading us into the kitchen.

"How has today been for you so far?"

"It's been good, considering. Candice and I did a pretty good job of fitting a lot of our memories of them into today. What are you making?"

"Food."

I feigned excitement. "My favorite!"

He turned to grin at me and put a dish in the oven, started the timer, and pulled me into his arms again. "I'm glad today was good for you."

"Me too."

Pulling a small remote out of his pocket, he pushed a button and soon the kitchen was filled with the beginning of a familiar song. My smile widened when I remembered the first time he sang it to me. "I'm sorry; I didn't mean to try to take that memory of your parents from you the night I sang their song." He curled one hand around mine and put it against his chest, and the other he wrapped around my waist as he slowly started rocking us back and forth.

My breath caught in my throat and I tried to choke out his name, but hardly any sound came out. Tears filled my eyes and I pressed my forehead against his chest next to our hands.

"So I'm gonna make our own memory, baby."

I slowly nodded my head against his chest and a few tears fell onto his shirt when his husky voice began singing in my ear along with Brantley Gilbert. Flashes of my dad singing "I'll Be" to my mom danced through my head for a few seconds before I let go and cherished this gift. Kash was taking my favorite memory of my parents and giving me our own version of it, and I somehow—impossibly—fell more in love with him as he sang "Fall into Me."

"*I'll be the love song, and I'll love you right off your feet . . . Until you fall into me.*"

Even after the song was over and other songs had begun playing . . . Kash didn't let me go, we didn't speak, and we didn't stop dancing. There was nothing to say; what he'd given me was beyond beautiful. It was a perfect way to end this day. And I knew if my dad were alive, Logan Hendricks would have his stamp of approval.

"Y'ALL NEED ANY help closing up?" Tina asked as she slung her purse over her shoulder.

"No, we're good, we're almost done anyway. Go home, I know you're exhausted."

"I swear, college kids are the worst. No offense, hon. But they're rowdy and the worst tippers."

"None taken." I smiled wide at her and walked her over to the door so I could lock it behind her. "See you later, drive safe!"

With an awkward wave of her hand, she ran to her car and I watched as she drove off. Bryce and Kash were closing up the restaurant, and I didn't need to be there, but I'd gotten a ride with Kash tonight and I usually waited until he was off anyway, so it didn't bother me to help them out. He was talking to Rod about something and pointing at papers in Rod's hand, and when he glanced up at me, he sent a wink my way without a pause in his sentence.

I walked over to Bryce and helped him put away some glasses before running to the back and grabbing another rack of glasses that had just been cleaned. When I walked back into the restaurant, Kash and Rod were both gone and Bryce was standing there waiting for me to come back. We were putting everything away when a guitar started coming through the speakers.

Figuring one of the guys had turned on the music, we thought nothing of it and I kept talking to Bryce until I heard a husky voice join in. I abruptly stopped talking and stood there with two glasses in my hands just staring at the wall that separated us from the area that held the stage. I bit my lip to contain my smile as I heard the first few lines of "Your Guardian Angel." It didn't matter what type of song it was; Kash could sing it. And in his deep voice? Lord, it was a treat.

He'd just started the second verse of the song by The Red Jumpsuit Apparatus when I rounded the corner and leaned up against the wall to watch him. His lips curled up when he saw me enter the dim room, and other than the few times he'd look down when he was only playing the guitar, he kept his gray eyes trained on me.

I took in the words like I was hearing them for the first time, because Kash had told me last week after dancing with me in my kitchen that he would only sing me songs that meant something for us. My heart beat wildly as I felt every word go straight to my soul, and I subconsciously grabbed at my warming chest. When his words trailed off and his hand stopped strumming the guitar, I was still leaning against the wall, hoping it would keep me standing as he set the guitar down and stepped off the stage. Much like the first night he sang to me in the bar, his stride was purposeful as he made his way toward me. Only this time, I didn't turn and run.

His smile grew when he got closer to me, but he didn't pull me into his arms like he normally would. Just as I started to push myself off the wall, he spoke, his voice gruff. "I didn't do this right the first time." Dropping slowly to one knee, he grabbed my left hand and brought a diamond solitaire up to my ring finger. "Rachel Masters, I promise to love you and take care of you . . . no matter the cost, every day for the rest of my life. Will you marry me?"

"Yes," I whispered, and bounced on my toes when he slid the ring onto my finger. Grabbing his face, I pulled him up and kissed him with every bit of passion in my body.

"Do you trust me to always protect you?"

Uh . . . Awkward question to follow up a proposal. I jerked back and smiled self-consciously. "Of course I do, why?"

"I just needed to make sure."

What on earth? Before I could ask where that deep and random question came from, he hooked his arm around my neck and pulled me toward the front of the restaurant.

"Come on, let's go home. I plan on keeping you up all night."

Random question officially forgotten.

Kash

"THAT BETTER HAVE been a Cracker Jack ring and this better just be some sick joke you're playing to get back at me for the honeymoon bullshit!" Mason slammed the door to my bedroom shut and began stalking back and forth.

"Did it *look* like a Cracker Jack ring?"

"What the fuck were you thinking?!"

That I'm in love with Rachel and I want to spend every fucking second of the rest of my life with her? I didn't say anything, I just continued getting ready. Once my badge and gun were on my belt, I pulled a shirt on and grabbed another button-up one to put over it, leaving the buttons undone. We'd learned early on that trying to hide your gun didn't work well if it bulged beneath your shirt.

"You're not going to say anything?"

I sighed and faced him. "What do you want me to say?"

"That it's a joke! That you didn't really propose to a girl who knows *nothing* about you!"

"She knows me, Mase. She knows who I am. Maybe not my last name or my actual profession, but who I am as a person? She knows me."

He looked at me like I'd lost it. Bringing his hand to his head before flinging it to the side, he shouted, "Do you even hear yourself right now?! Your. Last. Name. She doesn't know your last name! Which means she thinks that someday she's going to be Rachel Hendricks. Not Rachel Ryan. Didn't you think of that? And your profession *is* who you are. It makes up everything that *is* Logan fuckin' Ryan."

I started walking around him and opened my door. "Whatever, I don't need this from you right now. You're my best friend; I'm pretty sure you're supposed to be saying congrats or something similar."

"The hell I am! Candice isn't even happy about this! You

saw her. As soon as she saw the ring, she started screaming at Rachel and left. Rachel looked fucking crushed. She needs her best friend, and she needs a fiancé that isn't lying to her. Don't you understand that? You can't do this to her. You're going to kill her when she finds out the truth—"

"She'll understand."

"No, she won't, Kash! Either tell her about who we are or break off the engagement. Today."

"Fuck you."

"Fine, I'll call her and do it myself."

I turned and swung, connecting with his jaw. "I will end you if you get in the middle of this!"

He slammed me into the hallway wall and held me there. "I love her too; I won't let you hurt her like that! You shouldn't have proposed until she knew everything about you and me. You should have never put her in that kind of position." Shoving off me, he started walking away before abruptly turning back to me. "Honestly, what the hell were you thinking?"

"I wasn't, okay? I wasn't thinking about anything other than the fact that I love her and I know I want to spend the rest of my life with her. I got caught up in that weekend, and I could see it, Mase—God, I could see our entire freakin' lives and I wanted it so damn bad. The last night we were there, it hit me that I was fucking terrified of not having that with her, and I asked her then. We've been engaged since before we came back; I just gave her the ring this weekend though. I hate lying to her; you have no idea what it's doing to me, and you have no idea how many times I've almost told her everything. But I can't do it, I need to protect her."

"Then you shouldn't have asked her yet." He sighed and scrubbed his face with his hands.

"I know. But I did and I would never take that back. I love her, and I'll always love her. I'll tell her the truth, soon."

"Swear?"

"Yeah." Without another word, I walked out of the apartment and headed toward my Harley.

"Where are you going? We don't need to leave yet."

"Gonna go ride for a while first. I need time to think, and you sitting there looking at me like I'm the asshole I already know I am isn't going to help me."

I started up my baby and looked at the empty space where Rachel normally parked. I knew I needed to tell her, and I knew the way I'd gone about this had probably already fucked things up beyond repair. I just prayed that when she did find out, she would understand my reasons for keeping her in the dark.

14

Rachel

I QUICKLY STEPPED out of my clothes from work and jumped into the shower after piling my hair on top of my head. The hot water ran over my body and I moaned from how good it felt. I would have loved a bath to wash the grime from the day away, but Kash would be over soon after cleaning up from the long day as well. After running the loofah all over my body and washing the suds away, I stood there for another few minutes just enjoying the way my muscles relaxed under the spray. Candice had gone right over to one of her hook-ups' house after school today and said not to expect her until tomorrow, which, unfortunately, wasn't uncommon since she'd found out about the engagement.

I was positive she was trying to avoid being near me as much as possible. It didn't make sense, but then again, *she* didn't make sense to me anymore. Our entire friendship had drastically changed since the end of the last school year, and I didn't know how to fix it. There were moments that I'd see my Candice, and then in a split second, she was gone. I sighed and brought my thoughts back to what was going right in my life to avoid getting in a funk. Right now, work was going well, Kash was amazing, and this hot shower felt like heaven. If I hadn't been expecting Kash soon, I wouldn't have been able to force myself to leave. As it was, I was ready for alone time with my man. I smiled to myself and turned off the water, towel-dried my body, and got in some comfy clothes before going out to the kitchen to find something to snack on.

I stumbled when I turned into the kitchen and caught sight of the unexpected shadowed objects waiting for me, but laughed when I flipped on the light. This boy. I swear. I walked over to the large mixing bowl, measuring cups, and pancake mix on the counter and glanced at the skillet on the stove, which was already turned on. I could feel the heat coming off it from where I was standing, and after dribbling water over my fingers at the sink, I flicked some drops at the skillet and watched them instantly sizzle and evaporate. *Damn. He must've come in and turned it on right after I got in the shower.*

Taking the hint, I started in on the batter at the same time my phone went off.

KASH:
I'm starving, do you want anything?

Funny. See you when you get back over here.

I looked over at the door and my brow wrinkled when I noticed it was still locked. *It's official. He* must *have a key.* Grabbing the bowl, I continued to whisk the batter as I walked over and unlocked the handle for him anyway and walked back into the kitchen. The door opened just as I was pouring some batter onto the skillet and I smirked.

"I don't know what's funny about— Ahh, woman. You're perfect."

Raising an eyebrow, I just nodded and kept pouring until the skillet was full of pancakes.

Kash walked into the kitchen and wrapped his arms around my waist before nuzzling my neck. "It's like you read my mind."

A short laugh left me. "Well, you left a strong enough hint this time." Grabbing the spatula that had been laid out with everything else, I turned and pointed it at him. "But don't think I'll let you get away with this again. You could have at least asked nicely."

His head jerked back. "Uh, what?"

"But like I said, it was funny. So I'll let it slide." I gave him a chaste kiss, and when I pulled away, he still looked confused rather than giving me the wry smile he normally wore when he got his way. "And your secret is out, but I won't make you give me back the key you somehow got."

"What key?"

I scoffed and turned back to the pancakes. If he wanted to play dumb, I'd let him. At least now I knew how he was getting in and out of here all the time.

"Oh my God, hide me!" Mason hissed as he shut the door quietly behind him and began turning off lights. "Oh, are you making pancakes? Do you have bacon too?"

My face fell even though he couldn't see me. "Well, I *was* making pancakes until you made it pitch-black in here. And even if I did, I wouldn't make any. I'm tired. Why aren't you guys making me food? And why did you turn off all the lights?"

"I'm hiding," Mason yell-whispered at the same time Kash turned the kitchen light back on and said, "He's hiding from one of the managers at his bar."

"Uh, and you have to hide from your boss . . . here?" I actually pouted. I wanted alone time with Kash.

Kash chuckled beside me and kissed my cheek before grabbing the spatula out of my hand and moving me aside. "Considering he probably just left her naked in our apartment, yeah, he needs to hide here."

"Mason Hendricks!"

"Shut it, Rach!" He jumped away from the window like his boss would come flying through it. "She's freakin' crazy."

"Well, what'd you do to her? Er . . . besides sleep with her?"

"Nothing, I did nothing! She's just clingy as shit. She started crying because I told her she couldn't move in with me."

I stopped pouring syrup on my pancakes and looked up at him. "How long have you been sleeping with her?"

"This is the first time." When I shot him a look, he threw his hands in the air. "Swear, Rach. First. Time. When we finished she asked when she could move her stuff in; I wasn't even out of her yet."

"Ew, Mase! I don't want details!"

"Whatever. I thought she was joking so I just laughed and took care of some stuff. When I came back she asked again, and I told her she couldn't. She instantly started crying and screaming at me, asking me what tonight meant then. And she's refusing to leave!"

I grabbed a fork and my plate and walked to the front door, patting Mason's chest with my free hand on the way there. "You picked a good one."

"Where are you going?" Kash asked from the kitchen.

I didn't look back at him. I just shrugged and opened the door. "Damage control."

I walked over to the boys' apartment and made myself comfortable on the couch. As soon as the TV was on, Mason's bedroom door opened and a gorgeous mess of a woman stepped out. Still. Naked.

Awkward.

Focusing on her mascara-streaked face, I gave her a head nod and looked back at the TV before taking a bite of pancakes.

"Who are you?" She poured as much venom into her words as was possible while still crying, and I shrugged again as I spoke around the pancakes.

"Mason's sister. You?"

Her head jerked back. "Mason's sister? What are you doing here?"

"I live here. What'd you say your name was again?"

"Uh, I didn't." She looked quickly at Kash's bedroom door, then back to Mason's. "You live here?"

"Yep. Good performance, by the way. Sounded pretty impressive." Her eyes got huge and it took everything in me not to laugh and begin choking on the pancakes I was shoveling in at an alarming rate. "You know, my fiancé lives next door. Maybe next time we can have a screaming match. Or see who lasts longer. It could be fun."

I had put my attention back on the TV so I wouldn't have to look at her, but when I could still see her out of the corner of my eye and she didn't make a sound, I finally turned to look at her again. She looked like she was in shock and disgusted. At least she'd stopped crying.

We stared at each other for a few seconds longer and I finally held my plate out toward her. "Pancakes?"

Sanity seemed to settle back over her face and she darted into Mason's room. My shoulders shook with silent laughter and I had to fan at my face, which I knew was bright red from holding it in. I was taking another deep breath to control myself when she ran out, now clothed.

"See you next time, Melanie!"

She stopped short of the front door and looked at me like I belonged in an asylum. "My name's— Never mind. Tell Mason I'll, uh, see him at work."

I was laughing so hard that I was still crying by the time I made it back to my apartment. Both guys were standing at the window, eating pancakes.

"What'd you do?" Mason asked in awe. "She *ran* to her car."

Another giggle burst from my chest as I washed my plate and put it in the dishwasher. "I have no idea. I thought she was so sweet. Guess I smell bad."

Kash smirked at me and studied my red face and wet eyes.

"Is she coming back?"

"No, Mase, she's probably not. Sorry, homie, I know you're really upset about that one. But now that you have a free apartment, I gotta ask you to leave me and Kash to mine."

He put his plate down on the counter and picked me up in a big bear hug. "Thanks, sweetheart."

"Oh, full stomach. I'm gonna throw up all over you."

Setting me down quickly, he kissed the top of my head and slapped Kash's back as he rushed out of the apartment. Kash walked over to me and helped me clean up our breakfast-for-dinner mess, and after a few minutes of silence, he finally turned and asked, "So what really happened over there?"

Kash

WE'D JUST FINISHED a two-hour-long meeting of going around and around and coming up with absolutely nothing on the Carnation Murders or James Camden and were now in a private meeting with Detective Ryder. Everyone was getting discouraged with this case. For a while, Camden had been slipping up more and more, and then with the doubled meal receipts we'd been sure something was about to happen soon. Then when classes had started again at the colleges around Austin this last week, we'd all been working around the clock trying to find anything on him and even brought in more officers, sure that he'd do something drastic. But he'd been completely invisible for weeks now.

But along with the discouragement . . . I knew there were a few of us who were more scared now that he was quiet.

"I think he either, one, knows we're onto him, or two, has found his next victim and is doing whatever he does before he takes her. I just think it's weird that throughout the last school year, he would pop up every now and then, and then over the summer, when school was out, he popped up like mad . . . and now school is back in session and he's a ghost." Ryder nodded and I continued. "Something about that just seems wrong. Like he was getting himself ready for this? I don't know."

"No, you're onto something. Why would he disappear right before school starts up when he lives in a college city?" Ryder rolled up some papers in his hand and hit his other palm with them furiously. "Nights you aren't working, I need you looking for him at other places with me. Got it?"

"Yes, sir." Mason and I confirmed it, shook hands with him, and left his office.

Mason waited until we were in my truck before asking, "Are you going to be able to swing that without Rachel noticing?"

"Yeah, she had to cut back on hours anyway because of classes and she'll have a lot of homework. I'll just say they need me more, more business with the students being back and all."

"Kash, I know you think you're still protecting her, but I really think it's time you told her everything."

"We're not going over this again, Mase. Have you told your family where we are?" He didn't answer, and I knew he hadn't. "Then I'm not telling Rachel anything until this is all over."

"You asked her to *marry* you. That's a big fucking deal. And you swore you would tell her soon!"

"And I will."

He snorted. "When, Kash? At the altar? Wait until she says *I do* and then say everything really quick before you do the same?"

"Screw you. You know I'd never do that to her."

"Well you shouldn't be doing this to her, it's not fair to her."

"I get that, Mase! I fucking get that! I'm sorry you don't agree or approve of my situation, but it's not like I sat there and decided to hurt her by moving our relationship to this next step by asking her. I literally couldn't think about anything but asking her to marry me. I should have waited, but I didn't. I couldn't. Okay?"

"No. It's not. You need to tell her."

I ran a hand over my face and kept it over my mouth as I shook my head. I wanted to. I just wanted to keep her safe more.

Rachel

WALKING INTO THE gym, I stopped short and took a step back when I saw Candice and Blake talking right around the corner. It never got easier seeing him. I'd seen him almost every day for the last two weeks, and though he hadn't once spoken to me, there were always the notes . . .

A shiver climbed its way up my spine and I clutched at my bag to help with the shaking that always came when I saw or thought about Blake. When I began receiving awkward looks for just standing there, I acted like I was checking my phone as I focused on what Candice and Blake were saying. My mouth popped open when Candice confirmed with Blake that he was going to come back with us for Thanksgiving.

"Yeah, there's no reason to waste money on a plane ticket if you're driving. So I'll just go with you and Rachel."

"Okay, I'll let my mom know you're coming with. I told her I didn't know if we were coming back or not, but Rachel and I really want to see them."

Uh, Candice might be going. But if Blake is going to be there, and traveling with us, then I sure as hell won't. I can wait until Christmas to see them.

"Let's just hope Rachel is done with this game she's playing by then."

My body stiffened and I heard Candice sigh.

"I know, this whole thing she's doing is . . ." Her voice trailed off as they walked away and I forgot that I was supposed to be appearing inconspicuous.

Phone temporarily forgotten, my eyes were wide as I leaned around the corner and watched as they made their way toward the back of the gym. What game? I wasn't playing anything!

"Rachel."

"What?" I practically shrieked, and whirled around, only to see Marcus, a guy from my class, standing there looking like he thought I was going to explode . . . again. "Jesus, Marcus, I'm sorry. You scared the crap out of me."

"Uh, yeah. I figured that. Are you going to go all the way in, or are you just going to keep standing here on the side?"

"No, I'm . . . I'm going. I just—yeah, I'm going."

He tried to hide his smile as he gestured for me to go ahead of him. I didn't want to be here, but seeing as I had to be here to pass this class, I didn't really have an option right now. I heard the tail end of Candice and Blake making plans to grab dinner that night and had to force out an awkward conversation with Marcus so I wouldn't start screaming at Candice right there. I knew that Blake was her family, but I'd never felt as betrayed by her as I had these last three months.

I didn't look at either of them as I passed by them, I just walked with Marcus until we hit the very back of the gym and then said my good-byes to him, silently thanking him for being a distraction from them.

"Hey, Rach."

I ground my teeth and forced a closed-lip smile as I turned to look at Candice.

"Just letting you know I won't need a ride home today, but I'll be home tonight."

"Oh? You don't have practice today . . . do you?"

"No, but some of the girls are going out for an early dinner."

Liar. " 'Kay. Have fun."

"Hey." She touched my arm and I turned to look at her again. "Are you okay?"

"I'm great."

She actually looked concerned, and I think that pissed me off more. Because I knew she loved me, and I loved her. She would always be like my sister. But Blake was ruining us. "You sure? Are you and Kash fighting?"

"Ha, uh, no. Not any more than we usually do anyway, not anything that's serious. I'm really fine, Candi." I met her stare and hoped she understood my next words for what they were. "I hope you have fun at dinner tonight."

Her eyes widened and she bit on her cheek as she nodded with exaggerated slowness and pursed her lips.

Yeah, I'm calling you out on your lies, Candice. Keep them coming; all you're doing is showing me how much I don't matter to you.

"Are you staying at our apartment tonight? Or will you be with Kash, or . . ."

"Or . . . ?"

"Will you be somewhere else?" she asked, challenging me.

"Where else would I be?"

She shrugged. "I don't know, why don't you tell me?"

"I'd be happy to if I had any idea what you were even getting at."

"Whatever, Rach. I give up," she huffed, and stormed off in the other direction.

How the hell had that gone from me catching her in a lie to her being pissed at me?

15

Kash

RACHEL GIGGLED AS I made my way down her neck. "I'm gonna be late to class if you keep that up."

"Don't care." I nuzzled her throat and bit softly at the smooth skin. "Give me a little bit, I'll be ready for round two."

"You're going to be late for inventory at the restaurant. And I don't think I can go again, babe."

"Wimp."

"Ha! Uh, well, seeing as I woke up to one, and then you forced another one out of me right after . . . then as soon as we were done with breakfast you brought me back in here and I just had another two orgasms? No, I'm not a wimp, I'm just worn out, mister."

I smiled wolfishly up at her and kissed her lips softly, loving how swollen they were from kissing. "Good. When we're married, I'm gonna make you stay home so I can have my way with you whenever I want."

She laughed loudly. "Really now? You're going to *make* me stay home?"

I grunted some form of affirmation and said teasingly, "Gonna turn you into a fifties wife. Make you wear dresses, stay home, clean and cook for me. All day, nothing but pancakes."

"You're ridiculous. And I refuse."

"To marry me?" I raised an eyebrow at her.

"To be your fifties wife. But I can't wait to marry you." Her eyes unfocused as she continued to run her hands through my hair.

"Rach? Hey." When her blue eyes came back to me I rolled to the side and pulled her with me. "Where'd you just go?"

"Can we elope, Kash?"

That was definitely not what I was expecting when she'd just spaced out on me. "Why? Don't you want the big wedding and the dress? Don't you want the Jenkinses and your friends there?"

"No, I just want to marry you. Please? We can get married this weekend. Candice still won't talk to me about it. I just feel like no one really wants us together except for us, and there's no point in waiting."

"That's not true. My parents want us together."

She blinked her blue eyes quickly. "Wait . . . What? They do? You and Mason never talk about your families . . . like, ever. Mason told me I reminded him of his little sister and that is literally the only thing I've heard about either of your families since the weekend you moved here. And I know Mase loves me . . . but whenever we talk about getting married around him, he always looks mad. Have you noticed that?"

Yes. "He's not mad, I promise. And my parents do want us together, and they want to meet you. So we can't get married until that happens, sweetheart." My parents had no idea I was engaged. They just knew that I was seeing someone, because I'd accidentally let Rachel's name slip once in one of our very few conversations. I hated hiding her from them, but just as I had to hide them from her, she had to stay hidden from them until this James Camden case was over. And even though I would do anything to marry the girl in my arms as soon as possible, there was no way I could do that to her until she knew that I wasn't really Logan Hendricks. She needed to find out about Logan Ryan and his real life before I ever made her vow to spend forever with me.

"When—"

"Rachel," Candice said as she burst into the room, "can I use— Oh! Oh my God, that's Kash's ass. Um . . . I'm leaving . . . oh, wow." She shut the door quickly behind her and yelled from the other side. "And get ready, we're going to be late!"

Thank God for Candice's perfect timing.

Rachel turned a bright shade of red before bursting out laughing and crawling off the bed. "Come on, you need to go so we can both get ready."

I pulled on my clothes and kissed her thoroughly, hoping she knew how much I loved her and how keeping myself a secret was worse than any deception I'd ever been a part of, and that it was eating me alive. "I love you, Rach."

"Mmm, I love you too, Logan."

Rachel

ALL I WANTED was a long, hot bath. The two classes I had that day had been easy and flown by. That wasn't what was bothering me. It was the creepy glares that Blake had shot my way every time I saw him during the first class, and the note tucked into my windshield wiper *again*. There were never any on the days that Candice and I drove home together. But if she had cheer practice, it never failed. Every one of those days these first three weeks of school there had been a note. Three words. Never signed. Always typed. And always crumpled up and left in the parking lot after I got it.

                you. are. mine.

I cringed thinking about them and wished there was something I could do. But honestly, what could I say? That I *knew* they were from Blake? I couldn't prove it, and I knew Kash would most likely believe me, but he'd go crazy and I didn't need that right now.

As soon as I opened the door to my apartment, I knew something was off. It was the *what* that I wasn't sure of yet. I took a hesitant step inside the apartment but left the door open in case I needed to scream for one of the guys. Another step and my chest started burning from the breath I was holding. I let it out quietly and did a double take at the door to my room just as the noise from the kitchen filtered into my brain.

What the hell?

My body rocked back and forth as I debated which way to go

first. "Kash? Mase?" Other than the sound of the dishwasher going, silence greeted me. "Guys, this isn't funny . . ." I took quick and quiet steps to my open bedroom door and looked down.

Sitting in the middle of the door frame, all lined up next to each other, were my journal, a black lacy bra with purple ribbon going through it, a pair of dark purple lacy underwear laid out like it was on display at a store, and my laptop. I'd just bought the lingerie a few days ago and the tags were still on it; I hadn't even told Kash about it yet. The laptop was opened and had iTunes up. Nothing was playing, but "I'll Be" was highlighted.

This is so not funny. Only Kash knew where I kept my journal, and he knew it wasn't just private. It was incredibly personal and the only thing I had here that connected me to my parents. To take it out and leave it here with these things was disturbing, and if Kash had read it . . . a breath caught in my throat. That was an invasion of privacy to the extreme. Tears pricked the back of my eyes and my throat began burning as I tried to hold off on the tears. Grabbing at everything, I hastily returned it all to where it belonged and took deep breaths in an attempt to calm down. *This is going too far. Why would he do this to me?*

After looking around quickly and making sure nothing else was out of place, I made my way to Candice's room and searched around in there. Nothing seemed different about her room, but I couldn't be positive. Shutting her door behind me, I went to the front door, shut and locked it, then made my way into the kitchen.

The dishwasher was running and almost done with its cycle. I thought back to this morning. I could have sworn I'd emptied the dishwasher, because I needed clean plates and coffee mugs when

the boys came over. There was a possibility I hadn't fully emptied it since I was still in zombie-Rachel mode . . . but Candice
had left for classes with me and was still at practice, and I'd been
gone for four hours. Even if I had started the dishwasher before
I left, it would have been done by now. And I didn't even understand fully how to do the delay on it. *Oh my God, I'm going insane.*

Jumping up on the counter, I stared at the dishwasher until it
was done, it had gone through the heated dry cycle, and the door
unlocked. With one more deep breath and chanting to myself
that I was just losing it and had actually started the dishwasher
before I left, I opened the heavy door and blinked rapidly after
the steam gave me a facial.

It was empty.

What in the actual hell?!

I shut the dishwasher door roughly, opened it once more to
confirm that it *was* indeed empty, and shut it again. My phone
chimed and after staring at it like it might explode, I grabbed it
to check the text.

> KASH:
> *Hey babe, just got done doing inventory. You home yet?*
> *Gonna pick up dinner.*

I didn't respond. He'd left to do inventory at the same time we
left for campus. Why was he lying about this? He was the *only*
one who knew where I kept my journal. Granted, Candice knew
I had one and knew about the song as well . . . and she had given
me the approval on my new lingerie. But she'd been in classes all
day and was in practice now. She wasn't supposed to be home for
another hour. My head shook back and forth as I looked around

my apartment, which now looked exactly as I'd left it that morning, and I went to sit on the couch. *I just—I don't understand. Am I going crazy? Am I doing all this to myself and just not realizing it?*

Ten minutes later, Kash called, but I let it go to voice mail. Same with the next call from him a few minutes after that. I pulled my legs up onto the couch and rested my chin on my knees as I played the morning in my head over and over again. And that's how Kash and Mason found me some time later.

They didn't knock, but then again, they never did. They walked right in and both heaved sighs of relief. And I *knew* I'd locked that door earlier.

"Did you not get my messages?" Kash asked, and planted himself directly in front of me, legs spread, arms crossed over his chest.

"I didn't listen to them."

"Are you okay? What's—"

"Where have you been?" I demanded, and looked directly into his gray eyes.

His head jerked back. "Taking inventory at the restaurant. Exactly where I said I was going."

"Where have you actually been?" Turning my head to look at Mason, my eyes narrowed. "And where were you?!"

They exchanged a look that I didn't understand, but it made my heart beat faster, and not in a good way. They were lying to me. I knew it.

"I went to help Kash since he helped me with inventory at my bar the other day."

I shot up off the couch and leveled my glare at both of them. "Don't lie to me! What you guys did isn't funny!"

"Wait. What? What did we do?" Kash's eyes were massive and he looked . . . *nervous*?

"You're really going to act like all the shit around here wasn't done by either one of you?"

Now neither looked nervous. Just incredibly confused. "Babe. What the hell are you talking about?"

"The dishwasher and the—" I cut off quickly and pointed at the floor of my doorway. "The stuff there! Why would you do something like that to me? That's cruel." My voice shook and I tried to swallow past the lump in my throat. "Did you really think I would find all that shit funny? You're such an asshole, Kash!"

Kash looked over at the bare carpet before looking back to me. "Woman. You're starting to piss me off, always accusing me of doing something. We've been gone since you left this morning."

"It had to have been you," I whispered, my anger quickly fading. I looked at Mason. He looked lost. "It was one of you . . . right?"

"*What* was?"

I jerked away from the tone of Kash's voice. I'd never seen him mad at me like this. "It wasn't you?" My body collapsed onto the couch and I grabbed my head in my hands. *Oh my God, this is what going insane feels like!* "I'm going crazy."

Kash came to kneel in front of me and grabbed my chin in one hand to make me look up at him. His anger was gone and he looked just as lost as Mason. "Baby, what are you talking about? Tell me what was wrong in here."

I told him about the lingerie, journal, and laptop, how they were laid out, and I whispered to him about the song that had been clicked on. His expression grew darker with each new item, and when I told him about the dishwasher, he made Mason go look in it. "So . . . so the pancakes weren't you either?"

The boys stopped talking and looked at me again. "There were pancakes too?"

"No. Remember the night I was making pancakes for you when you came over? The night Mason came to hide from his boss." When Kash nodded, I continued. "When I got out of the shower that night, the skillet was out and turned on. There were bowls, measuring cups, the whisk, and pancake mix. I thought you were trying to hint that you wanted me to make them for you." Both of their eyebrows shot straight up. Oh my God, it really hadn't been them. What the hell was happening?!

"Shit," Kash mumbled, and his head fell back. He just looked at the ceiling for a few moments before whispering something to Mason. Mason walked quickly out of the apartment, his phone going to his ear. "Rach, I need to tell you something. But I don't want you upset with me. You need to know that Mason and I did this to protect you, all right?"

My stomach dropped and I could swear my heart skipped a few beats.

"Do you trust me?"

Of course I trust him . . . or I did, up until tonight. And after that intro to the conversation, I'm really starting to rethink all that. And why did Mason leave? I think I need him here with me. Where is Candice? Shouldn't she be home soon? Why the hell was the dishwasher on . . . Oh my God! Kash is going to tell me that I'm insane and he's going to send me away. I'm the crazy girl who turns on dishwashers with nothing in them and lays out lingerie!

"Do. You. Trust me?"

"I'm not crazy!" I snapped, and then my hands flew over my mouth. *That's exactly what crazy people say!* "Why is it so hot in here?"

"Rachel . . . Rach. Come on, babe, just breathe, you're going to make yourself pass out." Kash was suddenly on the couch with me, pulling me to the side and into him so my back was against his chest. He took deep breaths in and out and kept one hand on my chest, forcing me to breathe in sync with him. "Better?" he asked softly in my ear after a couple minutes of our breathing together.

My body slumped into his and I shut my eyes. "Yeah."

"You're not crazy, sweetheart. I need you to listen to me though, all right?"

I nodded. "And I do trust you."

With a kiss to my temple, he moved me out from between his legs and situated me so we were facing each other. "Now, let me say all of this before you respond, and try to keep an open mind." He cracked his neck and thought for too long before he began. "I didn't take you on the trip to The Vineyard for the sole purpose of us being alone. The trip was amazing. I loved every second with you. But I took you to get you away from here. A couple days before we left, Mason and I separately ran into a guy who was looking in your windows. When he was confronted, he said he was your dad."

I gasped and jerked back. *That's not possible.* My mouth opened but Kash spoke before I could get anything out.

"We both knew he wasn't. We didn't even have to know about your parents' being gone to know he wasn't. He was stumbling over his own words, and when I was talking to him he got a phone call. He said it was you, and whomever he was talking to let him go on acting like it was you. Said you were out eating breakfast with Candice and he was going to meet you. While all of this was going on, you were asleep in my bed and Candice was at camp.

"Mason and I kept a watch for the next couple days; that's why we tried to get you and Candice to go out so much. He kept coming back; he'd just sit in the parking lot in a dark green Explorer for hours on end, and every once in a while he'd come back and try to get in your apartment or just look in the windows. He got a few more calls while in the breezeway that we were able to listen to. And in the one I heard the morning that we left, he was calling the person he spoke to West."

My heart was pounding. I didn't understand what was happening now any more than I had earlier. "West, as in Blake?"

"We think so."

"Oh my God." Hyperventilating back full force.

Kash's face grew tense. "He also said that the package had come in and he'd be putting it on your car as soon as you came back . . . and then 'West' could track you."

"There's a tracking device on my car?!"

"Baby, no. He put one on but you and I were already gone. Mason took it off and destroyed it."

"Oh my God," I repeated, and dropped my head into my hands. "Why is he doing this?"

"That's not all." A whimper left my throat and I pulled my legs back up onto the couch to curl into a ball. "I knew I needed to get you out of here so I already had my stuff packed and was waiting for him to leave—he would randomly leave for anywhere from twenty minutes to an hour—and I heard another call. All I heard was him talking about you being at the mall, like he was confirming that's what someone said, and then he said he was on his way there. You and Candice came back fifteen minutes later. That's why I didn't give you time to pack or get ready, and Mason texted me saying he came back not even ten minutes after we left."

"How did they know we were at the mall?!"

Kash grimaced. "Is Candice in contact with Blake a lot?"

My head snapped back. "What? Why would you ask that?"

"Someone had to tell Blake that the two of you were at the mall. Was Candice texting or calling anyone that day? Does she tell you if she talks to him?"

"She knows I don't want to talk about him; she was so mad when I told her about what he did. That was the first time she'd ever gotten mad at me like that. So we don't talk about him or that day at all. I mean—she and Eli went to go see him that night Eli was in town, but that was . . . that was Eli who brought it up. Not her. But Candice is always texting someone—like, it's weird if she's *not* on her phone—so I can't say who she ever is or isn't talking to. But I do know she talks to him a lot at our classes and hangs out with him."

He nodded his head and sighed heavily as he held my stare. "I don't want to say this about her, but I think she's unknowingly giving Blake information about you."

I was going to throw up. Or pass out. Okay, maybe both. Trying to take deep breaths, I clasped my hands together and the shaking in my body seemed to only get worse. "She didn't believe me, but she wouldn't hurt me." *But she still may have told Blake where you work . . .*

"I'm not saying that. I said 'unknowingly.' *If* she's telling him anything, she doesn't realize she is, because he's probably asking in a way where she wouldn't realize it. I can't be sure though, we'd need her phone."

"Why is he doing this—why can't he just leave me alone? Wait. Why are you telling me all this now? Do you think that guy was in here?" All the blood drained from my face. "Oh God. Was it Blake? Was Blake in here?"

"I don't know, Rach. But who else knows about the journal and song other than me?"

"Um, C-Candice's entire family knows about the journal, but only Candice knows about the song."

"And who knows about pancakes besides us?" he asked softly, and reached for me.

"Oh God," I cried, and my vision instantly blurred as I let him pull me back into his lap.

"Shh. It's okay, sweetheart. I'm going to keep you safe. I swear." His lips brushed my forehead and he held me tighter to him. "If Candice hasn't told him about those things, then either Blake or the other guy is watching us a lot closer than we thought. Do you know a Marvin Cross?"

I tried to think, but my head was spinning with all this new information. "Um, I don't—I don't think so. It doesn't sound familiar. Why?"

"That's the guy's name. If you ever see a dark green Explorer, I want you to call me."

"How do you know his name?"

There was a short pause before his answer. "We called the police and had them run the license plate on the car."

I didn't think they would just give that information out. But I was so shaken up, I was sure I was just second-guessing everything right now. I shuddered when I thought about all the times

I'd been near Blake recently. The possessive gleam in his eyes . . . his smile, like he had a secret . . . his vows to remind me whom I belonged to. I thought I'd been terrified of him before, but after all this new information, I knew I'd had no idea what he was capable of and fear ran through my veins like ice. "I can't keep going to school. He's always there, I can't—I don't want to be near him. And what if he knows where our apartment is? What if Candice told him? I can't stay here, we need to leave! Oh, God—"

Kash grabbed my cheeks and kissed me soft and slow until my body sagged with exhaustion from everything I'd just learned. "I'll keep you safe, Rachel. If you want to get away from here again, I'll make it happen. Say the word and we're gone, I swear."

I sighed heavily and whispered against his lips, "Thank you."

16

Rachel

"WHY ARE YOU leaving so early?" Candice unwrapped her hair from the towel and vigorously rubbed at it before tossing the towel back into her room. "Or are you going to meet up with your man before class?"

I'd stayed with Kash last night and had only come back to change. "No, I'm, uh— Candice . . . I decided I'm going to withdraw from my courses."

She froze midstep; her gaze was one of complete shock. "What?! Why?"

I'd been worrying over whether or not I should tell her all night. I hadn't slept at all because I was so stressed about what was happening and over the fact that my best friend wouldn't believe me, and I still didn't know if telling her was the right decision. "Blake has been—"

"Oh my God, Rachel. Again? Seriously?"

"Candice, he's been breaking into our apartment!"

She rolled her green eyes and shook her head at me. "I swear to God, it's like I don't know you these last few months! First you accuse my cousin of rape, then you meet and get engaged to a guy that you *just* met, and now you're saying my cousin is breaking into our apartment when he doesn't even know where we live? Classy, Rach. You've turned into a real bitch."

I bent forward and exhaled roughly, as if she'd actually punched me. "Candice."

"And you know what pisses me off *more*? The fact that throughout all of this, all of this lying to me, all of this acting like you're so in love with Kash and like you're some fucking victim . . . you're *still* dating Blake!"

"Whoa, what?! I—*no*! Where did you hear that?"

"He hates that you treat him like crap at school and that you're hiding your relationship with him. He showed me all of your texts to him."

I shook my head furiously and attempted to swallow past the dryness in my throat. "I haven't texted him since our dates at the end of last school year, Candice, I swear to you."

"I'm so done with this, Rachel. I've been waiting for you to just come clean to me, but for whatever reason, our friendship doesn't mean anything to you anymore. But if you're actually going to go through with this marriage to Kash, at least be respectful to my cousin and break it off with him. Nicely."

"Our friendship doesn't mean anything to me?! You're the one who won't believe me and you're the only family I have left!"

She snorted and whirled around with her hand on the door. "And another thing. I'd *love* to know how you've been going be-

tween school, work, Kash, and Blake without Kash or me noticing. Share your secrets sometime, it could really come in handy
for me, seeing as *I'm* the slut and all."

The door to her bedroom slammed shut and I stood there unmoving, just staring as I tried to comprehend what the hell had
just happened. *How* had this happened? How had he not only
hurt me but hurt my relationship with Candice as well? I hated
Blake West with every fiber of my being, and I hated what he'd
done to my life.

When I could finally make myself move again, I turned and
jolted when I saw Kash and Mason standing at the door.

Kash moved toward me and pulled me into his arms. "I'm
sorry, Rach."

"How long were you standing there?"

"We just opened the door, but we could hear her from the
breezeway."

I nodded against his chest and my body shook on a sigh. "I
swear I'm not seeing Bla—"

"Don't. I know you're not, babe."

"Kash," Mason called from the door. "We *need* to go."

He released his hold on me and shot Mason a look before grabbing the back of my neck and kissing my forehead. "Wait for me
to get back from doing inventory with Mase, I'll go with you to
drop your classes."

I needed to get these classes dropped before things got too
busy on campus, and there was no way I was waiting until next
week to do it. "I'm fine, I'll just go get it done and come back here
to wait for you."

"You sure?"

"Yeah."

After another hard kiss he let me go. "We'll be back soon."

I forced myself to my car and over to campus. The woman in administration eyed me curiously before giving me a look that clearly said I'd just made her Friday morning awful. It took all of five minutes, and I wanted to let her know she should try smiling instead . . . but I couldn't even force a smile on my face at the moment. So, I just thanked her, left her presence as quickly as possible, and headed toward my car.

I was less than a row away when he grabbed my arm and dug his fingers right into a pressure point. "I would love to know why my cousin is beginning to question me."

"Let go of me or I'll scream."

"Scream and I'll kill someone you love."

I turned to finally look up at Blake's cold blue eyes. "W-what did you say?"

"Exactly what you thought you heard. Now, let's go."

I dug my feet into the ground and tried to walk toward my car. "No! Let me go."

"For shit's sake, Rachel," he growled, and leaned close so it looked like we were hugging, "don't be difficult or I'll make good on my promise." From the tone of his voice, I had no doubt he would.

"Please, just let me go home, how did you even know I was here?"

Blake blew out an annoyed breath and dug his fingers into the pressure point harder before walking us toward his car. "Candice called me this morning screaming at me. Demanding to know what I did that would make you go drop all of your classes today. I was already on campus, so I've just been waiting for you."

Wait. Does that mean she believed me? Hope and an ache for the friendship Candice and I had always had blossomed in my chest but was quickly replaced by fear when Blake put me in his car and lifted his shirt just enough to show me the gun holstered to his hip.

"Run, Rachel. I dare you."

MY CHEST TIGHTENED and I choked on a sob. "No." My horrified whisper was barely audible as I looked at the screen in my hands. "No, God. Please, no!"

"Now, Rachel . . . are you going to be difficult again?"

I cried out and gripped the iPad tighter, letting my fingers trail over the video feed. Shaking my head quickly, my legs gave out and I landed on the hardwood floor of Blake's studio apartment with a dull thud. "What—what do you want from me?"

"You, Rachel. Just you."

"You're sick, Blake."

Grabbing a good amount of my hair in his hands, he yanked back and a cry of pain left my chest as I fell from a sitting position to my back. "I'm going to pretend like you didn't say that. You're mine, and someday soon you'll understand that." He took the iPad from my shaky hands and zoomed in on the house of the people I loved. "If not, I can promise you they won't be the only people you lose. Just think, sweetheart, if it was this easy to get close to them, how easy do you think it'll be to get to Candice, or your precious boyfriend?"

"You can't do this to them! They're your family, how could you—how would you be able to live with yourself? What did I do to deserve *any* of this? You raped me and harassed me! *Why?!* All because I didn't want to be with you?"

How a guy like Blake West could turn into a monster of this

magnitude just floored me. He gripped my jaw hard and crushed his mouth to mine. I'd kissed him before, and I hadn't felt anything. But after this, I felt like I needed to scrub everywhere he'd touched me and brush my teeth until I no longer could taste him.

"You. Are. Mine." With that he released his grip and my head smacked against the floor. He straightened and pulled his phone out of his pocket. In seconds the person answered the phone. "Can you please show my guest that I'm not fucking around with this?" It sounded like more of a demand than a question, and as soon as his phone was back in his pocket, he was on the ground with me, pulling me up so I was sitting in between his legs, my back against his chest. Both his legs wrapped around mine, pinning them to the ground, and he maneuvered his arms so I couldn't move mine, all while he held the iPad up in front of us.

I wanted to squeeze my eyes shut, but I couldn't stop looking. It was like watching a train wreck, although nothing was happening on the screen. It was still just the video feed of the Jenkinses' house. Same as it had been for the last few minutes since he'd pulled it out. My breathing escalated as I continued to stare. Seconds felt like hours as I waited for something to happen. All of a sudden the silver Audi's alarm started going off in the driveway and I shook my head, trying to figure out what this proved. "No!" I screamed as Candice's dad walked outside, looking at his car, then around the street for whatever had made the alarm start. "George, no! Please go back inside. He's your uncle, Blake!" I stared in horror as he made his way down the long walkway. Halfway to the driveway his car exploded and I screamed again, thrashing against Blake as I watched George fly backward a few feet before landing on the grass. *"George!"*

"He'll be fine, sweetheart." Blake set down the iPad to better contain me and his lips were at my ear. "I want you to be a good girl and do exactly as I tell you. Or next time, he won't be walking away."

"Anything!" I promised, and craned my neck to look down at the screen to see George rolling over and getting up on his hands and knees as he looked toward the burning mass in his driveway. "Anything, I swear! Just please don't hurt him!"

"Smart girl."

"What do you need me to do?"

Once again his lips were on my neck before brushing against the lobe of my ear. "Be mine."

I HAD TO take deep, calming breaths before I could even open the door of my car. It felt like there was a weight on my chest, threatening to crush down, breaking my heart even more than it already was.

I'd called Kash, asking him to meet me outside of a coffee shop. I needed to do this in public, not just because I knew Blake was watching, but because if I went back to one of our apartments, I didn't think I'd be able to handle not being able to fall into his arms and tell him everything. I knew he would help if I told him what was going on, but I needed to keep Candice and her parents safe and alive. Just the same as I had to do for Kash.

He stood from where he'd been sitting at one of the outdoor tables and his wide smile had the weight on my chest pressing down. I couldn't do this, I couldn't crush him this way. Tears pricked the back of my eyes and I blinked quickly, trying to hold them off. Turning my head so I wouldn't see his face, I saw where Blake was parked, watching. Just as he said he would.

"Hey, did you get all your classes dropped?" Kash started to pull me into his arms, but I put my hands against his chest and pushed back. "Rach, what's wrong?"

"We, uh—we n-need to . . . we need to talk, Logan."

His head jerked back, and while he let me push him back, he kept his hands on my upper arms. His brow wrinkled as his eyes searched my face.

"Um . . ."

"Rachel, what is going on? Talk to me. Did something happen with Candice? With Blake?"

I inhaled sharply but shook my head and tried to put more distance between us; his hands kept me where I was. "No. Nothing about them." It had *everything* to do with them. "Look, Logan—"

"Why the fuck are you calling me Logan right now?"

"I'm sorry, so sorry to be doing this to you . . ." A short sob rose from my throat and I tried to hold it together as I removed my hands from his chest and grabbed my engagement ring, tugging it slowly off my finger.

Kash's eyes went wide and his face fell. "Rachel," he whispered, and the tears that had been threatening their release finally spilled down my cheeks at the heartbreak in that one word.

". . . but I can't marry you."

"What?"

"I don't love you, Logan."

He took a stumbling step away from me and another sob tore through me as I held the ring up to him. "You're—you're lying." His eyes turned glassy and I had to look down at my feet. "Why are you doing this?"

"Please, Logan, don't make this harder than it has to be. Just take the ring back. I don't want it, I don't want you." I cried the last words and took a step toward him, pushing the ring against his chest.

His hand came up to wrap around mine, but I dropped the ring into his palm and jerked my hand away. "Babe, you—I don't—just yesterday you begged me to go elope! If this is because I said no, babe, we'll do it. Whatever you want, we'll do it. If you don't want the wedding with your friends and Candice's family, I'll marry you today. But I don't understand! We were fine when I left with Mase a couple hours ago, and now you want to call off our engagement?"

My vision started blurring and it had nothing to do with the tears that wouldn't stop. I thought about George's car exploding right before my eyes. I thought about Blake's threats to kill his aunt and uncle *first*. I worked at breathing in through my nose and out through my mouth as I turned and began walking away.

"Rachel!" He grabbed my hand and I whirled on him, my voice rising in my near-hysteria.

"I don't want you, Logan! I've *never* wanted you! Can't you understand that? You were fun. That's it. You were dangerous, and new, and it was what I needed at the time. But all you're good for is a good time. I'm sorry I got caught up in the whole marriage thing, but at least I'm doing this before we go through with it!"

He recoiled like I'd slapped him and dropped my hand. A single tear fell down his cheek and he shook his head slowly back and forth as he continued to retreat from me.

Everything in me screamed to run into his arms, to take back all I'd said. But I needed to keep the only family I had left safe.

And though he might never understand it, I needed to keep Kash safe too. Forcing myself away, I put my head down and walked quickly to my car. As soon as I was in, the roar of his motorcycle starting up and speeding out of the parking lot had the weight finally crashing in on me and I slumped against the steering wheel as sobs overtook my body.

I was still sitting in the parking lot an hour later. My sobs had run their course, and all that was left was a steady stream of tears. I felt hollow. It didn't matter that *I* had just broken *his* heart or that I'd done it for him. I would never again get to enjoy being in his arms, feeling his lips on mine, or waking up with his tattooed arm curled tight around my waist. Knowing I'd just lost the most important person in my life had shattered me, and I didn't know how to begin to cope with that.

My phone chimed and I frantically looked through my purse, praying it was Kash.

> BLAKE:
> You're done being upset about this, sweetheart. Now, go back to your apartment and pack a bag before Candice gets back. You're staying with me this weekend.
>
> I hate you.
>
> BLAKE:
> We'll work on that.
>
> BLAKE:
> Drive. Now.

Dropping my phone in one of my cup holders, I slowly went through the process of putting on my seat belt, cranking the engine, and backing out of my parking space. My tears never stopped, and a few times I had trouble seeing the road, but ten minutes later I was pulling into the complex. My breath caught when I saw Kash's motorcycle and truck there. He was home. Would he try to talk to me? Hope blossomed in my chest and I prayed that he would, that he would demand to know what had changed in me all of a sudden.

I'd barely pulled into my spot when my phone was chiming again.

> BLAKE:
> My guy is trailing Candice's parents right now. Don't even think about it.

What the hell? How can he even possibly know what I'm thinking? Blake had followed me as far as the street I lived off of, and then turned around. I quickly looked around until my eyes fell on a green Explorer. *So this is the man that has been watching me?* Wiping hastily at my cheeks, I took three deep breaths and got out of my car, giving Blake's creepy guy my best glare before heading to my apartment.

While I knew I needed to keep Kash away, it still hurt that he didn't once come by while I was in there packing. I knew he knew I was there. The fact that Mason was standing at their window shooting daggers at me when I let myself into our unit left no doubt that Kash knew.

Just as I was pulling my duffel bag into the living room, a knock came from the door and I shot toward it. Opening it wide, a small sound of surprise escaped my mouth and I instinctively began to shut the door when I saw Blake was standing there. His hand held the door open and his eyes narrowed as he felt the pressure.

"If you make this look like anything other than me taking my girl for a weekend with me, you won't like the consequences."

I immediately stopped pushing and stood aside as he walked in. My shoulders hunched and as soon as the door was shut, I shakily asked, "Are they still okay? Candice's parents, they're still okay . . . right?" I wanted to ask about Eli, but he hadn't mentioned him today, and I was afraid if I brought him up, it would give Blake a reason to have someone follow him.

"For now. Write a note to Candice saying you'll be back Monday. And for God's sake, Rachel, hurry the fuck up. You wasted enough time, she's already on her way back here."

My hand froze from searching for paper and a pen in one of the kitchen drawers, and I slowly looked up at him. "H-how do you know that?"

Blake smirked. "You really thought I only had someone trailing her parents and you, sweetheart? That's cute." He huffed, "Hurry."

"How do you even have these people, Blake? These guys working for you, ready to—ready to . . . You're a monster, do you realize that? You're doing *all* of this for me, but you'll never have me! Why don't you get that?!"

He stalked toward me and pulled me away from the counter, shoving me roughly against the refrigerator. With one hand clasping both of mine in front of me and the other arm pressed hard against my chest, he looked straight into my eyes for tense, silent moments before letting go and finding a pen and paper himself. Laying them on the counter in front of him, he leaned casually against it and read every word I wrote to Candice.

When he was satisfied, he grabbed one of my hands and led me toward my bag, which I'd dropped in the living room on my way to answer the door. After he picked it up and pulled the strap over his shoulder, he yanked me toward him, his lips going to my neck, then my ear.

"It's a safe bet we'll have an audience, since the cousin saw me walk in here. When we leave, you *will* have your arm around me and you *will* lean into me. You won't look scared or upset, and if anyone approaches you, you won't say anything. Understand, Rachel?"

I sighed in defeat, and my head shook once before he grabbed my chin roughly. It was already sore from the numerous times he'd done it that morning, and I knew I would have bruises there soon.

"Unless you want another show like you got this morning"—he paused and smiled when I inhaled audibly—"you will tell me you understand and you will make this look believable." Blake kissed me deceptively softly and murmured against my lips, "Go on, sweetheart; say it again. I know you're thinking it. I'm a monster." He kissed me again once, then brushed his lips across mine, his grip on my chin never loosening. "But like I said, we'll work on your feelings. Now, do as I said."

I nodded and blinked back tears. I was shaking so hard, I didn't know how I was still standing. But figuring Blake would be upset, or just carry me out of there if I fell to the ground like my legs were threatening to make me do, I took another deep breath in and resolved to do this for the Jenkinses and Kash.

We walked outside, and Blake kept one hand on my hip as

I turned to lock the door. When I faced forward, he pulled me close to his side with his arm now hanging over my shoulders, and it was then I heard the door across from ours open. Kash stepped out, his eyes glassy and red, his jaw tight as he mashed his lips together. My heart ached something fierce, but I forced my arm around Blake's waist and let my weight fall into his side.

Just as Blake started walking us toward the parking lot, I heard Kash's strained voice. "What the fuck did you do to her? She hates you, she's *terrified* of you! What did you do to her?"

Blake didn't stop walking me, and in an effort to not turn and look back at the man I loved, I dropped my gaze down and a shaky sigh left me.

"Rachel, what does he have on you? I know you, you wouldn't just choose this."

"If he doesn't shut up soon, I'll make sure he *is* shut up," Blake whispered, and continued to walk.

"I will find out," Kash said in a low growl. "And if you hurt her, so help me God, Blake West, I will end. Your. Life."

"Rachel," Blake said, warning me.

I turned, and though it killed me, I looked up at Kash's murderous expression. "Lo—" Clearing my throat, I tried again. "Logan, don't you see? I lied to you."

"Babe—"

"I'm sorry this isn't what you want—"

"Not what I want? Rachel, he's been stalking you!"

I shook my head and Blake's grip on my shoulder got painful. "He wasn't," I whispered, "I've been seeing Blake for months, Logan. I never *stopped* seeing him." He opened his mouth again and I shook my head quickly. "Just stop. Kash, *please* understand . . . *please*," I begged. I needed to cut this relationship now. Give him a clean break. But part of me couldn't stand to see him hurt. Couldn't stand knowing he thought I'd really left him for Blake.

My eyes pleaded with him to understand what was happening, and when his head shook at my last sentence, Blake's grip tightened even more and he swung us back around toward the cars.

"You're done talking," Blake said, and led me to my car. "Just in case you feel like doing anything else that would piss me off . . ." He grabbed my purse and duffel bag and put them in his own car. I knew letting me drive myself was a test, so I forced myself not to consider driving to a police station instead. Acting on that fantasy would only hurt everyone. Not allowing myself to look at Kash one last time, I put my car in reverse and followed Blake back to his place.

17

Kash

I FELT NUMB.

Looking down at the solitaire that just that morning I had caught Rachel admiring when she thought I was still asleep, my heart broke even more. It didn't make sense. Something wasn't adding up.

"Kash, you're just going to let her go?" Mason asked incredulously when he found me sitting on the floor, my back up against the front door. "I'll admit, when you first came back I thought maybe she'd found out you'd been lying. But this? You can't just let this happen."

"She left me for him. I don't know what you expect me to do. She called off the engagement. I—I don't—I don't fucking understand." I rubbed at my aching chest and let my head fall back 'til it hit the door.

"Rachel *hates* that guy. He raped her!"

I shook my head. "It was all a lie. She's been lying this whole time. You heard Candice this morning."

"You and I both know what Candice said was bullshit. You've seen Rachel break down! You saw what he did to her emotionally and what his coming around did to her. Something's not right."

I agreed on the last part . . . but that was just because I wanted my girl back. I wanted to believe this was all some sick joke. Or a nightmare. I wanted to wake up to Rachel in my arms again, smiling softly as she studied the way the light caught on the diamond on her finger. My vision blurred again and I shut my eyes, letting the tears fall down my face. I didn't care that Mason could see them; I didn't care about anything anymore. My reason for living didn't want me.

"Kash, you can't—"

"It's over, Mase. It's over." I stood from my spot on the floor and took a few steps toward my room before stopping. Looking down at the ring pinched between my fingers, I felt my heart being ripped out of my chest again. I held my hand out to Mason and had to clear my throat a few times before I could speak. "Do something with this. I don't want it . . . I can't keep it."

"Kash—"

"Take the goddamn ring!"

As soon as it was out of my hand, I stormed into my room and shut the door. I could still smell Rachel in there, and that killed me even more. After stripping the bed, I opened up the windows to air out the room and fell onto the bare mattress. Scenes from that morning flashed through my mind and I groaned as I prayed for sleep to escape this new hell I was in.

I WAS WOKEN up by my cell phone blaring its ringtone and scrambled to answer, thinking it would be Rachel. It wasn't. After a few clipped sentences with Ryder, I woke Mason and we both changed quickly before rushing to the station for an emergency meeting. Since it was barely after three in the morning, there was an ominous tension in the truck at the possibilities of what this could mean.

Detective Ryder began and the room quieted down "All right, thank y'all for coming in on short notice. We've got something on the Camden case that's going to help us more than anything has since it was discovered he was in Austin. Seems our man finally slipped up when using Camden's credit card. He signed a different name on the receipt, and we have him on camera this time. The name he signed matches up with the man we caught on camera."

Mason and I shared a glance from across the table and you could feel the excited energy flowing through the room. This was big. Every time there'd been a hit on the card, there'd never been anyone to link it to; the bartenders never knew who it belonged to, and the cameras hadn't caught anyone. And every damn time, Mason and I hadn't been working.

"This man has lived in every city that the Carnation Murders have taken place in and conveniently moved quickly after. Obviously that's much too coincidental, and we have reason to believe he stole Camden's identity and this is our guy. We already have a location on the guy and the takedown to bring him in for questioning will happen at oh five hundred." Ryder began working his way around the room, passing out pieces of paper with the suspect's picture on it as he continued speaking.

"Now, he's only in the system for a bar fight a few years ago, but if this is our guy, he will be armed and is considered extremely dangerous. We will meet behind the Denny's a couple miles out from his property to suit up and go over the takedown once more. Any questions before we head out?"

"Oh shit," Mason harshly whispered, "no!"

My brow furrowed as his face went white and I held my hand out to Detective Ryder for my copy of the picture.

As soon as the paper touched my hand, Mason tried to jump over the table and yelled, "Someone grab Kash!"

I'd barely glimpsed at the photo before Mason made it across the table and tackled me out of my chair, restraining me on the floor. But it was enough. I'd already seen. I already knew.

Rachel

"*No!*" I CRIED as Blake continued to turn on different TVs and monitors. "What is this, why are you doing this? I'm here! I'm with you, I left Logan, what more do you want?!"

"You did," he said darkly as he walked back to my side and pulled me into his arms, "but this is assurance that you won't leave. You should have seen what was on these screens before, sweetheart. I loved watching you in your place."

It shouldn't have surprised me, but my eyes still widened and a sick feeling settled deep in my stomach. *He has cameras in my apartment?* I looked at the screens in front of me now. Candice on a date with Mike. Her parents at the insurance office. Kash and Mason's apartment door. And I was positive that was the town home we'd helped Eli move into two years ago. How many people did Blake have watching and following the people I loved? Tears streamed down my face and all I could do was shake my head back and forth, my hands covering my trembling mouth.

"Please," I finally managed to say, "please call them off. Don't do this. They're your family, Blake! I'll do anything, I swear." Turning in his arms to face him, I pleaded with my eyes. "I've already proved that!"

Gripping my chin roughly in his fingers, he leaned over until his face was directly in front of mine. "You're right. You will do anything. But you've already ruined a lot, Rachel. We need to rectify that . . . first."

"First? I don't—what?"

"Yes, first. Before we move on to the next . . . *step*." His blue eyes took on some weird form of heat that I couldn't name.

"Well, didn't I do that by telling Logan I'd lied about you? By having him watch us leave together and telling Candice I was spending the weekend with you?"

"You're oddly eager to get to that next step, sweetheart." He smiled, and the arm around my waist tightened.

"If it'll get you to leave all of them alone, then I'll do whatever it takes to get to that step!"

"I'm counting on that," he whispered, and crushed his lips to mine, pushing his tongue into my mouth and growling when he didn't get the reaction he was looking for. "We'll work on that. Until you're convincing enough to fool me, this"—he pointed at the various screens—"is how it'll be."

Blake started to unwrap his arms, so I grabbed the back of his neck and brought our mouths back together. I tried to picture Kash as our lips moved against each other and I sucked on his bottom lip. But this wasn't Kash. Even if there had been a lip ring, or if Blake had been chewing the cinnamon gum that Kash always did, I wouldn't have been able to make myself believe this was the man I was in love with.

A sob ripped from me and my arms fell limply to my sides. Blake moved his lips to my neck and made a trail to my ear. "While I appreciated that, like I said, we'll work on it. Now, go get ready for bed, I'll be back in a minute." My body went rigid and he laughed soft and low. "I won't touch you tonight. Now that I have you where I want you, I need you to realize you're in love with me. Scaring you wouldn't help with that right now."

"You are scaring me!" My hand shot out toward the screens. "This—this is terrifying! Everyone I care about is in danger. You blew up George's car, for shit's sake! Does it not bother you at all that you're related to them?"

"For the last damn time, sweetheart," he sneered, "nothing will happen to them if you do what I say. And the faster you realize you're mine and you acknowledge and embrace your true feelings for me, the faster my men leave them alone."

"You can't just force someone to fall in love with you, Blake."

He huffed. "I'm not. You *are* in love with me. You're just being difficult. Get ready for bed." With that he turned and left the room.

Tears continued to fall down my cheeks as I went through the motions of getting ready for bed. The entire time I wondered what Kash was doing and if he was okay. My eyes flicked over to my phone thousands of times, but I knew he wouldn't call. And with what had already happened today and how closely everyone was being watched, I knew I couldn't call him. Not that calling him would do either of us any good anyway. If anything I would just make things worse. I prayed for the hundredth time that he would someday forgive me.

When I walked back out of the bathroom, Blake was lying in the bed, propped up against the headboard, his upper body bare. I wondered how many women wanted this. How many fantasized about his body against theirs and downtime before or after. I wanted to laugh at how seriously mistaken they all were about this Adonis. No. Not Adonis . . . not anymore. He was the damn devil. Lucifer had been a beautiful angel. And that's exactly what Blake was. He was beautiful, but something had happened to him and he was now nothing but pure evil.

Forcing myself to climb into bed beside him, I kept myself as close to the edge of the bed as possible and tried not to cry out in protest when he stretched out beside me and pulled me close. My body was shaking so hard, the entire bed was shaking with me. I prayed he'd get tired of it, but he held me closer and began whispering soothing words in my ear. But I knew it was all a lie, and I knew what he was capable of. I stayed awake for hours shaking and silently crying until sleep finally claimed me.

MY EYES FLUTTERED open and I looked around the dark room. The first thing I noticed was the empty bed beside me before I heard my phone vibrating again. Trying to remain quiet, in case Blake was somewhere nearby, I crept back into the bathroom and my heart squeezed when I saw the name on the screen.

"Hello?" I whispered, and peeked behind me into the empty room.

"Rach, oh my God, you need to get out of there! I'm not just—"

"Kash, slow down and talk a little softer. What's wrong?"

He was breathing heavily and I could hear the rumble of his truck's engine in the background. "Are you okay? Has he hurt you?"

I wanted to tell him that I was sorry for everything and that I'd lied to him yesterday . . . but I needed to keep up with this pretense to keep him safe. I cleared my throat and tried to sound strong. "Of course he hasn't. B-Blake wouldn't do anything to me."

"Babe, you don't need to keep lying to me. I'm coming for you. I will keep you safe. Just try to stay safe until we can get there, okay? Rachel, I love you. I love you so much, I need you to know that."

My heart broke at his frantic declaration, but I didn't understand. "Who is 'we,' Kash? And don't come here, please don't. I'm fine, I promise."

"Is he right there next to you?"

"No."

He breathed a heavy sigh of relief. "Rach, he's bad. He's so much worse than you originally thought. Stay as far from him as you can. If you can escape, I need you to. If not, just stay where you are, I'm coming to get you."

"Kash, no!" I harshly whispered, and turned again to make sure I was still alone. "Don't come here, I'm fine. I'm sorry you're upset that we broke up." My voice hitched and my eyes began watering. "But you need—you need to move on. I'm so sorry. Wait. How do you even know where I am?"

"How is his house set up, babe? I need your help on this."

"What?"

"C'mon, Rach. How is it set up, where's the room that you're in?"

"Listen to me, you can't do this! You need to go back home, you're going to ruin ever—" I cut off and ran into the room to watch the screens. If Kash was coming for me, that meant one of Blake's guys was following and Blake would know soon. "You need to turn around! Turn around, Kash, *please*."

"What room are you in?" he yelled suddenly, startling me and causing me to drop the phone.

I knelt down onto the ground and swiped my hand under the bed until I felt it and pulled it back toward me. "Kash, are you there?"

"This is very important. I need you to tell me exactly how the house is laid out, what room you're in, and what room Blake is in. Can you do that for me?" His voice was strained and I didn't understand why he needed to know all this so badly.

"I don't know where Blake is. Really, this isn't a house, it's more like a studio apartment. It's just one big room with a bathroom, and when I woke up from the phone vibrating, he wasn't in bed with me any—" I broke off quickly at Kash's quick intake of breath. I slammed my eyelids shut and wanted to curl up in a corner and die. I wanted to assure him we hadn't done anything, but what was the point? Forcing my eyes back open, I studied the screens. Almost all were of shots of the Jenkinses' houses and our apartment complex, focused in on Candice's and my door and windows. But one was facing a building. I studied the nondescript outer walls for a few moments until I noticed the three cars in front. "Are you or Mason at the police station?"

"Why would you ask that?" His tone was harsh and clipped.

"Um, well, just tell me if you are."

"No, I'm coming to get you."

"Where's Mason?"

He paused for a few beats. "He's on his way to get you too. Did you—" He inhaled deeply and the pain in his voice when he spoke tore at my heart. "Rachel, did you sleep with him?"

"Kash . . . ," I whispered softly.

"Please, I need to know."

I turned to look at the empty room again and hung my head. "No. I'm so sorry for today, Kash. I didn't want to do that to you, please know that I would never just hurt you like that." I choked on a sob and pressed a shaking fist over my mouth while I collected myself. I knew I shouldn't be telling him. But I needed him to know I couldn't just do this to us, and maybe if he understood he would turn around and go back to his apartment. "Blake has these guys tailing everyone. He's watching you and Mase; he has someone on Candice, her brother, and their parents . . . I'm so sorry, this is all my fault. He blew up George Jenkins's car this morning." I willed him to understand how demented Blake was. "If you do something right now, I don't know what else he'll do. I need to do this; I need to be with him. So please, go home."

His hissed a string of curses away from the phone before asking quickly, "Why did you think we were at the station?"

"On one of the screens, there's a video, and it looks like he's sitting outside one. It's showing a normal building across the street, but there are three APD cruisers in front of it."

"Thank God. Okay, babe, listen to me. I'm going to call some people so everyone else will be safe in case Blake catches wind of us coming there. But try to keep yourself safe. We'll be there soon, okay?"

"Kash, please listen to me. It's not a good i— Oh, shit."

"What, what?!"

"All the screens just stopped their live feed!" I hissed, and looked wildly around the room as I stood up and backed myself into the corner.

"What do you mean?"

"I mean it's just a bunch of screens with flowers on them! Oh my God, what if something happens? I won't even know now. This is my fault."

"Flowers. Rach, did you say flowers?" I was still chanting over and over again that this was my fault, so he spoke louder, "What *flowers,* Rachel?!"

"It's just a bouquet of these flowers."

"What kind?" I heard his truck accelerate and wanted to know why flowers were so damn important right now when I couldn't see what was happening to my family!

"Why does—"

"Just tell me!"

"They're those—I can't remember what they're called. They're white and reddish, pinkish . . ." *Dear Lord, is this how people feel on* Jeopardy!? "Oh! Carnations!"

"Son of a bitch. Rachel, get the fuck out of the house and run. Baby, do you hear me? *Run!* I will find you and I will make sure you're safe. Just get out of the goddamn house!"

"But why?"

"I'll tell you later, don't grab anything, just go!"

The fear in his voice finally caught up to me and without another thought, I took off out of the room. The door was already open, and my feet had barely touched the grass outside when I was yanked back by my hair. A cry of pain clawed its way out of my throat and I landed hard on my hip. I searched for my phone in the grass around me but came up empty. I screamed for help as Blake began dragging me back into the house by my hair and prayed that Kash was close.

"I'm disappointed in you, sweetheart."

"Please, let me go!" I grabbed on to the wrist of the hand that was holding my hair and tried to pull myself closer, but he yanked my hands off and continued dragging me toward the bed.

"You really think I would leave you alone and not be near the door? How stupid do you think I am?" He laughed softly. "I'm not an amateur."

My mind raced. *Amateur?*

He tsked softly. "My mother will be so upset when she gets the news. I was *this* close to letting everyone live to see the morning. For a second there, you *almost* made me proud with your responses to your little friend." He yanked harder when we got to the bed. "Get up."

I did as I was told and the relief of his letting go of my hair was enough to make me sigh.

"Tell me something, sweetheart. Do you want your friends to live?"

"Yes!"

"And you're willing to do . . . what? To have me call off my boys."

"Anything! I told you, anything. Just please don't hurt them, and I need to know before that they're okay!"

He pulled a remote out of his pocket and instantly the dimly lit bouquet disappeared and the live feed was back on each screen. The one that had been in front of what I'd assumed was the police station was now sitting as a dash cam and the driver was weaving in and out of traffic on the highway.

"Now, lie down. Grab the center bar of the headboard."

I whimpered as I crawled onto the middle of the bed. *I can do this. I can do this. For Kash and the Jenkins family. I can do this.*

As soon as I was lying down and holding on, Blake was grabbing handcuffs out of the nightstand and handcuffed my wrists to the wrought-iron headboard.

I can do this. I can do this.

Another set of cuffs went to my left ankle, securing it to the foot of the bed, and the last to my right.

I can't do this. Holy shit, I can't do this. My body was trembling by the time Blake stretched his fully clothed body on top of mine and pressed his mouth firmly to my own.

"I waited, Rachel. I waited until you were old enough. I wasted my time looking for girls who came even remotely close to looking like you." His hand brushed through my hair as he studied it. "Long legs. Long, straight, near-black hair. Eyes the exact color of sapphires." A heavy sigh left him and his forehead creased. "But none of them were you. None of them had your temper; none of them had your fire for life. So none of them deserved to have your beauty."

"Like Jenn." I realized it with dread and watched his face twist with a look of disgust.

"Everything I've done up until this point has been for you and our future together. I only wish," he said against my lips, "that you would stop being so goddamn difficult." Suddenly he was off me and the bed and rummaging through the nightstand drawer again.

He fastened a gag around my mouth and as soon as I began wondering what kind of sick things Blake really was into, he began pulling knives and different-looking blades out as well. Once everything was sitting on top of the nightstand, he grabbed a pair of keys out of his pocket and unlocked the cabinet door of the nightstand. Standing slowly, I saw the vase of carnations that had been on the screens and he smiled widely at me. Like he was proud of something.

"These are for you, sweetheart, as soon as I finish putting my claim on you and then making you mine. I've never forgotten the day you showed up at my door with these."

My head shook back and forth as I searched every memory I had regarding carnations, but nothing stood out, and Blake roared in frustration as he pulled one flower out and threw the rest of the bouquet against the far wall. The sound of the glass vase shattering filled the open space and he flung the lone flower at my face.

"*My* Rachel wouldn't forget that she brought my family a bouquet of carnations this exact color."

Oh God, I did remember. That had been right after I'd thought I'd fallen in love with him and his grandma had passed. My mom had bought them, but I'd wanted to give them to Mrs. West. I'd completely forgotten about that and that'd been about a dozen years ago. How did he remember that?

Blake laughed sadly and grabbed the carnation that was lying haphazardly on my cheek before trailing it along my face and up my arms. "See, *my* Rachel wouldn't have forgotten, but something happened and you changed. You're no longer my Rachel. And like the other Rachel imposters, you don't deserve the whole bouquet. You'll only be needing one, sweetheart."

What in the actual fuck is wrong with this man?

Kash

I HIT MASON'S name again on my screen and prayed he'd answer the phone this time. "C'mon, c'mon, c'mon."

Ever since I'd heard Rachel scream, and her phone had gone straight to voice mail when I called back, I'd been calling Mason over and over again. But he hadn't once answered. I knew I shouldn't have freaked out in the meeting room. But when you realize the serial killer you've been after has your girl with him, all rational thought goes out the window. But I still couldn't believe Mason of all people had asked them to keep me at the damn station!

"What, Kash?"

"Why the hell haven't you been answering your phone?"

"We were getting ready for the takedown." He sounded defeated and after a few seconds he sighed into the phone. "She's not here, man."

My blood ran cold. "Yes she is, she has to be. I was just talking to her. Are we sure that's the correct address?"

"Positive, this is definitely West's place. But he isn't here either; we checked all the rooms and there isn't a sign of him. His Lexus is out front, so he must have another car we don't know about, or that Explorer that man who was stalking Rachel for him drove is actually Blake's. But it's not here."

"I don't think it's Blake's, Rachel said he has men tailing all of us."

"You serious?"

"Yeah, man. Even Candice's family."

He growled, "That sick fuck. Look, I know we were already pretty sure this would be the Carnation killer, but even if it's not . . . he needs to go. Every room is full of pictures of Rachel, her schedule, and just random things about her."

I flipped on my blinker and swerved across a couple lanes to take the exit I was about to miss, earning me a few horns. "You keep talking about multiple rooms. Rachel said where she's at is practically one big room. Is there a shed or a guesthouse, anything?"

Mason started calling for Ryder away from the phone and after another few seconds, I heard him asking Ryder about other possibilities when something else he'd said occurred to me.

"Mase! Mase, can you hear me?"

"Yeah?"

"You said Blake's Lexus is there, right?"

A pause and some shuffling. "Positive that's his, there's no way I'd forget that car. And it's parked right out front."

"Where's Rachel's Jeep?"

"I don't know, man, why?"

"When he came by to get her today, they both took their cars. Find her Jeep, you find Rach." I looked down at my GPS and let out a deep breath. "I'm not far out, I'll be there soon."

"No, Kash. You go back. You're too close to this case."

"And you're not? She's like your sister!"

"She's your goddamn fiancée! Turn the fuck around!"

The tires of my truck squealed as I took a corner too quickly. I hoped like hell there were no cops running radar on this road right now—not like I'd stop for them anyway—because I was still ten minutes away if I went the speed limit. But no way was I gonna have the patience to go thirty-five miles per hour when my reason for breathing could have been taking her last. Once my truck straightened out again, I gunned it until I was going eighty-five down the narrow neighborhood roads. "If she dies, and I did nothing, I wouldn't be able to live with myself, Mason. I'll be there soon. Look for her Jeep or a guesthouse and call me back if you find them." Before he could protest further, I hung up and looked wildly around at the thinning houses.

Just as I was coming up on the different squad cars and vans they'd all taken to get there, I caught a glimpse of white to my left and it took everything in me not to slam on my brakes in the middle of the road or turn and drive my truck into the small guesthouse. I'd never been so happy in my life to see a damn Jeep Liberty. I pulled up behind the end of the line of cars and started back down the long dirt driveway on foot as I called Mason again.

"We don't have anything yet, Kash, we're working on it."

"I found her," I said softly, and walked low to the ground but swiftly. "The property directly next to his on the west has a dirt driveway that heads back to a small guesthouse. Rachel's Jeep is peeking out of the side. I'm walking up."

"No, wait for us! We need to think about the best way to go in there first, and besides, you don't have on a vest or anything—did they even give you your gun back?"

"Mason, the last thing I heard from her was her screaming

before the call was lost. I'm not waiting another minute. Either get your ass over here with me, or I'm going in alone!" I hissed, and continued making my way up the drive.

"Shit! Ryder, Mackey, Barnes, come with me *now*." I could hear the wind in the phone and Mason's breathing pick up. "We went out the back, we're coming. Where exactly are— Never mind, I see you. Just stay there."

I shoved my phone in my pocket and kept going. I wasn't stopping yet; I was barely halfway there. By the time the guys made it over to me, no one looked exactly happy to see me, especially Ryder. But Mason's anger was fighting with his fear for Rachel, and right now I couldn't figure out which one was winning.

Detective Ryder cleared his throat until I focused on him. "Mason said she screamed. And then what happened?"

"The call was dropped. She had been trying to make a run for it. This is our guy; I know it is. She said in the room there are screens and on them are live feeds coming from different men watching people closest to her. While we were talking, the feed stopped and all that was on the screen was a bouquet of carnations." I began moving toward the house, but Ryder put a hand on my chest and stopped me.

"We'll take it from here."

I swallowed hard and shook my head. "With all due respect, sir, there isn't a chance in hell you are stopping me from getting my girl out of that house. If I lose my job over this, so be it. But she's my world, and the only reason she's in here is because I fucked up and didn't do my job in protecting her." I pushed past his hand, only to stop again when Mason held something in front of me.

A gun.

Good thing, because I hadn't ever gotten mine back at the station. I looked at my best friend, and with a nod, he pulled out his second duty weapon and we quickly moved in on the house. All the curtains were closed, and as the five of us quickly set up to kick in the door, muffled screams came from somewhere in the house and Mason didn't waste another second.

The door went in easily, and I rounded the frame followed by the others.

"*Austin Police Department,*" I yelled as I charged into the open room, "*show me your hands!*"

"*Travis County sheriff, drop your weapon!*"

My blood boiled as my eyes narrowed in on Blake leaning over Rachel's body on the bed. He straightened on his knees and slowly lifted his hands in the air, a scalpel in one hand and what looked like a sickle in the other.

A disturbed smile covered his face as we closed in on him. He looked completely at peace, even with five guns pointing at him. I chanced a glance at Rachel and it took me a moment to realize that the roar that filled the room had come from me. She had blood covering her bare upper body and running down her arms, which were cuffed to the bed. I automatically took a step in her direction before I could remember the safest way to go about this for her—to keep my eyes and weapon on the shitbag still straddling her knees.

"Drop your weapons," I said through gritted teeth, and forced my eyes not to move from Blake's hands. I wanted nothing more than to keep my gun aimed right at his head, but training took over and I put it at his chest instead. My finger itched to move closer to the trigger. Mason was right. I was too close to this and I wasn't thinking clearly. But I couldn't have left someone else to save Rachel.

Blake started lowering his body over Rachel again.

"Freeze or I will shoot you!"

"You really don't want to do that," he said calmly.

Want to fuckin' bet?

"If my men don't hear from me every fifteen minutes, they have orders to kill. Since I was listening to Rachel during your *touching* phone call earlier . . . I know *you* know who will die. So you decide. Shoot me or arrest me and have the deaths of Rachel's loved ones on your hands . . . or let me go and we can hope you can get an ambulance out here fast enough so that our poor Rachel doesn't bleed out."

My eyes betrayed me and flashed back over to Rachel, running over her blood-covered body. There was a lot of blood, and she was pale and drenched in sweat. I prayed one of the guys was calling in an ambulance; I didn't even have a radio on me and wasn't about to reach for my phone. Just before I looked back over at Blake, I caught her gaze and wished I hadn't. She wasn't even looking at the man practically lying on top of her with knives. She was looking at me as tears poured rapidly down her face. And it was a look I'd been dreading for months. Like she had no idea who I was.

I could hear the other sheriffs and detectives trying to get Blake to put down the knives, but I couldn't stop looking at her. I had failed her. And I hated myself for it. When I came to Austin, I'd had one job to do: find the Carnation Killer before he found another victim. When I met Rachel, I was given a new job: love her and keep her safe. Not only had I let her go with the killer I was supposed to find, I'd kept a part of my life from her to keep her safe, and in doing that had ultimately put this look in her eyes. This look of distrust mixed in with the fear. My chest ached and I prayed that one day she would understand why I'd kept all of this from her.

Tearing my eyes from her, I leveled my gaze back at Blake. He was still ignoring orders and was looking directly at me with the same smile he'd had when we'd first walked in. Detective Ryder switched out his gun for his Taser next to me and gave final warnings. At the last moment, Blake raised his hands up high, the sickle and scalpel hanging directly above Rachel dangling from his fingertips. I knew if he got tased or shot, those would fall down, and I had no doubt the sickle positioned directly over her throat would do serious damage.

Before anyone could act, I quickly holstered my weapon and threw myself over the bed at him. I knocked into him and we went flying over the other side of the bed; the sound of metal hitting hardwood had never been so beautiful as it was then. I heard the guys moving in behind me, and though Blake didn't even attempt to struggle against me, I couldn't stop myself from punching him over and over again until Mackey and Barnes were pulling me away and Ryder was rolling Blake over to cuff him.

Turning around, I found Mason taking the gag off Rachel and I pushed his hands away, taking over for him. "Get the cuffs, Mase." Running my hands down her tear-streaked face, my heart broke when her eyes met mine. She was looking at me, but she wasn't seeing me. There was nothing in those beautiful blue eyes. No pain. No fear. No betrayal. No love. They were empty and were looking right through me. "I'm so sorry, Rach. I'm sorry. We got you, baby. You're safe now."

I kissed the top of her head and looked down at the rest of her body. There was so much blood and her skin was turning an unnatural gray. I couldn't tell if the blood was coming from multiple wounds but ripped my shirt off to press down on her stomach, where some was still pooling out.

"We need an ambulance here."

"Already on the way. Dispatched one right before we caught up with you," Mackey said as he emerged from the bathroom with towels. He and Mason wrapped them around her arms.

Keeping my shirt pressed firmly to her stomach, I took one of the towels and began gently wiping where more blood was coming from her chest. Lifting the towel to make sure I was over the wound, I saw what looked like a word carved into her chest before blood was pooling out of it again. I pressed down harder and whispered over and over again how sorry I was as I searched the rest of her body to see if we were missing anything. Just before Barnes announced the ambulance was here, Rachel's body started gently shaking, then full-on convulsing.

"She's going into shock," Mason breathed. "Get EMTs in here, *now!*"

"Come on, babe, stay with us. Keep your eyes open, Rachel. I need you to stay awake, okay?" Her chapped lips were a chalky white and her eyes rolled back; fat tears were falling down her face and into her hair. "Stay awake, Rachel!" I felt someone pushing me back, and when I tore my eyes from her I saw three EMTs with a stretcher.

As they worked over her and loaded her onto the stretcher, Mason was handing me my blood-soaked shirt and pushing me out of the house. "They'll take care of her, but we're in the way, Kash. Let's go."

"I can't leave her."

"I know you don't want to, but we still have a job to do. The faster we start taking care of this, the sooner you can be with Rachel."

This was a case going back years, and investigations on this man went back months. No way this could be over quick enough. They'd just have to come find me in Rachel's hospital room. She was my priority.

We'd just reached Detective Ryder when Rachel was wheeled past us, and both he and Mason had to keep an arm on me to keep me from going after her.

"We'll get you out of here soon enough, Hendricks. I know you want to be with her."

Need. Need to. I turned and my mouth popped open. "Who the fuck gave him a phone?!"

Mason's head snapped to the right to see what I was looking at, and we both took off for the squad car Blake was in the back of. The back door was wide open; his hands were cuffed behind his back and a phone was between his shoulder and cheek.

"He's calling off his men," Mackey explained when we reached him. "I'm listening to the call, he's doing as he's been told." Grabbing the phone when Blake looked up at him, he put it in an evidence bag and stepped to the back of the car.

"Why are you smiling, dipshit? You're going down for three murders and an attempted murder." Mason was gripping the top of the door tightly as he stared over it and at Blake.

His shit-eating grin just got bigger.

"For those three girls, I will make sure you rot until you die.

But for Rachel, I will make sure every one of those days you are suffering more than any of them ever had to," I promised, and stepped back to let Mason shut the door.

Blake's smile somehow broadened even more. "Such harsh and unnecessary words. Too bad that won't be happening."

I heard the distant crack a split second after Blake's head flew back and blood sprayed me. Mason and I turned as yells that there was a shooter went through the scene. Another two shots and Mason hit the car before sliding to the ground. I'd barely registered he'd been hit when I felt the pain tearing through my body. My knees gave out, and as one arm struggled to keep me up, my other hand pulled away from my bare chest, which was covered in blood. The last thing I saw was Mason checking his bulletproof vest and reaching for me.

18

Rachel

"Hey there, sweetheart."

My eyelids fluttered against the harsh light and I turned toward the voice. Mason—if that was even his name—was sitting next to my hospital bed, holding the hand that wasn't completely covered in tubes and wires. Removing my hand from his, I looked straight ahead and continued to blink until my eyes adjusted to the buzzing fluorescent lights.

"How are you feeling?"

"You both lied to me," I whispered, and continued to stare at my door.

He sighed heavily. "Rachel, you have to understand something—"

"No. I need you to leave." Why was he here with me? Where was Kash? Or Logan . . . or were either of those even his name?

My vision got blurry and my chest heaved with a sob. The man I had fallen in love with, the man I was engaged to marry, had been lying to me the entire time. I had been about to marry a man I didn't know a thing about. Other than the fact that apparently he was a cop and a liar.

"There's something you—"

"Go."

A heavy sigh followed tense silence between us. "All right." Getting out of his chair, he bent over the bed and kissed my forehead. "Love you, sweetheart. I'll tell the nurses you're awake."

When he was almost to the door, I called his name. "Tell your cousin—or friend, or whatever he is—not to come in here. I don't want to see him and I don't want to hear from him. Ever again . . . okay?"

"Rach, he—"

"Tell him, Mason."

Mason grimaced and just continued to stare at me before turning and leaving the room.

I heard familiar voices mixed with Mason's, and a few seconds later, Candice stuck her head in. "You're awake!" she cried, and her smile shook before she burst into sobs. "Rachel, I'm so sorry!"

"Candi, it's—" All the air in my lungs left me in one big rush when Eli and her parents followed her in. "You guys are okay?! I-I-I watched it, I saw your car. It was all my fault!"

I was quickly surrounded by the only family I had left and could no longer hold back the tears when Candice and her mom covered me with hugs. "No, it wasn't. They told us everything, sweet girl. None of that was your fault. He was very sick, there was nothing you could have done to stop him."

"George," I whispered. "I thought he was going to make me watch you die." My voice cracked at the end and soon he was covering his wife in order to get in on the hugs. Eli stood at the foot of my bed with his hands resting on my feet, just staring at me with water-filled eyes. Being the strong and silent one as always.

"I'm okay, Rachie," George said. "We're all okay, just worried about you. How are you?"

I had no idea. My body ached from where Blake had cut me, and overall I felt like I'd been run over by a dump truck. But my broken heart was worse than any pain I'd ever known, and my exhausted mind was taking too long to numb myself to everything. So how was I? I was shattered. "I . . . I'm really not sure."

"You must be exhausted," Janet said. "The doctor said you should rest after everything that you went through. And I know now that you're awake they'll be coming in to give you something for the pain again soon; that should help you fall asleep."

Speak of the devil . . . the nurse walked in and started shooing Candice's parents aside so she could give the next dose of pain meds and check all the machines I was hooked up to. As soon as she was gone, Janet spoke up again.

"Rest, baby. Visiting hours are almost over and we came here straight from the airport. We're going to go get settled in at a hotel and we'll be back in the morning to take you home. Do you want us to bring you anything other than a change of clothes?"

Shaking my head, I studied each of their faces and thanked God for keeping them all safe. "Love you guys."

"We love you too, sweet girl. We're so—we're sorry." She cried and stepped back so George could hug me close, before Candice did.

When they were gone, Eli walked silently up to me and bent

low to press his forehead to mine. "I love you, sis. I'd kill him if I could for hurting you." I just nodded my head and squeezed his hand when he pulled the chair up next to the bed and sat down.

"You should go back to the hotel with the family, Eli."

"There's no way I'm leaving you alone. A guy I'd always looked up to just tried to kill you. I'm not going anywhere. Go to sleep."

I wanted to fight him on staying, but my eyelids were already drooping and I was asleep before I could try to say anything.

THE NEXT TIME I woke it was dark in the room. The only lights and sounds were coming off the multiple machines I was hooked up to and the hallway outside my cracked door. I wasn't in much pain this time, but the wraps on my torso and arms, as well as the bandages on my throat and chest, were making it impossible to forget why I was in there. My body felt heavy, like I was weighted down with bricks, and even turning my head was—

My body locked up and I tried to throw up my walls, but my heart was betraying me. It pounded just as hard as it always did when Kash . . . Logan . . . whoeverthefuckhewas, was near. I looked at his handsome face through the sliver of light peeking in the room and tried to figure out just who he was.

This man who had stolen my heart.

His expression was kept carefully blank, but I saw the haunted look in his eyes. And knowing Kash, I'd bet that if the room had been well lit, I'd have been able to see the muscle tic in his jaw. But . . . I didn't know him.

"Who are you?" I asked, my voice hoarse and raspy from a combination of too much sleep, stress, and trying to scream against the gag.

My haunted stranger's eyes widened and he jerked back in his chair. Looking at the door, to the machines, and back to me, his mouth opened and shut once before a horrified whisper filled the room. "Rach, you—y-you don't . . . remember who I am? They didn't—they didn't tell me you were having memory loss."

He stood quickly and grabbed the chart off the end of my bed. Laying it near my feet, he started flipping through pages and leaning close to read in the dark. It was only then that I noticed his right arm was in a sling. He was hurt? Had that happened when he tackled Blake off me?

A shudder rolled through my body and I cleared my throat. "I remember you. I remember everything." He stopped looking through the file and looked back at me. "But I don't know who you *are*."

His face looked pained as realization set in. "Rachel—"

"You look an awful lot like a guy I was engaged to. But that guy—" My voice shook and tears filled my eyes. "See, the funny thing about him . . . is he wasn't real."

"Rachel." His voice was full of anguish as he walked back to the side of the bed and pulled the chair close to me. "I didn't want you to find out that way . . ."

"Who. Are. You?"

"Babe, you *know* me."

"No. I don't, and you don't get to call me that." The tears were now falling freely down my face and my heart began cracking all over again. "What is your name?"

"Logan Ryan. Not Hendricks, and my middle name *is* Kash; I've gone by that my entire life."

"And Mason?"

"Mason Gates. And he's not my cousin. We met at the police academy almost five years ago."

I nodded and tried to swallow the lump in my throat. "So, you're a cop?"

"Uh, yeah. Mason and I are partners. Up until we moved here, we were undercover narcotics division. *Why* we're here is a long story, but we came to find the killer behind the Carnation Murders. We had to stay undercover as we looked for him. And, Rachel"—he leaned forward, putting a hand on my arm and keeping it there even when I tried to jerk it away—"I swear we had no idea it was Blake West. We were following a trail for someone else. If I had known, you wouldn't have ended up here. Babe, I'm so sorry."

I let the *babe* slip as my mind raced. "Carnation Murders? What— I don't— Wait. Plural? Blake . . . Blake killed people?" I remembered what Blake had said to me: *So none of them deserved to have your beauty . . . And like the other Rachel imposters . . . Oh my God.*

Kash's eyes roamed over me, his face twisted in what could only be described as agony. "He won't hurt anyone again. He's dead."

I couldn't have stopped them even if I tried. My steady tears as my heart broke over Kash suddenly turned into loud sobs as I took everything in. Blake was a killer. He'd tried to kill me. He was dead now. Kash was an undercover cop. Kash, the only person to see through my walls and knock them down, was a stranger.

He hunched over the bed and, with the arm that wasn't in the sling, cupped my cheek and attempted to brush the tears away. His forehead rested on mine as he tried to calm me.

"It's okay, Rachel. He'll never touch you, or anyone, again. I'm sorry. I'm so sorry I failed you. I didn't protect you, and God, I'm so damn sorry. I love you so much."

Turning my face away from his hand, I spoke through clenched teeth. "Please stop touching me." Another sob worked its way from my chest and I took a deep breath, trying to steel my body against the pain that wouldn't stop coming.

"Babe, you have no idea how many times I wanted to tell you. I'm so sorry. But everything we had was real."

"I need you to leave."

"Please don't ask me to do that. I love you, Rachel. More than life itself."

"I don't love you. I'm in love with an illusion. Please just— don't make this more difficult than it needs to be. I can't do this with you, Kash. You lied to me. And it wasn't just something as simple as you telling me I look beautiful when I'm sick. You lied to me about *you*. *That* is an unforgivable lie. You hated my shields and broke them all down. You didn't want anything between us. But you made me fall in love with a man who doesn't exist."

"He does. I'm that guy. I'm him, Rachel . . . everything about us was real, I swear to you."

"When I woke up today, I didn't even know what your name was. I thought you were a bartender, Kash! And now that I'm thinking about it, you've still never told me where you're from."

"Tampa Bay, Florida. Ask me anything and I'll tell you, but you know me."

I shook my head and blinked back the new tears pricking my eyes. "It's too little way too late. How can I ever believe anything you say?"

"Rachel—"

"Go. Please." He started to speak, so I cut him off again. "Don't come back, Kash. I don't want to see or hear from you again."

He stood there staring at me for countless minutes. I could see his eyes gloss over in the dim lighting in the room, and when he turned for the door, I saw the tears start falling down his face.

And then he was gone.

I barely held it together for ten seconds before I felt myself shatter into a million pieces and heard my sobs fill the room. I'd protected myself from ever experiencing this type of hurt again by making sure I never gave anyone my heart. But I had never stood a chance against Kash. From the minute he almost took my car door off, he had taken my heart and kept a firm hold.

And now there was nothing left to protect. I somehow knew that I would never have to worry about guarding my heart again. Because even now, through the pain in my chest, through the betrayal I felt down to my core, I knew that Logan Kash Hen— *Ryan* would always have my heart.

Kash

ON AUTOPILOT, I walked out to the waiting room, where Mason was sleeping on one of the chairs. I couldn't make sense of my emotions, and every bit of me was fighting to go back into Rachel's room despite her pleas. But I knew I'd fucked up the best thing I'd ever had and would ever have.

She was right. I had hated her shields, and I'd pushed her every day until they were gone. Funny that it would be my fault that they had all gone back up, thicker than ever.

Someone cleared his throat, and I glanced up to see Candice's brother standing there. He stuck his left hand out toward me and cleared his throat again. "Eli Jenkins. Thank you for saving her. She's always been like a sister to me." When I didn't respond at first, he looked at Mason, then back to me. "You're her fiancé, right?"

My stomach tightened. *Ex,* I thought to myself. *Ex-fiancé.*

He dropped his hand and it was only then I realized I still hadn't said anything. "I'm sure it's been a long day for you. We can talk later. I just wanted to say thank you."

When he started to turn around, I quickly spoke. "You don't need to thank me. I would do anything for her." *Including walk away.* "Watch out for her, okay?"

He gave me an odd look but nodded before walking back toward her room. I sighed heavily and ran my free hand down my face.

Mason shifted in the chair beside me, and a few seconds later he spoke gruffly. "Give her time, bro. She'll come around."

"I don't think so. She trusted me, and I broke that trust beyond repair."

"She's just stressed, it was a hard day. Give her—"

"And it's *my* fault, Mase! All of this was my fault. In less than forty-eight hours, my fiancée gave me back the ring I'd given her to protect the people she loves, was almost murdered, and then broke up with me *again*. For real this time, and it's because of what I am. I told you, who we are . . . what we do . . . we can't have relationships. And this is why. I don't blame Rachel for anything. I put her in this situation, she was in danger because of me."

Mason quickly stood up and began pacing. "No she wasn't. All that shit had gone down with her and Blake before we'd ever even shown up. It had been going on for *years,* and it had nothing to do with your job. You being a cop is what saved her yesterday morning. Like I said, give her some time. She's gone through a lot over the last few months, but she loves you."

I don't love you. I'm in love with an illusion. I'd known heartache before, but what was happening now couldn't be described as heartache. Those words had shattered my soul. I felt hollow and lost. And like I could easily drown in the searing pain making its way through my body. "She doesn't want to see me, Mason. She wants me gone. I couldn't keep her safe even after I promised her I would. The least I can do is give her what she asks. It's over."

"Kash—"

"Stop. She deserves a normal life, not the one I have to offer. I couldn't protect her before, but I will now, by walking away."

Before he could say anything else, I began walking out of the waiting room and hospital. I was at Mason's truck for almost half an hour before he joined me. "Both of our dads will be here later today," I said.

He paused with his door half-open. "What?"

"They're going to help us pack up and move back to Florida." I grabbed the handle just inside the door and hauled myself into the cab. Putting on the seat belt should have been a lot easier than it was, but the sling and the additional pain in my shoulder and right side of my chest were making it damn near impossible. Note to self: Don't get shot again. It doesn't tickle and makes putting seat belts on a bitch.

"When did you talk to them?"

"When I was waiting for you."

"Kash." He sighed and finally got in the driver's seat but didn't put the key in the ignition. "I don't think you should do this. Give her time, yeah, but don't fucking run away."

If I didn't feel so dead inside, I would have snorted at him. "I'm not running away."

"Yes you are. You're being a little bitch! You always think people are better off without you. You did this with Megan and now you're doing it with Rachel. But with Rachel, she's best *with* you. I didn't have to know her before the two of you met to know that. So some shit went down, and she's terrified. Understandable. But you're being a bitch thinking that you caused all of this and that running from her is going to keep her safe. God, you're so fucking dumb."

"She almost died, Mason!" I yelled, and turned to face him. "She almost fucking died!"

"And so did we! With us it was because of our job and a psycho. With Rach it was *only* because of the psycho. She is alive because of our job. Get that through your thick skull."

"We're done talking about this. I'm not running from her, Mase. I'm leaving for her. Think what you want about that, I really don't fucking care anymore. But she asked me to leave and our job here is done. Staying—" *Would be too painful.* "There's no reason to stay."

"You're such an idiot," he sneered, and cranked the engine.

It's too little way too late. The pain that had nothing to do with getting shot intensified and I sucked in a quick breath. "Yeah . . . I am."

19

Rachel

Just as I was raising my shirt over my head, there was a knock on the door and I barely had time to push the material back down before it opened to reveal Candice.

"Hey," she said softly.

I hated that tone. Everyone in my life, including Candice and her parents, had used that tone on me the entire year after my parents died. It'd been months since the incident with Blake, and they were *still* using this tone with me. Like I was going to break if they spoke to me like a normal human being. He was her cousin. I almost wanted to give her the tone right back and ask how she liked it.

"Hey."

"What are you up to?" she asked quietly as she walked into my room and lay down on my bed.

"I was just about to take a shower."

"What are you doing after?"

And this was now the norm as well. *What are you doing, what are you eating, why are you going to sleep, why don't you want to come out with us* . . . next she was going to ask why I was still wearing clothes.

"I'm probably going to go to sleep."

"Okay, that's fine."

Fine? It was almost midnight. "What are *you* doing, Candi?" *Yeah . . . I flipped that shit around onto you. How does it feel?*

"Just checking on you."

"Ah." This was awkward. "You know, it's been three months. I'm okay."

She sat up from her sprawled-out position on my bed. "I know you are, I just—I wish you . . ."

"Wish I would what?" What *more* could I do? I'd kept my job. I'd gone to a therapist like Janet had begged me to. I wasn't sitting in the corner rocking back and forth talking about the boogeyman that was coming to get me. I really didn't understand what else they could expect of me.

"Rachel, I've been talking to Mason—"

"Oh, no. No, no, no. Candice, we talked about this!"

"He's miserable, Rach! Mason's worried about him. His parents are worried about him. The chief made him take some time off because he's just not the same."

My chest tightened and I sucked in air quickly through my teeth. Turning so my back was facing her, I blinked rapidly until my vision was no longer blurry. "He lied to me about everything. I can't—why am I even talking about him right now?" I huffed a pathetic attempt at a laugh. "No more." *Besides, he hasn't even tried to contact me.*

"Rachel, you told him not to talk to you!"

Shit, did I say that out loud?

"I know." I sighed heavily. "I know I did. And I don't want him to, but he—he didn't even try to fight for us after. He left and that was it. My word, I'm being such a girl." Leaning against the wall so I was facing Candice again, I crossed my arms under my chest and worried my bottom lip. "I wasn't playing games with him, and I'm still not. I wasn't testing him to see what he would do. When I told him I wanted him to go and not come back, I meant it. But the fact that he did it is killing me now."

"You still love him, right?"

A pained laugh escaped me. "Of course I do. I always will."

"Then call him, I have his real number! You're both miserable, this is stupid." She grabbed my phone off my nightstand and started walking toward me.

"I can't, it's not that simple."

"Yeah, actually, it is!"

I pushed the hand that was holding my phone away. "Candice, no. What he did is unforgivable. I'm still in love with him, but that doesn't change what he did and what he could do to me again. I almost married him without knowing his real last name. How would he have even done that? Just continued to act like his last name was Hendricks forever?" I snorted. Snorting was good. It helped me not break down into a crying mess in front of her right now. "I'm done talking about this, and I'm done talking about him."

Candice looked like she wanted to argue, but she just nodded her head, dropped my phone on the bed, and gave me a hug before leaving the room. I waited until I heard the TV turn on before going to remove my clothes. I'd never had an issue with changing around Candice; we grew up with each other, it was normal for us. But if Candice was already acting weird anyway, seeing the scars her cousin had put on me was sure to make her start sobbing and apologizing to me over and over again. I didn't want that. I had been upset when she didn't believe me about Blake raping me, but I knew she had blinders on and thought Blake was perfect. None of what happened had been her fault; I didn't blame her and hated when she blamed herself.

Taking a deep breath, I looked up at the mirror, and my chin trembled when I saw myself. It never got easier. In fact, I'm pretty sure it got harder. At least when the cuts had been fresh, I could make myself believe they would go away. But now that they'd all turned into scars, there was no way to keep telling myself that. But at least the haunting memories behind them were growing smaller each time.

For the first two months of therapy, I'd gone twice a week, and for the last month it'd only been once a week. I'd had my last session with Dr. Markowitz a few days ago, and I owed a lot to that woman. I'd never wanted to go to therapy after my parents' death, and I wouldn't have gone after what happened with Blake. But I was so glad Candice's mom had all but forced me into a car and driven me there before they went back to California. Dr. Markowitz had helped me accept what had happened and learn to move on from it. I knew I couldn't be afraid of something like this happening again, and most importantly, I knew I couldn't blame myself for what had happened to Kash and Mason, Jenn, or the other three girls who were victims in the Carnation Murders.

Jason Ruiz was the man hired to follow Kash, and from what he said after he was arrested, the sentence Blake had said when he was supposed to be calling Ruiz off had been the signal to take Blake, Kash, and Mase out. Blake was disturbed, but he was smart. He made sure he would never go down for what he did. I just needed to be thankful for bulletproof vests, and for the fact that Kash had turned toward Mason at the last second so nothing major was hit.

After our apartment had been swept for cameras and bugs and the Jenkins family had gone back to California, Candice and I moved back in and I'd immediately looked up the Carnation Murders. I don't know how I'd never heard of them, and I felt sick knowing every one of them was done by Blake and was because of me. I studied the pictures of the three women for hours, blown away by the similarities between them and me, and spent days grieving for their families and for the girls whose lives were cut too short all because they were unlucky enough to look like me. Getting past that guilt took five sessions with Dr. Markowitz and Candice hiding my phone and laptop from me for a few weeks so I couldn't search anymore.

But I knew now that Blake was just a sick man. Always had been. I couldn't blame myself for what he'd done to other women just like I couldn't blame myself for what he'd done to me.

I looked down at the three-inch scars on each of my wrists and then glanced back up at the mirror as I traced the diagonal scars going across my torso before letting my fingers trail over the small scarred *MINE* on the left side of my chest. My breaths were shaky, but there were no tears. I wasn't in danger of hyper-ventilating or passing out as I had many times after I first saw what Blake had done to me. This was part of my own therapy, facing the nightmare that was on my body until I was no longer hit with flashes of that early morning.

No flashes. No memories of Blake's chilling words as I waited for someone to save me.

I smiled softly to myself and turned the shower on. *Getting better all the time.*

Kash

"COME ON IN, Ryan."

I shut the door behind me and took a seat across from Chief. "Good afternoon, sir."

"How are you holding up?"

I wanted to laugh out loud. I wasn't. "Uh, I'm getting there."

He nodded and tapped his pen against a stack of papers as he studied me. "Did your vacation help at all?"

"It gave me time to think, and that's why I'm here." Straightening in the chair, I took a deep breath and tried to hold his stare. "I think I should resign."

The tapping pen stopped immediately. "Excuse me?"

"I didn't do my job the way I should have. I let my relationship get in the way of what I was supposed to be doing, and because of that, someone got hurt."

"Your fiancée."

Ex. "Yes. If I had remained focused on what I was there for, none of that would have happened. We would have most likely caught West long before he could do anything."

"You know, I spoke with Gates before I told you to take your vacation. He said you were blaming yourself for this, and I've got to tell you, I disagree with your assessment of the situation." I started to argue but he continued. "I spoke with Detective Ryder in Austin, and from what he said, both you and Gates went above and beyond what was asked of you. You were supposed to be there looking for the killer at the bars, and I was told you would go in early and look through all the cameras, checking even the people who paid cash. That's hours of extra work every week you weren't asked to do and that weren't expected of you. Ryder said he didn't have a clue you were even dating someone, let alone engaged, until the meeting setting up the takedown of Blake West. That doesn't sound like someone who lost focus on his job."

"But, Chief—"

"And when I spoke with Gates, he told me about how your fiancée was being stalked by this same guy, and while you were doing your job, you were trying to take care of that without her knowing she was being stalked and without giving away your position. Both Ryder and Gates agree that if it had not been for you, Rachel Masters wouldn't have been found in time. And Blake West would more than likely be a ghost to us. So I'm sure you can understand why I do not agree with you."

Why didn't anyone else understand this? "I let her—"

"Ryan, tell me something." He waited until I was looking at him again before speaking. "Do you enjoy what you do?"

I sighed. "Of course I do."

"And you like working in the gang division now?"

"I do." To be honest, it was perfect.

"Then I'm not letting you quit. I can't imagine how hard it must be that your fiancée went through that, but you're being too hard on yourself. You're good at what you do, I'm proud to have you and Gates working for me. Until you decide you hate it here or you find something better, I'm not going to let you leave."

I ground my jaw and nodded once.

"Anything else?"

"No, Chief."

"Then get your ass out of my office. You still have two days of vacation left."

WHEN I GOT back to the apartment late that night, Mason was being more awkward than usual. I slammed the beer down on the coffee table and glared at him. "Can I help you? You've been staring at me for five minutes straight."

"Did your dad say anything . . . about . . ."

"Jesus, Mase. About Rachel? Did he say anything about Rachel? Yeah, he did. So did Mom, and I know you probably put them up to it. But you have got to let it go; she wanted me gone." Grabbing my beer again, I stood and headed for my room.

Three and a half months later, and I was worse now than when we'd moved back here. I snapped at everyone, I was in a constant state of being pissed off, and I spent hours each day thinking about everything I wished I could do over again. For the first couple months, I told myself I just had to give her time . . . wait for her to come back to me. But even Mason had stopped saying she would come around. Now he just kept trying to get me to go to her.

I froze and glared at the new addition to my bed for almost an entire minute before setting my beer on the dresser and walking over. I knew what would be in the black velvet box even though I hadn't given Mason the box too. Picking it up in my left hand, I flipped the top open and snapped it shut again when I saw Rachel's engagement ring nestled in the satin. Fisting my hand over the box, I put the hand to my mouth and grabbed the picture that had been lying underneath the box.

I don't remember what had been happening; I don't think we'd even realized someone had taken the picture. But we were in the girls' apartment, Rachel was grabbing my shirt like she'd been pulling me toward her, and I had her cheeks cupped in my hands and was kissing her hard. Pain radiated through my body and I had to force my hand not to crumple up the picture.

My breaths came hard and fast through my nose as I turned and stormed back into the living room. "The fuck is this? Where did you get this?"

Mason leaned back in the chair and crossed his arms. "Candice sent the picture."

"Why?"

"Kash, you can't keep doing this to each other."

I scoffed and turned back toward my room before spinning right back around and pointing the picture at myself. "I'm only doing exactly what she asked me to!"

"You're both too damn stubborn to get over your own problems with the situation, but you both want each other. This is so fucking stupid! Grow a pair and go get her!"

Crumpling up the picture, I dropped it and the box on the sofa. "Mase, this ends. Now."

Rachel

I STOOD UNSTEADILY and waited for the feeling to come back into my legs before bending over and pressing my fingers to my lips and then the headstones. "Bye, Mom and Dad," I whispered, and wiped the tears from my cheeks as I made my way back to Candice's car, which I'd borrowed.

It'd taken me almost four and a half years to finally visit my parents' graves, but I'd done it. I was happy I had gone and spent hours talking to them instead of writing today; it almost felt like I'd just gotten closure that I hadn't realized I'd needed. I let my right hand trail over my worn journal sitting in the passenger seat next to me and smiled. I would always be glad I had finally gone, but my journals were all I needed. They helped me feel connected to my parents in a way those headstones never could.

Turning the car off when I got into the driveway of the Jenkins home, I stepped out and zipped up my hoodie as the cooler January air hit me and started making my way across the long walkway. It wasn't freezing by any means—this was Southern California—but they were having a lot cooler weather than Texas had been having when we left. I was thankful for it though; I was able to hide the scars on my arms from Candice and her family much more easily this way.

Eli opened the door before I got there and flashed a crooked smile as I quickened my pace and wrapped my arms around his waist. "Candice told me where you went," was all he said after he kissed the top of my head. And I knew he wouldn't say anything else; that's just how he was. So I smiled and turned us to walk into the house.

"Yeah, and it was good. I'm glad I did it. Did you bring Paisley with you?"

Eli's face lit up at the mention of his girlfriend and I loved seeing that look on him. He'd always dated a lot of girls, but we didn't meet many of them, and if we did it was usually by accident. But Paisley had come with him to all the holiday dinners, plus some others, over the last week and a half, and it wasn't hard to see that Eli adored her.

"I did, Mom's trying to teach her to cook right now . . . so I'm staying out of the kitchen."

I laughed and bumped his side as I removed my jacket and made sure my wrists were still covered by my long-sleeved shirt.

"She's moving in with me as soon as her lease ends next month," he said a little sheepishly.

"Really? Eli, that's great!"

His eyes flickered over toward the kitchen and he smiled again. "Yeah, I think so too. You know, I finally realized one day that if I didn't grab her for myself, someone else would. And I knew I wouldn't be able to handle the thought of her with anyone but me."

My forehead creased as he led me back toward the bedrooms. I'd already heard all about him and Paisley getting together. She'd been in love with him for years, and he'd been too stupid to realize or do anything about it until just recently. So why was he telling me this again?

"I hadn't realized how empty I was without her until the moment it hit me that I might not be able to spend the rest of my life with her."

"I know, Eli . . ." I drew the words out slowly as we walked. "I really am happy for you." *Is he questioning that?* I laughed softly, trying to lighten the conversation. "I'm glad you finally pulled your stubborn head out of your ass."

"Glad you feel that way, sis," he said with the most serious expression as he put his hands on my shoulders and pushed me in front of him.

I turned to see Candice staring at me expectantly, and my mouth popped open to ask what was going on when Eli suddenly pushed me down in Candice's chair at her desk. "Sheesh, Eli. What is wrong with you?"

His hands let up a little on my shoulders but didn't move away, and Candice came to my side to fully open the half-closed laptop on her desk. As soon as I focused on the screen, I tried to stand up, but Eli slammed me back down, not even trying to be gentle.

"What is this?"

Candice and Eli snorted. It was so identical it was creepy. And the Skype version of Mason on the laptop smiled softly. "Just part two of our intervention." When I narrowed my eyes at him, his smile turned sheepish. "Hey there, sweetheart."

My eyes started burning and my throat tightened. *Oh my word, what is wrong with me?* I blinked quickly and crossed my arms under my chest as I tried to hold my glare. "What do you want, Mase?"

"I want to know if you're still in love with my best friend."

"I'm not."

"Liar," all three said at once.

"You're miserable," Eli said at the same time Candice huffed. "You just told me last month you would always love him."

"Traitors," I whispered, and looked back to Mason since he was being quiet.

He just continued to look at me for what felt like minutes

before saying anything. "I can see it in your eyes, Rach. They're the same as Kash's. Empty."

"It's the lens on the laptop." I shrugged, but it was an awkward movement since Eli was still holding me to the chair. "Makes everyone look like that."

"Bullshit. So next question."

"Ha. No, one was more than enough. We're done, Mason." I tried to stand but Eli wasn't letting me budge. I unlocked my arms and reached for the laptop, but Candice smacked them down and pushed the laptop out of my reach.

"Why are you still doing this to each other? He's miserable without you. Do you know that he tried to quit his job? That's how fucked up he is right now, Rach."

"That's not my problem!" I snapped. "He *lied* to me. He let me believe all of these false things about both of you, and you know what, Mase? I'm mad at you too! You were going to let me marry him when you knew I didn't know a damn thing about him? You told me I reminded you of your sister; would you let your sister do something like that— Wait. Do you even have a sister?!"

"I do, she's a year older than you. We told you as many truths as we could, Rachel. I was pissed when the two of you got engaged—not because I didn't want you together," he hurried to say, "but because of the fact that we were still undercover and you didn't know who we really were. He fell for you hard and fast; nothing was going to be enough until you were completely his, and he got caught up in it. He wouldn't have married you before you knew everything, I know that for a fact. I promise you, he's killing himself for ever keeping anything from you."

I wanted to say something like *good* but I couldn't. I hated that

Kash was miserable. I hated what he'd done to me, but the fact that he was hurting . . . hurt me more.

"But you don't understand, Rach. When we came to Austin, we were hiding from a hit placed on both of us for some under-cover work we did here in Florida. We didn't have a choice about going by false names; we didn't even have a choice about moving to Austin. We had to leave the night we found out about it. Be-cause of the case we were on, we were going undercover *again,* to find the Carnation killer. Our jobs were set up for us; once again, we didn't have a say, but this is what Kash and I did for close to four years. We would go undercover, and we would be whatever they needed us to be. And once the hit on us was gone, we both agreed we still couldn't let you girls know, it was too dangerous. Obviously."

I winced and Mason grimaced.

"Kash tried to fight his feelings for you in the beginning, though. I swear he was constantly lecturing me on why we can't have relationships, and I know it was to try to remind himself why he couldn't be with you. But he's never met anyone like you, he couldn't stay away from you . . . and I know all you see is that he lied to you, but you didn't see how much the lies killed him during the time you two were together. Like I said, I was mad when he told me you were engaged, and I know that's one of the things that hurts you the most. Try to look at it from his side though: with the kind of undercover work we've done, and just being in law enforcement in general, we see a lot of death. We know life is short. So we don't waste it."

"But he shouldn't—"

"Hold on, Rach . . . let me finish. There was this girl Kash had dated for a long time, and he told me he was going to ask her to marry him when we got out of our first undercover assignment. By the time we got out, she was engaged to someone else. He never once looked at Megan the way he looked at you, and when he found out about her engagement, he wished her the best, knowing the other guy could give her the life she needed. Sure, he was upset, but it was nothing compared to what is happening to him still after all these months without you. So try to see it from his side, and know that he'd found the girl who meant the world to him. He wanted it all with you. Should he have waited to ask you to marry him until you knew the truth? Yeah, he should've. But he didn't; he was too in love with you to wait."

Silent tears were streaming down my face and I brought up my hands to try to wipe them away, but it was useless. They wouldn't stop.

Swallowing past the lump in my throat, I spoke softly. "I just don't know, Mason. He—what he did hurt me worse than anything has in my life. And he could easily do it again."

I watched as he reached forward and guessed he was touching my image on the screen. "I can promise you all day long that he wouldn't. But you're the one who has to decide to trust him. I know you're hurting, sweetheart . . . he is too. None of us can stand this for either of you. I've tried to get him to go to you, but he won't. He thinks that he's hurt you enough for one lifetime and that his job is too dangerous for you. He honestly believes he can't give you a life you deserve. He's always going to blame himself for what happened to you." He ended on a whisper.

A sob broke through and I buried my face in my hands.

"Rach, one of you has to end this, and he thinks he's protecting you by staying away."

My chest tightened in pain and a wave of what can only be described as the deepest sorrow I've ever known washed over my body. This full-body ache had become so familiar to me over the last four months, but it never once got any easier to deal with. Each time it knocked the air from my body just as it had the first time, and every time it took a little longer for the ache to subside.

Can people die from a broken heart?

I don't think so. But I do know that when you keep yourself, or are kept, from the person who holds your heart, your body cripples under the knowledge that it isn't whole and won't be until you're with them again.

Minutes passed as I stayed curled in on myself, and at some point, Eli pulled me up into his arms and sat back in the chair with me in his lap. "Rach," he whispered, "I finally pulled my head out of my ass . . . are you ready to do the same?"

20

Kash

"MASE? I'M HOME." I loosened my tie and unbuttoned the first two buttons on my shirt.

"Did you tell your mom I want more banana nut bread?"

I huffed a laugh and opened the fridge to grab a bottled water. "I did. She said if you come visit she'll make some."

"All right. Well, I'll see you later." He grabbed his keys off the counter and headed toward the door.

"Whoa. Wait. What? She's not going to make you some to-night. And you told me to get back here immediately and now you're leaving? I only see my parents once a week and I'd just barely gotten there."

"Yeah, well . . . I gotta go. I'll probably see you tomorrow. Or something."

My jaw dropped as I watched him walk out the door. I'd just spent all day in court and then missed a home-cooked meal for that? *Fuck this. I'm changing and going back over there. You just don't pass up my mom's cooking for no reason.*

Walking quickly into my room, I yanked off my tie and shirt and had begun taking my badge, gun, and cuffs off my belt when my eyes finally noticed the new item on my dresser. My heart skipped a couple painful beats before drumming quickly. My chest tightened and I had to force myself to set the cuffs down before grabbing the mason jar sitting there. It was full of Sour Patch Kids—only the green ones. I squeezed my eyes shut when I felt another person come into the room and swore that if Mason was playing a trick on me, or just trying to get me to go see her again, I'd shoot him.

Blowing out a deep breath, I turned slowly and looked up to see Rachel standing there, looking more beautiful than I remembered. Before any type of hope could fill me, the memory of our last conversation replayed in my mind and pain sliced through my chest. I hadn't seen her in just over four months, and not one day in that time had passed without my wishing I could go back and change everything.

Neither of us said anything, we just stared at each other. But then her eyes filled with tears and they spilled over, and I couldn't stay away from her anymore. I didn't know what she was doing here, and I didn't know what she wanted from me. All I knew was that I loved her more now than I had when I left, and my girl was crying.

"Rachel," I breathed when I pulled her into my arms.

A sob hitched in her throat and she buried her face in my neck, her arms tightening around my waist when I kissed the top of her head. I breathed in her sweet scent and almost thanked God out loud for bringing her back to me. Walking us toward the bed, I sat down and pulled her onto my lap before wrapping my arms around her again. I didn't say anything; I was afraid to. Right then, she was in my arms, and I knew how quickly that could change. So I would keep her there and try to prolong the moment while I memorized the way her body felt against mine.

"I'm sorry," she whispered, and pulled away.

I started to keep her there but knew she wasn't mine to keep, so I gritted my teeth and let her slide off my lap and to the other side of the bed.

"I—that wasn't—I wasn't going to cry. I wanted to talk to you, and I had this whole thing planned out that I was going to say, but then I saw you and . . . and I'm just sorry. That wasn't sup-posed to happen."

I didn't know how to respond to what she was saying. Rachel was here, in Florida. She'd come to me. If she wanted to say something bad, she wouldn't have come to the other side of the U.S., right? She would have called, or . . . well, she would have just continued to not talk to me.

"How are you?" It was one of the worst questions I could have come up with. But it was better than letting loose with the dozens of others I was dying to ask.

Her mouth opened but then snapped shut, and her eyes drifted to something behind me as she thought. "Honestly, I'm not okay."

My fault. It's my fault she's not okay. My stomach twisted and I had to clench the comforter so I wouldn't grab for her.

"The thing that happened with Blake, I'm doing better with.

I have nightmares every now and then. But they're really rare. I went back to work for the rest of the semester, and I decided I'm not going to enroll in classes next semester because I really only went to stay with Candice. I hate what I was majoring in and don't want to do anything with it." She smiled shakily and glanced at me. "And I finally visited my parents' grave."

"That's great. I'm really proud of you."

"I hated you," she whispered suddenly, and it felt like someone had shot me all over again. "Since the phone call I made to Candice after I found out about it, I'd never told anyone about my parents. I never wanted to. And granted, I told you in a fight, but I realized after that I'd wanted you to know. I wanted you to know everything about me. You always saw through my bullshit, and you didn't let me hide. I loved that about you."

My eyes shut and a harsh breath left me at her use of the past tense.

"I was trying so hard to cling to the thought of you coming to save me," she said, choking, and had to clear her throat. "When you ran into that house . . . God, I just remember thinking, *He's here, he came for me.* But then it hit me what you were saying, who you were with, and I—I couldn't even focus on Blake anymore. My heart shattered when I realized that you'd lied to me. And when I woke up, all I knew was that I'd fallen in love with a lie. You'd broken down every wall I had so that there was nothing between us, and I didn't even know who you were, Kash," she whispered, and wiped at a few new tears.

"Rachel, I couldn't tell you—"

"I know. Mason and Candice told me everything. I know about the hit, all your undercover work. I know. But you should have never pursued a serious relationship with me when you were hiding something that big. And you should have never asked me to marry you. If you couldn't give me you, you should have never asked me to give myself to you. That wasn't fair to me."

"I'm sorry for not telling you. But I loved you then, and I love you now . . . I'll never be sorry for asking you to marry me." Her eyes shut and she took a deep breath in, and before she could respond, I said the words I'd been thinking since the second Detective Ryder put West's picture in my hand. "I'm so sorry I didn't keep you safe, Rachel."

Her eyes flew open. "Are—"

"I hate myself for letting that happen to you. I swore I would never let him, or anyone else, touch you again, and I couldn't even keep that promise."

"Kash, stop." Her blue eyes were searching my face incredulously. "How can you even say any of that? You saved me. I owe you my life—"

I shook my head. "You don't owe me anything."

"Yes, I do. That's the reason I'm here."

I flinched. *The reason she's here is because she feels like she owes me her life? I have to live through the heartbreak again for this?* Getting off the bed, I ran my hands through my hair roughly and growled as I paced, "I don't want you to feel like you owe me shit. That was my *job,* Rachel. I was supposed to find him before he could hurt anyone else, not come in at the last minute and fucking save you! You should have never been there in the first place! I literally watched you walk away with a killer, and I did nothing." I stopped pacing with my back to her, planted my shaking fists on my hips, and hung my head. "The minute I realized I was in love with you, my purpose in life changed to taking care of you . . . to keeping you safe . . . and to loving you. I failed at almost all of those, along with my job. So no, Rachel, you don't owe me a damn thing. And I'm sorry you came all this way because you felt like you did."

"Kash," she said softly, "I didn't come here because I felt like I owed you something. I meant you saving me is the reason I'm here . . . here as in *alive*. And I do owe you my life, but that's not why I'm in Florida, in your bedroom. I'm here because I'm miserable."

God, I knew how she felt.

"Like I said, I'm moving on from what happened and I've healed more in the last few months from my parents' death than I did in four years. But I feel like I'm lost. I tried telling myself that you and I were all wrong for each other and that I couldn't forgive you for what you did. I kept saying that *tomorrow* it wouldn't hurt so much and tried to convince myself that you were moving on with your life because you never cared about me."

I turned quickly to tell her how wrong she was, but she kept talking.

"But I finally realized that even with the lies, what you and I had was more real than anything I've ever experienced. And no matter how hard I tried, I couldn't fool myself into thinking that I could ever get over you." She licked her lips and looked at me before looking at her lap. "I told you that first night we were together that you made me feel like I was in love and terrified at the same time. And that's still true. I'm terrified at the depth of my feelings for you. I'm terrified of how easily you can hurt me. And I'm *terrified* of living the rest of my life without you. I physically moved on with my life, but a part of me died each day I was away from you."

My breathing was heavy as I stared at her. She was still looking at her lap and I needed to see her, I needed to know what this meant for us. Squatting down in front of her, I placed my hands on either side of her hips on the bed and looked at those beautiful blue eyes. "Rachel, what are you saying?"

"I'm saying I can't live without you. I still love you." Her words were so soft they were almost inaudible, but I'd heard, and it was all I needed to know.

I sat up and crushed my mouth to hers as I laid her back on the bed and hovered over her. Her hands gripped my shirt and she moaned my name before deepening the kiss.

"I've missed you so much," I whispered against her skin, and sucked on that sensitive spot behind her ear. "Forgive me, Rachel."

Her breath hitched as I made my way back to her lips. They trembled against mine and I opened my eyes.

"Babe, why are you crying?" I brushed the tears away and held her face in my hands.

"I don't know." A sound that was half laugh and half sob left her. "I feel like I'm being ridiculous right now, but I'm just happy. I feel like everything is right again. God, that sounds so stupid and cliché."

"You're not being ridiculous." I kissed her forehead before brushing my lips against her cheek to catch more tears. "And you're right, that is pretty cliché." She laughed and pushed against my chest. I just smiled and kissed her nose. "But I feel the exact same way." Pressing my lips to hers once more, I rolled to the side and pulled her so she was facing me. "My name is Logan Ryan, but everyone calls me Kash," I said, and she laughed softly. "I was born and raised in Tampa Bay, Florida, and for almost four and a half years now I've worked in law enforcement. I'll be twenty-six soon and don't have any siblings. I'll do just about anything for pancakes and green Sour Patch Kids." She smiled and I stroked her jaw with my thumb. "And I *will* do anything to make sure I never lose you again."

"My name is Rachel Lynn Masters, I'm twenty-one, and I'm from Yorba Linda, California . . . formerly known as far West Texas." She winked and wiggled closer to me. For a few moments she just looked at me before taking a big breath and laying the rest of it out there. "I don't know what I want to do for the rest of my life, but I know that whatever it is, I want to do it with you." Closing the distance between us, she kissed me softly and spoke against my mouth. "I forgive you, but no more lies."

"None."

She leaned away and propped herself up on an elbow. "I'm serious, Kash. Not even the forgiving lies to save me from getting my feelings hurt. If I ask you if my butt looks big, you can't lie."

"Woman, you barely even have an ass. That was the worst example you could have used."

Rachel grinned wryly and launched herself at me. Rolling so she was on top of me, I pulled her close and kissed her deeply. She groaned when I nipped at her bottom lip and I reveled in the taste of her.

I'd missed everything about her, and I wanted nothing more than to spend the rest of the night worshipping her body, but I couldn't believe that she was even here, and I didn't want to push anything. Forcing my hands to stay on her hips was damn hard, but she was calling the shots right now.

She dragged her teeth against my jaw, and my fingers flexed on her hips. She laughed low before whispering in my ear, "I need you. Now. Stop holding back."

No need to tell me twice. I flipped us over so her back was to the bed, grabbed the bottom of her shirt, and yanked it off her body. My hands went to the button on her jeans and my mouth went to her right, lace-covered breast at the same time she pulled my undershirt off me and attacked my belt.

Worshipping her was going to have to wait until later. I didn't have the patience for that just yet.

I finally got the button and zipper undone and had just started pulling off her jeans when I saw it and I wanted to die. "God, Rach." My body froze and one of my hands slowly came up to trace the scars covering her stomach. "I'm sor—"

"Don't. It's not your fault." Her hands left my hips and cupped my cheeks, pulling my head up to look into her beautifully pained blue eyes. "Okay?"

Shaking my head, I kissed the inside of her wrist and pulled it back when I remembered. I looked at the long scar running up her wrist and let my lips trail the length of it before grabbing her other arm and doing the same. "Rachel, you're beautiful," I said softly, and leaned down to kiss the scarred word above her left breast. "And I love you." Crawling farther down, I kissed every inch of the scars on her stomach and vowed, "Somehow, I will make up for every mark he ever put on your body."

Frenzied passion forgotten, I spent the rest of the night loving and worshipping every part of her.

Rachel

I SLIPPED OUT of Kash's bed and tiptoed around his room looking for my clothes, which had been thrown around last night. My eyes landed on the midnight-blue button-down shirt he'd been wearing when he walked in and I shrugged into it, buttoning only a few of the middle buttons. I walked back over to the bed, kissed his cheek, and quietly walked out into the living room, shutting his bedroom door behind me.

After walking into Mason's empty room and grabbing my purse, I pulled out my phone and decided against checking the dozens of texts and voice mails Candice had left, and called her instead.

"Mmm 'lo?"

I looked at the clock in the kitchen and figured it was almost eight in California. "Sorry for waking you, Candi."

She gasped and I heard rustling. "No, no. It's fine, I've been waiting for you to call. Tell me everything— *Wait.* What time is it?!" I heard her counting, "Almost eleven there? Does that mean it went well?"

A blush stained my cheeks and I bit back a smile. "Yeah, you could say that."

"I knew it would!" she squealed. "So you guys are back together? Did you tell him you want to move there?"

"Ah, no, I didn't exactly say those words. But I will today. I'm pretty sure from how it went last night it was kind of assumed I want to be here with him." After searching through all the cabinets, I finally found the skillet and pulled it out, but a bunch of the pans in there clanked together. "Shit. Shh." I winced and hushed the pots and pans.

"What are you doing?" Candice whispered, like she needed to be quiet too.

"I'm making pancakes. But Kash is still asleep."

"Pfft. Figures. He should be making *you* pancakes."

I paused with my hand on the pancake mix and thought back over everything Kash had done for me last night. "That man definitely deserves pancakes." My voice got breathy and a huge smile crossed my face.

"Tell. Me. Everything!"

"Do I, now?" a husky voice asked from behind me.

I gasped and whirled around to face Kash, who was looking sexier than any man had a right to in nothing but a pair of gray boxer-briefs.

"Candice . . . ," I said.

"Go! Go, and call me later. I want details! Love you."

"Love you back." I had barely pressed the *end* button when Kash pushed me up against the counter and claimed my mouth. "Morning." I giggled against his lips when he lifted me onto the counter.

"You weren't there when I woke up," he said, and ran his hands over my bare thighs.

"I wanted to make you breakfast."

"I can see that. Lie back, Rachel."

My eyes widened but I didn't say anything as he gently pushed me back until I was lying on the counter, my legs hanging off the end. When he spread my legs farther and I felt his breath on me, my heart instantly sped up and then began skipping beats when he hooked my legs over his shoulders.

"Kash!" I gasped and my back tried to arch off the granite

when he swiped his tongue against me in one long stroke. He laughed softly against me and the things the vibrations did to me were almost enough to send me over the edge right then. My body heated and the knot in my lower stomach tightened as he continued to work me with his tongue, and just as I began shivering in anticipation, he added his fingers and my body shattered.

He rode me through my orgasm, and when my body fell limp, he gently lowered my legs, sat me up, and scooted me to the very edge of the counter before filling me with his length. I hadn't even realized he'd taken his boxer-briefs off. I cried out and wrapped my arms around his shoulders to attempt to hold on as he teased me by alternating between slow and gentle strokes, and slamming into me hard and fast, over and over again. When that familiar tightening started low in my stomach, I begged him to go faster and growled in frustration when he would get me as close to the edge as possible and then back off completely. I caught sight of his wicked grin and vowed to return the favor. Soon. Resting his forehead against my neck, he quickened and held his pace as my fingernails dug into his back. A pleasured scream started tearing through my chest as I crashed down around him and I bit down on his shoulder to muffle any other noises I might make as he continued to drive into me until he found his release inside me.

We stayed just like that as our breathing returned to normal, and Kash peppered my neck and throat with soft kisses. "Amazing breakfast, babe."

I laughed but quickly broke off when I felt it where I was aching from the multiple orgasms I'd had last night and this morning. "Smart-ass."

"Go wash up, I'll clean the counter."

When I came back out to the kitchen, he was just about to pour some pancake batter on the skillet. Smiling widely at me, he sat the bowl back down and pulled me into his arms before placing a kiss on my jaw and lips. "We need to talk about a few things."

I raised an eyebrow at him and wrapped my arms around his narrow hips. "Do we?"

"Now that you're healing from your parents' death, do you want to be in California?" I shook my head and he continued. "Then will you move here to be with me?"

"I'd, uh, already kind of planned on it."

"All right." He huffed a soft laugh. "We'll start looking for a place for just us. And I want this time to be different for us, Rach. I love you more now than I did before, but I'm going to wait until I know you're ready before I ask you again. I just need you to know now that I do plan on marrying you; that has not changed for me at all."

" 'Kay." I smiled at him and wiggled closer.

"I want you to meet my parents . . . today or tomorrow, it doesn't matter, but soon. I know they'll love you."

My heart started racing and I nodded my head against his chest.

"Every day for the rest of our lives, I want you to spend the mornings in nothing but my shirt." I laughed and he tightened his arms around me. "And we really need to talk about getting you on birth control. Because after last night and this morning, I don't know how I could ever go back to using a condom with you."

"But I am on birth control."

He jerked his head back and tilted mine up to look at him, his brow furrowed. "Then why am I always wearing one?"

I shrugged. "Neither is one hundred percent effective, and since Candice was always with guys I made her use both so she wouldn't have mini Candices running around. I guess my own argument just followed me."

His scowl deepened. "Do you want to marry me?"

"Yes."

"Do you want to have kids with me?"

"Someday," I whispered.

"Do you ever miss taking your pill?"

"Never."

His gray eyes turned silver and the heat in them warmed my body. "Bed. Now. We're never using condoms again."

"Pancakes?" I argued miserably.

He turned off the skillet, put the batter in the fridge, and pointed in the direction of his bedroom. "We'll make them later. Go."

"But—"

"Woman, I just found out that you've been on the Pill this whole time. Right now I'm struggling not to spank the hell out of you. Last time I'm going to tell you." He leaned in close and ordered gruffly, "Bed, Rachel. Now."

Goose bumps covered my skin and a pleasant shiver made its way through my body as I turned to leave the kitchen. I'd barely made it two steps when his hand came down across my butt, which was still covered in his shirt. "Whoa!" I yelled, and covered myself with my hands as I turned to face him. "Ow! That hurt, you jerk!" I went to smack him but he caught my hand and smiled as he kissed my palm.

"Don't lie, Sour Patch, you enjoyed it." When he lifted me

up, I automatically wrapped my legs around his hips and let him walk me back to the bedroom. "And you're gonna get another one for making me take you to the bed."

I didn't even try to argue. The way his heated eyes mixed with that arrogant smile I'd fallen in love with made for one delicious combination. And I decided right then that I liked this side of Kash.

Epilogue

Four months later . . .

Kash

"You good?" I asked Mason as we headed back toward the elevators.

He shrugged and punched at the buttons on the wall. "There's only so much you can do to get them to go in a different direction. He wanted to follow his brother."

We'd gotten a call late last night from homicide detectives about a murder that looked gang related. It had ended up being a drive-by involving a newer gang that we'd come across recently, and one of the two victims was a thirteen-year-old Mason had been trying to get off the streets over the last few months named Lil Tay. And though Mason was acting like this was just another case, I knew this was harder for him than the rest.

Knowing there was nothing I could say, I clapped his shoulder and let him be alone with his thoughts. Grabbing my phone, I smiled when I finally saw Rachel's text from last night.

> SOUR PATCH:
>
> *Just so you know . . . cleaning up from a whipped cream war without you isn't nearly as fun. See you when you get home. Love you.*
>
> *We just finished up, be home soon babe. Love you too.*

Rachel had moved to Tampa Bay the week after she showed up in my apartment and I'd never been happier. My parents loved her just as much as she loved them, and she fit in with my life well. Mason's younger sister and Rachel were practically inseparable and his parents viewed her as an extension of their family, the same way they did me.

Candice was graduating at the end of this month and we were taking a two-week vacation to be there and spend time with the Jenkinses in California before Candice came back with us for a month. Rachel couldn't wait to see her, and honestly, I think Mason was excited to have that particular hookup back.

Work was going well; Mase and I—as well as our parents— were happy we were out of the inner parts of narcotics. Living that way isn't something that any cop would want; the reward of bringing down an entire drug ring was what had made it worthwhile. For us to go to the gang division was natural. We knew the ins and outs of different gangs, already knew a lot of the members, and were no longer undercover. It was perfect for us, and we were good at what we did. Most importantly, Rachel supported me one hundred percent.

A month after Rachel had moved here, I'd asked her to marry me again. This time, there was absolutely nothing between us and everything about it felt different . . . felt right. We talked about everything, there were never secrets kept unless there was a surprise involved, and there were never any lies. And even when my family and Mason's asked for her side of the story about our time in Texas and when we broke up, Rachel never held it against me. She'd gotten everything out the night she came here and left it there. She wasn't one to hold grudges, and I loved her for it. I would always hate myself for what happened, but whenever I started to bring it up, she would kiss me to shut me up and say we were moving forward.

We were getting married at the end of June, and Rachel and my mom had been busy planning the wedding since we set the date. I loved that she was enjoying this and that she was going to get the wedding she deserved, but I didn't care about the details. I just wanted her to be mine, and in a month and a half, she would be.

The doors to the elevator opened and we stepped in. Just as they were closing, someone started yelling my name from down the hall and Mason caught the door just in time.

"Ryan! Gates!" Sergeant Ramirez ran toward us and as soon as he was in the elevator, he started pounding on the *Close Doors* button.

I suppressed a groan. I was exhausted and wanted to get home to my fiancée.

"We already have three units at the scene, and I'll be following you there."

Ramirez was a K-9 unit; why did they want his dog, Crush, there? And what scene? "Wha—"

"I know you're anxious to get there, but you know we're doing everything we can for this." The elevator was already moving but Ramirez kept stabbing at the ground-level button. "How are you holding up? You look really calm, are you in shock? Maybe you should let Gates drive."

That seemed to snap Mason out of his thoughts. His head jerked up and his eyes widened. "Why would I need to drive?"

"And why would I be in shock?" My heart started racing as Ramirez started hitting the *Open Doors* button.

Ramirez gave both of us an awkward sympathetic look before ushering us out to the underground parking lot. "You weren't informed?"

"Of what?" I was supposed to be the one in shock. So it had something to do with me. *My parents, my— Oh God . . .* "What happened?!"

"I'm sorry, I thought someone already told you, you were supposed to be informed already. I didn't understand why I saw you two walking down the hall. I figured you would have already been there." He mumbled to himself as he kept walking toward the lot. "Look, I'm sorry I'm the one who has to tell you this." He stopped walking abruptly and turned to look at me. His expression was one I had seen so many times and had even had to use myself. My stomach dropped and it felt like time slowed as I waited for him to tell me one of fifty scenarios that were flashing through my mind. "A call came into dispatch about an hour ago. It was your fiancée, Ryan. The only thing that came from her end of the call was her saying her name, that someone had broken in—"

I didn't wait to hear the rest. I took off running for my truck and had just gotten to the driver's door when Mason slammed me into the side and ripped the keys from my hand. After barking at me to get in the passenger seat, he fired up the engine and peeled out of the lot.

"This isn't happening. This isn't happening, Mase, tell me this isn't fucking happening!"

"Kash—"

"Damn it!" I roared, and punched at the dashboard. "I don't even know if she's okay, Mason! What was Ramirez saying, did he say if she's okay?! Is she—oh God. Rach, baby, please be alive," I whispered, and slumped into my seat, raking my hands over my face.

I heard Mason on the phone calling into dispatch and asking questions about what happened, but I couldn't focus on his exact words or the muffled response coming from the dispatcher. I just kept praying over and over again that she was okay. I could deal with our place being broken into. I could replace our things. But I couldn't replace Rachel. Ramirez came up next to us running code three and pulled in front of us so we could follow him safely with his lights and sirens going.

Mason nudged my arm and I snapped my head to the left to look at him. "Sorry, you weren't responding." He looked quickly back and forth between me and Ramirez's Tahoe in front of us, his face solemn. "They don't know if she's alive." I sucked in air quickly, and Mason continued, loud enough so I would listen. "But there's no blood. So just focus on that, Kash."

"W-what?! No . . . what do you mean?"

He took a deep breath and gripped the steering wheel. "From what units at the scene—uh, your place—are saying, whoever broke in . . . they, uh, they took Rachel."

Mason was saying something else, but I couldn't hear anything past the blood rushing through my ears. This had to be a nightmare. There was no way something like this was happening to us again. I grabbed my phone and called her number, praying that all this was a misunderstanding and they had the wrong girl, the wrong address. It rang until her voice mail picked up. I quickly hung up and called again with the same result.

By the time her voice mail came on the second time, we were pulling up to our house and I didn't wait for Mason to stop; I threw open the door and sprinted past the neighbors standing around in our cul-de-sac and ducked under the crime-scene tape before rushing into the house. The front door was hanging like it had been kicked in, and my first thought was, *No one heard that happening and came to help her?* It had been barely eight in the morning when Mason and I had started to head home; someone had to have been awake, or at least woken up when all this happened.

Officers were trying to talk to me, but all I could see was that other than the front door being kicked in, the front of our house looked completely normal. Save for the dozens of officers and detectives who were walking in and out of it. Someone tapped my shoulder but I walked quickly to the hallway, barely paying attention to the other officers taking pictures of our bedroom, which looked like a hurricane had just gone through it. I turned into the bathroom and went to the large closet. We had a faux wall set up that was really just flimsy material. But with all the clothes around it, it looked legit, and I'd put it up for times just like this. Rachel had joked that I was going overboard, and at the time I'd agreed I probably was. But now, I hoped like hell she'd used it and that I would find her behind it. Alive.

Opening the closet door, I flipped on the light, and my heart sank when I saw the drag marks on the carpet. I called one of the officers over to take pictures before I walked in there. The female officer snapped photos and I stepped in cautiously.

"Rach?" I said softly. *Please, God, be in here.* "Rach?" With one last breath, I grabbed the edge of the faux wall and yanked it back. I sank to my knees and a sound of pain left my chest as my eyes fell on our puppy, Trip, backed into the corner whining softly. There was no Rachel. She was really gone. "C'mere." I grabbed him and pulled him into my chest as I fell back against the wall and the tears that had been threatening started spilling over.

"Kash, you need to see this," Mason said softly from the doorway to the closet. I looked over at him, rolled to my knees, and stood. "Give me Trip. Go into the bedroom and look at the wall. We'll find her, okay? I swear to you we'll find her."

I handed him the golden retriever and rushed into the bedroom, my eyes widening when they finally landed on the wall opposite our bed. A roar filled the room, and before I could realize it had come from me, two officers were holding me back and trying to get me to sit down on the bed.

On the wall in red spray paint were the words *DID YOU THINK WE WOULD FORGET?* Underneath was a symbol both Mason and I'd had tattooed on our left forearms before we'd gotten them covered up. The sign for Juarez's gang, the one we'd had to join on our last undercover narcotics assignment.

"How?" Mason was asking a detective who was in the room with us. And that was a damn good question. The hit on Mase and me had died when the guys hired were thrown in prison for murder. And I knew for a fact Juarez and his boys were all in prison. "Recruiting people from the inside who got out? Or just using people he trusts? Set up questioning with each of them separately."

I looked up when Detective Byson's cell rang. His mouth snapped shut as he stopped talking to Mason and took the call. "Byson." His eyes flashed over to me and a grim look crossed his face as he listened. "Mmm-hmm . . . Yeah. Set up something with Romero Juarez and his attorney immediately. I'm on my way." He turned to face me fully and slid his phone back in the holder on his belt. "Rachel is alive."

"Thank God," I breathed, and tried to stand, but the officers were still holding me there.

"A call was placed about fifteen minutes ago, they said they had Rachel and demanded that every charge against Juarez's gang be dropped. Before the dispatcher could ask anything, the caller said they would call back in two days and expected progress on the charges being dropped, and would continue to call every two days until the gang was released. They said if there wasn't progress, there would be consequences, and if they aren't released within the month . . . she dies."

"Kash, Kash, Kash, calm down. Come on, man. Calm down. I know."

Mason gripped my shoulders and I tried to focus on him. The other two officers were now struggling to keep me down as I thrashed against them. Where I was going to go when I got away from them, I didn't know; I just needed to go. They had my girl. I needed to find out who *they* were and I needed to get her back.

"I know this is hard. But we'll find her. I swear." Mason looked just as panicked as I felt, and it was then I noticed the wetness in his eyes he was trying to keep back.

When I finally stopped struggling, the officers let me go at Mason's request, but he kept me seated on the bed. "I need to get her back, Mason. I have to."

"We will."

"I'll do anything."

A determined look settled over his face and he whispered low enough that only I could hear him, "Anything to bring the fuckers down, right?"

I slammed my fist against his and replied, "Always."

The End for Now . . .

Want more Kash and Rachel?

Keep reading for a sneak peek of
Deceiving Lies!

Prologue

Rachel

I NERVOUSLY FLIPPED my long hair over my shoulders and smoothed my hands down my shirt a few times as I took deep breaths in and out. My back was to Kash's truck, hiding me from his parents' house while I collected myself, but I was starting to consider taking off running. *Why the hell did I buy and wear heels today?*

"Rach?" He laughed when he came around the truck and caught sight of me. "What are you doing? You look amazing."

I grimaced when I glanced down at my dark, skinny jeans and electric blue top that I'd gone out to buy today, since I hadn't brought any clothes to Florida that I'd deemed acceptable to meet his parents in. "It's not the clothes."

He grabbed my chin and tilted my head back until I was looking at him, and waited until I stopped fidgeting. "They're going to love you," he assured me as he brushed his lips across mine. "You have nothing to worry about."

"How can you say that? I was engaged to their son without ever meeting them, they hardly knew I existed, Kash." *And I got their son shot* . . . I knew it wasn't my fault, my therapy sessions with Dr. Markowitz at the end of last year had helped me realize that. But that didn't mean Kash and Mason's family would feel the same. "Honestly, at the time I just thought you weren't close with them, it didn't seem weird to me because, well . . . because I didn't have parents for you to meet either. But now—"

"Stop. You're overthinking this, they know everything that happened now, and you have no idea how excited my mom was when I called her this morning to tell her you were here. Right now, they're just happy because they know I've been miserable without you. But, babe, they're going to love you."

I exhaled roughly and nodded my head. "Okay, let's do this."

"That's my girl." He kissed me hard before wrapping his arm around my waist and walking me toward the house. "I mean, honestly, how could they not love you and your bitchy personality?"

"You're such an asshole, Kash," I hissed at the same second the front door opened and his mom stepped out. *Oh good Lord, kill me now. This is where I need to run away.*

Mrs. Ryan's eyebrows shot up to her hairline and Kash tried to choke back his laugh but failed miserably. It felt like my stomach was simultaneously on fire and dropping. Not a good feeling, I was going to be sick. I was the freaking Queen of first impressions with the Ryan family. When I'd met Kash at the beginning of last summer, I'd been a bitch to the extreme and our first three run-ins had gone over about as well as a bale of turtles in a sprinting race. Now there I was cussing in front of his mom in the first seconds of ever seeing her.

I started feeling lightheaded as I held my breath waiting for Mrs. Ryan to tell me I was not good enough for her son, or to reprimand me. Instead, she crossed her arms over her chest and leveled a glare at Kash that impressed even me.

"What on earth did you say to the poor girl?"

He raised his hands in surrender before wrapping his arm around me again. "No clue what you're talking about. And why do you automatically think it had to be something I did?"

"Because I know you, Logan."

"Eh . . . so anyway. Mom, this is Rachel. Rachel, this is my mom."

She brushed back a chunk of black hair that had fallen into her eyes and smiled brightly at me. I still felt like I was frozen and didn't know how to breathe properly. "Rachel, it's so good to meet you, honey!"

I almost blurted out, *"But I just called your son an asshole right in front of you!"* Instead, I plastered a smile on my face and tried to relax my body as Kash let go of me and she wrapped me in a hug. "It's nice to meet you too. Thank you for having us for dinner."

"Of course"—and then softer so only I could hear—"he gets the obnoxious, asshole gene from his father. But, unfortunately, its one of the things I love most about my guys. You just get used to it and become a master at slyly flipping them off with a smile."

My eyes widened and I blinked rapidly as we pulled away from each other. *Is she being serious?*

She smiled at me again and kissed Kash on the cheek before

slapping his shoulder. "Be nice to her, she just got here! But always remember this, honey, the minute Richard and Logan stop giving you a hard time, is the minute they stop loving you. So, as long as he's pissing you off, you know he loves you. Now come on, your dad just started the grill and I'm going to make margaritas for Rachel and me. Oh, do you like margaritas?"

I nodded and then had to shake my head to get my mind working properly again. "Uh, yeah. Yeah, I do, I love them."

"Well then, I think we're going to get along just fine. C'mon, now!" She turned and walked into the house, and Kash pulled me into his side, his lips going to my ear.

"Now was that so bad?"

"Aside from the fact that the first time your mom saw me, I was cussing . . . I think I just fell in love with her."

He laughed low and pulled me into the house. "Just wait 'til you meet my dad."

1

Kash

"RACH, DO YOU really need this many shoes?" I watched as she unpacked the third box in our closet, and wondered how any person could ever have a need for that many pairs of shoes.

Her hand stopped mid-way to the shelf with another pair, and her bright blue glare turned on me. I took a step back.

"Are you actually asking me that right now?"

"Say no," my dad whispered from behind me. " 'Course it wasn't, Rachel. He's just mad that he won't have anywhere to put his sparkly hooker heels."

Rachel laughed and went back to putting her dozens of shoes away. "No worries about that one, Rich. I put them up already, they even have their own little place away from everything so they don't get ruined."

My mom pushed through Dad and me to get into the closet with an armful of clothes to hang up. "Really, Logan. Give the girl a break, I have more shoes than this."

"Oh, Marcy! I forgot to tell you—"

"Is this gonna be a long story?" Dad drawled, cutting Rachel off.

"Actually, it is," she snapped right back with a playful smirk. "So get comfy!" As soon as she launched into her story about whatever the hell those two always talked excitedly about, my dad turned and gave me a shove.

"Have I taught you nothing when it comes to women?" he asked softly.

"What? That's a shit ton of shoes!" I hissed and looked back to see her pull more out. I swear this last box was like Mary Poppins's purse. It was a never-ending pit of shoes.

"Okay, we're gonna do this quick and easy. One, your woman can never have too many shoes, clothes, purses or jewelry. Two, it doesn't matter if you know you're right—because God knows your mother is wrong about . . . well . . . just about everything—but it doesn't matter. They are *always* right. Just say a simple, 'Yes sweetheart, I'm sorry I'm a dumbass' and you'll be fine. Three, them asking if they look okay is a trick question. Because, let's face it, even if we think it's the ugliest shirt we've ever seen, it's probably in style and we wouldn't know either way. So they always look *amazing,* remember that word."

I laughed. Rachel *did* always look amazing. She could wear a sack and I would think that . . . or nothing. I preferred her in nothing.

"Four, and probably the most important if you want to keep your manhood, do not *ever* ask if she is PMS-ing. No matter what. Might as well dig your own grave if you do that."

Too late. I was always asking Rach if that's why she was in a bad mood. And if I was right, there was no way in hell I was going to tell her I was in the wrong. She could bitch about it if she wanted, but I wasn't going to go easy on her for the sake of getting out of an argument. Arguing with her was one of my favorite things.

Nodding, I slapped my dad's shoulder and smiled. "Thanks, Dad, I'll remember all that."

". . . have to go back and see if they're still there." Mom was excited about something, and from the look of it, Rachel was too.

"Yeah, we do! Anyway, I just had to tell you about that, I knew you'd flip," Rach mumbled as she flattened the last box of shoes. Thank God Mary Poppins' box had officially emptied out.

"That was a *lovely* story,"—Dad drawled again—"and you tell it so well, with such enthusiasm."

Mom rolled her eyes and shook her head as she smiled, and Rachel just looked at my dad like she was about to let him have it. At the last second, her head jerked back. "Wait. *Forrest Gump* . . . really, Rich? You're using *Forrest Gump* quotes to insult me?"

"You have met your match, honey!" Mom cheered, and Dad just huffed in annoyance toward them, but shot me a wink.

"She doesn't put up with your bullshit or mine. Son, I'm telling you, you better hold on tight to that one."

"I will, Dad. Rach, are you done with the shoes?"

"I'm not sure. If you bring up my shoes again, I could probably sit here and re-arrange them, maybe set them up by color, size of the heel, and length of the boot."

"Woman, get out of the damn closet. I have to put this up, and if you coordinate your shoes, I swear to you they will be in a pile on the floor the next time you come in here."

"Logan Kash Ryan!" Mom chided at the same time Rachel swore, "I will gut you."

My little Sour Patch. So damn cute when she's threatening my life.

"Wait, what are you putting up?" she asked as she walked out of the closet that could fit a car inside it.

"Fake wall."

"Uh. Why?"

"Kind of like a really cheap safe room. Actually, that's a lie. It's just for you to hide behind if someone were to break in or something."

She laughed loudly and kissed my throat. "Kash, really? You're being just a little bit paranoid. We're not putting up a fake wall."

Before she could move away, I wrapped an arm around her and pulled her close. "I almost lost you once, I'll be working shitty hours and there will be a lot of nights you're here alone. This is for my peace of mind, don't be difficult."

"Nothing is going to—"

"Rachel, stop. We're putting up the wall."

"You're being paranoid!"

I kissed her hard once before pushing her gently away. "I probably am, but I don't care. With all the clothes hung up, you won't even notice it's there. And if something happens, it's there for you to hide behind. I love you, but I'm getting my way on this, okay?"

She rolled her eyes and gave my mom a look that Mom clearly understood since she started laughing. "All right, Kash. If you want to put up the fake wall to help you sleep at night—err, to keep you happy when you're away—then have at it."

Rachel

"Oh my word this is going to be a disaster," I whispered as I pulled yet another shirt off my body and threw it on the bed before heading back to the closet.

I was so done meeting people in Florida. I had already established I was the Queen of first impressions gone horribly wrong with Floridians, and I could only imagine this one going the same. And, to make it worse, it was Mason's family. Which meant I got to meet another family of someone that got shot because of me. Well, Blake . . . but still.

I'd been in Florida for two weeks, and though we saw Mason practically every day, I had yet to meet his parents or sister. To be honest, I'd much rather go through meeting Kash's mom and dad again. Other than the humiliating first few seconds of meeting Marcy, the dinner had gone smoothly and I absolutely loved both of them.

But this particular meeting? I had a bad feeling about it. Call it bad juju, paranoia, premonition or an omen. I'd had my first dream about Blake in over a month the night before, and to make matters worse, Kash had been gone because he'd gotten a call for work as we were getting ready for bed. Ever since I'd woken up in a cold sweat at three AM, I'd been positive that this dinner was going to go wrong on so many levels. Blake being one of them. I was ready for him to be gone from my life. It was ridiculous that even in death, he still found ways to torture me.

Now I was running fifteen minutes late and I still couldn't find something that would cover all my scars. I didn't pay a lot of mind to them now, but after the dream, it was like they were neon signs on my body screaming, *"Look, look, look, look, looooooook!"*

I grabbed a thin, long-sleeved shirt and threw it on, but the MINE on my chest was flashing its bitchy, bright lights at me; so I grabbed a button-up shirt and pulled it over. Even though the top buttons couldn't button without looking all kinds of messed up because of the size of my chest, the collar still covered the little scar.

There. I'm ready now.

"Rach, what are you wearing? It's hot outside."

Don't care. "It's winter," I reasoned as I caught Kash's gaze in the mirror.

His gray eyes were heating as they trailed over my non-existent ass, and while I loved that he was appreciating the view, this was about to be an epic fail of a dinner. I wasn't in the mood to be checked out right now. I was having a mini-freak out.

"Yeah, but it's also seventy today. Take off the shirt underneath."

"I'm fine."

Wrapping an arm around my waist, he pulled me so my back was against his chest and brought his lips to the sensitive spot behind my ear. "I know you're fine, but you're gonna be too hot," he whispered, his voice dropping even lower as he began slowly unbuttoning my shirt.

Goose bumps covered my body when the cool metal of his lip ring brushed against my skin, and I felt myself getting ready to say I would do whatever he asked of me. He was such a cheater. He knew what that ring did to me.

"Open your eyes, Rachel."

I did as I was told and found his gunmetal gray eyes looking directly into mine. Even through the reflection of the mirror, I could feel the heat from them and sense the want. His hands trailed over my chest, waist, and stomach; the pressure so light

I almost couldn't feel it, but it was doing insane things to my stomach and my breathing quickly escalated. I watched as he slowly took my top shirt off, the movement of his hands so calculated and controlled, I felt like we had just entered some form of foreplay. If I'd thought I had wanted to stay home earlier, I was definitely all for skipping this dinner now.

After he tossed the first shirt onto the bed, his hands did their barely-there touches over the swell of my breasts and down my waist again until he hit the hem of the long-sleeved shirt. One hand slipped under, and a breathy whimper of need sounded in the back of my throat when his warm hand caressed my bare skin. He smiled against my neck and nipped on it lightly. I wanted to shut my eyes and enjoy every touch, but everything in me was screaming to watch the most erotic undressing I'd ever witnessed or been a part of.

Like with the first, his movements were slow and controlled as he pulled this shirt higher, but now he gave little teases of fingertips being brushed against my skin. By the time it was over my head and he was letting it fall to the ground, my entire body was on fire and I was practically panting with need.

"Rachel," his voice traveled over my bare shoulder like a caress, and I let my bodyweight fall against him.

"Hmm?"

Suddenly he was gone and I stumbled back a step before catching myself. I turned to see where he'd gone and my button-up shirt hit me in the face.

"What the—"

"Get dressed, we gotta go."

"The hell, Kash? You can't do stuff like that to me and then stop!"

"Have you forgotten what frustration feels like?" He asked huskily and I wanted to punch him in the face.

"I hate you."

His lips curved up into my favorite smirk and he winked. "I love you too, Sour Patch."

Douche.

OKAY SO I GUESS I should be thankful that the meeting went off relatively smooth. Mason's parents and sister were actually really nice, and although we'd gone through the mandatory introductions for me, Marcy and Richard had come to dinner also and made the introduction fast and flawless. I'd just kept my mouth shut for the first five minutes unless I was saying the customary *hellos* and *it's so nice to meet you toos,* and I didn't have anything to worry about.

Until dinner started anyway.

"So, Rachel," Mrs. Gates began and took another sip of her tea before continuing. "We've heard bits and pieces of what happened in Texas from the boys. But you know how men are with details," she teased.

Mother effing shit. Bad juju! I knew it!

"I've really been wanting to hear your side of what went down."

I got your sons shot! I had to bite down on my cheek so I wouldn't say something of that nature as I took a breath to collect my thoughts. "What went down at the end?"

"The whole time they were there. We had no clue where they even were and didn't talk to them more than once or twice a month, so we don't know what was happening."

Memories of the few months in Texas with the guys went

flying through my mind and I swallowed hard. I knew this was coming at some point, Marcy and Richard had never asked and I knew it was only a matter of time. But I was fine with never reliving those three months again.

Kash seemed to sense the unease pouring off me and stopped talking to Mason and Mr. Gates. "You okay?" he asked softly, and sat back when he realized the other half of the table was completely silent. "What's going on?"

I looked up and caught Marcy and Richard giving me sympathetic looks. They had to want to know this too, and it hit me then that Kash must have told them not to ask me. There was no way we could have gone this many days together without them saying something unless he had talked to them.

"Nothing, I just asked Rachel to tell us her side of what happened in Tex—"

"No," Kash stated firmly at the same time Mason hissed, "Mom!"

"What? Is it so wrong for us to want to know what went on there?" Mrs. Gates asked, and I couldn't blame her.

"Rachel, you don't have to say anything."

"He's right," Kash agreed with Mason before whispering in my ear, "If you want to get out of here we can."

"It's fine, we can't keep avoiding the elephant in the room, can we?"

His eyes shut tight and he exhaled roughly. "Babe, please—"

"Kash, they deserve to know what happened to you guys."

When his eyes met mine they were pained, and I squeezed his hand tightly before looking back toward Kash's parents and Mrs. Gates. "Where do you want me to start?"

There was an uncomfortable silence for a few moments before

Mrs. Gates spoke, "So, you knew the boys because they lived near you?"

"Yeah, they lived in the apartment directly across the hall from mine. My best friend, Candice, saw them moving in and introduced herself, we all went out for dinner that first night."

"And you had no idea what they were really doing there?"

"Not at all, the only thing that seemed off to me was where they were from. Kash was kind of evasive with his answer, but I had my own secrets so I didn't really push it. But Candice and I were in college, moving somewhere for a new start was kind of what everyone was doing after graduation anyway unless they went back to their hometowns . . . so I didn't have a reason to think them being there and looking for work was weird."

Mrs. Gates fidgeted a bit. "Mason told us they would have meetings a few times a week at the police department. Even when you started spending more time with them, you never noticed them going off to these meetings?"

I laughed softly thinking back to all the times the guys would up and leave suddenly. "At the time, they played it off well to the point I thought they were going to work out or something. After I found out about everything, it all made more sense though. They were good liars," I teased and winked at Mason as I nudged Kash. Neither looked happy right now.

"They are very secretive, that's for certain." She rolled her eyes but still looked lovingly at both. "So tell us about Blake. We know the boys' side, but I know that has to be so different from your experiences with him."

Something that sounded dangerously close to a growl came from Kash and my eyes widened when I saw his murderous expression.

"Um, Blake was . . ." I trailed off and attempted to tear my eyes from Kash's face to look back at Mrs. Gates. "He's Candice's cousin, I grew up with him." The icy feeling that always accompanied thoughts of Blake began making it's way through my veins, and I took deep breaths in as I spoke to keep myself calm. "I had a crush on him growing up, but he was so much older than me that it was just one of those schoolgirl crushes."

"I didn't know you'd known him before," Marcy whispered, and after a glance in Kash's direction, snapped her mouth shut.

"Yeah, we were all really close, but he left for the Air Force and I didn't see or hear from him until fall of my junior year of college. He started working for the school and began asking me out immediately." I waved a dismissive hand and tried to smile. "Long story, short, I finally agreed at the end of that school year and almost immediately there was a change in him. I didn't want to keep dating him and—uh, some stuff happened between us right before the year ended. I met Kash and Mason just a couple weeks after that."

From the sympathetic looks the majority of the people at the table were giving me, they knew exactly what had happened between Blake and me. Part of me felt . . . embarrassed. Knowing that they knew, wondering what they must think. Kash was gripping the table and staring off into nothing as I swallowed down my unfounded embarrassment and kept talking.

"I didn't see or hear from him until the end of July, he showed up where Kash and I were working one night . . . and from there things just kind of escalated. Things kept going missing or being moved around in my apartment, he was always leaving me anonymous notes on my car when school started back up. But in front of anyone else, he was the perfect Blake everyone was in love with. And really—what he'd done in the apartment, none of it was anything bad, it was just enough for him to show me that he still had control over me. Like turning on the dishwasher with nothing in there when we'd all been gone for hours, putting out things in my kitchen to make pancakes because he knew Kash was always having me make them . . . just random, stupid things that separately were harmless. It was the fact that he was getting in and was watching us that closely without us realizing it that made it bad.

But, honestly, I didn't even know that any of it had been Blake until the night before everything happened. I'd been blaming Mason and Kash, and then the next day he was there waiting for me when I came out of the administrative building from dropping my classes in an attempt to avoid him. He forced me to break up with Kash. He had one of his guys blow up Candice's dad's car as he was walking to it—I watched the whole thing on a live feed and Blake swore he would kill her parents first if I didn't do what he wanted."

My breathing had been escalating, but stopped altogether when Kash shoved away from the table and stalked out of the room. I swallowed roughly and tried to straighten my back from how I'd unknowingly curled in on myself.

"I think you all know the rest of what happened that night and the next morning," I whispered and excused myself before going after him.

Even if Kash hadn't left, there would be no sense in repeating what I was sure they already knew. That was the night and morning that brought everything crashing down. Kash and Mason had been undercover looking for a serial killer for the Carnation Murders while simultaneously keeping their lives from Candice and me, and making sure that Blake and the men he had stalking me couldn't get close to me. Even with all that had happened between Blake and me, no one had been expecting him to be the murderer Kash and Mase had been looking for. And by the time the guys had found out, I was stuck in a studio apartment with him against my will. What happened later is what led to my body being permanently scarred before I could be saved.

But, Blake, well he had been insane, and smart . . . aren't all the genius' the crazy ones? He'd set it up so he wouldn't do time for the crimes he'd committed, and he never would. Blake set up his own death, as well as Kash and Mason's. I thank God every day that Mason had been wearing a bulletproof vest and Kash had turned at the last second so nothing major had been hit.

I found Kash outside pacing back and forth with his hands in his nearly black hair. When I stepped outside and shut the door behind me, he stopped pacing, and after a few seconds, turned to face me.

"I'll never forgive myself for what he did—"

"Stop," I begged and stepped up to him, wrapping my arms around his narrow waist. "Just stop. You can't keep doing this to yourself."

"Rachel, I *let* all that happen to you!"

I had to blink back tears when I brought my left hand up to his right shoulder, then down a little onto his chest. Even through the shirt, I could feel the scarred skin from the gunshot wounds. "Then I let this happen to you," I murmured and stared, fixated on my fingers as they lightly brushed against the fabric covering the scars.

He brushed strands of hair away from my face, and held my hair back. "No you didn't, this had nothing to do with you."

"It's only fair; if what happened to me is your fault, then what happened to you is mine."

A low growl built up in the back of his throat. "I was supposed to be protecting you, and I—"

I crushed my mouth to his to stop whatever he had been about to say, and waited until I felt his body relax beneath my fingertips. "It wasn't your fault, and it wasn't mine. We can't keep doing this, Kash. We're moving on with our lives and we're moving on from what happened. Okay?"

He stayed silent as his gray eyes bounced back and forth between mine.

"No more blaming yourself," I pleaded and kissed him softly again before letting my forehead rest against his.

"Fine." He sighed heavily after another minute. "I'm sorry about their questions. They weren't supposed to ask you anything about it. Mason and I told them that at least a dozen times."

"Really it's fine, they deserve to know. It's a weird situation all around, and I had more information that they wanted . . . I'm sure they still want more details. But the details I have won't change anything for them."

Kash got silent again before pressing his lips to my forehead. "You're amazing for reliving that . . . and you handled it well. But don't feel like you need to answer their questions. Mase and I have answered enough. And that's not what tonight was about. They're like my second family, and they've been dying to meet you for months."

"I like them. They're really nice, and Maddie is hilarious. Another girl that doesn't put up with your shit is great in my book."

He laughed when I pushed against his toned stomach. "I'm sorry for getting frustrated."

I took a few steps back and grabbed his hand to pull him with me. "Don't be, let's just go back in there and enjoy the rest of the night. Deal?"

He drew me back to his body and kissed me firmly. "Deal."

Don't Miss NEW BOOKS from your
FAVORITE NEW ADULT AUTHORS

Cora Carmack

LOSING IT A Novel
Available in Paperback and eBook

FAKING IT A Novel
Available in Paperback and eBook

KEEPING HER An Original eNovella
eBook on Sale August 2013

FINDING IT A Novel
Available in Paperback and eBook Fall 2013

Jay Crownover

RULE A Novel
Available in eBook
Available in Paperback Fall 2013

JET A Novel
Available in eBook
Available in Paperback Fall 2013

ROME A Novel
Available in Paperback and eBook Winter 2014

Lisa Desrochers

A LITTLE TOO FAR A Novel
Available in eBook Fall 2013

A LITTLE TOO MUCH A Novel
Available in eBook Fall 2013

A LITTLE TOO HOT A Novel
Available in eBook Winter 2014

Abigail Gibbs

THE DARK HEROINE A Novel
Available in Paperback and eBook

AUTUMN ROSE A Novel
Available in Paperback and eBook Winter 2014

Sophie Jordan

FOREPLAY A Novel
Available in Paperback and eBook Fall 2013

J. Lynn

WAIT FOR YOU A Novel
Available in eBook
Available in Paperback Fall 2013

BE WITH ME A Novel
Available in Paperback Winter 2014

TRUST IN ME A Novella
Available in eBook Fall 2013

Molly McAdams

FROM ASHES A Novel
Available in Paperback and eBook

TAKING CHANCES A Novel
Available in Paperback and eBook

STEALING HARPER
An Original eNovella
Available in eBook

FORGIVING LIES A Novel
Available in Paperback and eBook Fall 2013

DECEIVING LIES A Novel
Available in Paperback and eBook Winter 2014

Shannon Stoker

THE REGISTRY A Novel
Available in Paperback and eBook

THE COLLECTION A Novel
Available in Paperback and eBook Winter 2014

Visit www.betweencoversbooks.com to download a free eBook samp